序　言

　　ECL（English Comprehension Level）測驗，旨在測試考生的英文理解程度，軍方人員要出國受訓、進修時，都必須通過這項考試。近幾年來，我國對外購買武器數目增多，因此 ECL 考試舉行的次數也較爲頻繁。

　　爲服務三軍將士，我們特別費心蒐集了歷年來的 ECL 全眞試題，彙編成精彩的「ECL 聽力測驗詳解」一書，資料十分珍貴，希望能提供考生充分的練習機會，以增加應考信心。

　　本書包括 16 回聽力模擬測驗，錄音帶的説話速度及間隔秒數完全模擬 ECL 考試，能增加考生應考的臨場感。而試題後並附詳解及中文翻譯，希望讀者們認眞練習。藉由密集的聽力訓練培養，必能爲考生們奠定良好的聽力佳績。

　　本書試題及詳解雖經多次校對，但仍恐有疏漏之處，祈請各界先進不吝批評指教。

編者　謹識

CONTENTS

ECL 聽力測驗準備方向

1. 考試型式：

新版 ECL 測驗中，聽力測驗（Listening Part）占 **60** 題，考試
時間約 **25** 分鐘，旨在評量考生對口語英文的理解程度。考試方式
類似**托福考試**，考生必須根據錄音帶中的問題或提示，選出正確
的答案。

2. 聽力訓練：

聽力部分對中國學生而言令人較頭痛，因為平常缺乏練習機會，
故要準備這一方面，一定要先**訓練自己的聽力**。平時可多收聽**英
文廣播**及觀賞**原音播出**的外國影集，多熟悉單字的發音，及老外
說話的速度及音調，這不僅訓練聽力，更有助於早日適應日後留
美的環境。

3. 答題技巧：

考試時錄音帶**只播放一次**，考生必須全神貫注聆聽題目，若怕四
個選項來不及看完，可在錄音帶尚未正式發問之前，先看前二個
選項，等錄音帶唸完後，再看後二個選項，如此可有更充裕的時
間考慮正確答案。此外，先看過選項有一點印象時，再聽題目，
就會比較輕鬆，而且容易掌握**關鍵字**，便可正確地選出答案。

ECL分數換算表

QCA	ESC	QCA	ESC	QCA	ESC	QCA	ESC
100	100	75	72	50	46	25	20
99	98	74	71	49	45	24	19
98	96	73	71	48	44	23	19
97	94	72	70	47	42	22	18
96	92	71	69	46	41	21	17
95	90	70	69	45	40	20	16
94	88	69	68	44	39	19	15
93	86	68	67	43	37	18	14
92	84	67	66	42	36	17	13
91	82	66	66	41	35	16	12
90	82	65	65	40	34	15	12
89	81	64	64	39	33	14	11
88	81	63	63	38	32	13	11
87	80	62	62	37	31	12	10
86	80	61	61	36	30	11	9
85	79	60	60	35	29	10	8
84	78	59	58	34	28	9	8
83	77	58	56	33	27	8	7
82	76	57	54	32	26	7	6
81	75	56	53	31	25	6	5
80	75	55	52	30	24	5	5
79	74	54	51	29	23	4	4
78	73	53	50	28	22	3	3
77	73	52	49	27	21	2	2
76	72	51	48	26	20	1	1

QCA = questions correctly answered 答對題數
ESC = equivalent scores contrasted 相對分數

LISTENING TEST 1

● *Directions for questions 1-25. You will hear questions on the test tape. Select the one item A, B, C or D which answers the question correctly, and mark your answer sheet.*

1. A. Barbara
   B. Martha
   C. They are of the same age.
   D. We don't know.

2. A. She had a flat tire.　　　　　B. The engine didn't start.
   C. She ran out of gas.　　　　　D. She had an accident.

3. A. 140 dollars　　　　　B. 60 dollars
   C. 200 dollars　　　　　D. 100 dollars

4. A. June　　　　　B. May
   C. August　　　　　D. February

5. A. He can be appointed by the President.
   B. He can be installed immediately.
   C. He can be removed.
   D. He can be awarded with honors.

6. A. He wanted to see them in color.
   B. He wanted a close view of them.
   C. He wanted to see them during the day.
   D. He wanted to see the moon behind the sun.

7. A. an animal　　　　　B. a vegetable
   C. a color　　　　　D. a field

8. A. an officer　　　　　B. a doctor
   C. a farmer　　　　　D. a merchant

9. A. a pair of scissors   B. a razor
   C. a cutting device   D. a machine tool

10. A. travel around the world
    B. donate money to charity
    C. buy whatever he wants
    D. help poor people

11. A. He made the mistake out of curiosity.
    B. He made the mistake by accident.
    C. He made the mistake gradually.
    D. He made the mistake intentionally.

12. A. He has a perfect score.   B. He has a medal.
    C. He behaves well.   D. He has been a bad boy.

13. A. a story   B. a rock
    C. a storm   D. a ball

14. A. break the door by hitting it
    B. make a noise by hitting the door
    C. throw a stone at the door
    D. lean on the door

15. A. give   B. demand
    C. lend   D. bend

16. A. jet fuel   B. an apple
    C. a type of table   D. a kind of food

17. A. too hard   B. too soft
    C. very delicious   D. too rare

18. A. a type of wood   B. the bark of a tree
    C. a very hard metal   D. the hair of sheep

19. A. delighted　　　　　　B. hungry
　　C. afraid　　　　　　　D. pleased

20. A. a mechanic　　　　　B. a baker
　　C. a plumber　　　　　D. a butcher

21. A. It is expensive.　　　B. It is boring.
　　C. It is enjoyable.　　　D. It is bad.

22. A. his money back　　　B. receipt for money
　　C. a front seat　　　　D. an exchange ticket

23. A. chocolate　　　　　　B. black
　　C. well-done　　　　　D. boiled three minutes

24. A. the sun　　　　　　B. the window
　　C. brightness　　　　　D. electricity

25. A. listening to ICRT
　　B. watching TV
　　C. doing her homework
　　D. talking to her friend on the phone

- *Directions for questions 26-50. You will hear statements on the test tape. Select the one answer A, B, C, or D which comes closest to the meaning of the statement and mark your answer sheet.*

26. A. Jack left in the middle of lunch.
　　B. Jack left home for lunch.
　　C. Jack left for home to take his lunch box.
　　D. Jack didn't bring his lunch.

27. A. I'll ring the door bell.　　B. I'll visit you.
　　C. I'll call on you.　　　　D. I'll telephone you.

28. A. Wayne apologized to me.
    B. I thanked Wayne for his help.
    C. We became friends again.
    D. Wayne made me angry.

29. A. We had lunch late.
    B. We bought some food.
    C. We bought a little pet snake.
    D. We decided to eat lunch early.

30. A. He doesn't resemble an American.
    B. His native country is America.
    C. He looks like an American.
    D. He speaks English fluently.

31. A. She went to Singapore a long time ago.
    B. She has never had the opportunity to go.
    C. She never cared to go there.
    D. She lived in Singapore before.

32. A. Everybody should hear today's lecture.
    B. Everybody needn't hear today's lecture.
    C. Everybody has heard the lecture today.
    D. The lecture will be delivered by everybody.

33. A. He has stopped dancing.
    B. He dances very fast.
    C. He dances when he is well.
    D. He dances very well.

34. A. The ship appeared to be very small.
    B. It was difficult to see the ship.
    C. The ship seemed very far away.
    D. The fog was barely visible from the ship.

35. A. Did you recognize the place?
    B. Did anyone know who you are?
    C. Did anyone guess the answer?
    D. Did you remember the right way?

36. A. I enjoyed the picnic very much.
    B. He likes funny pictures, doesn't he?
    C. He doesn't like picnicking.
    D. The picnic wasn't enjoyable.

37. A. You've been here already.
    B. Why did you hide it here?
    C. It was hard to find you.
    D. Where did you find that?

38. A. That's a very bad error.
    B. What's wrong with the steak?
    C. Is he afraid of making mistakes?
    D. I know what happened there.

39. A. The typewriter was small.
    B. The typewriter cost a great deal.
    C. The typewriter did not cost much.
    D. The typewriter was large.

40. A. Kate was late.   B. Kate was early.
    C. Kate was on time.   D. Kate was absent.

41. A. I have good looks.   B. I am very lucky.
    C. The door is locked.   D. The lock is a strong one.

42. A. Tom has only been here for a week.
    B. Tom has been here the longest.
    C. Tom felt lonely once in a while.
    D. Tom has been alone for a week.

43. A. I saw him walking.
    B. I saw him going down.
    C. I saw him running.
    D. I saw him drinking.

44. A. The sun is shining.
    B. The humidity is high.
    C. The weather is dry.
    D. The weather is very pleasant.

45. A. I want to be an operator.
    B. I am more than an operator.
    C. I am ready to cooperate.
    D. I'll be a cooperative executive.

46. A. He had much money with him.
    B. He didn't have enough money.
    C. He had a few dollars left over.
    D. He bought the coat without any trouble.

47. A. It is all right to park there.
    B. Parking is permitted there.
    C. It is unlawful to park there.
    D. Parking is always done there.

48. A. She made the suggestion.
    B. She agreed to the suggestion.
    C. She changed the suggestion.
    D. She typed the suggestion.

49. A. The girl went out twice yesterday.
    B. The girls went to the party.
    C. The girl will go to the party.
    D. The girls didn't attend the party.

50. A. We were very glad when the train left.
　　B. Getting nearer to the station made us happy.
　　C. Leaving the station made us happy.
　　D. We were very glad when we visited the station.

● *Directions for questions 51-60. You will hear dialogs on the test
tape. Select the correct answer A, B, C, or D and mark your
answer sheet.*

51. A. to an officer　　　　B. to a doctor
　　C. to a patient　　　　D. to a driver

52. A. not getting what he wanted
　　B. calling up customers
　　C. a custom that's new to him
　　D. some of his good friends

53. A. It's not important how he dances.
　　B. If he's careful, no one will notice.
　　C. No one knows the steps to the dance.
　　D. It's too crowded to dance anyway.

54. A. as soon as possible　　B. the next day
　　C. in a week or two　　　D. at some time in the future

55. A. a ticket to Boston and back
　　B. a one-way ticket
　　C. a ticket purchased on credit
　　D. a ticket paid for with cash

56. A. It was broken to small pieces.
　　B. It was dirty.
　　C. It was locked in the closet.
　　D. It was full of paint.

57. A. a big box of vegetables
    B. a good price for vegetables
    C. only a few vegetables
    D. a good selection of vegetables

58. A. He had not been there.   B. He didn't care.
    C. He didn't like it.   D. He wasn't careful.

59. A. She was misunderstood.
    B. She was hungry.
    C. She was confused.
    D. She was afraid.

60. A. He swam across it.   B. He jumped over it.
    C. He climbed it.   D. He crawled under it.

In a perfect world, the mail would always be early,
the check would always be in the mail, and it would
be written for more than you expected.

在完美的世界中，郵件總是提早到達，支票總是在郵件裏，
而且上面的金額總是比你預期的多。

ECL 聽力測驗 [1] 詳解

1. (**B**) Martha was born before Barbara was. Who is older?
瑪莎比芭芭拉早出生。/ 誰年紀較大？

    (A) 芭芭拉　　　　(B) 瑪莎　　　　(C) 一樣大　　　(D) 不知道

2. (**C**) Mary went to the gas station to have her tank filled.
What happened?
瑪麗到加油站加油。/ 發生了什麼事？

    (A) 車子爆胎。　　　　　　　(B) 引擎發不動。
    (C) 沒有汽油了。　　　　　　(D) 她發生意外。

    * tank (tæŋk) *n.* 油槽　　***flat tire*** 爆胎
    run out of 沒有～；用完　　accident ('æksədənt) *n.* 意外

3. (**A**) This skirt costs 200 dollars and Jane got a thirty percent
discount. How much did Jane pay for the skirt?
這件裙子二百元，而珍得到百分之三十的折扣。
珍付多少錢買這件裙子？

    (A) 一百四十元　　(B) 六十元　　(C) 二百元　　(D) 一百元

    * discount ('dɪskaunt) *n.* 折扣

4. (**D**) Which is the shortest month in a year?
一年當中最短的月份是幾月？

    (A) 六月　　　　(B) 五月　　　　(C) 八月　　　(D) 二月

5. (**C**) An official of the United States government can be
dismissed. What can happen to him?
一位美國政府官員可能受免職處分。/ 他會發生什麼事？

    (A) 他可能被總統任命。　　(B) 他可能會馬上就職。
    (C) 他可能會被免職。　　　(D) 他可能榮獲頒獎。

    * dismiss (dɪs'mɪs) *v.* 解雇　　appoint (ə'pɔɪnt) *v.* 任命
    install (ɪn'stɔl) *v.* 就職　　remove (rɪ'muv) *v.* 解雇
    award (ə'wɔrd) *v.* 頒發；授與

6. (**B**) Why did the teacher use the telescope to look at the stars?
為什麼老師要用望遠鏡觀看星星？

(A) 他想看彩色的星星。　　　　　(B) <u>他想要看得更清楚。</u>
(C) 他想要在白天看到星星。　　　(D) 他想看躲在太陽後的月亮。

* telescope (ˈtɛləˌskop) *n.* 望遠鏡

7. (**C**) The house is gray. What is gray?
房子是灰色的。／什麼是灰色？

(A) 一隻動物　　(B) 一株植物　　(C) <u>一種顏色</u>　　(D) 一片田野

* gray (gre) *adj.* 灰色的

8. (**A**) I spoke to the Captain. With whom did I speak?
我跟上尉說話。／我和誰說話？

(A) <u>一位軍官</u>　　(B) 一位醫生　　(C) 一位農夫　　(D) 一位商人

* captain (ˈkæptɪn) *n.* 隊長；上尉　　merchant (ˈmɝtʃənt) *n.* 商人

9. (**C**) She bought a new knife. What did she buy?
她買了一把新的刀。／她買了什麼？

(A) 一把剪刀　　　　　　　　　　(B) 一把剃刀
(C) <u>一個剪裁工具</u>　　　　　　　(D) 機器工具

* scissors (ˈsɪzɚz) *n., pl.* 剪刀　　razor (ˈrezɚ) *n.* 剃刀
device (dɪˈvaɪs) *n.* 設備；儀器

10. (**C**) Bob said, "I wish I were a millionaire. I would buy everything I want."
What would Bob do if his dream came true?
鮑伯說：「我希望我是個百萬富翁。我會去買任何我想要的東西。」
如果鮑伯的夢想實現，他會做什麼？

(A) 環遊世界　　　　　　　　　　(B) 捐錢給慈善機構
(C) <u>買任何他想要的東西</u>　　　　(D) 幫助窮人

* *come true* 實現　　donate (ˈdonet) *v.* 捐贈
charity (ˈtʃærətɪ) *n.* 慈善機構

11. (**D**) Frank made this mistake on purpose.
　　　How did Frank make the mistake?
　　　法蘭克故意犯下這個錯。／法蘭克怎麼會犯這個錯呢？

　　　(A) 他出於好奇犯錯。　　　　(B) 他意外地犯錯。
　　　(C) 他逐漸地犯錯。　　　　　(D) 他故意犯錯。

　　　* **on purpose** 故意地　　curiosity〔ˌkjʊrɪˈɑsətɪ〕n. 好奇心
　　　　by accident 意外地　　gradually〔ˈgrædʒʊəlɪ〕adv. 逐漸地
　　　　intentionally〔ɪnˈtɛnʃənlɪ〕adv. 故意地

12. (**C**) What does it mean if Bob's conduct is good?
　　　鮑伯的行為良好代表什麼意思？

　　　(A) 他得到完美的分數。　　　(B) 他得到一面獎牌。
　　　(C) 他表現良好。　　　　　　(D) 他一直是個壞男孩。

　　　* conduct〔ˈkɑndʌkt〕n. 行為；品行　　score〔skor〕n. 分數
　　　　medal〔ˈmɛdl̩〕n. 獎牌　　behave〔bɪˈhev〕v. 行為舉止

13. (**B**) If Collins broke the window with a stone, what did he throw?
　　　如果柯林斯拿石頭打破窗戶，他拿什麼丟？

　　　(A) 故事　　(B) 石塊　　(C) 暴風雨　　(D) 球

14. (**B**) Steve wants to knock on the door.
　　　What would he do?
　　　史蒂夫想要敲門。／他要怎樣做？

　　　(A) 把門撞破　　　　　　　(B) 藉由敲門發出聲音
　　　(C) 對著門扔石頭　　　　　(D) 靠在門上

　　　* lean〔lin〕v. 倚靠

15. (**C**) What is the opposite of "borrow"?
　　　借入的相反意思是什麼？

　　　(A) 給　　(B) 要求　　(C) 借出　　(D) 折彎

　　　* demand〔dɪˈmænd〕v. 要求；請求
　　　　bend〔bɛnd〕v. 彎曲

16. (**D**) That beef is cheap. What is beef?
  牛肉很便宜。／牛肉是什麼？
      (A) 噴射機燃料   (B) 蘋果
      (C) 一種桌子   (D) <u>一種食物</u>
      * fuel〔'fjuəl〕*n.* 燃料

17. (**A**) The meat was so tough that we couldn't cut it. How was the meat?
  肉太硬了，以至於我們都切不動。／肉怎麼樣？
      (A) <u>太硬了</u>   (B) 太軟了
      (C) 非常好吃   (D) 太生了
      * tough〔tʌf〕*adj.* 硬的   rare〔rɛr〕*adj.* （牛排）半熟的；生的

18. (**D**) This product is made of wool. What is it made of?
  這產品是由羊毛做成的。／它是由什麼做成的？
      (A) 一種木頭   (B) 樹皮
      (C) 一種非常堅硬的金屬   (D) <u>羊毛</u>
      * *be made of* 由～做成   bark〔bɑrk〕*n.* 樹皮
      sheep〔ʃip〕*n.* 綿羊

19. (**C**) The girl was frightened. How did the girl feel?
  這女孩嚇壞了。／這個女孩覺得怎樣？
      (A) 愉快   (B) 飢餓   (C) <u>害怕</u>   (D) 高興
      * frighten〔'fraɪtn〕*v.* 使驚嚇   delight〔dɪ'laɪt〕*v.* 使高興

20. (**B**) Mr. Gram makes bread, cakes, and pies. What is he?
  葛拉姆先生做麵包、蛋糕，和派。／他的職業是什麼？
      (A) 技工   (B) <u>麵包師傅</u>
      (C) 水管工人   (D) 肉店老板
      * mechanic〔mə'kænɪk〕*n.* 技工
      baker〔'bekɚ〕*n.* 麵包師傅
      plumber〔'plʌmɚ〕*n.* 水管工人
      butcher〔'butʃɚ〕*n.* 屠夫；肉店老板

21. (**C**) Captain Oscar said that television is entertaining.
What did he mean?

奧斯卡上尉說電視很有趣。/ 他的意思是什麼？

(A) 電視很貴。　　　　　　(B) 電視很無聊。

(C) 電視很有趣。　　　　　(D) 電視不好。

22. (**D**) The bus driver gave Lieutenant William a transfer.
What did Lieutenant William get?

公車司機給威廉中尉一張轉車車票。/ 威廉中尉得到什麼？

(A) 歸還他的錢　　(B) 錢的收據　　(C) 前面的座位　　(D) 轉車車票

* lieutenant (lu'tɛnənt) *n.* 中尉　　transfer ('trænsfɜ) *n.* 轉車 (車票)
receipt (rɪ'sit) *n.* 收據　　exchange (ɪks'tʃendʒ) *n.* 交換

23. (**B**) How do you like your coffee?

你要喝怎樣的咖啡？

(A) 巧克力　　　　　　　　(B) 黑咖啡（不加糖及奶精）

(C) 全熟（指牛排煮法）　　(D) 煮三分鐘

24. (**D**) What makes artificial light?

人造燈是利用什麼發亮的？

(A) 太陽　　　　(B) 窗戶　　　　(C) 亮光　　　　(D) 電力

* artificial (ˌɑrtə'fɪʃəl) *adj.* 人造的

25. (**B**) Laura had the TV on when her parents entered the room.
What was she doing at that time?

當蘿拉的父母親進房間時，她正開著電視。/ 她當時正在做什麼？

(A) 收聽 ICRT　　　　　　(B) 看電視

(C) 做作業　　　　　　　　(D) 和朋友講電話

26. (**D**) Jack left his lunch box at home.

傑克把便當留在家裏了。

(A) 傑克在午餐中離開了。　　(B) 傑克離開家去吃午餐。

(C) 傑克回家拿便當。　　　　(D) 傑克沒有帶午餐。

27. (**D**) I'll give you a ring sometime after 8:00 tonight.
我會在今晚八點後打電話給你。

    (A) 我會按門鈴。   (B) 我會去拜訪你。

    (C) 我會去拜訪你。   (D) 我會打電話給你。

    * *give sb. a ring* 打電話給某人   *call on sb.* 拜訪某人

28. (**C**) Wayne accepted my apology and we made up again.
韋恩接受我的道歉，我們又和好如初了。

    (A) 韋恩向我道歉。   (B) 我謝謝韋恩的幫忙。

    (C) 我們再次成為朋友。   (D) 韋恩讓我生氣。

    * apology〔ə'pɑlədʒɪ〕*n.* 道歉   *make up* 和好
    apologize〔ə'pɑlə,dʒaɪz〕*v.* 道歉

29. (**B**) We decided to buy a little snack since lunch had been several hours ago.
午餐吃完好幾個小時之後，我們決定買一點點心吃。

    (A) 我們很晚吃午餐。   (B) 我們買了一點食物。

    (C) 我們買了一隻小寵物蛇。   (D) 我們決定早點吃午餐。

    * snack〔snæk〕*n.* 點心   snake〔snek〕*n.* 蛇

30. (**A**) It's easy to tell that he isn't a native American.
很容易看出他不是土生土長的美國人。

    (A) 他不像美國人。   (B) 他的祖國是美國。

    (C) 他看起來像美國人。   (D) 他說英文很流利。

    * native〔'netɪv〕*adj.* 當地的；土生土長的
    resemble〔rɪ'zɛmbl〕*v.* 相像   fluently〔'fluəntlɪ〕*adv.* 流利地

31. (**B**) Cindy has wanted to go to Singapore for a long time, but she was never able to.
辛蒂想去新加坡已經很久了，但是她一直沒能去。

    (A) 她很久以前去過新加坡。   (B) 她一直沒有機會去。

    (C) 她從來不想去那兒。   (D) 她以前住在新加坡。

    * opportunity〔,ɑpə'tjunətɪ〕*n.* 機會
    care to 想要（用於否定句和疑問句）

32. (**A**) Today's lecture ought to be heard by everybody.
今天的演講每個人都應該聽。

　　(A) 每個人都應該聽今天的演講。
　　(B) 每個人都不需要聽今天的演講。
　　(C) 每個人都已經聽了今天的演講。
　　(D) 每個人都要演講。

　　* lecture (ˈlɛktʃɚ) *n.* 演講　　***ought to*** 應該
　　　deliver (dɪˈlɪvɚ) *v.* 陳述；發表

33. (**D**) He dances quite well.
他舞跳得相當好。

　　(A) 他已經停止跳舞。　　　　(B) 他舞跳得很快。
　　(C) 他身體健康時就跳舞。　　(D) 他舞跳得很好。

34. (**B**) The ship was hardly visible through the dense fog.
在濃霧中這艘船幾乎看不見。

　　(A) 這艘船看起來很小。　　　　(B) 很難看到這艘船。
　　(C) 這艘船似乎很遙遠。　　　　(D) 從船上霧幾乎看不見。

　　* visible (ˈvɪzəbl) *adj.* 看得見的　　dense (dɛns) *adj.* 濃密的
　　　barely (ˈbɛrlɪ) *adv.* 幾乎不

35. (**B**) Were you recognized right away?
你立刻被認出來了嗎？

　　(A) 你認得這個地方嗎？　　　　(B) 有人知道你是誰嗎？
　　(C) 有人猜到答案嗎？　　　　　(D) 你記得正確的路嗎？

　　* ***right away*** 立刻
　　　recognize (ˈrɛkəɡˌnaɪz) *v.* 認得

36. (**A**) The picnic is fun, isn't it?
這次野餐真有趣，不是嗎？

　　(A) 我很喜歡這次野餐。　　　　(B) 他喜歡有趣的照片，不是嗎？
　　(C) 他不喜歡野餐。　　　　　　(D) 這次野餐並不愉快。

　　* enjoyable (ɪnˈdʒɔɪəbl̩) *adj.* 令人愉快的

37. (**C**)　Here you are! Where have you been hiding?
　　　　你在這裏！你都躲到哪兒去了？

　　　　(A) 你已經在這裏了。　　　　(B) 你為何把它藏在這裏？
　　　　(C) 你很難找。　　　　　　(D) 你在哪兒找到的？

38. (**A**)　What a terrible mistake!
　　　　錯得太嚴重了！

　　　　(A) 那是個嚴重的錯誤。　　(B) 牛排怎麼了？
　　　　(C) 他害怕犯錯嗎？　　　　(D) 我知道那裏發生的事。
　　　　* error〔'ɛrə〕*n.* 錯誤

39. (**C**)　The student bought an inexpensive typewriter.
　　　　這位學生買了一台便宜的打字機。

　　　　(A) 打字機很小。　　　　　(B) 打字機花很多錢。
　　　　(C) 打字機沒有花多少錢。　(D) 打字機很大。
　　　　* inexpensive〔ˌɪnɪk'spɛnsɪv〕*adj.* 便宜的　　***a great deal*** 很多

40. (**A**)　Kate arrived 20 minutes after the class has started.
　　　　凱特在上課後二十分鐘才來。

　　　　(A) 凱特遲到了。　　　　　(B) 凱特來早了。
　　　　(C) 凱特準時到。　　　　　(D) 凱特缺席。
　　　　* ***on time*** 準時　　　absent〔'æbsnt〕*adj.* 缺席的

41. (**B**)　I had very good luck.
　　　　我運氣非常好。

　　　　(A) 我有好看的外表。　　　(B) 我很幸運。
　　　　(C) 這扇門鎖上了。　　　　(D) 這個鎖很堅固。

42. (**B**)　Only Tom has been here for more than a week.
　　　　只有湯姆來此超過一星期了。

　　　　(A) 湯姆來此才一星期。　　(B) 湯姆在這兒待得最久。
　　　　(C) 湯姆有時會感到寂寞。　(D) 湯姆單獨一人一星期了。
　　　　* lonely〔'lonlɪ〕*adj.* 寂寞的　　***once in a while*** 偶爾；有時
　　　　　alone〔ə'lon〕*adj.* 獨自的

43. (**B**) I saw the boy sink.
　　我看到那男孩沈下去。

(A) 我看到他走路。　　　　(B) 我看到他往下沈。
(C) 我看到他跑步。　　　　(D) 我看到他喝酒。

* sink〔sɪŋk〕v. 下沈

44. (**B**) There's a lot of water in the air.
　　空氣中有許多水分。

(A) 陽光普照。　　　　　　(B) 濕度很高。
(C) 天氣乾燥。　　　　　　(D) 天氣很怡人。

* humidity〔hju'mɪdətɪ〕n. 濕度

45. (**C**) I am more than willing to cooperate.
　　我非常願意合作。

(A) 我要成為接線生。　　　(B) 我不只是一個接線生。
(C) 我非常樂意合作。　　　(D) 我將成為合作的幹部。

* *more than* 非常；不只是　　cooperate〔ko'ɑpə,ret〕v. 合作
operator〔'ɑpə,retə〕n. 接線生　　executive〔ɪg'zɛkjutɪv〕n. 幹部

46. (**B**) Samuel wanted to buy the coat for 90 dollars; however,
　　he ran short of cash.
　　山米爾想買這件九十元的外套，然而他錢不夠。

(A) 他身上有很多錢。　　　(B) 他錢不夠。
(C) 他還剩一點錢。　　　　(D) 他順利買到外套。

* *run short of* sth. 不夠~

47. (**C**) It is illegal to park in front of the water hydrant.
　　在消防栓前停車是違規的。

(A) 在那兒停車沒關係。　　(B) 那裏准許停車。
(C) 在那裏停車違法。　　　(D) 總是有車停在那裏。

* illegal〔ɪ'ligḷ〕adj. 非法的　　hydrant〔'haɪdrənt〕n. 消防栓
permit〔pə'mɪt〕v. 准許　　unlawful〔ʌn'lɔfəl〕adj. 非法的

48. (**B**) Mary went along with our suggestion.
　　　　瑪麗贊成我們的提議。

　　(A) 她提出建議。　　　　　　(B) 她贊成提議。
　　(C) 她改變提議。　　　　　　(D) 她將提議打字出來。
　　* *go along with* 贊成

49. (**D**) The girl said, "We were not able to go to the party yesterday."
　　　　那女孩說：「我們昨天沒有辦法去舞會。」

　　(A) 那女孩昨天出去兩次。　　(B) 那些女孩子去參加舞會。
　　(C) 那女孩要去參加舞會。　　(D) 那些女孩子沒有參加舞會。
　　* attend (ə'tɛnd) *v.* 參加

50. (**B**) We were very glad when we approached the station.
　　　　當我們快到車站時，我們好高興。

　　(A) 火車離開時我們好高興。
　　(B) 接近車站使我們感到快樂。
　　(C) 離開車站使我們快樂。
　　(D) 當我們去參觀車站時，我們很高興。
　　* approach (ə'protʃ) *v.* 接近

51. (**D**) M : Watch where you're going, Madam.
　　　　W : Why do you say that, officer?
　　　　M : Because if you are not more careful, you might end up in the hospital.
　　　　To whom is the policeman talking?
　　　　男：看路啊，太太。
　　　　女：這話怎麼說，警官？
　　　　男：因為妳如果再不小心，可能就得進醫院了。
　　　　警察在跟誰說話？

　　(A) 一位警官　　(B) 一位醫生　　(C) 一位病人　　(D) 一位駕駛
　　* *end up* 結果

52. (**C**) M：I wish I could get used to this American custom of using first names.

W：I usually call just my good friends by their first names.

What's the man complaining about?

男：我希望我能習慣美國這種直接叫人名字的習俗。

女：我通常只有好朋友才會直接叫名字。

這位男士在抱怨什麼？

(A) 無法得到他要的東西　　(B) 打電話拜訪顧客

(C) 一種對他很陌生的習俗　(D) 他的一些好朋友

* *get used to* 習慣於～　　*call up* 打電話

53. (**D**) M：I'd love to dance, but I don't know the steps.

W：It doesn't matter. No one will be looking at us in this crowd.

What does the woman mean?

男：我很想跳舞，但我不知道怎麼跳。

女：沒關係。這兒這麼多人，沒有人會看我們。

這位女士是什麼意思？

(A) 他跳得如何不重要。

(B) 如果他小心一點，就沒人會注意。

(C) 沒人知道這個舞怎麼跳。

(D) 反正太擁擠了也無法跳。

54. (**D**) W：When is Virginia coming home?

M：Oh, she will come home eventually.

When will she be home?

女：維吉妮亞什麼時候會回家？

男：哦，她終究會回來的。

她什麼時候會回來？

(A) 儘快　　　　　　　　　(B) 隔天

(C) 再過一、二個星期　　　(D) 未來的某個時間

* eventually (ɪˈvɛntʃʊəlɪ) *adv.* 結果地；最後地

55. (**A**)　M：Where are you going, Sarah?
　　　　W：To Boston.
　　　　M：What kind of ticket are you buying?
　　　　W：A round trip ticket.
　　　　What kind of ticket is Sarah buying?
　　　　男：莎拉，妳要去哪裏？
　　　　女：去波士頓。
　　　　男：妳買什麼票？
　　　　女：來回票。
　　　　莎拉買什麼票？

　　(A) 到波士頓的來回票　　　　　(B) 單程票
　　(C) 記帳買的票　　　　　　　(D) 付現買的票
　　* **round trip ticket** 來回票　　**one-way ticket** 單程票
　　　purchase (ˈpɝtʃəs) v. 購買　　**on credit** 記帳

56. (**A**)　W：Good Heavens! What happened?
　　　　M：As you see, the glass was shattered.
　　　　What did he say about the glass?
　　　　女：老天！發生什麼事了？
　　　　男：如你所見，玻璃破了。
　　　　他說玻璃怎麼？

　　(A) 破成碎片了　　　(B) 髒了　　　(C) 鎖在櫃子裏　　　(D) 滿是油漆
　　* shatter (ˈʃætɚ) v. 破碎　　　lock (lɑk) v. 上鎖
　　　closet (ˈklɑzɪt) n. 櫥櫃

57. (**D**)　M：I am hungry.
　　　　W：We have a good choice of vegetables today.
　　　　What did the woman say she had?
　　　　男：我餓了。
　　　　女：我們今天有精選的蔬菜。
　　　　這位女士說她有什麼？

　　(A) 一大箱蔬菜　　　　　　(B) 價錢好的蔬菜
　　(C) 只有幾棵蔬菜　　　　　(D) 精選的好蔬菜
　　* selection (səˈlɛkʃən) n. 選擇

58. (**C**) W : You didn't care for that restaurant, did you?

M : I'll say I didn't.

What did the man mean?

女：你不喜歡那家餐廳，是嗎？

男：我會說我不喜歡。

這位男士是什麼意思？

(A) 他沒去過那兒。　　　　　(B) 他不在乎。

(C) 他不喜歡那兒。　　　　　(D) 他不小心。

　* *care for* 喜歡

59. (**C**) M : What's the trouble with your daughter, Mrs. Lee?

W : She's all mixed up.

What was the trouble with the daughter?

男：李太太，妳女兒有什麼問題嗎？

女：她全搞混了。

這位女兒有什麼問題？

(A) 她被誤解。　　　　　　　(B) 她餓了。

(C) 她搞混了。　　　　　　　(D) 她害怕。

　* *mix up* 搞混　　misunderstand〔͵mɪsʌndɚ'stænd〕*v.* 誤解

60. (**B**) M : Be careful. There's a ditch here.

W : Mark is on the other side. I wonder how he got there.

M : He leaped over it.

How did Mark get to the other side of the ditch?

男：小心。這裏有個水溝。

女：馬克已經在另一邊。我懷疑他是怎麼過去的。

男：他跳過去的。

馬克如何到水溝的另一邊？

(A) 游泳過去　　　　　　　　(B) 跳過去

(C) 爬上去　　　　　　　　　(D) 從底下爬過去

　* ditch〔dɪtʃ〕*n.* 水溝　　leap〔lip〕*v.* 跳

　crawl〔krɔl〕*v.* 爬行

LISTENING TEST 2

- *Directions for questions 1-25. You will hear questions on the test tape. Select the one item A, B, C or D which answers the question correctly, and mark your answer sheet.*

1. A. later on
   C. at once
   B. at any time
   D. some other time

2. A. at a large table
   C. in a small enclosed place
   B. at the counter
   D. in a large room

3. A. a kind of ball game
   B. a popular sport
   C. an area for hunting
   D. a license to kill wild animals

4. A. study hard
   C. go to the movies
   B. fall asleep
   D. watch TV

5. A. It was cleaned.
   C. It was returned.
   B. It got dirty.
   D. It was destroyed.

6. A. answer his phone
   C. call someone on the phone
   B. stamp his letter
   D. write a letter

7. A. cars and trucks
   C. tables and chairs
   B. pens and pencils
   D. books and tapes

8. A. Some will sing.
   C. A few will sing.
   B. None will sing.
   D. All will sing.

9. A. He has a lot of heredity.
   C. He is very brave.
   B. He is very cautious.
   D. He has a lot of fear.

10. A. Several members were absent.
    B. Not one member was absent.
    C. None of the members were absent.
    D. Members with numbers were absent.

11. A. They are on both sides of the valley.
    B. They are on both sides of the street.
    C. They are on both sides of the view.
    D. They are on both sides of the sidewalk.

12. A. air   B. spare tire
    C. spare room   D. parking space

13. A. strange music   B. a knock on the door
    C. bright lights   D. a low-flying jet

14. A. leave it   B. get on it
    C. inspect it   D. buy it

15. A. movement   B. motor
    C. station   D. moment

16. A. two dimes and a nickel B. a half-dollar
    C. twenty pennies   D. two quarters

17. A. because he was hungry B. for a break
    C. at eight thirty   D. to a place to eat

18. A. They drew plans for it. B. They constructed it.
    C. They built an apartment. D. They lived in it.

19. A. Cadet Smith   B. lost it
    C. next week   D. some days later

20. A. quite well   B. not very well
    C. couldn't sleep at all D. quite suddenly

21. A. the professor
    C. a story

    B. some money
    D. an announcement

22. A. a postman
    C. a salesman

    B. a weatherman
    D. a clergyman

23. A. fifteen
    C. last Monday

    B. fifty
    D. a fifth of them

24. A. some place
    C. Sunday night

    B. nowhere
    D. anywhere

25. A. water
    C. traffic

    B. space
    D. forest

● *Directions for questions 26-50. You will hear statements on the test tape. Select the one answer A, B, C, or D which comes closest to the meaning of the statement and mark your answer sheet.*

26. A. There will be a game regardless of the weather.
    B. The game is temporarily delayed because of rain.
    C. There will be no game if it rains.
    D. It rains every time there is a game.

27. A. Henry studied every day, but he didn't do well in the exams.
    B. Henry hasn't studied for a while, but he thinks he will pass the exams.
    C. Henry is so lazy that he seldom passes the exams.
    D. Henry probably won't pass because he hasn't studied.

28. A. He seems to be angry.
    C. He likes to be angry.

    B. He's angry.
    D. He isn't angry.

29. A. He examined it.
    B. He paid and left.
    C. He bought the hotel.
    D. He arrived and moved in.

30. A. It seems that John forgot about our meeting.
    B. John never forgets his meetings.
    C. John should have canceled the meeting.
    D. John has to come to the meeting.

31. A. Knowing that he lacked experience, Phil still applied.
    B. Even though he was experienced, Phil didn't apply for the job.
    C. Phil was highly qualified for the job, so he applied.
    D. Phil didn't have much experience working in the field.

32. A. He is a good driver.   B. He is a good swimmer.
    C. He is a good father.   D. He is a good student.

33. A. She was not interested in it.
    B. It was exciting.
    C. She was impressed with it.
    D. She likes long movies.

34. A. Go and see him.   B. Call him on the phone.
    C. Take someone to see him.   D. Attract his attention.

35. A. She has little money now.
    B. She has too much change.
    C. She has more money than usual.
    D. She has a lot of cash at present.

36. A. They must study the lesson carefully.
    B. They should study the lesson carefully.
    C. They might study the lesson carefully.
    D. They won't study the lesson carefully.

37. A. The building has just been planned.
    B. The building is not yet finished.
    C. The building was built underground.
    D. The building is being torn down.

38. A. It can be controlled with water.
    B. It can be frozen into water.
    C. It can be changed into water.
    D. It can be mixed with water.

39. A. He was pleasing his wife.
    B. He was bothering his wife.
    C. He suddenly remembered his wife.
    D. He resembled his wife.

40. A. Mrs. Carl wanted her children to leave the dinner table.
    B. Mrs. Carl wanted her children to be more polite while eating.
    C. Mrs. Carl wanted her children to eat a little more slowly.
    D. Mrs. Carl wanted her children to remember meal times.

41. A. Mike enjoyed the sounds at the party.
    B. Mike didn't like the sounds at the party.
    C. It seems that Mike had a good time.
    D. Mike himself didn't like the party.

42. A. It drops down the engine.
    B. It holds up the engine.
    C. It covers the engine.
    D. It supplies the engine.

43. A. It is necessary to regulate it.
    B. It is necessary to issue it.
    C. It is necessary to compare it.
    D. It is necessary to upset it.

44. A. The professor was upset.
    B. The new schedule annoyed him
    C. He set off on his summer vacation.
    D. The professor arranged the schedule.

45. A. The suitcase is much heavier since you packed it.
    B. I prefer a lighter suitcase.
    C. The suitcase is not as light as the other one.
    D. You don't know how heavy the suitcase really is.

46. A. My uncle borrowed my typewriter.
    B. I can type well on my uncle's typewriter.
    C. I can use my uncle's typewriter.
    D. My uncle isn't a good typist.

47. A. He is trying to design a fast car.
    B. He is trying to design one that makes no sound.
    C. He is trying to design one that is cheaper.
    D. He is trying to design a car that is easy to drive.

48. A. He cannot hear.   B. He cannot see.
    C. He cannot talk.   D. He cannot walk.

49. A. He was tired of hearing complaints.
    B. He was tired of hearing music.
    C. He was tired of hearing the pipes.
    D. He was tired of hearing the noise.

50. A. There isn't enough dormitory space for the students.
    B. Students must pay for living expenses separately.
    C. The university cannot pay for new buildings.
    D. Students cannot live in the dormitory.

● *Directions for questions 51-60. You will hear dialogs on the test tape. Select the correct answer A, B, C, or D and mark your answer sheet.*

51. A. Jim   B. Carol
    C. the bakery   D. Susan

52. A. temperatures   B. the seasons
    C. zones   D. climates

53. A. in an area near the city
    B. downtown
    C. in the country
    D. on the crossroads

54. A. increase his speed
    B. decrease his speed
    C. move very fast
    D. take a long time to move

55. A. They were busy once in a while.
    B. They were busy last week.
    C. They arrived very late.
    D. Recently they have been busy.

56. A. The roof is touching the ground.
    B. The roof is perpendicular to the ground.
    C. The roof is level with the ground.
    D. The roof is parallel to the ground.

57. A. "I can't dissolve it."   B. "I can't solve it."
    C. "I can't add it."   D. "I can't subtract it."

58. A. Everyone participated in them.
    B. Everyone anticipated them.
    C. Everyone accepted them.
    D. Everyone divided them.

59. A. You'll have a chance to speak German.
    B. It's a good practice to speak German.
    C. You'll learn German quickly.
    D. You won't have any occasion to speak German.

60. A. one hundred persons
    B. a dozen persons
    C. less than one hundred persons
    D. a minimum of one hundred persons

"My father made a scarecrow so good that crows would not come within three miles of his farm," the farm boy boasted.

"That's nothing," his friend said. "My uncle made a scarecrow so good that the crows brought back all the corn they had stolen the previous year."

「我爸爸做了一個非常棒的稻草人，以至於烏鴉都不敢靠近他的農場三哩之內。」農場男孩如此吹噓。

「那沒什麼。」他的朋友說：「我叔叔做的稻草人，好得讓烏鴉把它們前一年偷的玉米都送還回來了。」

ECL 聽力測驗 [2] 詳解

1. (**C**) Henry must leave right away. When must Henry leave?
亨利必須立刻離開。/ 亨利何時必須離開？
(A) 等會兒　　(B) 隨時隨地　　(C) 立刻　　(D) 改天

2. (**C**) Tony said to Sunny, "Let's eat in this booth."
Where did Tony want to eat?
湯尼對桑尼說：「咱們在這座位吃吧。」/ 湯尼想在哪裏吃？
(A) 在一張大桌子上　　　　　(B) 在櫃台
(C) 在一個小又封閉的空間　　(D) 在一個大房間
* booth〔 buθ 〕 *n.* 隔開的空間；（餐廳的）座位
counter〔 'kauntɚ 〕 *n.* 櫃台　　enclose〔 ɪn'kloz 〕 *v.* 圍繞

3. (**D**) What is a hunting permit?
什麼是狩獵許可證？
(A) 一種球類遊戲　　　　(B) 一種受歡迎的運動
(C) 打獵的場地　　　　　(D) 一種可以捕殺野生動物的執照
* permit〔 'pɝmɪt 〕 *n.* 許可證；執照　　license〔 'laɪsn̩s 〕 *n.* 執照

4. (**B**) He should have studied last night, but he was too tired.
What was he likely to do last night?
他昨晚該讀書，可是他太累了。/ 他昨晚可能做了什麼事？
(A) 努力用功　　　　(B) 睡著了
(C) 去看電影　　　　(D) 看電視
* *be likely to* 可能　　*fall asleep* 睡著

5. (**D**) Jane's book burned up. What happened to it?
珍的書燒掉了。/ 珍的書怎麼了？
(A) 被清理乾淨了　　(B) 變髒了
(C) 被找回來了　　　(D) 毀壞了
* *burn up* 燒掉；燒盡

6. (**C**) Private Hardy is going to make a call.
What is he going to do?

士兵哈蒂要去打個電話。/ 他要做什麼?

(A) 接電話　　　　　　　　　(B) 在信上貼郵票
(C) 打電話給某人　　　　　　(D) 寫信

* private ('praɪvɪt) *n.* 士兵 (階級最低)
stamp (stæmp) *v.* 在~上貼郵票

7. (**C**) The sons picked up the new furniture for their mother.
What did they pick up?

兒子們爲他們的母親挑選家具。/ 他們在挑選什麼?

(A) 汽車及卡車　　(B) 筆與鉛筆　　(C) 桌椅　　(D) 書及帶子

* *pick up* 挑選　　furniture ('fɜnɪtʃə) *n.* 家具

8. (**D**) If the entire group will sing, how many will sing?

如果整個團體要唱歌,那是多少人要唱?

(A) 一些人要唱。　　　　　　(B) 沒人要唱。
(C) 一些人要唱。　　　　　　(D) 全部的人要唱。

* entire (ɪn'taɪr) *adj.* 全部的　　*a few* 一些

9. (**C**) If someone has a lot of courage, what does it mean?

假使某人勇氣十足,這意味著什麼?

(A) 他遺傳了很多特點。　　　(B) 他非常小心。
(C) 他非常勇敢。　　　　　　(D) 他很害怕。

* heredity (hə'rɛdətɪ) *n.* 遺傳
cautious ('kɔʃəs) *adj.* 小心的;謹愼的　　brave (brev) *adj.* 勇敢的

10. (**A**) A number of members were absent this morning.
How many were absent?

有一些會員今早缺席。/ 多少人缺席?

(A) 一些會員缺席。　　　　　(B) 沒人缺席。
(C) 沒人缺席。　　　　　　　(D) 有號碼的會員缺席。

* *a number of* 一些　　absent ('æbsnt) *adj.* 缺席的

11. (**B**) Flowers grow on both sides of the avenue.
Where are the flowers?
街道兩旁長滿了花。/ 花兒在哪裏？

(A) 在山谷兩側。

(B) 在街道兩旁。

(C) 在視野兩側。

(D) 在人行道兩邊。

* avenue 〔'ævə,nju 〕 *n.* 大街；林蔭大道
valley 〔'vælɪ 〕 *n.* 山谷　　view 〔 vju 〕 *n.* 景色；視野
sidewalk 〔'saɪd,wɔk 〕 *n.* 人行道

12. (**C**) Do you have space in the car for another person?
What does the "space" in the sentence mean?
你車內還有空位可容下一個人嗎？
句中的 "space" 意思為何？

(A) 空氣

(B) 備胎

(C) 多餘的空間

(D) 停車位

* space 〔 spes 〕 *n.* 空間　　spare 〔 spɛr 〕 *adj.* 剩下的；多餘的
tire 〔 taɪr 〕 *n.* 輪胎

13. (**D**) The students looked up from their books when they
heard the roar. What did they hear?
聽到了隆隆聲，原本在看書的學生們都抬起頭來。
他們聽到了什麼？

(A) 奇怪的音樂

(B) 敲門聲

(C) 明亮的燈光

(D) 低飛的噴射機

* ***look up*** 抬頭　　roar 〔 ror 〕 *n.* 轟鳴聲；隆隆聲
jet 〔 dʒɛt 〕 *n.* 噴射機

14. (**B**) Alex will probably board the plane this afternoon.
What will he do?
艾利斯也許今天下午會搭飛機。/ 他將會做什麼？

(A) 離開飛機

(B) 上飛機

(C) 檢查飛機

(D) 買下飛機

* board 〔 bord 〕 *v.* 上（船、車、飛機等）
inspect 〔 ɪn'spɛkt 〕 *v.* 檢查

15. (**A**) The workman cut the wood in quick motion.
What do we mean by motion?
工人快速地伐木。/「動作」的意思是什麼?

(A) 動作　　　　(B) 馬達　　　　(C) 車站　　　　(D) 片刻

* motion〔'moʃən〕*n.*（物體的）運動；移動　　motor〔'motɚ〕*n.* 馬達

16. (**A**) If a boy asks you to change a quarter, what would you give him?
如果一個男孩要求你把二十五分的硬幣換開,你會給他什麼?

(A) 二個一角、一個五分　　　　(B) 一個五角
(C) 二十分錢　　　　　　　　　(D) 二個二十五分硬幣

* quarter〔'kwɔrtɚ〕*n.* 二十五分硬幣　　dime〔daim〕*n.* 一角硬幣
nickel〔'nɪkl̩〕*n.* 五分硬幣　　penny〔'pɛnɪ〕*n.* 一分錢

17. (**D**) Mr. Walker went to the café at 8:30. Where did he go?
渥克先生八點三十分到咖啡廳去。/ 他去哪兒了?

(A) 因為他餓了。　　　　(B) 去休息一下。
(C) 八點三十分。　　　　(D) 去一個地方吃東西。

* café〔kə'fe, kæ'fe〕*n.* 小餐館；咖啡廳

18. (**A**) Mr. White said, "The engineers designed an apartment."
What did Mr. White mean?
懷特先生說:「工程師設計了一棟公寓。」/ 他指的是什麼?

(A) 他們為它畫設計圖。　　　　(B) 他們建了它。
(C) 他們建了一棟公寓。　　　　(D) 他們住在那裏面。

* engineer〔͵ɛndʒə'nɪr〕*n.* 工程師　　construct〔kən'strʌkt〕*v.* 建造

19. (**D**) It was several days before Cadet Smith discovered that he had lost his keys.
When did he find out that his keys were missing?
幾天之後,實習生史密斯才發現他的鑰匙掉了。
他什麼時候發現鑰匙不見了?

(A) 史密斯本人　　(B) 丟了鑰匙　　(C) 下個禮拜　　(D) 幾天之後

* cadet〔kə'dɛt〕*n.* 軍校學生；見習生

20. (**A**) Ryan said, "I couldn't have slept more soundly last night." How well did Ryan sleep last night?

萊恩說:「昨晚我睡得好極了。」／昨晚萊恩睡得如何?

(A) 滿不錯的　　(B) 不是很好　　(C) 根本睡不著　(D) 十分突然

* soundly ('saʊndlɪ) *adv.* 完全地;酣然地(入睡)
suddenly ('sʌdn̩lɪ) *adv.* 突然地

21. (**D**) The professor put a notice on the bulletin board. What did he place on the bulletin board?

教授在公告欄上貼了一張通告。／他在公告欄上貼了什麼東西?

(A) 教授　　(B) 一些錢　　(C) 一個故事　　(D) 通告

* notice ('notɪs) *n.* 公告;通知　　bulletin ('bʊlətɪn) *n.* 公告
professor (prə'fɛsə) *n.* 教師;教授
announcement (ə'naʊnsmənt) *n.* 公布;通告

22. (**C**) Harry spent five hours knocking on doors, but he didn't sell a single magazine.
What's the possible occupation of Harry?

哈利花了五個小時挨家挨戶敲門,但他一本雜誌也沒有賣出去。
哈利的職業可能是什麼?

(A) 郵差　　(B) 氣象播報員　　(C) 推銷員　　(D) 牧師

* clergyman ('klɜdʒɪmən) *n.* 神職人員;牧師

23. (**B**) Fifty students went to the coast last Monday.
How many students went to the coast?

五十個學生上星期一去海邊。／有多少學生去海邊?

(A) 十五人　　　　　　　(B) 五十人
(C) 上星期一　　　　　　(D) 五分之一的人

* coast (kost) *n.* 海岸

24. (**A**) Alan said that he was going somewhere Sunday night. Where did he say he was going?

亞倫說他禮拜天晚上要去某個地方。／他說他到哪兒去了?

(A) 某個地方　　(B) 哪兒也沒去　　(C) 星期天晚上　(D) 任何地方

25. (**B**) When men traveled between the earth and the moon, what did their ships travel through?

當人類在地球與月球之間旅行時,他們的太空船穿越了什麼?

(A) 水　　　　 (B) <u>太空</u>　　　　 (C) 交通　　　　 (D) 森林

* space (spes) *n.* 太空　　　 traffic ('træfɪk) *n.* 交通

forest ('fɔrɪst) *n.* 森林

26. (**A**) The game will be held, rain or shine.

不論晴雨,比賽都會舉行。

(A) <u>不論天氣如何都有比賽。</u>

(B) 因為下雨,比賽暫時延後。

(C) 如果下雨就沒有比賽。

(D) 每次比賽就下雨。

* *be held* 舉行　　 *rain or shine* 不論晴雨　　 *regardless of* 不管

temporarily ('tɛmpə,rɛrəlɪ) *adv.* 暫時地

27. (**B**) Although Henry hasn't studied in weeks, he's sure he'll pass the exams.

雖然亨利幾星期沒念書,可是他確信他會通過考試。

(A) 亨利每天念書,但考試還是沒考好。

(B) <u>亨利有一陣子沒念書,可是他認為他會通過考試。</u>

(C) 亨利很懶,所以很少通過考試。

(D) 亨利可能不會通過考試,因為他沒念書。

28. (**A**) Bruce sounds like he's angry.

布魯斯聽起來像是在生氣。

(A) <u>他似乎在生氣。</u>　　　　 (B) 他生氣了。

(C) 他喜歡生氣。　　　　　　 (D) 他沒生氣。

29. (**B**) Peter checked out of the hotel yesterday.

彼得昨天結帳離開旅館。

(A) 他檢查它。　　　　　　 (B) <u>他付帳然後離開。</u>

(C) 他買下旅館。　　　　　 (D) 他抵達並且搬進去。

* *check out* 結帳退房　　 examine (ɪg'zæmɪn) *v.* 檢查

30. (**A**) John must have forgotten about our meeting.
約翰一定忘了我們的會議了。

(A) 約翰似乎忘了我們的會議了。　(B) 約翰從不會忘記他的會議。
(C) 約翰早該取消這次會議了。　(D) 約翰必須來參加會議。

31. (**A**) Despite his inexperience in the field, Phil applied for the job.
儘管對這方面沒有經驗，菲爾還是去應徵這份工作。

(A) 知道缺乏經驗，菲爾還是去應徵。
(B) 即使有經驗，菲爾也不去應徵這份工作。
(C) 菲爾對這份工作非常合格，所以他去應徵。
(D) 這方面菲爾沒有很多工作經驗。

* **apply for** 申請；應徵

32. (**D**) Michael has a good academic record.
邁可擁有優秀的學業成績。

(A) 他是個優秀的駕駛。　(B) 他是個優秀的泳者。
(C) 他是個好爸爸。　(D) 他是個好學生。

* academic〔ͺækəˋdɛmɪk〕 *adj.* 學術的；學業的
record〔ˋrɛkəd〕 *n.* 成績；紀錄

33. (**A**) Amy was bored with the movie. It was too long.
這部電影讓艾美感到無聊。它太長了。

(A) 她對它不感興趣。　(B) 它很刺激。
(C) 她對它印象深刻。　(D) 她喜歡長的電影。

* **be bored with** 對～感到無聊　impress〔ɪmˋprɛs〕 *v.* 使印象深刻

34. (**B**) Give the captain a ring after you land.
著陸後打電話給上尉。

(A) 去看他。　(B) 打電話給他。
(C) 帶某人去看他。　(D) 吸引他的注意。

* **give** *sb.* **a ring** 打電話給某人
captain〔ˋkæptɪn〕 *n.* 船長；機長；首領；上尉
land〔lænd〕 *v.* 登陸；降落　attention〔əˋtɛnʃən〕 *n.* 注意

35. (**A**) She is running short of cash at present.
她現在缺少現金。

    (A) 她現在的錢很少。   (B) 她有太多零錢。

    (C) 她的錢比平常多。   (D) 她現在有很多現金。

    * ***run short of*** 缺少   cash〔kæʃ〕 *n.* 現金
      at present 目前；現在   change〔tʃendʒ〕 *n.* 零錢

36. (**B**) The students ought to study this lesson carefully.
學生們應該仔細地研讀這一課。

    (A) 他們必須仔細地研讀這一課。

    (B) 他們應該仔細地研讀這一課。

    (C) 他們可能仔細地研讀這一課。

    (D) 他們將不會仔細地研讀這一課。

    * ***ought to*** 應該

37. (**B**) Across the street, a new building is under construction.
在對街，有棟新大樓正在施工中。

    (A) 大樓剛設計好。   (B) 大樓還沒完成。

    (C) 大樓建在地底下。   (D) 大樓正在拆除。

    * construction〔kən'strʌkʃən〕 *n.* 建築   ***under construction*** 建築中
      tear〔tɛr〕 *v.* 撕裂   ***tear down*** 拆除

38. (**C**) Ice can be converted into water.
冰可以變化成水。

    (A) 冰可以由水來控制。   (B) 冰可以凍結成水。

    (C) 冰可以變化成水。   (D) 冰可以和水混合。

    * convert〔kən'vɝt〕 *v.* 轉變
      frozen〔'frozn̩〕 *v.* 結冰（freeze 的過去分詞）

39. (**B**) The man was disturbing his wife.
那個男士正在打擾他太太。

    (A) 他正在取悅他太太。   (B) 他正在打擾他太太。

    (C) 他突然想起他太太。   (D) 他長得像他太太。

    * disturb〔dɪ'stɝb〕 *v.* 打擾   resemble〔rɪ'zɛmbl̩〕 *v.* 相似

40. (**B**) Mrs. Carl reminded her children of table manners.
   卡爾太太提醒她的孩子注意餐桌禮儀。

   (A) 卡爾太太要她的孩子離開餐桌。
   (B) 卡爾太太要她的孩子吃飯時更有禮貌。
   (C) 卡爾太太要她的孩子吃飯慢一點。
   (D) 卡爾太太要她的孩子記住用餐時間。

   * ***remind*** sb. ***of*** sth. 提醒某人某事
     meal〔mil〕n. 一餐

41. (**C**) It sounds like Mike enjoyed himself at the party.
   聽起來麥克在舞會玩得很開心。

   (A) 麥克喜歡舞會的聲音。
   (B) 麥克不喜歡舞會的聲音。
   (C) 麥克似乎玩得很開心。
   (D) 麥克自己不喜歡舞會。

   * ***enjoy*** oneself 玩得開心 (= have a good time)

42. (**B**) This attachment supports the engine.
   這個零件支撐著引擎。

   (A) 它降下引擎。   (B) 它支撐住引擎。
   (C) 它蓋住引擎。   (D) 它補充引擎。

   * attachment〔ə'tætʃmənt〕n. 配件；附屬物
     support〔sə'port, -'pɔrt〕v. 支持
     engine〔'ɛndʒən〕n. 引擎   drop〔drɑp〕v. 降下
     hold up 支持   cover〔'kʌvɚ〕v. 遮蓋
     supply〔sə'plaɪ〕v. 補充

43. (**A**) It is necessary to adjust the piano correctly.
   有必要將鋼琴的音調整正確。

   (A) 有必要調整它。   (B) 有必要發行它。
   (C) 有必要比較它。   (D) 有必要顛覆它。

   * adjust〔ə'dʒʌst〕v. 調整   regulate〔'rɛgjə,let〕v. 調整
     issue〔'ɪʃu, 'ɪʃju〕v. 發行   compare〔kəm'pɛr〕v. 比較
     upset〔ʌp'sɛt〕v. 顛覆

44. (**D**) The schedule was set up by the professor this summer.
今年夏天課表由教授排定。

(A) 教授很難過。　　　　　　(B) 新課表使他煩惱。
(C) 他出發去度暑假。　　　　(D) 教授安排課表。

* schedule ('skɛdʒul) *n.* 時間表；課表　　*set up* 設立；安排
upset (ʌp'sɛt) *adj.* 難過的　　annoy (ə'nɔɪ) *v.* 使煩擾
arrange (ə'rendʒ) *v.* 安排

45. (**D**) The suitcase is heavier than you think it is.
這個旅行箱比你所認為的更重。

(A) 自從你打包後，這個旅行箱更重了。
(B) 我比較喜歡輕一點的旅行箱。
(C) 這個旅行箱沒有另外一個輕。
(D) 你不知道這個旅行箱實際有多重。

* suitcase ('sut,kes) *n.* 旅行箱　　pack (pæk) *v.* 打包

46. (**C**) My uncle says I can borrow his typewriter.
我的舅舅說我可以借用他的打字機。

(A) 我的舅舅借用我的打字機。
(B) 我用我舅舅的打字機可以打得很好。
(C) 我可以用我舅舅的打字機。
(D) 我舅舅不是一個好打字員。

47. (**B**) He is trying to design a silent car.
他正嘗試設計無聲的車。

(A) 他正嘗試設計快速車。　　(B) 他正嘗試設計沒有聲音的車。
(C) 他正嘗試設計便宜的車。　(D) 他正嘗試設計容易開的車。

* design (dɪ'zaɪn) *v.* 設計　　silent ('saɪlənt) *adj.* 無聲的

48. (**A**) Be careful with Mr. Roberts. He is deaf.
小心羅勃茲先生。他是聾子。

(A) 他聽不到。　　　　　　　(B) 他看不見。
(C) 他不會說話。　　　　　　(D) 他不會走路。

* deaf (dɛf) *adj.* 聾的

49. (**A**) The lieutenant was tired of hearing gripes.
中尉聽煩了怨言。

(A) 他聽煩抱怨。 (B) 他聽煩音樂。

(C) 他聽煩笛聲。 (D) 他聽煩噪音。

* lieutenant (lu'tɛnənt) *n.* 中尉　　gripe (graɪp) *n.* 怨言

50. (**B**) The university fees don't include room and board.
大學學費不包括食宿費用。

(A) 給學生的宿舍空間不夠。

(B) 學生們的生活費用必須另外付。

(C) 大學無法付新大樓的費用。

(D) 學生不能住在宿舍裏。

* board (bord) *n.* 膳食　　expense (ɪk'spɛns) *n.* 費用

51. (**D**) M：Carol, did you bake the cake for Jim's party?
W：I had Susan do it.
Who baked the cake?
男：卡羅，妳替吉姆的舞會烤好蛋糕了嗎?
女：我叫蘇珊去烤了。
蛋糕是誰烤的?

(A) 吉姆　　(B) 卡羅　　(C) 麵包店　　(D) 蘇珊

* bakery ('bekərɪ) *n.* 麵包店

52. (**B**) M：Do you like winter better than summer?
W：Not really. Actually, I like spring and fall better than either.
What are they talking about?
男：妳喜歡冬天勝於夏天嗎?
女：不見得。事實上，我比較喜歡春天和秋天。
他們在談論什麼?

(A) 溫度　　(B) 季節　　(C) 地帶　　(D) 氣候

* temperature ('tɛmprətʃɚ) *n.* 溫度　　zone (zon) *n.* 地帶
climate ('klaɪmɪt) *n.* 氣候

53. (**A**) M：Where do you do your shopping?
　　　　W：In a shopping center, of course.
　　　　M：Which shopping center?
　　　　W：The one in the suburbs.
　　　　Where is this shopping center located?
　　　　男：妳去哪裏買東西？
　　　　女：當然是去購物中心。
　　　　男：哪個購物中心？
　　　　女：市郊的那一家。
　　　　這家購物中心位在哪裏？

　　　　(A) <u>靠近城市的地區</u>　　　　(B) 市中心
　　　　(C) 鄉下　　　　　　　　　　(D) 十字路口

　　　　* suburb (ˊsʌbɝb) *n.* 市郊　　locate (loˊket) *v.* 位於
　　　　downtown (ˊdaʊnˊtaʊn) *adv.* 在市中心
　　　　crossroads (ˊkrɔs͵rodz) *n.pl.* 十字路口

54. (**B**) W：Watch out, Eric. You'll hit that dog.
　　　　M：Don't worry. I'm careful.
　　　　W：Well, go more slowly.
　　　　What does the woman want the man to do?
　　　　女：小心，艾瑞克。你會撞到那隻狗。
　　　　男：別擔心。我很小心。
　　　　女：喂，再開慢一點。
　　　　這位女士要男士怎麼做？

　　　　(A) 加速　　　(B) <u>減速</u>　　　(C) 快速移動　　　(D) 慢慢移動

55. (**D**) M：Are the police kept busy in this city?
　　　　W：Lately they've been busy because of the heavy traffic.
　　　　What did the woman say about the police?
　　　　男：這城市的警察一直保持忙碌嗎？
　　　　女：最近他們一直在忙，因爲交通繁忙。
　　　　這位女士說警察怎麼樣？

　　　　(A) 他們偶爾忙碌。　　　　(B) 他們上星期忙碌。
　　　　(C) 他們很晚才到。　　　　(D) <u>最近他們一直在忙。</u>

　　　　* *once in a while* 偶爾

56. (**D**)   M : What kind of roof does your cabin have?
      W : A horizontal one.
      What kind of roof does the woman's cabin have?
      男：妳的小木屋屋頂是什麼樣的？
      女：水平的。
      這位女士的小木屋屋頂是什麼樣的？

   (A) 屋頂和地面接觸。　　　　　　(B) 屋頂和地面垂直。
   (C) 屋頂和地面同高。　　　　　　(D) 屋頂和地面成平行。

   * roof〔ruf〕 *n.* 屋頂　　cabin〔'kæbɪn〕 *n.* 小木屋
     horizontal〔,harə'zantḷ〕 *adj.* 水平的
     perpendicular〔,pɝpən'dɪkjələ〕 *adj.* 垂直的
     level〔'lɛvḷ〕 *adj.* 相同高度的　　parallel〔'pærə,lɛl〕 *adj.* 平行的

57. (**B**)   M : What's your problem, Jane?
      W : I can't figure this out.
      What did Jane say?
      男：珍，妳的問題是什麼？
      女：我不了解這個。
      珍說什麼？

   (A) 我無法溶解它。　　　　　　(B) 我無法解決。
   (C) 我無法將它加起來。　　　　(D) 我無法減掉它。

   * ***figure out*** 理解　　dissolve〔dɪ'zalv〕 *v.* 溶解
     solve〔salv〕 *v.* 解決　　subtract〔səb'trækt〕 *v.* 減去

58. (**A**)   M : Did everyone enjoy the activities?
      W : Well, everyone took part in them.
      What did the woman say?
      男：每個人都喜歡這些活動嗎？
      女：嗯，每個人都參加了。
      這位女士說了什麼？

   (A) 每個人都參加活動。　　　　　(B) 每個人都期待活動。
   (C) 每個人都接受活動。　　　　　(D) 每個人都將活動分開。

   * ***take part in*** 參加　　participate〔pɚ'tɪsə,pet , par-〕 *v.* 參與
     anticipate〔æn'tɪsə,pet〕 *v.* 期待　　divide〔də'vaɪd〕 *v.* 分開

59.(**A**)　M：I have no friends with whom to practice German.

W：I'll see to it that you soon have an opportunity to speak German.

What did the woman say?

男：我沒有朋友可以練習德文。

女：我來處理，你很快就有機會說德文。

這位女士說了什麼？

(A) 你將有機會說德文。　　　(B) 說德文是很好的練習。

(C) 你很快就可以學會德文。　(D) 你將不會有任何機會說德文。

* **see to** 照料；負責　　opportunity (͵ɑpə'tjunətɪ) *n.* 機會

occasion (ə'keʒən) *n.* 時機；場合

60.(**D**)　M：How many people were at the concert last night?

W：At least one hundred.

How many people were at the concert?

男：昨晚的音樂會有多少人？

女：至少一百人。

音樂會有多少人？

(A) 一百人　　(B) 十二個人　　(C) 不到一百人　　(D) 至少一百人

* minimum ('mɪnəməm) *n.* 最小量

　　Did you hear about the cat that gave birth in a Singapore street? It got fined for littering.

　　你聽說過有一隻貓在新加坡的馬路上生產嗎？牠因為製造垃圾被罰了。

LISTENING TEST 3

● *Directions for questions 1-25. You will hear questions on the test tape. Select the one item A, B, C or D which answers the question correctly, and mark your answer sheet.*

1. A. an engineer
   C. a meteorologist
   B. a chemist
   D. a physiologist

2. A. a cold wind
   C. a light breeze
   B. a warm wind
   D. an east wind

3. A. She stopped to smoke.
   B. She no longer smokes.
   C. She has to smoke less.
   D. She told me not to smoke.

4. A. five
   C. fifteen
   B. fifty
   D. three

5. A. a sheep
   C. a ship
   B. a chip
   D. a jeep

6. A. a good student
   C. an inexpensive car
   B. a good boy
   D. a good driver

7. A. at 1030
   C. to the city
   B. to buy a dog
   D. in a park

8. A. making a turn
   C. taking a trip
   B. building a tower
   D. getting off the bus

9. A. warm
   C. not too hot
   B. very hot
   D. cool

10. A. He peeled the banana.
    B. He ate the banana peel.
    C. He dropped the banana peel.
    D. He fell down.

11. A. I failed the test.
    B. I studied harder than before.
    C. I passed the test.
    D. I stayed up studying.

12. A. for measuring lengths B. for painting boards
    C. for holding objects D. for sharpening tools

13. A. Yes, she stopped it. B. Yes, she prepared it.
    C. Yes, she pressed it. D. Yes, she presented it.

14. A. English B. spelling
    C. grammar D. organization

15. A. It's exciting. B. It's good.
    C. It's very plain. D. It's very sad.

16. A. a doctor B. a trader
    C. a swimmer D. a laborer

17. A. an engine B. an automobile
    C. an airplane D. a train

18. A. a book cover B. a table cover
    C. a window cover D. a fan cover

19. A. very good B. very bothersome
    C. very surprising D. very promising

20. A. an opportunity B. a talent
    C. a fear D. a desire

21. A. fast
    C. dark
    B. light
    D. heavy

22. A. at 1200
    C. at 2400
    B. just at dark
    D. tomorrow night

23. A. last
    C. wrong
    B. secondary
    D. most important

24. A. He needed to take his time.
    B. He had a lot of time.
    C. His time was not limited.
    D. He didn't have much time.

25. A. because he was angry
    B. because he was in a hurry
    C. because he was excited
    D. because of a fit of coughing

● *Directions for questions 26-50. You will hear statements on the test tape. Select the one answer A, B, C, or D which comes closest to the meaning of the statement and mark your answer sheet.*

26. A. She is small.
    C. She has big feet.
    B. She is large.
    D. She talks a lot.

27. A. His feet are ugly.
    B. He hurt his feet.
    C. His socks are full of holes.
    D. He did not have shoes on.

28. A. Some of the items of the dresses were the same.
    B. Everyone's dress was different.
    C. Some of the items of the dresses were different.
    D. Everyone was dressed the same.

29. A. Some parts have no people.
    B. Some parts have mountains.
    C. Some parts have no water.
    D. Some parts have no plants.

30. A. It was changing.   B. It was going faster.
    C. It was always the same. D. It was going slower.

31. A. The condition is good.
    B. The circumstances are excellent.
    C. The circumstances are poor.
    D. The solution is not very good.

32. A. She is on her way home now.
    B. She will read it at home.
    C. She is reading it at home.
    D. She will read it as she goes home.

33. A. He signed the report.   B. He changed the report.
    C. He copied the report.   D. He typed the report.

34. A. Peter could not go to the dentist.
    B. The dentist might visit Peter.
    C. Peter needs a new tooth.
    D. Peter should go to the dentist.

35. A. He somewhat liked the visits.
    B. He enjoyed the visits.
    C. He feared the visits.
    D. He refused the visits.

36. A. Mark must hurry up.
    B. It seems that there is plenty of time.
    C. Mark is pressed for time.
    D. There's a problem with the train.

37. A. A clerk in the store sold the jewels.
    B. A clerk in the store made the jewels.
    C. A clerk in the store stole the jewels.
    D. A clerk in the store bought the jewels.

38. A. The path rolls.   B. The path winds.
    C. The path skips.   D. The path dips.

39. A. He breaks the rock.
    B. The rock is too small.
    C. He doesn't go to move the rock.
    D. He can't move the rock.

40. A. They were too surprised.
    B. They were happy to see her walk.
    C. They thought she would get lost.
    D. They were very scared at what could happen.

41. A. He joined them.   B. He weighed them.
    C. He corrected them.   D. He separated them.

42. A. He knows how to inspect it.
    B. He knows how to fix it.
    C. He knows how to open it.
    D. He knows how to run it.

43. A. He has discussed that part.
    B. He has closed that part.
    C. He has overlooked that part.
    D. He has omitted that part.

44. A. It was not properly operated.
    B. It was not properly finished.
    C. It was not considered in good condition.
    D. It was not kept in good condition.

45. A. It could be wrong.
    B. It was almost right.
    C. It was wrong.
    D. It would be wrong with some changes.

46. A. They teach the activities.
    B. They study the activities.
    C. They take part in the activities.
    D. They watch movies of the activities.

47. A. Mark's car costs more.
    B. Both cars are damaged.
    C. The two cars are for sale.
    D. Allen's car costs more than Mark's.

48. A. He came this morning.
    B. He left this morning.
    C. He was given some money this morning.
    D. He was out of cash this morning.

49. A. Help me take the food out.
    B. Help me get the basket.
    C. Help me buy food from the basket.
    D. Help me put the food in the basket.

50. A. Sam is now in class.
    B. Sam has been in class for two weeks.
    C. Sam is in good health.
    D. Sam is ill.

● *Directions for questions 51-60. You will hear dialogs on the test tape. Select the correct answer A, B, C, or D and mark your answer sheet.*

51. A. He has a very good watch. B. He doesn't wear it.
    C. It doesn't keep good time. D. It is too tight.

52. A. humidity   B. atmospheric pressure
    C. temperature   D. wind velocity

53. A. 2   B. 5
    C. 7   D. 9

54. A. before five   B. on the hour
    C. within an hour   D. by the next day

55. A. windy   B. hot and dry
    C. cool   D. very damp

56. A. It's warm.   B. It's red.
    C. It's small.   D. It's wool.

57. A. a good supply of fresh fish
    B. a good supply of copper and iron
    C. a good supply of wheat and vegetables
    D. a good supply of beef cattle and sheep

58. A. Mark's son   B. Mark's wife
    C. Mark's daughter   D. the girl Mark will marry

59. A. He caused the accident.
    B. He survived the accident.
    C. He avoided the accident.
    D. He died because of the accident.

60. A. She would not pay any attention.
    B. She would argue with him.
    C. She would follow his advice.
    D. She would change her dress.

ECL 聽力測驗 [3] 詳解

1. (**C**)　Who　studies　the　weather？
　　　誰研究天氣？

　　　(A) 工程師　　　(B) 化學家　　　(C) 氣象學家　　　(D) 生理學家
　　　* engineer (ˌɛndʒəˈnɪr) *n.* 工程師　　chemist (ˈkɛmɪst) *n.* 化學家
　　　meteorologist (ˌmitɪəˈrɑlədʒɪst) *n.* 氣象學家
　　　physiologist (ˌfɪzɪˈɑlədʒɪst) *n.* 生理學家

2. (**A**)　Frank　said,　"The　wind　is　as　sharp　as　a　knife."
　　　What　kind　of　wind　is　it？
　　　法蘭克說：「風利得跟刀子一樣。」／這是什麼樣的風？

　　　(A) 冷風　　　(B) 溫暖的風　　(C) 輕微的涼風　　(D) 東風
　　　* knife (naɪf) *n.* 刀子　　breeze (briz) *n.* 微風

3. (**B**)　Nancy　has　stopped　smoking.　What　did　Nancy　do？
　　　南茜戒煙了。／南茜做了什麼了？

　　　(A) 她停下來抽煙。　　　　　(B) 她不再抽煙了。
　　　(C) 她必須少抽一點。　　　　(D) 她叫我不要抽煙。

4. (**B**)　There　are　50　officials　in　the　three　rooms.
　　　What　was　the　total　number　of　officials？
　　　在三個房間內有五十個官員。／官員的總數是多少？

　　　(A) 五個　　　(B) 五十個　　　(C) 十五個　　　(D) 三個
　　　* official (əˈfɪʃəl) *n.* 官員　　total (ˈtotḷ) *adj.* 全部的

5. (**D**)　The　teacher　pointed　to　a　picture　and　said,　"This　is　a　jeep."
　　　What　picture　did　he　point　to？
　　　老師指著一張圖並說：「這是一輛吉普車。」／他指著什麼圖？

　　　(A) 一隻綿羊　　(B) 一個碎片　　(C) 一艘船　　　(D) 一輛吉普車
　　　* jeep (dʒip) *n.* 吉普車　　chip (tʃɪp) *n.* 碎片

6. (**C**) Ted got a good bargain on a car.
What did Ted get?
泰德買到一台便宜的車。／泰德得到什麼？

(A) 一個好學生   (B) 一個好男孩

(C) 一台不貴的車   (D) 一位好司機

* bargain ('bɑrgɪn) *n.* 便宜品

7. (**C**) Alan is going to town at 1030 to buy a dog.
Where is Alan going?
阿倫十點半要到城裏買一隻狗。／阿倫要到哪裏去？

(A) 在十點半   (B) 買一隻狗

(C) 到城裏去   (D) 在公園裏

8. (**C**) We were making a tour when the typhoon came.
What were we doing when the typhoon came?
我們正在旅行時颱風就來了。／颱風來時我們在做什麼？

(A) 轉彎   (B) 建造一座塔   (C) 旅行   (D) 下車

* *make a tour* 參觀；旅行   typhoon (taɪ'fun) *n.* 颱風
make a turn 轉彎   tower ('tauɚ) *n.* 塔
get off 下車

9. (**B**) When Peter stepped outside, he said, "It's mighty hot!"
How hot was it?
當彼特走到外面時，他說：「眞是熱死了！」／有多熱？

(A) 溫暖的   (B) 非常熱   (C) 不會太熱   (D) 涼爽

* mighty ('maɪtɪ) *adv.* 很；非常

10. (**D**) He slipped on the banana peel.
What happened to him?
他踩到香蕉皮滑倒了。／他怎麼了？

(A) 他剝下了香蕉皮。   (B) 他吃掉香蕉皮。

(C) 他丟掉香蕉皮。   (D) 他跌倒了。

* slip (slɪp) *v.* 滑倒   peel (pil) *n.* 皮   *v.* 剝皮

11. (**A**) If I had studied more, I would have passed the test.
What happened?
如果我再用功點，我就通過考試了。／ 發生了什麼事？

   (A) 我考試不及格。   (B) 我比以前更用功。
   (C) 我通過考試。   (D) 我熬夜看書。

   * *stay up* 熬夜

12. (**C**) Steven has a new vise in his workshop.
What does he use it for?
史蒂文在工廠裏有把新的虎頭鉗。／ 他用它來做什麼？

   (A) 測量長度 (B) 畫板子   (C) 夾緊物品 (D) 削利工具
   * vise (vaɪs) *n.* 虎頭鉗   measure ('mɛʒɚ) *v.* 測量
   length (lɛŋθ) *n.* 長度   sharpen ('ʃɑrpn̩) *v.* 使銳利

13. (**A**) Did she prevent the accident?
她阻止意外了嗎？

   (A) 是的，她阻止了。   (B) 是的，她準備了。
   (C) 是的，她壓迫了。   (D) 是的，她提出了。
   * press (prɛs) *v.* 壓迫   present (prɪ'zɛnt) *v.* 提出

14. (**B**) Bill's grammar and organization are above average, but
his spelling needs improving.
What is he poor at?
比爾的文法和組織都在水準之上，但他的拼字需要改進。
他什麼部分較差？

   (A) 英文 (B) 拼字   (C) 文法   (D) 組織
   * grammar ('græmɚ) *n.* 文法   organization (,ɔrgənə'zeʃən) *n.* 組織
     above average 一般水準之上

15. (**C**) Last night my friend and I saw a mediocre movie.
How was the movie?
昨天晚上我和朋友看了一部平凡的電影。／ 這部電影如何？

   (A) 很刺激 (B) 很好   (C) 很平淡   (D) 很悲哀
   * mediocre (,midɪ'okɚ) *adj.* 平凡的   plain (plen) *adj.* 平淡的

16. (**C**) Cynthia's brother is an athlete. What is he?
辛西亞的哥哥是運動員。／他是做什麼的？

    (A) 醫生　　　　(B) 貿易商　　(C) 游泳選手　　(D) 勞工

    * athlete (ˈæθlɪt) *n.* 運動員
      trader (ˈtredɚ) *n.* 貿易商　　　laborer (ˈlebərɚ) *n.* 勞工

17. (**A**) Our unit received a new motor. What did we get?
本單位領到一台新馬達。／我們拿到什麼？

    (A) 引擎　　　　(B) 汽車　　　(C) 飛機　　　　(D) 火車

    * unit (ˈjunɪt) *n.* 單位　　motor (ˈmotɚ) *n.* 馬達
      engine (ˈɛndʒən) *n.* 引擎　　automobile (ˈɔtəməˌbil) *n.* 汽車

18. (**C**) Susie's mother closed the curtain.
What did she close?
蘇西的母親拉上窗帘。／她把什麼合上？

    (A) 書的封面　　(B) 餐桌罩　　(C) 窗帘　　　(D) 風扇的蓋子

    * curtain (ˈkɝtn̩) *n.* 窗帘　　cover (ˈkʌvɚ) *n.* 封面；蓋子
      fan (fæn) *n.* 風扇

19. (**B**) Our neighbors were annoyed at our son's practicing the
trumpet all day long.
How do they find our son's playing?
我們鄰居對我們兒子整天練習吹喇叭感到很煩。
他們認為我們兒子的吹奏如何？

    (A) 很好　　　　(B) 很煩　　　(C) 很驚人　　(D) 很有前途

    * annoyed (əˈnɔɪd) *adj.* 煩擾的　　trumpet (ˈtrʌmpɪt) *n.* 喇叭
      bothersome (ˈbɑðɚsəm) *adj.* 煩人的
      promising (ˈprɑmɪsɪŋ) *adj.* 有前途的

20. (**B**) George has the ability to learn languages.
What does George have?
喬治有學習語言的能力。／喬治擁有什麼？

    (A) 機會　　　　(B) 才能　　　(C) 恐懼　　　(D) 慾望

    * talent (ˈtælənt) *n.* 才能　　desire (dɪˈzaɪr) *n.* 慾望

21. (**D**) When cars are moving bumper to bumper, how is traffic?
當車子行進時大排長龍，交通如何？
(A) 快速　　　(B) 輕巧　　　(C) 黑暗　　　(D) 擁塞
* bumper ('bʌmpə) n. 保險桿（保險桿抵到保險桿，形容車子大排長龍）

22. (**A**) The train will leave at noon.
When will the train leave?
火車將在正午出發。／火車何時出發？

(A) 十二點　　(B) 天剛黑　　(C) 零時　　(D) 明天晚上

23. (**D**) This is the primary cause.
What does "primary" mean?
這是主要的原因。／ "primary" 是什麼意思？

(A) 最後的　　(B) 次要的　　(C) 錯誤的　　(D) 最重要的

* primary ('praɪ,mɛrɪ , -mərɪ) adj. 首要的；主要的
secondary ('sɛkən,dɛrɪ) adj. 次要的

24. (**D**) Tony had better take a taxi. Why did he take a taxi?
東尼最好搭計程車去。／他為何要搭計程車？

(A) 他必須慢慢來。　　　　(B) 他有很多時間。
(C) 他的時間沒有限制。　　(D) 他沒有很多時間。

25. (**A**) In a fit of rage, Allen left the room.
Why did he leave?
一時氣憤之下，艾倫離開了房間。／他為何離開？

(A) 因為他很生氣　　　　(B) 因為他很匆忙
(C) 因為他很興奮　　　　(D) 因為他忽然一陣咳嗽

* fit (fɪt) n. 一陣；發作　　rage (redʒ) n. 憤怒

26. (**A**) Jean is tiny.
琴很瘦小。

(A) 她很小。　　(B) 她很大。　　(C) 她的腳很大。　　(D) 她話很多。

27. (**D**) The boy was barefoot.
   這個男孩赤著腳。
   (A) 他的腳很醜。   (B) 他的腳受傷了。
   (C) 他的襪子都是洞。   (D) <u>他沒有穿鞋子。</u>
   * bare〔bɛr〕*adj.* 赤裸的   sock〔sɑk〕*n.* 襪子   hole〔hol〕*n.* 洞

28. (**D**) Everyone's dress was uniform.
   每個人的服裝都一樣。
   (A) 服裝的有些部份相同。   (B) 每個人的服裝都不同。
   (C) 服裝的有些部份不同。   (D) <u>每個人都穿得一樣。</u>
   * uniform〔'junə,fɔrm〕*adj.* 相同的;一律的

29. (**A**) Some parts of the plain are uninhabited.
   平原有些地方沒有人煙。
   (A) <u>有些地方沒有人。</u>   (B) 有些地方有山。
   (C) 有些地方沒有水。   (D) 有些地方沒有植物。
   * uninhabited〔,ʌnɪn'hæbɪtɪd〕*adj.* 無人居住的

30. (**C**) Her speed was constant.
   她的速度一定。
   (A) 速度在改變。   (B) 速度加快。
   (C) <u>速度一直一樣。</u>   (D) 速度減慢。
   * constant〔'kɑnstənt〕*adj.* 不變的;一定的

31. (**C**) The situation is not very good.
   情況不是很好。
   (A) 情況良好。   (B) 狀況極佳。   (C) <u>狀況不良。</u>   (D) 答案不佳。
   * circumstance〔'sɝkəm,stæns〕*n.* 情形   solution〔sə'luʃən〕*n.* 解答

32. (**B**) Jenny is going to read the book at home.
   珍妮將要在家裏看這本書。
   (A) 她正在回家路上。   (B) <u>她將會在家裏看書。</u>
   (C) 她正在家裡看書。   (D) 當她要回家的時候,她將會看書。

33. (**B**) The supervisor made a correction on the report.
主管在報告上做了訂正。

(A) 他在報告上簽字。　　　(B) 他修改報告。
(C) 他影印報告。　　　　　(D) 他將報告打字。

* supervisor〔͵supɚˋvaɪzɚ〕 *n.* 管理者
correction〔kəˋrɛkʃən〕 *n.* 更正

34. (**D**) Peter needs to visit a dentist for treatment of his tooth.
彼得需要去看牙醫治療他的牙齒。

(A) 彼得不能去看牙醫。　　　(B) 牙醫可能會拜訪彼得。
(C) 彼得需要一顆新牙齒。　　(D) 彼得應該去看牙醫。

* dentist〔ˋdɛntɪst〕 *n.* 牙醫　　treatment〔ˋtritmənt〕 *n.* 治療

35. (**C**) My roommate always dreaded visits to his aunt's house.
我的室友一直害怕去他姑媽家拜訪。

(A) 他有點喜歡這樣的拜訪。　(B) 他喜歡這樣的拜訪。
(C) 他害怕這樣的拜訪。　　　(D) 他拒絕這樣的拜訪。

* dread〔drɛd〕 *v.* 害怕　　fear〔fɪr〕 *v.* 恐懼
refuse〔rɪˋfjuz〕 *v.* 拒絕

36. (**B**) Mark, the train leaves at 5:00, so please take your time.
馬克，火車五點才開，所以請你慢慢來。

(A) 馬克必須趕快。　　　　　(B) 似乎還有很多時間。
(C) 馬克的時間緊迫。　　　　(D) 火車有問題了。

* *plenty of* 許多；充足的　　pressed〔prɛst〕 *adj.* 緊迫的

37. (**C**) One of the clerks in the store made off with the jewels.
商店裏的一個職員偷走了珠寶。

(A) 商店裏一個職員賣掉了珠寶。
(B) 商店裏一個職員製成了珠寶。
(C) 商店裏一個職員偷了珠寶。
(D) 商店裏一個職員買了珠寶。

* *made off with* 偷走；搶走　　jewel〔ˋdʒuəl〕 *n.* 珠寶

38.(**B**) The path curves in and out of the trees.
這條小路蜿蜒於樹林中。

    (A) 這條小路滾動。   (B) 這條小路彎曲。
    (C) 這條小路跳躍。   (D) 這條小路傾斜。

    * path〔pæθ〕*n.* 小路   curve〔kɜv〕*v.* 彎曲
      wind〔waɪnd〕*v.* 彎曲；蜿蜒   skip〔skɪp〕*v.* 跳躍
      dip〔dɪp〕*v.* 傾斜

39.(**D**) Lieutenant Johnson doesn't have sufficient strength to move the rock.
強森中尉沒有足夠的力氣去搬動這顆石頭。

    (A) 他打碎石頭。   (B) 這塊石頭太小了。
    (C) 他沒有去搬石頭。   (D) 他無法搬動石頭。

    * lieutenant〔lu'tɛnənt〕*n.* 中尉
      sufficient〔sə'fɪʃənt〕*adj.* 足夠的
      strength〔strɛŋ(k)θ〕*n.* 力氣

40.(**D**) Everybody held their breath when they saw the child walk into the street.
當他們看到那個小孩走到街上，每個人都屏住呼吸。

    (A) 他們太吃驚了。
    (B) 他們很高興看到她走路。
    (C) 他們認為她可能會迷路。
    (D) 他們對於可能發生的事感到很害怕。

    * **hold** *one's* **breath** 屏息
      scared〔skɛrd〕*adj.* 害怕的

41.(**A**) After looking things over, James connected the two wires together.
檢視過後，詹姆斯將兩條電線接起來。

    (A) 他將它們接合。   (B) 他稱它們的重量。
    (C) 他將它們修正。   (D) 他將它們分開。

    * **look over** 看一遍；校閱   connect〔kə'nɛkt〕*v.* 接連
      wire〔waɪr〕*n.* 電線   weigh〔we〕*v.* 稱重量

42. (**D**) The soldier knows how to operate the machine.
這名士兵知道如何操作這部機器。

    (A) 他知道如何檢查它。   (B) 他知道如何修理它。
    (C) 他知道如何打開它。   (D) 他知道如何操作它。

   * soldier ('sodʒɚ) *n.* 士兵；軍人   operate ('ɑpə,ret) *v.* 操作
    inspect (ɪn'spɛkt) *v.* 檢查   run (rʌn) *v.* 執行；運作

43. (**A**) The instructor has already covered that part of the lesson.
老師已經講過這課的那部份。

    (A) 他已經討論過那部份。   (B) 他已經結束那部份。
    (C) 他已經略過那部份。   (D) 他遺漏掉那部份。

   * instructor (ɪn'strʌktɚ) *n.* 講師；老師
    cover ('kʌvɚ) *v.* 包括；論及
    overlook (,ovɚ'luk) *v.* 忽略   omit (o'mɪt , ə'mɪt) *v.* 遺漏

44. (**D**) The machine was not maintained in good condition.
這部機器沒有維持在良好的狀態。

    (A) 它遭到不當的操作。
    (B) 它沒有被適當地磨光。
    (C) 它沒有被認為狀況良好。
    (D) 它沒有被維持在良好的狀態。

   * maintain (men'ten) *v.* 維持   properly ('prɑpəlɪ) *adv.* 適當地

45. (**C**) The answer was incorrect.
這個答案不正確。

    (A) 它可能是錯的。   (B) 它幾乎是正確的。
    (C) 它是錯誤的。   (D) 做些改變就會是錯的。

   * incorrect (,ɪnkə'rɛkt) *adj.* 不正確的

46. (**C**) The children participate in the activities.
這些小孩參加活動。

    (A) 他們教導活動。   (B) 他們研究活動。
    (C) 他們參加活動。   (D) 他們觀賞有關活動的電影。

   * participate (pə'tɪsə,pet , pɑr-) *v.* 參加 <*in*>   *take part in* 參加

47. (**D**) Mark's car is almost as expensive as Allen's.

　　馬克的車幾乎和亞倫的一樣貴。

　　(A) 馬克的車價錢較貴。　　　(B) 兩部車都損壞。

　　(C) 兩部車要出售。　　　　　(D) <u>亞倫的車比馬克的貴。</u>

　　* damage ('dæmɪdʒ) v. 損壞

48. (**B**) Mr. Kelly checked out this morning.

　　凱利先生今早結帳退房。

　　(A) 他今天早上來。　　　　　(B) <u>他今天早上離開。</u>

　　(C) 他今天早上拿到一些錢。　(D) 他今天早上沒有現款。

　　* *check out* 結帳退房　　　*out of* 沒有；失去

49. (**A**) Help me get the food out of the basket and we can eat right away.

　　幫我把食物從籃子裏拿出來，這樣我們馬上就可以吃。

　　(A) <u>幫我把食物拿出來。</u>　　(B) 幫我拿籃子。

　　(C) 幫我從籃子裏買食物。　　(D) 幫我把食物放進籃子裏。

50. (**D**) Sam is not in class because he has been sick for two weeks.

　　山姆沒有來上課，因為他已經生病兩星期。

　　(A) 山姆現在在上課。　　　　(B) 山姆已經上了兩星期的課。

　　(C) 山姆身體健康。　　　　　(D) <u>山姆生病了。</u>

51. (**C**) W : What do you think of your watch?

　　M : Its accuracy varies.

　　What did the man say about his watch?

　　女：你覺得你的錶怎麼樣？

　　男：它的準確性會改變。

　　這位男士說他的錶如何？

　　(A) 他有支非常好的錶。　　　(B) 他沒有戴錶。

　　(C) <u>它不準。</u>　　　　　　　(D) 太緊了。

　　* accuracy ('ækjərəsɪ) n. 準確性　　vary ('vɛrɪ) v. 改變
　　　keep good time (鐘、錶) 準時　　tight (taɪt) adj. 緊的

52. (**C**) W：What are you looking for?

　　　　M：A thermometer.

　　　What does he want to measure?

　　　女：你在找什麼?

　　　男：溫度計。

　　　他想要量什麼?

　　　(A) 濕度　　　　(B) 氣壓　　　　(C) 溫度　　　　(D) 風速

　　　* thermometer (θə'mɑmətə) *n.* 溫度計
　　　　humidity (hju'mɪdətɪ) *n.* 濕度
　　　　atmospheric (ˏætməs'fɛrɪk) *adj.* 大氣的
　　　　pressure ('prɛʃə) *n.* 壓力　　temperature ('tɛmprətʃə) *n.* 溫度
　　　　velocity (və'lɑsətɪ) *n.* 速度

53. (**C**) W：Every time I see you, Bob, you are wearing a
　　　　　　different tie.

　　　　M：That's because I have one for every day of the week.

　　　How many ties does the man have?

　　　女：鮑伯，每次我看到你，你都戴不同的領帶。

　　　男：那是因為我整個星期中每天換一條。

　　　這位男士有幾條領帶?

　　　(A) 二條　　　　(B) 五條　　　　(C) 七條　　　　(D) 九條

54. (**A**) W：Do you rent bicycles here?

　　　　M：Yes, we rent them by the hour or by the day. Either
　　　　　　way you have to have them back here by five.

　　　When must the bicycles be returned?

　　　女：你們這兒出租腳踏車嗎?

　　　男：是的，我們有按小時和按日出租。不管那一種，你都必須在五
　　　　　點之前把腳踏車還回這兒。

　　　腳踏車必須在何時歸還?

　　　(A) 五點以前　　　　　　　(B) 整點時

　　　(C) 一小時內　　　　　　　(D) 第二天之前

　　　* rent (rɛnt) *v.* 出租　　***by the hour*** 按小時計費

55. (**D**) W : What kind of climate does your country have ?
M : We average about 80 percent humidity.
What kind of climate does his country have ?
女：你們國家是屬於哪一型氣候？
男：我們的平均溼度是百分之八十。
他的國家是屬於哪種氣候？

(A) 多風　　　(B) 乾熱　　　(C) 涼爽　　　(D) <u>極潮溼</u>

* climate (ˊklaɪmɪt) *n.* 氣候　　average (ˊævərɪdʒ) *v.* 平均有
　windy (ˊwɪndɪ) *adj.* 多風的　　damp (dæmp) *adj.* 潮溼的

56. (**B**) W : How do you like Emma's new winter coat ?
M : It's nice and it's the brightest red I've seen.
What did the man say about Emma's coat ?
女：你覺得艾瑪的新冬裝外套怎麼樣？
男：很好，是我見過最亮麗的紅色。
這位男士認為艾瑪的外套怎麼樣？

(A) 暖和　　　(B) <u>紅色的</u>　　　(C) 很小　　　(D) 羊毛製的

* bright (braɪt) *adj.* 明亮的

57. (**C**) W : Are the crops going to be good this year ?
M : Yes, they should be, because we've had an excellent
combination of rain and sunshine.
What are the woman and man talking about ?
女：今年的收成將會很好嗎？
男：是的，應該會，因為雨水和陽光非常調和。
這位女士和男士在談論什麼？

(A) 鮮魚的豐收　　　　　　(B) 銅鐵的豐收
(C) <u>小麥和蔬菜的豐收</u>　　　(D) 牛羊的豐收

* crop (krɑp) *n.* 收成；農作物
　combination (ˌkɑmbəˊneʃən) *n.* 組合
　supply (səˊplaɪ) *n.* 貯藏量　　copper (ˊkɑpə) *n.* 銅
　iron (ˊaɪən) *n.* 鐵　　wheat (hwit) *n.* 小麥
　cattle (ˊkætl̩) *n.* 牛　　sheep (ʃip) *n.* 羊；綿羊

58. (**D**) W：Were Mark's parents happy to meet his fiancée?

M：Yes, they were delighted to meet her.

Who were Mark's parents glad to meet?

女：馬克的父母很高興認識他的未婚妻嗎？

男：是的，他們很高興認識她。

馬克的父母很高興認識誰？

(A) 馬克的兒子　　　　　　(B) 馬克的太太

(C) 馬克的女兒　　　　　　(D) 馬克要娶的女孩

* fiancée〔͵fiən'se , fi'ɑnse〕*n.* 未婚妻

delighted〔dɪ'laɪtɪd〕*adj.* 高興的

59. (**B**) M：Did your friend live after his terrible traffic accident?

W：I haven't gone to the hospital today, but I heard

that he made it O.K.

What did the woman hear about her friend?

男：妳的朋友在那場可怕的車禍中存活下來了嗎？

女：我今天還沒有去醫院，但是我聽說他已經沒事了。

這位女士聽到關於她朋友什麼事？

(A) 他造成那場意外。　　　(B) 他在意外中存活下來。

(C) 他避開了意外。　　　　(D) 他死於意外。

* survive〔sə'vaɪv〕*v.* 存活

60. (**A**) M：What would you do if one of your friends told you

he didn't like the color of your dress?

W：I would probably ignore him.

What did the woman mean?

男：如果妳的朋友告訴妳說，他不喜歡妳衣服的顏色，妳會怎樣？

女：我大概不會理他。

這位女士的意思是什麼？

(A) 她不會去注意。　　　　(B) 她會和他理論。

(C) 她會聽從他的勸告。　　(D) 她會換衣服。

* ignore〔ɪg'nor〕*v.* 不理

LISTENING TEST 4

- *Directions for questions 1-25. You will hear questions on the test tape. Select the one item A, B, C or D which answers the question correctly, and mark your answer sheet.*

1. A. It's about a ten-minute drive.
   B. I always walk to work.
   C. I go to work by car.
   D. I ride to work with Tom.

2. A. France   B. Norway
   C. Spain   D. Greece

3. A. Yes, I go.   B. No, I haven't.
   C. Yes, I have to.   D. Yes, he has to.

4. A. a closet
   B. a fireproof liquid
   C. something that burns easily
   D. a liquid with a bad smell

5. A. many   B. quick
   C. some   D. new

6. A. unexpected   B. short
   C. planned   D. long

7. A. Carry the cake.   B. Have some cake.
   C. Don't eat the cake. D. Buy the cake.

8. A. one month after delivery   B. during delivery
   C. before delivery   D. right after delivery

9. A. made a fire
    C. reported the fire
    B. extinguished the fire
    D. put the fire outside

10. A. the approaching exam
    C. an uncomfortable noise
    B. a kind of insect
    D. a difficult problem

11. A. He found the book boring.
    B. He read the book attentively.
    C. He lost his way.
    D. He lost his book.

12. A. He approved of my request.
    B. He disagreed with me.
    C. He fell asleep.
    D. He made a mistake.

13. A. an animal
    C. a building
    B. a vegetable
    D. a field

14. A. The officer will be here.
    B. The doctor will be here.
    C. The farmer will be here.
    D. The merchant will be here.

15. A. He paints pictures.
    B. He repairs old boats.
    C. He grows fruits and vegetables.
    D. He enforces the law.

16. A. a little
    C. a few times
    B. often
    D. seldom

17. A. poor
    C. not considered
    B. fair
    D. excellent

18. A. visit him   B. introduce him
     C. bring him   D. phone him

19. A. when Allen could bring the fuel tank for repair
     B. how much fuel the tank could hold
     C. where Allen had bought the fuel tank
     D. what kind of fuel the tank was carrying

20. A. She enjoyed the trip.   B. She finished the trip.
     C. She canceled the trip.   D. She put off the trip.

21. A. It contains many facts.
     B. The paper has calculations.
     C. The paper contains mistakes.
     D. It has many figures.

22. A. He liked to predict the future.
     B. He built a large machine.
     C. He made a lot of money.
     D. He met many people.

23. A. It was hot and humid.   B. It was cold.
     C. It was stormy.   D. It was sunny.

24. A. He carries a bag.
     B. He carries a sack.
     C. He has a light load.
     D. He has many responsibilities.

25. A. He was considered a person with skill.
     B. He was considered an average fellow.
     C. He was considered a person with no skill.
     D. He was considered a man without any experience.

● *Directions for questions 26-50. You will hear statements on the test tape. Select the one answer A, B, C, or D which comes closest to the meaning of the statement and mark your answer sheet.*

26. A. The gasoline tank stayed empty.
    B. The full tank was on the right.
    C. The right hand indicator had no needle.
    D. The indicator showed a full tank.

27. A. You could see the wires.
    B. The wires were in front of the walls.
    C. You could not see the wires.
    D. The wires were outside the walls.

28. A. I have bread and butter every day.
    B. I don't have bread and butter every day.
    C. I like to eat bread and butter in the evening.
    D. Occasionally I have bread and butter for breakfast.

29. A. They don't like milk shake and apple pies.
    B. They bought some milk shake and apple pies.
    C. They like milk shake and apple pies.
    D. They don't care for them too much.

30. A. We don't mind it.   B. We do not want it.
    C. We will do without it.   D. We are arguing about it.

31. A. He is never on time.
    B. He likes to punch holes.
    C. He is always late.
    D. He is always on time.

32. A. It was a square hole.   B. It was very shallow.
    C. It was a big hole.   D. It was only a small hole.

33. A. My leg hurts.
    B. My leg has paint on it.
    C. I have a cut on my leg.
    D. I have no feelings in my leg.

34. A. Mary didn't know that David was lying.
    B. Mary thought that David was testing her.
    C. Mary didn't know what to tell David.
    D. Mary didn't know that David was joking.

35. A. The bookstore sent Steven the books.
    B. Steven carried the books to the bookstore.
    C. Steven got the books from the bookstore.
    D. Steven went to the bookstore to buy some magazines.

36. A. We will have dinner next Saturday.
    B. Our neighbor invited us to dinner.
    C. We asked him to have dinner with us.
    D. Our next dinner will be on Saturday.

37. A. It rained very hard.
    B. It rained on and off.
    C. It didn't rain very much.
    D. The clouds prevented the rain.

38. A. He went in last night.
    B. He didn't tell anyone he was competing.
    C. There was no one watching him.
    D. He announced his participation.

39. A. It is raining because we will not go hiking.
    B. We will not go hiking, so it is raining.
    C. It is raining, so we will not go hiking.
    D. It is raining for we will not go hiking.

40. A. He will read the handouts to the students.
    B. He forgot to give the handouts to the students.
    C. The students won't receive the handouts.
    D. He will give the students the handouts.

41. A. The movie is a war film.
    B. I hated to see the movie.
    C. I really want to see the movie.
    D. The movie makes me sad.

42. A. They decided to attend the party.
    B. They did not worry about the party.
    C. They could not decide about the party.
    D. They are not going to the party.

43. A. The panel is on the right of the instrument.
    B. The instrument panel on the right is useless.
    C. The instrument panel is not on the right.
    D. The panel on the right is very useful.

44. A. Ralph talked to his father.
    B. Ralph yelled at his father.
    C. They didn't talk to each other.
    D. Ralph didn't try very hard to talk to his father.

45. A. She never came late.   B. She was tardy.
    C. She was usually late.   D. She was absent.

46. A. Don't take these seeds.   B. Don't take these sheets.
    C. Don't sit on the chairs.   D. Don't take these sweets.

47. A. You must present your identification.
    B. You must complete an application form.
    C. You must keep it flat at all times.
    D. You must write your name on the back.

48. A. He ate his meal at ten.
    B. He went to bed at ten.
    C. He went to class at ten.
    D. He took his laundry at ten.

49. A. Tina enjoys tea best.   B. Lisa enjoys coffee best.
    C. Lisa likes tea better.   D. Lisa never drinks tea.

50. A. Nancy wants coffee and pie.
    B. Nancy already had pie and coffee.
    C. The waiter likes pie and coffee.
    D. The waiter gave Nancy a menu.

● *Directions for questions 51-60. You will hear dialogs on the test tape. Select the correct answer A, B, C, or D and mark your answer sheet.*

51. A. They would have worked if asked.
    B. The work was not difficult.
    C. They did not want to work.
    D. They had finished the work.

52. A. She wants dessert.   B. She likes dessert.
    C. She is full.   D. She hates dessert.

53. A. The order was expensive.
    B. The instrument was expensive.
    C. The small vise was expensive.
    D. The job was expensive.

54. A. Frequently it was a bomber.
    B. Finally it was a bomber.
    C. Formerly it was a bomber.
    D. Now it is a bomber.

55. A. He finally arrived.
    B. His arrival was satisfactory.
    C. He arrived immediately.
    D. He would arrive later.

56. A. The man submitted it.   B. The man omitted it.
    C. The man required it.   D. The man accepted it.

57. A. He gained weight.
    B. He increased his vocabulary.
    C. He gained acceleration.
    D. He improved his speech.

58. A. that it would rain   B. that rain was possible
    C. that it would not rain   D. that rain was impossible

59. A. He refused the woman's request to drive the car.
    B. He granted the woman permission to drive the car.
    C. He told the woman the car is brand-new.
    D. He told the woman the car is not in good condition.

60. A. Robert did poorly and cannot be retested again until
       next month.
    B. Robert cannot be retested even if he wants it.
    C. Robert should take the test again next week.
    D. Robert did well and won't be tested again until next
       month.

ECL 聽力測驗 [4] 詳解

1. (**A**) How far do you have to go to get to work?
   你去上班必須走多遠的路程?
   (A) 大約十分鐘的車程。　　　(B) 我一向走路去上班。
   (C) 我開車去上班。　　　　　(D) 我和湯姆騎車去上班。

2. (**B**) They spent their last vacation in Northern Europe.
   Which country did they possibly go to?
   他們上次到北歐度假。 / 他們可能去了哪個國家?
   (A) 法國　　　(B) 挪威　　　(C) 西班牙　　　(D) 希臘
   ＊ Norway (ˈnɔrˌwe) n. 挪威　　Greece (gris) n. 希臘

3. (**C**) Do you have to go to school today?
   你今天必須去上學嗎?
   (A) 是的,我去。　　　　　(B) 不,我還沒有。
   (C) 是的,我必須去。　　　(D) 是的,他必須去。
   ＊ (A)(B)(D) 文法錯誤。

4. (**C**) The container in the closet is marked flammable.
   What's in the container?
   櫥櫃裏的容器標示著易燃。 / 容器裏有什麼?
   (A) 櫥櫃　　　　　　　　(B) 一種防火的液體
   (C) 易燃的物品　　　　　(D) 一種有臭味的液體
   ＊ container (kənˈtenɚ) n. 容器　　closet (ˈklɑzɪt) n. 櫥櫃
   　flammable (ˈflæməbḷ) adj. 易燃的
   　fireproof (ˈfaɪrˌpruf) adj. 防火的　　liquid (ˈlɪkwɪd) n. 液體

5. (**B**) In the month of April, we often have sudden changes in
   the weather. What kind of changes do we have?
   在四月,天氣常常會突然改變。 / 天氣有什麼樣的改變?
   (A) 很多　　　(B) 快速　　　(C) 一些　　　(D) 新的

6. (**A**) Mary made a surprise visit to her husband's office.
What kind of visit was it?
瑪麗意外地造訪她先生的辦公室。/ 這是什麼樣的拜訪？

(A) 意外的　　　　　　　　　(B) 短暫的
(C) 計劃過的　　　　　　　　(D) 長時間的

＊ unexpected〔͵ʌnɪk'spɛktɪd〕*adj.* 意外的；突然的

7. (**B**) Donna said, "Please try this cake." What did she say?
唐娜說：「請嚐嚐這塊蛋糕。」/ 她說了什麼？

(A) 帶走蛋糕。　　　　　　　(B) 吃點蛋糕。
(C) 不要吃蛋糕。　　　　　　(D) 買蛋糕。

8. (**C**) Kim paid for his card in advance of delivery.
When did he pay?
金在寄送之前先付了卡片的錢。/ 他什麼時候付錢？

(A) 寄送後一個月　　　　　　(B) 在寄送期間
(C) 寄送之前　　　　　　　　(D) 寄送後馬上

＊ *in advance* 事先　　delivery〔dɪ'lɪvərɪ〕*n.* 寄送

9. (**B**) They put out the fire. What did they do?
他們將火熄滅。/ 他們做了什麼？

(A) 生火　　　　　　　　　　(B) 熄滅火
(C) 報告火災　　　　　　　　(D) 將火拿到外面

＊ *put out* 熄滅　　*make a fire* 生火
extinguish〔ɪk'stɪŋgwɪʃ〕*v.* 熄滅

10. (**B**) The mosquitoes are driving us crazy.
What's bothering us?
蚊子快把我們逼瘋了。/ 什麼東西在煩我們？

(A) 即將來臨的考試　　　　　(B) 一種昆蟲
(C) 令人不舒服的噪音　　　　(D) 困難的問題

＊ mosquito〔mə'skito〕*n.* 蚊子　　*drive sb. crazy* 把某人逼瘋
bother〔'bɑðə〕*v.* 煩擾　　approach〔ə'protʃ〕*v.* 將近

11. (**B**) John was completely lost in his book.
    What did he do?
    約翰完全沈迷於他的書中。／ 他做了什麼?

    (A) 他發現這本書很無聊。　　(B) 他很專心地讀這本書。
    (C) 他迷路了。　　　　　　　(D) 他的書不見了。

    * *be lost in* 沈迷　　attentively〔əˈtɛntɪvlɪ〕*adv.* 專心地

12. (**A**) When I asked Father whether I could go out or not,
    he nodded his head.
    What did he mean?
    當我問爸爸我能不能出去時,他點點頭。／ 他是什麼意思?

    (A) 他同意我的請求。　　　　(B) 他不同意我的意見。
    (C) 他睡著了。　　　　　　　(D) 他犯了一個錯誤。

    * nod〔nɑd〕*v.* 點頭　　approve〔əˈpruv〕*v.* 同意
    　request〔rɪˈkwɛst〕*n.* 請求

13. (**C**) What is a mansion?
    mansion 是什麼?

    (A) 動物　　　(B) 蔬菜　　　(C) 大樓　　　(D) 場地

    * mansion〔ˈmænʃən〕*n.* 大廈　　field〔fild〕*n.* 場地

14. (**A**) If the Captain visits us, who will be here?
    如果上尉來探視我們,是什麼樣的人物會來此?

    (A) 長官會來此。　　　　　　(B) 醫生會來此。
    (C) 農夫會來此。　　　　　　(D) 商人會來此。

    * captain〔ˈkæptɪn〕*n.* 上尉　　officer〔ˈɔfəsə, ˈɑf-〕*n.* 長官;官員
    　merchant〔ˈmɝtʃənt〕*n.* 商人

15. (**C**) Fred is a peasant. What does he do?
    弗瑞德是農夫。／ 他從事什麼工作?

    (A) 他畫畫。　　　　　　　　(B) 他修理舊船。
    (C) 他種植水果和蔬菜。　　　(D) 他執行法律。

    * peasant〔ˈpɛznt〕*n.* 農夫　　enforce〔ɪnˈfors〕*v.* 執行;實施

16. (**B**)　Jacob visited us frequently.
　　　　　When did we see him?
　　　　　雅各時常拜訪我們。／ 我們什麼時候見到他?

　　(A) 有一些　　　(B) 時常　　　(C) 有幾次　　　(D) 不常

　　＊ frequently (ˈfrikwəntlɪ) adv. 時常地；頻繁地
　　　　seldom (ˈsɛldəm) adv. 不常地；很少地

17. (**D**)　The performance of that dancer was outstanding.
　　　　　How was her performance?
　　　　　那位舞者的表演很傑出。／ 她的表演如何?

　　(A) 差勁　　　　　　　　　　(B) 普通
　　(C) 未經深思熟慮　　　　　　(D) 卓越

　　＊ performance (pəˈfɔrməns) n. 表演
　　　　outstanding (autˈstændɪŋ) adj. 傑出的　　　fair (fɛr) adj. 普通的
　　　　considered (kənˈsɪdəd) adj. 考慮過的
　　　　excellent (ˈɛkslənt) adj. 卓越的

18. (**A**)　Edna is going to call on him sometime.
　　　　　What is Edna going to do?
　　　　　艾德娜將找個時間去拜訪他。／ 艾德娜將要做什麼?

　　(A) 拜訪他　　　　　　　　　(B) 介紹他
　　(C) 帶他　　　　　　　　　　(D) 打電話給他

　　＊ *call on* 拜訪 (＋人)　　　introduce (ˌɪntrəˈdjus) v. 介紹

19. (**B**)　The mechanic asked Allen what the capacity of the fuel
　　　　　tank was. What did the mechanic want to know?
　　　　　技工問艾倫燃料槽的容量是多少。／ 技工想知道什麼?

　　(A) 艾倫什麼時候可以帶燃料槽來修理
　　(B) 槽裏可以容納多少燃料
　　(C) 艾倫在哪裏買燃料槽
　　(D) 槽裏裝的是什麼種燃料

　　＊ mechanic (məˈkænɪk) n. 技工　　　capacity (kəˈpæsətɪ) n. 容量
　　　　fuel (ˈfjuəl) n. 燃料　　　tank (tæŋk) n. 槽

20. (**D**) Linda postponed the trips. What did Linda do?
琳達將旅行延後。／琳達做了什麼?

(A) 她非常喜歡這趟旅遊。　　(B) 她完成旅遊。
(C) 她取消旅遊。　　　　　　(D) <u>她延後旅遊。</u>

* postpone〔post'pon, pos'p-〕v. 延後　　cancel〔'kænsḷ〕v. 取消
put off 延後

21. (**C**) If a paper has many errors, what does it contain?
如果一份報告有許多錯誤,裏面包含了什麼?

(A) 它包含了很多事實。　　(B) 這份報告有計算。
(C) <u>這份報告包含錯誤。</u>　(D) 它有很多數據。

* error〔'ɛrə〕n. 錯誤　　contain〔kən'ten〕v. 包含
calculation〔,kælkjə'leʃən〕n. 計算　　figure〔'fɪgjə, 'fɪgə〕n. 數字

22. (**C**) He made a fortune by writing. What did he do?
他靠寫作賺了大錢。／他做了什麼?

(A) 他喜歡預測未來。　　(B) 他造了一部大機器。
(C) <u>他賺了很多錢。</u>　　(D) 他遇見很多人。

* fortune〔'fɔrtʃən〕n. 財富　　predict〔prɪ'dɪkt〕v. 預測

23. (**A**) Sally didn't enjoy the trip because of the muggy weather.
How was the weather?
莎莉不喜歡這次旅行,因為天氣悶熱。／天氣如何?

(A) <u>又熱又濕</u>　(B) 很冷　(C) 狂風暴雨　(D) 陽光普照

* muggy〔'mʌgɪ〕adj. 悶熱的

24. (**D**) If we say that the Mayor carries a heavy burden, what
do we mean?
如果我們說市長背負重擔,我們是指什麼?

(A) 他提著一個袋子。　　(B) 他提著一個袋子。
(C) 他的負擔很輕。　　　(D) <u>他有許多責任。</u>

* mayor〔'meə, mɛr〕n. 市長　　burden〔'bɝdn〕n. 負擔
sack〔sæk〕n. 袋子　　load〔lod〕n. 負擔
responsibility〔rɪ,spɑnsə'bɪlətɪ〕n. 責任

25. (**A**)　Larry was considered an expert by many people.
What did the people think of him?
賴瑞被許多人認爲是專家。／人們對他的看法是什麼？

　　(A) 他被認爲是有專長的人。
　　(B) 他被認爲是個普通人。
　　(C) 他被認爲是個沒有一技之長的人。
　　(D) 他被認爲是個沒有經驗的人。

　　* expert (ˈɛkspɝt) n. 專家　　skill (skɪl) n. 技能
　　average (ˈævərɪdʒ) adj. 一般的　　fellow (ˈfɛlo) n. 人

26. (**D**)　The needle moved to the right when the tank was full.
當油箱滿的時候，針指向右邊。

　　(A) 油箱保持空的。　　　　　(B) 裝滿的油箱在右邊。
　　(C) 右邊的指示器沒有針。　　(D) 指示器顯示油箱裝滿。

　　* needle (ˈnidl) n. 針　　gasoline (ˈgæsl̩ɪn , ˌgæsl̩ˈin) n. 汽油
　　indicator (ˈɪndəˌketɚ) n. 指示器

27. (**C**)　The wires were hidden between the walls.
電線隱藏在牆壁之間。

　　(A) 你可以看到電線。　　　　(B) 電線在牆壁前面。
　　(C) 你看不到電線。　　　　　(D) 電線在牆壁外。

　　* wire (waɪr) n. 電線　　*in front of* 在前面

28. (**D**)　I sometimes have bread and butter for breakfast.
我早餐有時候吃奶油麵包。

　　(A) 我每天吃奶油麵包。　　　(B) 我沒有每天吃奶油麵包。
　　(C) 我晚上喜歡吃奶油麵包。　(D) 我早餐偶爾吃奶油麵包。

　　* occasionally (əˈkeʒənl̩ɪ) adv. 偶爾

29. (**C**)　They are very fond of milk shakes and apple pies.
他們很喜歡奶昔和蘋果派。

　　(A) 他們不喜歡奶昔和蘋果派。　(B) 他們買了一些奶昔和蘋果派。
　　(C) 他們喜歡奶昔和蘋果派。　　(D) 他們不是很喜歡它們。

　　* *be fond of* 喜歡

30. (**A**) We do not object to the food in the mess hall.
　　　　我們不反對餐廳的食物。

　　　　(A) 我們不介意。　　　　　(B) 我們不想要。
　　　　(C) 沒有也可以。　　　　　(D) 我們爲它在爭吵。

　　　　* object (əb'dʒɛkt) v. 抗議；反對　　mess (mɛs) n. 食堂；會餐室
　　　　hall (hɔl) n. 餐廳　　*do without* 沒有也可以

31. (**D**) Mr. Lee is very punctual.
　　　　李先生很準時。

　　　　(A) 他從不準時。　　　　　(B) 他喜歡打洞。
　　　　(C) 他總是遲到。　　　　　(D) 他一向準時。

　　　　* punctual ('pʌŋktʃuəl) adj. 準時的　　*on time* 準時
　　　　punch (pʌntʃ) v. 打洞

32. (**C**) Albert found a pretty large hole in the floor.
　　　　亞柏特發現地板上有個相當大的洞。

　　　　(A) 是個四方形的洞。　　　　(B) 洞很淺。
　　　　(C) 是個大洞。　　　　　　(D) 只是個小洞。

　　　　* square (skwɛr) adj. 方形的　　shallow ('ʃælo) adj. 淺的

33. (**A**) I have a pain in my leg.
　　　　我的腿痛。

　　　　(A) 我的腿痛。　　　　　　(B) 我的腿上面有顏料。
　　　　(C) 我的腿上有傷口。　　　　(D) 我的腿沒有感覺。

　　　　* pain (pen) n. 疼痛　　paint (pent) n. 顏料
　　　　cut (kʌt) n. 切口

34. (**D**) Mary didn't realize that David was only kidding her.
　　　　瑪麗不知道大衛只是和她開玩笑。

　　　　(A) 瑪麗不知道大衛說謊。
　　　　(B) 瑪麗以爲大衛在試探她。
　　　　(C) 瑪麗不知道要告訴大衛什麼。
　　　　(D) 瑪麗不知道大衛在開玩笑。

35. (**B**) The books were taken to the bookstore by Steven.
這些書被史帝文帶到書店。

(A) 書店寄書給史帝文。　　　(B) 史帝文將書帶到書店。
(C) 史帝文從書店拿到書。　　(D) 史帝文到書店買些雜誌。

36. (**B**) The man next door asked us to dinner on Saturday night.
隔壁的人請我們星期六晚上吃飯。

(A) 我們下星期六要吃晚飯。
(B) 我們的鄰居邀請我們吃晚飯。
(C) 我們請他和我們一起吃晚飯。
(D) 我們下一頓晚飯在星期六。

37. (**C**) Though it was really cloudy, it hardly rained.
雖然雲很多，卻幾乎沒有下雨。

(A) 下了很大的雨。　　　　　(B) 雨斷斷續續地下。
(C) 沒下什麼雨。　　　　　　(D) 雲防止下雨。

＊ *on and off* 斷斷續續地

38. (**B**) No one knew Harold had entered the contest.
沒有人知道哈洛德參加了比賽。

(A) 他昨晚加入了。　　　　　(B) 他沒有告訴任何人他要比賽。
(C) 沒有人看著他。　　　　　(D) 他宣布參賽。

＊ contest (ˈkɑntɛst) *n.* 比賽　　compete (kəmˈpit) *v.* 比賽
announce (əˈnaʊns) *v.* 宣布
participation (pɑˌtɪsəˈpeʃən , pɑr-) *n.* 參加

39. (**C**) It is raining. We will not go hiking.
現在正在下雨。我們將不去健行。

(A) 現在正在下雨，因為我們將不去健行。
(B) 我們將不去健行，所以正在下雨。
(C) 現在正在下雨，所以我們將不去健行。
(D) 現在正在下雨，因為我們將不去健行。

＊ hike (haɪk) *v.* 健行

40. (**D**) The instructor will distribute the handouts to the students.
老師將發講義給學生。

(A) 他將念講義給學生聽。　　(B) 他忘記將講義交給學生。
(C) 學生將不會拿到講義。　　(D) 他將把講義交給學生。

* instructor〔ɪnˈstrʌktɚ〕*n.* 老師　　distribute〔dɪˈstrɪbjut〕*v.* 分發
handout〔ˈhændˌaʊt〕*n.* 講義

41. (**C**) I'm dying to see that new movie.
我很渴望去看那部新電影。

(A) 那部電影是戰爭片。　　(B) 我討厭去看那部電影。
(C) 我真的想去看那部電影。　　(D) 那部電影讓我很難過。

* *be dying to* 渴望

42. (**A**) The students made up their minds to go to the party.
學生們下定決心要參加舞會。

(A) 他們決定要參加舞會。　　(B) 他們不擔心舞會。
(C) 他們無法對舞會做決定。　　(D) 他們將不去參加舞會。

* *make up* one's *mind* 下定決心　　attend〔əˈtɛnd〕*v.* 參加

43. (**A**) That instrument panel is very important. It is on the right.
那個工具的儀表板很重要。它在右邊。

(A) 儀表板在工具的右邊。　　(B) 在右邊的工具儀表板沒有用。
(C) 工具儀表板不在右邊。　　(D) 在右邊的儀表板非常有用。

* instrument〔ˈɪnstrəmənt〕*n.* 工具　　panel〔ˈpænl〕*n.* 儀表板

44. (**C**) Ralph tried to communicate with his father, but in vain.
羅夫試著和他父親溝通，但沒有用。

(A) 羅夫和他父親談話。
(B) 羅夫對他父親大叫。
(C) 他們彼此不說話。
(D) 羅夫並沒有努力嘗試和他父親說話。

* *in vain* 徒勞　　yell〔jɛl〕*v.* 大叫

45. (**A**) The secretary was always on time for work.
    這位祕書上班一向準時。

    (A) 她從不遲到。 (B) 她遲到。
    (C) 她經常遲到。 (D) 她缺席。

    * tardy〔'tardɪ〕*adj.* 遲緩的 absent〔'æbsn̩t〕*adj.* 缺席的

46. (**C**) Please don't take these seats.
    請不要坐這些位子。

    (A) 不要拿這些種子。 (B) 不要拿這些被單。
    (C) 不要坐在這些椅子上。 (D) 不要拿這些糖果。

    * seat〔sit〕*n.* 位子 seed〔sid〕*n.* 種子
    sheet〔ʃit〕*n.* 被單 sweet〔swit〕*n.* 糖果

47. (**D**) Before you cash the check, you must endorse it.
    在兌現支票前,你必須背書。

    (A) 你必須表明身份。 (B) 你必須完成一張申請表。
    (C) 你必須隨時將它保持平坦。 (D) 你必須在背後簽名。

    * cash〔kæʃ〕*v.* 兌現 check〔tʃɛk〕*n.* 支票
    endorse〔ɪn'dɔrs〕*v.* 背書 present〔prɪ'zɛnt〕*v.* 提出
    identification〔aɪ,dɛntəfə'keʃən〕*n.* 身份
    application〔,æplə'keʃən〕*n.* 申請 flat〔flæt〕*adj.* 平坦的

48. (**B**) Mr. Jones turned in at 10 o'clock.
    瓊斯先生十點睡覺。

    (A) 他十點吃飯。 (B) 他十點睡覺。
    (C) 他十點去上課。 (D) 他十點去拿送洗的衣服。

    * *turn in* 睡覺 laundry〔'lɔndrɪ, 'lɑn-〕*n.* 送洗的衣服

49. (**C**) Tina likes coffee; on the other hand, Lisa prefers tea.
    蒂娜喜歡咖啡,不過,麗莎偏愛茶。

    (A) 蒂娜最喜歡茶。 (B) 麗莎最喜歡咖啡。
    (C) 麗莎比較喜歡茶。 (D) 麗莎從不喝茶。

    * *on the other hand* 另一方面 prefer〔prɪ'fɝ〕*v.* 偏愛

50. (**A**) The waiter said, "What would you like ?" Nancy answered, "I think I'll have pie and coffee."

服務生說：「您要什麼？」南西回答：「我想我要點派和咖啡。」

(A) <u>南西要咖啡和派。</u>   (B) 南西已經有了派和咖啡。

(C) 服務生喜歡派和咖啡。   (D) 服務生給南西菜單。

51. (**C**) M : Do those men have jobs?

W : Yes, but they are reluctant to work.

What did the woman mean?

男：那些人有工作嗎？

女：有，但是他們不願工作。

這位女士的意思是什麼？

(A) 如果人家要求，他們才會工作。 (B) 工作不難。

(C) <u>他們不想工作。</u>   (D) 他們已經完成工作。

* reluctant〔rɪˈlʌktənt〕*adj.* 不情願的

52. (**C**) M : Would you like some dessert?

W : No, thanks. I am stuffed.

What does the woman mean?

男：妳要來些甜點嗎？

女：不了，謝謝，我好飽了。

這位女士是什麼意思？

(A) 她要甜點。   (B) 她喜歡甜點。

(C) <u>她吃飽了。</u>   (D) 她討厭甜點。

* dessert〔dɪˈzɝt〕*n.* 甜點

53. (**B**) W : Did you buy that gadget?

M : Yes, I did, and this small device is very expensive.

What was very expensive?

女：你買了那個小機械嗎？

男：是的，我買了，這小玩意相當貴。

什麼東西很貴？

(A) 訂單很貴。   (B) <u>工具很貴。</u>

(C) 小老虎鉗很貴。   (D) 工作很貴。

* gadget〔ˈgædʒɪt〕*n.* 設計精巧的小機械   vise〔vaɪs〕*n.* 老虎鉗

54. (**C**)　W：What kind of plane is that?

M：Well, originally it was a bomber.

What did he say about the plane?

女：那是哪一種飛機？

男：嗯，它原本是轟炸機。

他說飛機怎麼樣？

(A) 它通常是一架轟炸機。　　　　(B) 它最後成爲一架轟炸機。

(C) 它以前是一架轟炸機。　　　　(D) 它現在是一架轟炸機。

　* originally〔ə'rɪdʒənlɪ〕adv. 原本；最初

　　bomber〔'bɑmɚ〕n. 轟炸機　　frequently〔'frikwəntlɪ〕adv. 時常地

　　formerly〔'fɔrməlɪ〕adv. 從前

55. (**A**)　W：Why are the people running over there?

M：Because at last their leader has arrived.

What did the man say about their leader?

女：這些人爲什麼跑到那裏去？

男：因爲他們的領袖終於到了。

這位男士說他們的領袖怎麼樣？

(A) 他終於抵達。　　　　　　　　(B) 他的到達令人滿意。

(C) 他馬上到達。　　　　　　　　(D) 他會晚點到達。

　* *at last* 最後；終於

56. (**A**)　W：What happened to that proposal you are supposed

to prepare for the manager?

M：I turned it in.

What happened to the proposal?

女：你要準備給經理的提案進行得如何？

男：我交了。

提案怎麼了？

(A) 男士交出去了。　　　　　　　(B) 男士遺漏掉了。

(C) 男士需要。　　　　　　　　　(D) 男士收下了。

　* proposal〔prə'pozl〕n. 提議　　*turn in* 交出

　　submit〔səb'mɪt〕v. 提出　　omit〔o'mɪt, ə'mɪt〕v. 遺漏

　　require〔rɪ'kwaɪr〕v. 需要

57. (**C**) M : What did you say about Thomas?

W : I said that he has picked up a little speed.

What did Thomas do?

男：妳說湯瑪士怎麼了？

女：我說他將速度加快了一點。

湯瑪士做了什麼？

(A) 他增加體重。 (B) 他增加他的字彙。

(C) 他增加速度。 (D) 他改進他的演說。

* ***pick up*** 增加 (速度)　　gain (gen) v. 增加

vocabulary (və'kæbjə,lɛrɪ) n. 字彙

acceleration (æk,sɛlə'reʃən) n. 加速　　improve (ɪm'pruv) v. 改善

58. (**B**) W : Do you think it will rain?

M : Well, it might.

What did the man predict about the weather?

女：你認為會下雨嗎？

男：嗯，可能會。

這位男士預測天氣會如何？

(A) 會下雨 (B) 可能會下雨

(C) 不會下雨 (D) 不可能會下雨

* predict (prɪ'dɪkt) v. 預測

59. (**B**) W : That used car is in very good condition. May I drive it?

M : Sure, try it out.

What did the man do?

女：那輛二手車狀況良好。我可以開嗎？

男：當然，請試車。

這位男士做了什麼？

(A) 他拒絕女士試車的請求。 (B) 他答應讓女士試車。

(C) 他告訴女士車子是全新的。 (D) 他告訴女士車子狀況不佳。

* ***try out*** 試用　　request (rɪ'kwɛst) n. 請求

grant (grænt) v. 允許；答應　　permission (pə'mɪʃən) n. 許可

brand-new ('brænd'nju) adj. 全新的

60. (**A**)　M：Did I pass the test?

　　　　W：I'm sorry, Robert. You failed it. You have to wait
　　　　　　until next month before you can take it again.

　　　What did the woman say?

　　　男：我通過考試了嗎？

　　　女：我很抱歉，羅勃特。你沒有通過。你必須等到下個月才能重考。

　　　這位女士說了什麼？

　　　(A) 羅勃特表現不佳，必須到下個月才能重考。

　　　(B) 羅勃特不能重考，即使他想要。

　　　(C) 羅勃特下星期應該重考。

　　　(D) 羅勃特考得很好，下個月不必重考。

　　　One of my son Keith's university applications
included questions about his intended major. After
reviewing the long list of options, he checked off
"Undecided." The next question was: "Are you sure?"
Without a moment's hesitation he checked off his
answer: "No."

　　　我兒子吉斯的大學申請書中，有一份包括了打算主修哪個科
目的問題。看完了一長串的選擇後，他在「尚未決定」處打勾。
下一個問題是：「你確定嗎？」他毫不遲疑地勾出了他的答案
「不」。

LISTENING TEST 5

● *Directions for questions 1-25. You will hear questions on the test tape. Select the one item A, B, C or D which answers the question correctly, and mark your answer sheet.*

1. A. examine it
   C. repair it
   B. turn it off
   D. turn it on

2. A. well done
   C. meat cooked in oil
   B. slightly bloody meat
   D. salted meat

3. A. add more
   C. fail them
   B. check the number
   D. reduce the number

4. A. now and then
   C. countless times
   B. many times
   D. all at once

5. A. to drive nails
   C. to turn screws
   B. to bend or cut wire
   D. to cut wood

6. A. a little over thirty
   C. about thirteen
   B. more than thirty
   D. exactly thirteen

7. A. football
   C. tennis
   B. scuba diving
   D. badminton

8. A. They are made of lead.
   B. They are made of synthetic rubber.
   C. They are made of tree bark.
   D. They are made of animal skin.

9. A. thunder
   C. tail wind
   B. cross wind
   D. north wind

10. A. Do you have any identification ?
　　B. Do you want traveler's checks ?
　　C. Shall I get a check for you ?
　　D. How do you want this money ?

11. A. advertisements　　　　B. editorials
　　C. local news　　　　　　D. comics

12. A. inaccurate　　　　　　B. confusing
　　C. strict　　　　　　　　D. easy

13. A. hail　　　　　　　　　B. a solid
　　C. snow　　　　　　　　　D. a liquid

14. A. The jam she bought tasted bad.
　　B. She got stuck in traffic.
　　C. The traffic jam she met was terrible.
　　D. She has a serious problem.

15. A. He would ask about your patient's name.
　　B. He would ask about your family.
　　C. He would ask about your work.
　　D. He would ask what the occasion was.

16. A. She congratulated me.
　　B. She questioned me about the tour.
　　C. She worked for our company.
　　D. She went along with me.

17. A. sent a letter home
　　B. went home to see her mother
　　C. missed her class
　　D. bought some envelopes

18. A. in a visitor's room　　　B. in the living room
　　C. in the study room　　　 D. in the dining room

19. A. if my clothes were proper
    B. where I was going
    C. where I lived
    D. if my ID was valid

20. A. It is not well.   B. It is excited.
    C. It is not calm.   D. It is serious.

21. A. a nurse   B. a housewife
    C. a salesclerk   D. a teacher

22. A. the case   B. the box
    C. the suitcase   D. the briefcase

23. A. He was on the train.
    B. He lost his way.
    C. He didn't like Chicago.
    D. He was at a busy train station.

24. A. dangerous   B. wonderful
    C. dull   D. well-paying

25. A. He drove recklessly.   B. He drove carefully.
    C. He drove too fast.   D. He drove too slowly.

• Directions for questions 26-50. You will hear statements on the
  test tape. Select the one answer A, B, C, or D which comes
  closest to the meaning of the statement and mark your answer
  sheet.

26. A. He is well known.
    B. He is not known.
    C. He does not know anyone.
    D. He is a dangerous person.

27. A. He is a foreign teacher.
　　B. He is able to speak seven languages.
　　C. He is a language instructor.
　　D. He has been an assistant professor for a long time.

28. A. It's an influential speech.
　　B. It's an uninteresting speech.
　　C. It's a boring speech.
　　D. It's an inconsistent speech.

29. A. Sheep are cheap animals.
　　B. By boat is inexpensive.
　　C. Shipping goods by train is cheaper.
　　D. By plane is expensive.

30. A. She forgot her lesson.
　　B. She didn't forget her lesson.
　　C. She wasn't a member of her class.
　　D. She forgot to go to class.

31. A. Stuart completed his classroom.
　　B. Stuart was late for class.
　　C. Stuart finished highest in his class.
　　D. Stuart had an accident in class.

32. A. His temperature is above normal.
　　B. His temperature is below normal.
　　C. His feet are cold this weekend.
　　D. He has eaten this weekend.

33. A. I don't need milk.
　　B. I must get some milk.
　　C. I have two bottles of milk.
　　D. I just bought some milk.

34. A. I want to know it.   B. I don't care about it.
    C. I'm happy with it.   D. I know it.

35. A. Only the ending was read to me.
    B. The beginning was read to me.
    C. He read the conclusion only.
    D. The conclusion was read to me.

36. A. I listen to a tape.   B. I hear a plane.
    C. I hear a car.   D. I see a train.

37. A. He likes winter.
    B. He enjoys snow in winter.
    C. There isn't much snow.
    D. He doesn't enjoy much snow in winter.

38. A. I'm buying it.   B. I'm sharing it.
    C. I'm preparing it.   D. I'm comparing it.

39. A. She fell sick.
    B. She felt sick.
    C. She was sick when she fell.
    D. She found me sick.

40. A. He was in training.   B. He was becoming sick.
    C. He was bored.   D. He was becoming tired.

41. A. It could not be done.
    B. It was hard.
    C. It was easy.
    D. It could be done with some difficulties.

42. A. It was interesting.
    B. It was not safe.
    C. It was a good assignment.
    D. It was pretty challenging.

43. A. His French is excellent.
    B. He doesn't speak French at all.
    C. He speaks a little French.
    D. His French is only fair.

44. A. He had many.   B. He had some.
    C. He had a few.   D. He had none.

45. A. Food may be kept in a refrigerator.
    B. Food may be bought in a store.
    C. Food stores buy refrigerators.
    D. We can buy it at the food store.

46. A. I ought to like tea.
    B. I might like tea.
    C. I would like tea
    D. Tea isn't stimulating.

47. A. I didn't have any visitors last Monday.
    B. I had a few visitors at home.
    C. We didn't have a holiday last Monday.
    D. I had a lot of visitors.

48. A. The desk belongs to Jane.
    B. The desk belongs to John.
    C. The desk belongs to both.
    D. The desk belongs to neither.

49. A. We have to receive it.   B. We can receive it.
    C. We might receive it.   D. We won't receive it.

50. A. He criticized his patient.
    B. He examined his patient.
    C. He treated his patient.
    D. He dismissed his patient.

● *Directions for questions 51-60. You will hear dialogs on the test tape. Select the correct answer A, B, C, or D and mark your answer sheet.*

51. A. The student starts class at 0720.
    B. The student is late for class.
    C. The class will not begin until later.
    D. The class will be held downtown.

52. A. replace it   B. repair it
    C. inflate it   D. rotate it

53. A. The parents will provide transportation.
    B. The parents aren't worried about the zoo.
    C. There won't be enough cars for everybody.
    D. The parents aren't going to the zoo.

54. A. She wants to buy a transistor radio.
    B. She wants to listen to overseas radio stations.
    C. She wants to trade an old television set for a radio.
    D. She wants to sell transistor radios.

55. A. clear weather   B. temperature
    C. heavy fog   D. cloudless sky

56. A. She needs some work.
    B. She needs some sticky material.
    C. She needs some tape.
    D. She needs some paper.

57. A. The rates are too high.
    B. The rates are too low.
    C. The rates are fair.
    D. The rates are unreasonable.

58. A. His thigh hurts.   B. He feels good.
    C. His thigh is weak.   D. He feels numb.

59. A. He would repair it, but he wouldn't replace it.
    B. He wouldn't replace or repair it.
    C. He would replace it rather than repair it.
    D. He would repair it and replace it.

60. A. ask for his picture   B. tell him a story
    C. see his smile   D. take his picture

Boy to mother: "I've decided to stop studying."

"How come ?" asked the mother.

"I heard on the news that someone was shot dead in Italy because he knew too much."

兒子對媽媽：「我決定不要讀書了。」

媽媽問：「為什麼呢？」

「我聽新聞說，有人在義大利被射殺，因為他知道得太多了。」

ECL 聽力測驗 [5] 詳解

1. (**D**) If William tells you to switch on the light, what should you do?
如果威廉告訴你打開電燈,你應該怎麼做?

(A) 檢查它　　(B) 關掉它　　(C) 修理它　　(D) 打開它

* **switch on** 打開(開關)　　examine〔 ɪgˈzæmɪn 〕 v. 檢查
turn off 關掉(開關)　　**turn on** 打開(開關)

2. (**A**) When you are in a restaurant, you can order meat just the way you like it. If you like meat cooked thoroughly, what kind of meat would you order?
當你在餐廳時,你可以依自己的喜好來點肉食。如果你喜歡烹調徹底的肉,你要點什麼樣的肉?

(A) 全熟的　　　　　　　(B) 稍微帶血的肉
(C) 用油調理的肉　　　　(D) 用鹽醃製的肉

* thoroughly (ˈθɝolɪ) adv. 徹底地　　**well done** 全熟
slightly (ˈslaɪtlɪ) adv. 輕微地;稍微

3. (**D**) Miss Lee will cut down the number of students in the class. What would Miss Lee do to the class?
李小姐要減少班上的學生人數。/ 李小姐對班上學生要如何處理?

(A) 增加更多　　(B) 檢查數目　　(C) 當掉學生　　(D) 減少人數

* **cut down** 減少　　fail〔 fel 〕 v. 使不及格
reduce〔 rɪˈdjus 〕 v. 減少

4. (**A**) You should wash your coat occasionally.
When should the coat be washed?
你偶爾應該洗洗你的外套。/ 外套應該何時洗?

(A) 有時候　　(B) 很多次　　(C) 無數次　　(D) 突然

* occasionally〔 əˈkeʒənlɪ 〕 adv. 有時;偶爾　　**now and then** 有時
countless (ˈkauntlɪs) adj. 數不盡的　　**all at once** 突然

5. (**C**) What is a screwdriver used for?
　　螺絲起子的用途是什麼？

　　(A) 釘釘子　　　　　　　　(B) 彎曲或剪斷電線
　　(C) 鎖螺絲釘　　　　　　　(D) 砍樹木

　　* screwdriver〔'skru,draɪvɚ〕*n.* 螺絲起子　　drive〔draɪv〕*v.* 釘入
　　　bend〔bɛnd〕*v.* 使彎曲　　screw〔skru〕*n.* 螺絲釘

6. (**C**) There are approximately 13 dogs in the yard.
　　How many dogs are there?
　　院子裏大約有十三隻狗。／有多少隻狗？

　　(A) 比三十隻多一點　　　　(B) 超過三十隻
　　(C) 大約十三隻　　　　　　(D) 剛好十三隻

　　* approximately〔ə'prɑksəmɪtlɪ〕*adv.* 大約　　yard〔jɑrd〕*n.* 院子
　　　exactly〔ɪg'zæktlɪ〕*adv.* 精確地

7. (**B**) Tennis, football, and badminton are popular sports, but
　　recently scuba diving has become popular.
　　What has become popular lately?
　　網球，美式足球，羽球都是流行的運動，可是最近水肺潛水變得很熱
　　門。／最近什麼變得熱門？

　　(A) 美式足球　　　　　　　(B) 水肺潛水
　　(C) 網球　　　　　　　　　(D) 羽球

　　* badminton〔'bædmɪntən〕*n.* 羽毛球　　recently〔'risṇtlɪ〕*adv.* 最近
　　　scuba〔'skubə〕*n.* 水下呼吸器；水肺　　diving〔'daɪvɪŋ〕*n.* 潛水
　　　lately〔'letlɪ〕*adv.* 最近

8. (**D**) The shoes are made of leather.
　　What are they made of?
　　這鞋子是皮製的。／它們是什麼製的？

　　(A) 它們是鉛製的。　　　　(B) 它們是合成塑膠製的。
　　(C) 它們是樹皮製的。　　　(D) 它們是動物皮製的。

　　* leather〔'lɛðɚ〕*n.* 皮革　　lead〔lɛd〕*n.* 鉛
　　　synthetic〔sɪn'θɛtɪk〕*adj.* 合成的　　rubber〔'rʌbɚ〕*n.* 橡膠
　　　bark〔bɑrk〕*n.* 樹皮

9. (**C**) What is the opposite of head wind?
逆風的相反是什麼？

(A) 雷　　　(B) 逆風　　　(C) 順風　　　(D) 北風

* opposite〔'ɑpəzɪt〕*n.* 相反的事物　　***head wind*** 迎面風；逆風
cross wind 逆風　　***tail wind*** 順風

10. (**D**) The teller at the bank said, "What denominations of
bills would you like?" What did the teller mean?
銀行的出納員說：「你要什麼面額的鈔票？」
出納員的意思為何？

(A) 你有任何的身份證明嗎？　(B) 你要旅行支票嗎？
(C) 要我拿張支票給你嗎？　　(D) 你的錢要怎麼換？

* teller〔'tɛlɚ〕*n.* 出納員
denomination〔dɪˌnɑmə'neʃən〕*n.* 單位；面積
bill〔bɪl〕*n.* 鈔票　　identification〔aɪˌdɛntəfə'keʃən〕*n.* 身份證明
traveler's check 旅行支票

11. (**A**) What can a person usually find in the classified ads
section of the newspaper?
在報紙的分類廣告版可以找到什麼？

(A) 廣告　　(B) 社論　　　(C) 地方新聞　　(D) 連環漫畫

* classified〔'klæsəfaɪd〕*adj.* 分類的
ads〔ædz〕*n.* 廣告（advertisements 的縮寫）
section〔'sɛkʃən〕*n.* 版面；部門
advertisement〔ˌædvɚ'taɪzmənt, əd'vɝtɪz-〕*n.* 廣告
editorial〔ˌɛdə'torɪəl〕*n.* 社論　　local〔'lokḷ〕*adj.* 地方的
comic〔'kɑmɪk〕*n.* 連環漫畫

12. (**C**) The new regulations were very rigid.
How were the regulations?
新規定非常嚴格。／規定如何？

(A) 不正確　(B) 困惑的　　(C) 嚴格　　　(D) 容易

* regulation〔ˌrɛgjə'leʃən〕*n.* 規定　　rigid〔'rɪdʒɪd〕*adj.* 嚴格的
inaccurate〔ɪn'ækjərɪt〕*adj.* 不正確的　　strict〔strɪkt〕*adj.* 嚴格的

13. (**D**)　When ice is exposed to heat, it changes to water.
What does it change to?
冰暴露於熱下會變為水。／冰會變成什麼？

(A) 冰雹 　　(B) 固體 　　(C) 雪 　　(D) 液體

* expose〔ɪk'spoz〕v. 暴露　　hail〔hel〕n. 冰雹
solid〔'sɑlɪd〕n. 固體　　liquid〔'lɪkwɪd〕n. 液體

14. (**D**)　She told me she's in a terrible jam.
What happened to her?
她告訴我她陷入嚴重的困境。／她怎麼了？

(A) 她買的果醬很難吃。　　(B) 她被困在交通阻塞中。
(C) 她所遇到的塞車很糟糕。　　(D) 她遇到一個嚴重的問題。

* jam〔dʒæm〕n. 果醬；困境　　*traffic jam* 交通阻塞；塞車

15. (**C**)　If someone asked about your occupation, what would
he ask?
如果有人詢問你的職業，他會問什麼？

(A) 他會詢問你病人的名字。　　(B) 他會詢問你的家庭。
(C) 他會詢問你的工作。　　(D) 他會問是何種場合。

* occupation〔ˌɑkjə'peʃən〕n. 職業　　occasion〔ə'keʒən〕n. 場合

16. (**D**)　She accompanied me on the tour. What did she do?
她陪我去旅行。／她做了什麼？

(A) 她恭喜我。　　(B) 她詢問我關於旅行的事。
(C) 她在我們公司上班。　　(D) 她和我一起去。

* accompany〔ə'kʌmpənɪ〕v. 陪伴

17. (**A**)　Mary mailed a letter to her mother yesterday after class.
What did Mary do yesterday?
瑪麗昨天下課後寄了一封信給她母親。
瑪麗昨天做什麼？

(A) 寄一封信回家　　(B) 回家看母親
(C) 沒有去上課　　(D) 買了一些信封

18. (**A**) John will stay in the guest room.
Where will he stay?
約翰將暫時住在客房。／他將住在哪兒？

 (A) 客房 (B) 客廳   (C) 書房   (D) 餐廳

19. (**C**) The policeman asked me about my address.
What did he want to know?
警察詢問我的地址。／他想知道什麼？

 (A) 我的衣服是否合宜 (B) 我要去哪裏
 (C) 我住在哪兒   (D) 我的身份證是否有效

 * address (ə'drɛs , 'ædrɛs) *n.* 地址 ID 身份證 (= *identification*)
  valid ('vælɪd) *adj.* 有效的

20. (**A**) That dog needs to be watched very carefully because it
is sick. What is the matter with the dog?
那隻狗需要非常小心地照料，因爲它生病了。／小狗怎麼了？

 (A) 牠不舒服。   (B) 牠很興奮。
 (C) 牠不冷靜。   (D) 牠很嚴肅。

 * calm (kɑm) *adj.* 平靜的 serious ('sɪrɪəs) *adj.* 嚴肅的

21. (**D**) Edith is a teacher like her mother.
What is her mother?
愛蒂絲和她母親一樣是位老師。／她母親是做什麼的？

 (A) 護士 (B) 家庭主婦 (C) 店員   (D) 老師

  * housewife ('haʊs,waɪf) *n.* 家庭主婦
   salesclerk ('selz,klɜk) *n.* 店員；售貨員

22. (**B**) This box holds more than that suitcase.
Which is larger?
這個箱子裝得比那個手提箱多。／哪一個比較大？

 (A) 箱子 (B) 箱子 (C) 手提箱   (D) 公事包

  * suitcase ('sut,kes) *n.* 手提箱 briefcase ('brif,kes) *n.* 公事包

23. (**B**) John got lost at a train station in Chicago and he became very confused. Why did John become confused?

約翰在芝加哥的火車站迷路，他非常迷惑。／約翰爲什麼迷惑？

(A) 他在火車上。　　　　　(B) 他迷路了。
(C) 他不喜歡芝加哥。　　　(D) 他在繁忙的火車站。

＊ *get lost* 迷路

24. (**A**) That job is hazardous. What kind of job is it?

那個工作很危險。／那是什麼性質的工作？

(A) 危險的　　　　　　　　(B) 奇妙的
(C) 沈悶的　　　　　　　　(D) 待遇好的

＊ hazardous〔'hæzədəs〕*adj.* 有危險的　　dull〔dʌl〕*adj.* 沈悶的

25. (**C**) He was fined 500 dollars for speeding.
Why was he fined?

他因超速被罰款五百元。／他爲何被罰款？

(A) 他開車鹵莽。　　　　　(B) 他開車小心。
(C) 他開太快。　　　　　　(D) 他開太慢。

＊ fine〔faɪn〕*v.* 罰款　　speeding〔'spidɪŋ〕*n.* 超速
recklessly〔'rɛklɪslɪ〕*adv.* 鹵莽地

26. (**A**) The chairman of the convention is a famous person.

會議的主席是個名人。

(A) 他很有名。　　　　　　(B) 他沒有名氣。
(C) 他不認識任何人。　　　(D) 他是個危險人物。

＊ chairman〔'tʃɛrmən〕*n.* 主席　　convention〔kən'vɛnʃən〕*n.* 大會

27. (**C**) Prof. Dixon teaches several foreign languages.

狄克生教授教幾種外國語言。

(A) 他是個外國老師。　　　(B) 他會講七國語言。
(C) 他是教語言的老師。　　(D) 他當助教很久了。

＊ Prof. 教授（＝professor〔prə'fɛsə〕*n.*）
instructor〔ɪn'strʌktə〕*n.* 老師　　*assistant professor* 助敎

28. (**A**) The speech changed people's minds.

這場演講改變了人們的想法。

(A) 這是一場有影響力的演講。 (B) 這是一場無趣的演講。

(C) 這是一場無聊的演講。 (D) 這是一場矛盾的演講。

* influential〔ˌɪnfluˈɛnʃəl〕*adj.* 有影響力的

uninteresting〔ʌnˈɪntrɪstɪŋ〕*adj.* 無趣的

boring〔ˈbɔrɪŋ〕*adj.* 無聊的

inconsistent〔ˌɪnkənˈsɪstənt〕*adj.* 不一致的；矛盾的

29. (**B**) To ship goods by sea is cheaper.

由海運運貨較便宜。

(A) 綿羊是便宜的動物。 (B) 海運便宜。

(C) 用火車運貨較便宜。 (D) 空運很貴。

* ship〔ʃɪp〕*v.* 運送

30. (**A**) Mary didn't remember her lesson.

瑪麗不記得她的功課。

(A) 她忘了她的功課。 (B) 她沒有忘記她的功課。

(C) 她不是班上的一員。 (D) 她忘了去上課。

31. (**C**) Stuart ended up at the top of his class.

史都華結果成為班上的第一名。

(A) 史都華完成教室。

(B) 史都華上課遲到。

(C) 史都華最後在班上成績最高。

(D) 史都華上課時發生意外。

* ***end up*** 結果 complete〔kəmˈplit〕*v.* 完成

32. (**A**) Captain White had a fever this weekend.

懷特上尉這個週末發燒了。

(A) 他的體溫高於正常。 (B) 他的體溫低於正常。

(C) 這個週末他的腳發冷。 (D) 這個週末他已吃過飯。

* fever〔ˈfivɚ〕*n.* 發燒 normal〔ˈnɔrml̩〕*n.* 正常

33. (**B**) I have got to buy some milk.
　　　我必須買些牛奶。
　　　(A) 我不需要牛奶。　　　　　(B) <u>我必須買些牛奶。</u>
　　　(C) 我有二瓶牛奶。　　　　　(D) 我剛買了些牛奶。

34. (**D**) I am familiar with it.
　　　我對那很熟。
　　　(A) 我想知道它。　　　　　　(B) 我不關心它。
　　　(C) 對它我感到很快樂。　　　(D) <u>我知道它。</u>
　　　* familiar (fə'mɪljə) *adj.* 熟悉的　　*care about* 關心

35. (**B**) He read the preface to me.
　　　他唸序言給我聽。
　　　(A) 只有結局唸給我聽。　　　(B) <u>開頭唸給我聽。</u>
　　　(C) 他只唸了結論。　　　　　(D) 結論唸給我聽。
　　　* preface ('prɛfɪs , -fəs) *n.* 序言　　conclusion (kən'kluʒən) *n.* 結論

36. (**B**) I hear an aircraft.
　　　我聽到飛機聲。
　　　(A) 我在聽卡帶。　　　　　　(B) <u>我聽到飛機聲。</u>
　　　(C) 我聽到汽車聲。　　　　　(D) 我看到火車。
　　　* aircraft ('ɛr,kræft) *n.* 飛行器

37. (**D**) He can't stand snowy weather.
　　　他無法忍受下雪的天氣。
　　　(A) 他喜歡冬天。　　　　　　(B) 他很喜歡冬天下雪。
　　　(C) 沒有下很多雪。　　　　　(D) <u>他不喜歡冬天下很多雪。</u>
　　　* stand (stænd) *v.* 忍受　　snowy ('snoɪ) *adj.* 下雪的；多雪的

38. (**C**) I'm making some tea now.
　　　我正在泡茶。
　　　(A) 我正在買茶。　　　　　　(B) 我正在分配茶。
　　　(C) <u>我正在準備茶。</u>　　　　(D) 我正在比較茶。

39. (**B**) My sister felt sick yesterday.
   我姊姊昨天覺得噁心不舒服。
   (A) 她生病了。   (B) 她覺得噁心不舒服。
   (C) 當她跌倒時，她覺得不舒服。   (D) 她認爲我不舒服。

40. (**D**) He was getting tired from walking all morning.
   走了一早上的路，他覺得愈來愈累。
   (A) 他在受訓中。   (B) 他變得不舒服。
   (C) 他覺得無聊。   (D) 他變得疲倦。

41. (**A**) The mission was impossible.
   這件任務是不可能的。
   (A) 它不可能做到。   (B) 它很困難。
   (C) 它很容易。   (D) 有困難，但可以做到。
   * mission ('mɪʃən) *n.* 任務　　impossible (ɪm'pɑsəbḷ) *adj.* 不可能的

42. (**B**) Joe was given a dangerous assignment.
   喬被指派一項危險的任務。
   (A) 它很有趣。   (B) 它不安全。
   (C) 那是項好任務。   (D) 它相當有挑戰性。
   * assignment (ə'saɪnmənt) *n.* 任務　　pretty ('prɪtɪ) *adv.* 相當地
   　 challenging ('tʃælɪndʒɪŋ) *adj.* 有挑戰性的

43. (**A**) He speaks French fluently.
   他法語說得很流利。
   (A) 他的法語很棒。   (B) 他根本不會講法語。
   (C) 他會說一點法語。   (D) 他的法語只有普通程度。
   * fluently ('fluəntlɪ) *adv.* 流利地　　fair (fɛr) *adj.* 普通的

44. (**A**) He has numerous telephone calls.
   他有許多通電話。
   (A) 他有很多通電話。   (B) 他有一些電話。
   (C) 他有幾通電話。   (D) 他沒有電話。
   * numerous ('njumərəs) *adj.* 衆多的

45. (**A**) We can store food in the refrigerator.
　　　我們可以將食物貯存在冰箱。

　　(A) 食物可以貯存在冰箱。　　(B) 食物可以在商店買到。
　　(C) 食品店買冰箱。　　　　　(D) 我們可以在食品店買到。

46. (**C**) I would like tea because it's stimulating.
　　　我要茶，因爲它可提神。

　　(A) 我應該喜歡茶。　　　　　(B) 我可能喜歡茶。
　　(C) 我要茶。　　　　　　　　(D) 茶不能提神。

　　* stimulating (ˈstɪmjəˌletɪŋ) *adj.* 刺激的；提神的

47. (**D**) Since last Monday was a national holiday, I had many
　　　visitors at home.
　　　因爲上星期一是國定假日，所以我家裏有許多訪客。

　　(A) 上星期一我沒有訪客。　　(B) 我有一些訪客。
　　(C) 上星期一不是假日。　　　(D) 我有很多訪客。

48. (**B**) This is John's desk and not Jane's.
　　　這是約翰的桌子，不是珍的。

　　(A) 桌子屬於珍的。　　　　　(B) 桌子屬於約翰的。
　　(C) 桌子屬於兩人的。　　　　(D) 桌子不屬於任何人。

　　* belong (bəˈlɔŋ) *v.* 屬於 < *to* >

49. (**C**) We may receive the check tomorrow.
　　　我們明天可能會收到支票。

　　(A) 我們必須收到它。　　　　(B) 我們可以收到它。
　　(C) 我們可能會收到它。　　　(D) 我們將收不到它。

50. (**B**) The doctor looked over his patient but didn't find
　　　anything wrong with him.
　　　醫生檢查病人，但是沒有發現異樣。

　　(A) 他批評病人。　　　　　　(B) 他檢查病人。
　　(C) 他治療病人。　　　　　　(D) 他把病人打發走。

　　* ***look over*** 檢查　　dismiss (dɪsˈmɪs) *v.* 使離開

51. (**C**) M : My name is Sergeant Scott. Can you tell me where my new class meets?

W : Yes, it's upstairs in Room 504. You are early though. Class doesn't start until 7:30.

What did the woman tell Sergeant Scott?

男：我是史考特下士。妳能告訴我新課程在哪裏上課嗎？

女：是的，在樓上的五〇四室。不過你來早了，課要七點半才開始。

這位女士告訴史考特下士什麼？

(A) 學生七點二十分開始上課。　(B) 學生上課遲到。
(C) <u>課程要晚一點才開始。</u>　(D) 課程在市區上課。

52. (**A**) W : This tire is in bad shape. What should I do with it?

M : Change it.

What did the man tell the woman to do with the tire?

女：這個輪胎變形了。我該怎麼處理？

男：換掉它。

這位男士告訴女士如何處理輪胎？

(A) <u>換掉它</u>　(B) 修理它
(C) 充氣　(D) 旋轉它

* inflate〔ɪnˋflet〕*v.* 充氣　rotate〔ˋrotet〕*v.* 旋轉

53. (**A**) W : Will there be enough transportation to take us to the zoo?

M : You don't have to worry about that. The parents will provide enough cars.

What did the man mean?

女：有足夠的交通工具可以載我們到動物園嗎？

男：這妳不必擔心。家長們會提供足夠的車子。

這位男士的意思為何？

(A) <u>家長會提供交通工具。</u>　(B) 家長不擔心動物園。
(C) 車子不夠每個人用。　(D) 家長不去動物園。

* transportation〔͵trænspɚˋteʃən〕*n.* 交通工具

54. (**A**)　W：I want to listen to some of the local radio stations. Do you sell any inexpensive transistor radios?

M：Yes, we have several different kinds and they pick up all local stations.

What does the woman want to do?

女：我想收聽一些地方電台。你們有賣便宜的電晶體收音機嗎？

男：有，我們有幾種不同的款式，都可以收到所有的地方電台。

這位女士想要做什麼？

(A) 她想要買一台電晶體收音機。

(B) 她想要聽海外的電台節目。

(C) 她想要用舊電視機換一台收音機。

(D) 她想要賣電晶體收音機。

　＊ transistor (trænˊzɪstɚ, -ˊsɪs-) *n.* 電晶體　　***pick up*** 收聽
　　overseas (ˏovɚˊsiz) *adj.* 海外的　　trade (tred) *v.* 交換

55. (**C**)　W：I can hardly see.

M：Neither can I. The visibility is bad.

What made the visibility bad?

女：我幾乎看不見。

男：我也是，能見度不佳。

什麼使得能見度不佳？

(A) 晴朗的天氣　　(B) 氣溫　　　(C) 濃霧　　(D) 沒有雲的天空

　＊ visibility (ˏvɪzəˊbɪlɪtɪ) *n.* 能見度

56. (**B**)　M：What do you need to finish your work?

W：I need some paste.

What did the girl need?

男：妳需要什麼來完成妳的工作？

女：我需要一些漿糊。

這位女孩需要什麼？

(A) 她需要一些工作。　　　　　　(B) 她需要一些黏性物質。

(C) 她需要一些膠帶。　　　　　　(D) 她需要一些紙。

　＊ paste (pest) *n.* 漿糊　　sticky (ˊstɪkɪ) *adj.* 黏性的
　　tape (tep) *n.* 膠帶

57. (**C**) M : How are the prices in the hotel?

W : The rates are very reasonable.

What did the woman say about the rates?

男：旅館的價格如何？

女：價格非常合理。

這位女士說價格如何？

(A) 價格太高。 (B) 價格太高。

(C) 價格合理。 (D) 價格不合理。

* rate〔ret〕*n.* 費用   reasonable〔'riznəbḷ〕*adj.* 合理的

58. (**A**) W : You don't look like you feel good.

M : I have a pain in my thigh.

What did the man say?

女：你看起來不太舒服。

男：我的大腿在痛。

這位男士說什麼？

(A) 他的大腿痛。 (B) 他感覺很好。

(C) 他的大腿無力。 (D) 他感覺麻木。

* thigh〔θaɪ〕*n.* 大腿   numb〔nʌm〕*adj.* 麻木的

59. (**C**) W : Will you repair this tire for me?

M : I will replace it instead of repairing it.

What did the man mean?

女：你幫我修這個輪胎好嗎？

男：我會將它換掉而不是修理。

這位男士的意思為何？

(A) 他會修理它，但是他不會換掉它。

(B) 他不會換掉或修理它。

(C) 他會換掉它，而不是修理它。

(D) 他會換掉並修理它。

* replace〔rɪ'ples〕*v.* 取代；換掉

  instead of 而不是（ = *rather than* ）

60. (**D**) M : What are you doing with that camera?

W : Smile, I want a picture of you.

What is the woman going to do?

男：妳拿那台照相機要做什麼？

女：笑一個，我幫你照張相。

這位女士要做什麼？

(A) 要他的照片　　　　　　(B) 告訴他一個故事

(C) 看他微笑　　　　　　　(D) 替他照相

When my 89-year-old grandmother checked into the hospital, she was more upset by her wrist tag, which displayed her age, than she was about the impending surgery. "Now, Mrs. Stone," said a perceptive nurse, "we'll just turn the wristband upside-down. Then everyone will think you're 68."

當我八十九歲的祖母住院時，她手腕上的籤條寫出了她的年紀，比她即將動的手術，更使她難過。一位敏銳的護士說：「現在，史東太太，我們只要把妳手腕上的帶子弄顛倒，那麼大家就會認為妳六十八歲了。」

LISTENING TEST 6

• *Directions for questions 1-25. You will hear questions on the test tape. Select the one item A, B, C or D which answers the question correctly, and mark your answer sheet.*

1. A. after getting a haircut   B. after eating his dinner
   C. at the barbershop   D. at the cafeteria

2. A. The temperature went up.
   B. It got colder.
   C. The temperature stayed the same.
   D. The fall season arrived.

3. A. That's a big boy for a small load.
   B. His brother is a big load.
   C. His brother is handsome.
   D. The load is rather large.

4. A. on top of the TV set
   B. in front of the TV set
   C. behind the TV set
   D. on the left side of the TV set

5. A. He replaced the tire.   B. He filled the tire with air.
   C. He patched the tire.   D. He removed the tire.

6. A. because he went to a party
   B. because he wasn't busy
   C. because he didn't have a party
   D. because he had a party

7. A. headlines   B. news
   C. stories   D. drawings

8. A. to sharpen it   B. to light it
    C. to carry it   D. to nail it

9. A. pieces of ice   B. flood water
    C. water vapor   D. drizzle

10. A. movies   B. fashions
     C. prices   D. menus

11. A. He replied quickly.   B. He caught her.
     C. He didn't get her.   D. He understood her reply.

12. A. He sells cars.
     B. He files records and letters.
     C. He repairs machines.
     D. He manages a company.

13. A. He worked out the problem.
     B. He continued working on it.
     C. He gave up.
     D. He worked too long.

14. A. He doesn't like appointments.
     B. He's always late.
     C. He always stands me up.
     D. He's always punctual.

15. A. a pharmacist   B. a physician
     C. a physicist   D. a supervisor

16. A. She has a strong heart.   B. She hears every word.
     C. She works hard.   D. She worries a lot.

17. A. a position   B. an attack
     C. a support   D. an advance

18. A. a parking job   B. a permanent job
     C. a part time job   D. a difficult job

19. A. Monday and Tuesday   B. Wednesday and Thursday
     C. Monday to Friday   D. Saturday and Sunday

20. A. They have become poorer.
     B. They have become richer.
     C. They have become worse.
     D. They have gone from bad to worse.

21. A. I left it behind somewhere.
     B. It's broken.
     C. It's sold.
     D. It gains a minute a day.

22. A. 16 gallons of gas   B. 30 gallons of gas
     C. 32 gallons of gas   D. 8 gallons of gas

23. A. The room was too cold.
     B. The room was too windy.
     C. The room was too small.
     D. The room was too warm.

24. A. Mark   B. Kevin
     C. Neither of them is loud.   D. Either of them is loud.

25. A. once in a week   B. once in two weeks
     C. every two months   D. once in a month

● *Directions for questions 26-50. You will hear statements on the test tape. Select the one answer A, B, C, or D which comes closest to the meaning of the statement and mark your answer sheet.*

26. A. He didn't get any money.
    B. He got extra money.
    C. He got just enough money.
    D. He didn't get enough money.

27. A. He is not working.   B. He is sick.
    C. He is out of town.   D. He moved away.

28. A. He lost his money.   B. He lost his ball.
    C. He fell down.   D. He walked down the steps.

29. A. Cars are more popular than bicycles.
    B. More students ride bicycles.
    C. More cars park on campus.
    D. This campus is crowded with cars and bicycles.

30. A. They will set it on fire.
    B. They will take it apart.
    C. They will repair it.
    D. They will paint it.

31. A. My lawyer is interested in the will.
    B. I will lower the interest rate.
    C. My lawyer charges interest on the bill.
    D. I will rest inside.

32. A. There is little doubt about it.
    B. The rain relieved our pain.
    C. A rain wouldn't help much.
    D. A rain could relieve the drought.

33. A. I joined in September.
    B. I joined in December.
    C. I joined before graduation.
    D. I graduated from the service.

34. A. They are not in the shipment.
    B. They are part of the shipment.
    C. They are separated in the shipment.
    D. They are apart from the shipment.

35. A. Mark kept on walking.
    B. Mark's foot hurt.
    C. Mark was exhausted.
    D. Mark's car had two flat tires.

36. A. My letter contained important knowledge.
    B. My letter may never have been received.
    C. The company insured my letter.
    D. The company said my letter had arrived.

37. A. She is going to throw them away.
    B. They belong to her.
    C. Some of them are lost.
    D. They are sent to her for free.

38. A. She thinks she'll do well on the exam.
    B. She is sure she'll be flunked.
    C. She is going to see an eye doctor.
    D. She plans to change her major.

39. A. I wrote Peter yesterday.
    B. I called Peter yesterday.
    C. Peter called me yesterday.
    D. We discussed our letters yesterday.

40. A. The cat and the boy played together.
    B. The cat made the boy happy.
    C. The boy chased the ball.
    D. The cat frightened the boy.

41. A. She is not ugly. B. She is in bad health.
    C. She is not thin. D. She is pretty.

42. A. Carl would like his wife to stop working and stay at home.
    B. Carl would like his wife to continue working.
    C. Carl wants to quit his job.
    D. Carl wants to stay home.

43. A. Someone said he was coming.
    B. He was late.
    C. Everyone ignored him.
    D. No one knew he was coming.

44. A. She spoke for two more hours.
    B. She walked two more hours.
    C. She entered the classroom.
    D. She remained in the classroom.

45. A. Jane worked in graduate school.
    B. Jane finished graduate school quickly.
    C. Right after graduate school, Jane started to work.
    D. Right after work, Jane went to graduate school.

46. A. Leslie wanted to read a book about cards.
    B. Leslie found the card in the book.
    C. Leslie found the book she needed.
    D. Leslie was ordering from a catalogue.

47. A. The doctor was supposed to cure me of my cold.
    B. I think the medicine may have worked.
    C. You are supposed to take the medicine.
    D. You helped me a lot when I was sick.

48. A. He is afraid of work. B. He likes to work.
    C. He works slowly. D. He is a poor worker.

49. A. Eight people are on board.
    B. The plane fly from New York to here.
    C. Passengers can board at Gate Eight.
    D. The plane has departed for New York.

50. A. Go out of the room, please.
    B. I like to smoke outside.
    C. Please smoke outside.
    D. I prefer the door to be open.

● *Directions for questions 51-60. You will hear dialogs on the test tape. Select the correct answer A, B, C, or D and mark your answer sheet.*

51. A. California
    C. Michigan
    B. New York
    D. The South

52. A. at or before five
    C. late at night
    B. after five
    D. in the morning

53. A. Patient-Doctor
    C. Wife-Husband
    B. Waitress-Customer
    D. Secretary-Boss

54. A. Yes, he is not.
    C. No, he is not.
    B. No, he is.
    D. Yes, he is.

55. A. Their hobbies are much alike.
    B. Their hobbies are the same.
    C. They work at their hobbies together.
    D. They work at their hobbies separately.

56. A. He is not prepared.
    C. He is almost ready.
    B. He is well prepared.
    D. He will soon start.

57. A. They couldn't find their dog.
　　B. They rested with their dog.
　　C. They saved their dog.
　　D. They looked for their dog.

58. A. bring some food to the table
　　B. help herself to some food
　　C. use the phone on the table
　　D. move the table over there

59. A. study them　　　　B. obey them
　　C. disobey them　　　D. rewrite them

60. A. Scott is angry with her.
　　B. Scott has the same opinion as she.
　　C. Scott has a different opinion.
　　D. Scott doesn't care to say anything.

"I'd like some vitamins for my son."
"Vitamin A, B, or C?" asked the pharmacist.
"It doesn't matter, he can't read yet."

「我要買維他命給我兒子。」
「維他命 A、B 還是 C 呢？」藥劑師問道。
「那不重要，他還不識字。」

ECL 聽力測驗 [6] 詳解

1. (**A**) Lieutenant Steward is going to the barber shop to get a haircut, and then he is going to the cafeteria to eat dinner. When will Lt. Steward have his dinner?

司徒雅德中尉要到理髮店剪頭髮，然後再到自助餐廳吃晚餐。
司徒雅德中尉何時要吃晚飯？

(A) 剪完頭髮後
(B) 吃完晚餐後
(C) 在理髮店
(D) 在自助餐廳

* lieutenant〔lu'tɛnənt〕*n.* 中尉　　barber〔'bɑrbɚ〕*n.* 理髮師
cafeteria〔ˌkæfə'tırıə〕*n.* 自助餐廳

2. (**B**) The temperature fell rapidly when the cold front hit. What happened when the cold front arrived?

冷鋒來襲時，溫度快速下降。／冷鋒到時發生了什麼事？

(A) 溫度上升。
(B) 天氣變得更冷。
(C) 溫度維持一樣。
(D) 秋天來臨。

3. (**D**) Joe told his brother, "That's a pretty big load for such a small boy." What did Joe mean?

喬告訴他哥哥：「對這麼小的男孩而言，那是個很大的負擔。」
喬意指什麼？

(A) 對大男孩而言是小負擔。
(B) 他哥哥是大負擔。
(C) 他哥哥很帥。
(D) 負擔相當大。

* load〔lod〕*n.* 負擔

4. (**C**) The cable was concealed in back of the television set. Where was the cable hidden?

纜線隱藏在電視機後面。／纜線藏在哪兒？

(A) 電視機上面
(B) 電視機前面
(C) 電視機後面
(D) 電視機左邊

* cable〔'kebḷ〕*n.* 纜線　　conceal〔kən'sil〕*v.* 隱藏

5. (**B**) I took the tire to the service station and had the mechanic inflate it. What did the mechanic do?

我把輪胎拿到加油站,請技工充氣。／技工做了什麼事?

(A) 他換掉輪胎。 　　　　　　(B) 他替輪胎充氣。
(C) 他修補輪胎。 　　　　　　(D) 他卸下輪胎。

＊ *service station* 加油站　　 inflate (ɪn'flet) *v.* 充氣
patch (pætʃ) *v.* 修補　　 remove (rɪ'muv) *v.* 清除;卸下

6. (**D**) Joseph had a party last night and couldn't finish his homework. Why didn't he finish his homework?

約瑟夫昨晚辦了一場舞會,而沒有完成他的作業。
為何他沒有完成他的作業?

(A) 因為他去參加舞會 　　(B) 因為他不忙
(C) 因為他沒有辦舞會 　　(D) 因為他辦了一場舞會

7. (**D**) Miss Bush likes the cartoons in the evening newspaper. What are they?

布希小姐喜歡看晚報的漫畫。／那是什麼?

(A) 標題　　 (B) 新聞　　 (C) 故事　　 (D) 圖畫

＊ cartoon (kɑr'tun) *n.* 漫畫;卡通　　 headline ('hɛd,laɪn) *n.* 標題

8. (**A**) The gardener used the electric grinder on the knife. Why did he use it?

園丁使用電動磨刀機磨刀。／他為什麼用它?

(A) 把刀磨利　　 (B) 照亮它　　 (C) 攜帶它　　 (D) 釘住它

＊ gardener ('gɑrdn̩ə) *n.* 園丁　　 grinder ('graɪndə) *n.* 研磨機

9. (**A**) Hail did much damage to crops. What damaged crops?

冰雹造成農作物嚴重損失。／什麼損害了農作物?

(A) 冰塊　　 (B) 洪水　　 (C) 水蒸氣　　 (D) 毛毛雨

＊ hail (hel) *n.* 冰雹　　 *do damage to* 造成~損失
flood (flʌd) *n.* 洪水;氾濫　　 vapor ('vepə) *n.* 蒸氣
drizzle ('drɪzl̩) *n.* 毛毛雨

10. (**B**) Anna is very interested in the latest styles.
What is she interested in?
安娜對最新的風格很感興趣。／她對什麼感興趣？

    (A) 電影   (B) 流行   (C) 價格   (D) 菜單

    * latest〔'letɪst〕*adj.* 最新的   fashion〔'fæʃən〕*n.* 流行

11. (**C**) She responded so quickly that he didn't catch her reply.
What's the problem with him?
她回答得太快，以至於他沒有聽到她的答案。／他有什麼問題？

    (A) 他回答得很快。   (B) 他捉住她。

    (C) 他沒有聽懂她的話。   (D) 他了解她的回答。

    * respond〔rɪ'spand〕*v.* 回答   reply〔rɪ'plaɪ〕*n., v.* 回答

12. (**B**) Paul is an office clerk. What does he do?
保羅是辦公室職員。／他做什麼事？

    (A) 他賣車。   (B) 他將記錄和信件歸檔。

    (C) 他修理機器。   (D) 他管理一家公司。

    * file〔faɪl〕*v.* 歸檔   manage〔'mænɪdʒ〕*v.* 管理

13. (**B**) Doctor Gilbert had worked on the project too long to
give up. What happened later?
吉伯特醫生從事這個計畫太久了，他不能放棄。
後來發生什麼事？

    (A) 他解決問題了。   (B) 他繼續從事這個計畫。

    (C) 他放棄了。   (D) 他工作太久了。

    * ***work on*** 從事   ***work out*** 解決

14. (**D**) It's not like Ted to be late for an appointment.
What kind of person is Ted?
約會遲到這不像泰德。／泰德是怎樣的人？

    (A) 他不喜歡約會。   (B) 他總是遲到。

    (C) 他總是放我鴿子。   (D) 他總是準時。

    * appointment〔ə'pɔɪntmənt〕*n.* 約會

      stand *sb.* ***up*** 爽約；放某人鴿子   punctual〔'pʌŋktʃʊəl〕*adj.* 準時的

15.(**B**)　When Billy was sick, he went to a man who cured him.
Who cured Billy?
比利生病時，他去找一個能治好他的人。／什麼人把比利治好？

(A) 藥劑師　　　(B) 醫師　　　(C) 物理學家　　　(D) 上司

* pharmacist (ˈfɑrməsɪst) *n.* 藥劑師
physician (fəˈzɪʃən) *n.* 內科醫生　　physicist (ˈfɪzəsɪst) *n.* 物理學家
supervisor (ˌsupəˈvaɪzə) *n.* 監督者；上司

16.(**C**)　Karen is a hard worker. How does she do?
凱倫是個努力的員工。／她做得如何？

(A) 她心臟功能很強。　　　(B) 她聽到每個字。
(C) 她工作努力。　　　　　(D) 她非常擔憂。

17.(**B**)　What is the opposite of "defense"?
「保衛」的相反是什麼？

(A) 位置　　　(B) 攻擊　　　(C) 支持　　　(D) 前進

* defense (dɪˈfɛns) *n.* 保衛　　attack (əˈtæk) *n.* 攻擊
advance (ədˈvæns) *n.* 前進

18.(**C**)　Some local businesses hire students on a part time basis.
What kind of job do students do?
有些當地企業以兼職方式雇用學生。／學生做怎樣的工作？

(A) 停車的工作　　　(B) 永遠的工作
(C) 兼職的工作　　　(D) 困難的工作

* local (ˈlokḷ) *adj.* 當地的　　hire (haɪr) *v.* 雇用
on a ~ basis 以~基礎；以~方式　　***part time*** 兼職
permanent (ˈpɜmənənt) *adj.* 永遠的

19.(**D**)　He must work overtime on weekends.
When must he be working?
他週末必須加班。／他何時仍必須工作？

(A) 星期一和星期二　　　(B) 星期三和星期四
(C) 星期一到星期五　　　(D) 星期六和星期日

* overtime (ˈovəˌtaɪm) *adv.* 超出時間地；加班

20. (**B**) They have become better off after working hard for many years. After many years, what has become of them？

努力工作多年後，他們已變得更富有。／ 多年後，他們怎麼了？

(A) 他們變得更窮。　　　　　　(B) 他們變得更有錢。
(C) 他們變得更糟。　　　　　　(D) 他們每下愈況。

　＊ *better off* 更富有　　*What became of* ～？　～怎麼了？
　　 from bad to worse 愈來愈糟；每下愈況

21. (**A**) I looked everywhere but couldn't find my watch. What happened to my watch？

我到處找，但找不到我的錶。／ 我的錶怎麼了？

(A) 我把它掉在某處了。　　　　(B) 壞掉了。
(C) 賣掉了。　　　　　　　　　(D) 每天快一分鐘。

　＊ *leave behind* 遺留　　gain〔gen〕*v.* （鐘、錶）時間變快

22. (**C**) Sixteen gallons of gas filled up my gas tank, and now it's half-empty. How much can my gas tank hold？

十六加侖的油加入我的油箱，現在它是半滿的。
我的油箱可以裝多少？

(A) 十六加侖　　(B) 三十加侖　　(C) 三十二加侖　　(D) 八加侖

　＊ gallon（'gælən）*n.* 加侖（液體單位）　　hold〔hold〕*v.* 裝載

23. (**D**) When the room became too warm, we opened the window. Why did we open the window？

當房間太溫暖時，我們把窗戶打開。／ 我們為何要開窗？

(A) 房間太冷。　　　　　　　　(B) 房間風太大。
(C) 房間太小。　　　　　　　　(D) 房間太溫暖。

24. (**C**) Mark and Kevin are both rather quiet. Which one of them is louder？

馬克和凱文都很安靜。／ 他們當中誰比較吵？

(A) 馬克　　　　　　　　　　　(B) 凱文
(C) 他們二個都不吵。　　　　　(D) 他們二個有一個很吵。

25. (**B**) Our club members meet every other Wednesday.
How often do our members meet?
我們俱樂部會員每二個星期三聚會一次。
我們的會員多久聚會一次?

    (A) 一星期一次   (B) <u>二星期一次</u>
    (C) 每隔二個月一次   (D) 一個月一次

26. (**B**) Anthony received additional money for his good service.
安東尼因爲他的服務好,收到額外的錢。

    (A) 他沒有得到錢。   (B) <u>他得到額外的錢。</u>
    (C) 他得到剛好足夠的錢。   (D) 他沒有得到足夠的錢。

    * additional〔ə'dɪʃən!〕*adj.* 額外的

27. (**A**) Jonathan is on vacation this week.
強納生本週去度假。

    (A) <u>他沒有上班。</u>   (B) 他生病了。   (C) 他出城了。   (D) 他搬走了。

28. (**C**) He lost his balance.
他失去平衡。

    (A) 他錢不見了。   (B) 他失去了他的球。
    (C) <u>他跌倒了。</u>   (D) 他走下樓梯。

    * balance〔'bæləns〕*n.* 平衡   step〔stɛp〕*n.* 樓梯

29. (**B**) There are more bicycles than cars on this campus.
這個校園裏腳踏車比汽車多。

    (A) 汽車比腳踏車受歡迎。   (B) <u>較多學生騎腳踏車。</u>
    (C) 較多汽車停在校園裏。   (D) 這個校園擠滿了汽車和腳踏車。

30. (**B**) The workman will tear down that building.
工人們將拆毀這棟大樓。

    (A) 他們將放火把它燒掉。   (B) <u>他們將把它拆毀。</u>
    (C) 他們將修復它。   (D) 他們將粉刷它。

    * ***tear down*** 拆毀   ***set ~ on fire*** 放火燒~   ***take ~ apart*** 把~拆毀

31. (**A**) The will interests my lawyer.
這份遺囑使我的律師很感興趣。

(A) 我的律師對這份遺囑很感興趣。　　(B) 我將會降低利率。
(C) 我的律師帳單裏多收利息。　　　　(D) 我將到裏面休息。

* will〔wɪl〕*n.* 遺囑　　interest〔'ɪntrɪst〕*v.* 使感興趣　*n.* 利息
rate〔ret〕*n.* 比率　　charge〔tʃɑrdʒ〕*v.* 收費

32. (**C**) A day of rain would do little to relieve the drought.
下一天的雨對減輕乾旱幫助不大。

(A) 沒有疑問。　　　　(B) 雨減輕了我們的痛苦。
(C) 一場雨幫助不大。　　(D) 一場雨可以減輕乾旱。

* relieve〔rɪ'liv〕*v.* 減輕　　drought〔draʊt〕*n.* 乾旱

33. (**A**) I graduated from high school in July and joined the
military service two months later.
我七月從中學畢業，二個月後即入伍當兵。

(A) 我九月入伍。　　　　(B) 我十二月入伍。
(C) 我畢業前入伍。　　　(D) 我從軍中退伍。

* *military service* 兵役

34. (**B**) Spare parts of the instruments are included in the
shipment.
工具的備用部分也包含在這次裝運之內。

(A) 它們不在這次裝運內。　　(B) 它們是裝運的一部分。
(C) 它們和裝運分開。　　　　(D) 它們和裝運分開。

* spare〔spɛr〕*adj.* 備用的　　instrument〔'ɪnstrəmənt〕*n.* 工具
shipment〔'ʃɪpmənt〕*n.* 裝運

35. (**C**) Mark was too tired to move another foot.
馬克太累了，一步也走不動。

(A) 馬克繼續走。　　　　(B) 馬克的腳痛。
(C) 馬克筋疲力竭了。　　(D) 馬克的車有二個爆胎。

* exhausted〔ɪg'zɔstɪd〕*adj.* 筋疲力竭的　　*flat tire* 爆胎

36. (**D**)　The insurance company acknowledged receiving my letter.
　　　　保險公司確認收到我的信。

　　　　(A) 我的信包含重要知識。　　　(B) 我的信可能從未被收到。
　　　　(C) 這家公司替我的信保險。　　　(D) 這家公司說我的信到了。

　　　　* insurance (ɪnˋʃʊrəns) *n.* 保險　　acknowledge (əkˋnɑlɪdʒ) *v.* 承認
　　　　　insure (ɪnˋʃʊr) *v.* 爲～投保

37. (**B**)　Those are her personal belongings.
　　　　那些是她的個人物品。

　　　　(A) 她將要把它們丟掉。　　　　(B) 它們屬於她。
　　　　(C) 它們當中有一些丟掉了。　　(D) 它們是被免費送給她的。

　　　　* belongings (bəˋlɔŋɪnz) *n., pl.*　(個人的) 物品；財產
　　　　　for free 免費地

38. (**A**)　Susan is optimistic about her final exam.
　　　　蘇珊對她的期末考試很樂觀。

　　　　(A) 她認爲她會考得很好。　　　(B) 她確定她會被當掉。
　　　　(C) 她要去看眼科醫生。　　　　(D) 她計畫要更改主修科目。

　　　　* optimistic (ˌɑptəˋmɪstɪk) *adj.* 樂觀的　　flunk (flʌŋk) *v.* 使不及格
　　　　　major (ˋmedʒɚ) *n.* 主修科目

39. (**C**)　I heard from Peter yesterday.
　　　　我昨天收到彼德的音信。

　　　　(A) 我昨天寫信給彼德。　　　　(B) 我昨天打電話給彼德。
　　　　(C) 彼德昨天打電話給我。　　　(D) 我們昨天討論我們的信件。

　　　　* *hear from sb.* 收到某人的音信 (信、電話等)

40. (**B**)　The little boy laughed with delight while the cat chased
　　　　the ball.
　　　　當貓咪追著球時，小男孩笑得很開心。

　　　　(A) 貓咪和小男孩一起玩。　　　(B) 貓咪讓男孩很開心。
　　　　(C) 男孩追著球。　　　　　　　(D) 貓咪嚇到男孩了。

　　　　* delight (dɪˋlaɪt) *n.* 高興　　chase (tʃez) *v.* 追
　　　　　frighten (ˋfraɪtn̩) *v.* 使驚嚇

41. (**C**) The woman who will come to see you is rather fat.

要來看你的那位女士很胖。

(A) 她不醜。　　　　　　(B) 她健康情形不佳。

(C) 她不瘦。　　　　　　(D) 她很漂亮。

＊ rather (ˊræðɚ) *adv.* 相當地

42. (**A**) Carl wants his wife to quit working and stay home with the children

卡爾要他太太辭職，待在家裏陪小孩。

(A) 卡爾要他太太辭職待在家裏。

(B) 卡爾要他太太繼續工作。

(C) 卡爾要辭職。

(D) 卡爾要待在家裏。

＊ quit (kwɪt) *v.* 放棄；辭掉

43. (**D**) He arrived unannounced.

他未經宣布突然出現。

(A) 有人說他來了。　　　(B) 他遲到了。

(C) 每個人都忽略了他。　(D) 沒有人知道他來了。

＊ unannounced (ˌʌnəˊnaʊnst) *adj.* 沒有預告的；突然出現的
　 ignore (ɪgˊnɔr) *v.* 忽略

44. (**D**) She sat in the classroom for two more hours.

她在教室裏多坐了二個小時。

(A) 她多講了二個小時。　(B) 她多走了二個小時。

(C) 她進入教室。　　　　(D) 她待在教室裏。

＊ remain (rɪˊmen) *v.* 停留

45. (**C**) Jane finished graduate school and got a job immediately.

珍研究所畢業，立刻找到工作。

(A) 珍在研究所工作。　　(B) 珍很快從研究所畢業。

(C) 一畢業，珍就開始工作。(D) 工作完，珍就去唸研究所。

＊ *graduate school* 研究所

46. (**C**) Leslie first checked the card catalogue and then located the book.

萊斯莉先查卡片目錄，然後找出那本書。

(A) 萊斯莉要讀一本關於紙牌的書。 (B) 萊斯莉找到書中的卡片。

(C) 萊斯莉找到她需要的書。 (D) 萊斯莉從目錄中訂貨。

* catalogue ('kætl,ɔg) *n.* 目錄

　locate (lo'ket) *v.* 找出；發現位置　order ('ɔrdə) *v.* 訂貨

47. (**B**) The medicine was helpful, I suppose.

我想這個藥有效。

(A) 醫生應該治好我的感冒。 (B) 我認為這個藥有效。

(C) 你應該吃這個藥。 (D) 我生病時，你幫助我很多。

* suppose (sə'poz) *v.* 認為　*be supposed to* 應該

　cure sb. of ～ 治好某人的～

48. (**B**) Sam is an eager worker.

山姆是個努力的員工。

(A) 他害怕工作。 (B) 他喜歡工作。

(C) 他工作緩慢。 (D) 他是個差勁的員工。

* eager ('igə) *adj.* 熱切的

49. (**C**) The plane to New York is now ready for boarding at Gate No. 8.

到紐約的班機在八號門可以準備登機了。

(A) 八個人在飛機上。 (B) 這架飛機從紐約飛到這裏。

(C) 乘客可以在八號門登機。 (D) 飛機已出發前往紐約了。

* board (bord) *v.* 登機　gate (get) *n.* 大門

　on board 在機上　depart (dɪ'part) *v.* 出發；離開

50. (**C**) I would prefer if you would smoke outside.

我比較喜歡你到外面抽煙。

(A) 請離開房間。 (B) 我喜歡到外面抽煙。

(C) 請到外面抽煙。 (D) 我比較喜歡門開著。

51. (**B**) W : Where are you from?

M : I was born in California, but I was brought up in
New York and studied in Michigan.

Where did the man grow up?

女：你是從哪裏來的？

男：我在加州出生，但在紐約長大，在密西根唸書。

這位男士在哪裏長大？

(A) 加州　　　　(B) <u>紐約</u>　　　(C) 密西根　　(D) 南方

* ***bring up*** 撫養

52. (**A**) W : It's no use going to the store now.

M : You're right. It's after five already.

When does the store probably close?

女：現在去商店已經沒有用了。

男：妳說得對。已經過五點了。

這家商店可能何時關門？

(A) <u>五點或五點之前</u>　　　(B) 五點以後

(C) 深夜　　　　　　　　　(D) 早上

* ***It's no use + V-ing*** ～是沒有用的

53. (**B**) W : Would you like to see a menu?

M : No, thank you. I already know what I want to order.

What is the probable relationship between the two
speakers?

女：您要看菜單嗎？

男：不，謝謝。我已經知道要點什麼了。

這二位說話者之間的關係可能為何？

(A) 病人對醫生　　　　　(B) <u>女服務生對客人</u>

(C) 妻子對先生　　　　　(D) 祕書對老板

* menu ('mɛnju) *n.* 菜單　　order ('ɔrdɚ) *v.* 點菜
relationship (rɪ'leʃən,ʃɪp) *n.* 關係
patient ('peʃənt) *n.* 病人
waitress ('wetrɪs) *n.* 女服務生

54. (**D**)　W : Are you a member of the officer's club, Lieutenant?

　　　M : Yes, Madam.

　　　Is the man a member of the club?

　　　女：中尉，你是軍官俱樂部的會員嗎？

　　　男：是的，女士。

　　　這位男士是俱樂部會員嗎？

　　　(A) 是，他不是。(B) 不，他是。　(C) 不，他不是。(D) 是，他是。

55. (**A**)　W : Do your children have hobbies?

　　　M : Yes, in fact their hobbies are similar.

　　　What did the man say about his children's hobbies?

　　　女：你的孩子們有嗜好嗎？

　　　男：有，實際上他們的嗜好都很類似。

　　　這位男士說他的孩子們嗜好怎樣？

　　　(A) 他們的嗜好很像。　　　　(B) 他們的嗜好相同。

　　　(C) 他們一起從事嗜好。　　　(D) 他們分開從事嗜好。

56. (**A**)　W : Are you ready?

　　　M : Ready? I haven't even started.

　　　What does the man mean?

　　　女：你準備好了嗎？

　　　男：準備好？我根本還沒開始。

　　　這位男士是什麼意思？

　　　(A) 他還沒準備好。　　　　(B) 他準備得很充分。

　　　(C) 他快準備好了。　　　　(D) 他很快就要開始了。

57. (**C**)　M : Why are Mr. and Mrs. Wharton so excited?

　　　W : They rescued their dog.

　　　What did the woman say about Mr. and Mrs. Wharton?

　　　男：爲什麼瓦爾頓先生和瓦爾頓太太如此興奮？

　　　女：因爲他們救了他們的狗。

　　　這位女士說瓦爾頓先生和瓦爾頓太太怎麼了？

　　　(A) 他們找不到他們的狗。　　(B) 他們和他們的狗在休息。

　　　(C) 他們救了他們的狗。　　　(D) 他們尋找他們的狗。

58. (**C**)　W : Excuse me, but would you mind if I use your phone?
　　　　　　M : Help yourself. It is on the table over there.
　　　　　　What did the man tell the woman to do?
　　　　　　女：對不起，你介意我借用你的電話嗎？
　　　　　　男：請自便。電話就在那邊的桌上。
　　　　　　這位男士告訴女士做什麼？

　　　　(A) 帶些食品擺在桌上。　　　　(B) 自行取用食物。
　　　　(C) <u>用桌上的電話。</u>　　　　　　(D) 移動那邊的桌子。
　　　　＊ *help oneself* (*to* ～) 自行取用～

59. (**B**)　W : Do people adhere to the laws in your country?
　　　　　　M : Oh, yes. They certainly do.
　　　　　　What do the people of the country do about the laws?
　　　　　　女：貴國人民都守法嗎？
　　　　　　男：是的，當然。
　　　　　　該國的人民對法律都怎樣？

　　　　(A) 研究它們　　　　　　　　　(B) <u>服從它們</u>
　　　　(C) 不服從它們　　　　　　　　(D) 重寫它們
　　　　＊ adhere〔əd'hɪr〕v. 堅守＜ *to* ＞　　obey〔ə'be, o'be〕v. 服從
　　　　　disobey〔‚dɪsə'be〕v. 不服從

60. (**C**)　M : Did you speak with Scott about your suggestion?
　　　　　　W : Yes, but he disagrees with me.
　　　　　　What did the woman mean?
　　　　　　男：妳向史考特談過妳的建議了嗎？
　　　　　　女：談過了，但他不同意我的意見。
　　　　　　這位女士是什麼意思？

　　　　(A) 史考特對她很生氣。　　　　(B) 史考特和她意見相同。
　　　　(C) <u>史考特有不同的意見。</u>　　　(D) 史考特不想說任何事。
　　　　＊ *care to* 想要

LISTENING TEST 7

● *Directions for questions 1-25. You will hear questions on the test tape. Select the one item A, B, C or D which answers the question correctly, and mark your answer sheet.*

1. A. He's going to work as a doctor.
   B. He's going to teach first aid.
   C. He's going to see the doctor.
   D. He's going to study medicine.

2. A. fold the tablecloth on the table
   B. spread the tablecloth on the table
   C. roll the tablecloth on the table
   D. take the tablecloth away from the table

3. A. It measures rainfall.
   B. It measures atmospheric pressure.
   C. It measures the temperature.
   D. It measures the velocity of the wind.

4. A. before the movie ended   B. after the movie ended
   C. before the movie started   D. after the movie started

5. A. Good afternoon.   B. Good evening.
   C. Good night.   D. Good morning.

6. A. steel   B. cloth
   C. radios   D. flour

7. A. break his promise
   B. buy a necklace for his mother
   C. give him a new watch
   D. grant him a wish

8. A. to give an order
   C. to complete a statement

   B. to answer a question
   D. to explain a statement

9. A. It hit the dock.
   C. It missed the pillar.

   B. It stayed intact.
   D. It broke into pieces.

10. A. saluted a captain
    C. gave a perfect salute

    B. saluted quickly
    D. gave two salutes

11. A. It was raining hard.
    C. The sun was shining.

    B. Light rain was falling.
    D. It was pretty cloudy.

12. A. because they like it
    C. two hours every night

    B. Mr. and Mrs. Wood
    D. at home

13. A. No, they wasn't.
    C. Yes, they weren't.

    B. Yes, they were.
    D. No, they were.

14. A. They are 55 ¢ a dozen.
    B. There are twelve in a carton.
    C. They have protein in them.
    D. I like them boiled.

15. A. He is my English teacher.
    B. He is thirty years old.
    C. He wears a gray jacket.
    D. He is standing over there.

16. A. funny
    C. interesting

    B. sad
    D. terrible

17. A. farms
    C. factories

    B. residences
    D. parks

18. A. begin   B. stop
     C. finish   D. improve

19. A. a type of weapon   B. a type of rifle
     C. a publication   D. a kind of machine gun

20. A. to love company   B. to love freedom
     C. to love friends   D. to love life

21. A. a book   B. a passage
     C. a name   D. a position

22. A. Yes, it isn't.   B. No, it is.
     C. Yes, I don't think so.   D. Yes, it is.

23. A. gradually   B. suddenly
     C. laughingly   D. quickly

24. A. went to make lunch for Linda
     B. went to have lunch with Linda
     C. left Linda's house before lunch
     D. went to buy lunch for Linda

25. A. his dues   B. his bill
     C. his billfold   D. his room

- *Directions for questions 26-50. You will hear statements on the test tape. Select the one answer A, B, C, or D which comes closest to the meaning of the statement and mark your answer sheet.*

26. A. They have not eaten yet.
     B. They are eating now.
     C. They have to eat quickly.
     D. They were late for breakfast.

27. A. She no longer drinks coffee.
    B. She stopped to drink some coffee.
    C. She couldn't find any coffee to drink.
    D. She dislikes coffee but drinks it.

28. A. The air is thin.   B. The air is thick.
    C. The air is hot.   D. The air is cool.

29. A. I don't have any pens.
    B. I have a few pens.
    C. I don't have much use for pens.
    D. I have a lot of pens.

30. A. The yellow hat is cheaper.
    B. The gray hat is cheaper.
    C. They are the same price.
    D. The red hat is cheaper.

31. A. Jane remembered her father.
    B. Jane did what her father said.
    C. Jane disobeyed her father.
    D. Jane's father was always gone.

32. A. Dennis caught the train.
    B. Dennis took the train.
    C. Dennis missed the train.
    D. Dennis usually load the train.

33. A. Paul will not go.   B. Paul doesn't think he'll go.
    C. I think Paul will go.   D. Everyone but Paul will go.

34. A. He has only money.
    B. He has only a small amount of money.
    C. He usually has some money.
    D. He never has any money.

35. A. Jim did some schoolwork at home.
    B. Jim cleaned up the living room.
    C. Jim rearranged the books in his study.
    D. Jim picked out a book with a red cover.

36. A. Control the class.   B. Leave the class.
    C. Study the class.   D. Dismiss the class.

37. A. It looks like it is raining.
    B. It is raining outside.
    C. It will be raining.
    D. It might rain.

38. A. I won't call you.   B. I'm sure that I'll call.
    C. I will call tonight.   D. I'll try to call.

39. A. I want you to go.   B. I don't want you to go.
    C. I believe you will go. D. I think you can't dance.

40. A. They are reliable.   B. They work by themselves.
    C. They are popular.   D. They are very large.

41. A. We went to the party after finishing the test.
    B. We'll go to the party if we finished on time.
    C. We have to go to a party after class.
    D. We're going to have a party when the test is over.

42. A. It won't work.
    B. It will go very fast.
    C. I ordered a new one.
    D. I have bought a new one.

43. A. I did not know her name.
    B. I remembered what she looked like.
    C. I suddenly remembered her name.
    D. I couldn't say her name.

44. A. He must have bought a house.
    B. He ought to buy a house.
    C. He would like to buy a house.
    D. He could have bought a house.

45. A. Kelly told her to be aware of it.
    B. Kelly told her to consider it.
    C. Kelly told her to delete it.
    D. Kelly told her to forget it.

46. A. Kevin's friend is always late.
    B. Kevin's friend is always rushing.
    C. Kevin's friend does everything slowly.
    D. Kevin's friend always asks for more time to finish.

47. A. The group had to work until quitting time.
    B. The group came back to finish the job.
    C. The group was permitted to leave early.
    D. The group took more time to do the job.

48. A. He wanted to review the lesson.
    B. He asked the students to write the lesson.
    C. He thought the lesson was well explained.
    D. He thought he overlooked the lesson.

49. A. Paul didn't bring his book, but I did.
    B. Paul and I have bought our books.
    C. Paul and I should have brought our books.
    D. The book I brought belongs to Paul.

50. A. A committee selected the class representative.
    B. The committee gave her a present.
    C. She has chosen us to be on the committee.
    D. She will represent us on the committee.

● *Directions for questions 51-60. You will hear dialogs on the test tape. Select the correct answer A, B, C, or D and mark your answer sheet.*

51. A. Her smile disappeared all at once.
    B. Her smile began to show up beautifully.
    C. She always has a pretty smile.
    D. Her smile lingered on.

52. A. decorated   B. lacking
    C. repaired   D. furnished

53. A. She can stay a little longer.
    B. She must go home now.
    C. Her parents never worry about her.
    D. Her parents are too nervous.

54. A. The attendant refused to check water and oil.
    B. The major wants her tank half full.
    C. The filling station is out of gas.
    D. The major wants her tank full.

55. A. ordinary type   B. small type
    C. little letters   D. large type

56. A. frozen rain   B. light rain
    C. a heavy rain   D. a sudden shower

57. A. give her a piece of jewelry
    B. visit her
    C. telephone her
    D. look her up

58. A. He finished a new lesson.
    B. He began a new lesson.
    C. He forget to introduce a new lesson.
    D. He put the new lesson aside.

59. A. crowded   B. far away
    C. a place to eat   D. handy

60. A. a senior job   B. an excellent job
    C. a temporary job   D. a job for life

    I heard *Women in a Bathhouse* was a very
interesting play, and decided to see it. When I
grumbled about the expensive admission fee, my
brother was surprised. "You mean you can get in
the ladies' bathhouse for just 10,000 yens?" he
asked enviously.

    我聽說「公共澡堂的女人」是一齣很有趣的戲劇,所以決
定去看。我在抱怨入場費非常貴時,我弟弟非常驚訝。他很嫉
妒地問:「你的意思是說,你只要付一萬元,就可以進去女人
的公共澡堂了嗎?」

ECL 聽力測驗 [7] 詳解

1. (**A**) He is going to practice medicine this summer.
   What is he going to do?
   今年夏天他即將開始行醫。/ 他將做什麼?
   (A) 他將開始當醫生。　　　　　(B) 他將敎急救課程。
   (C) 他將去看醫生。　　　　　　(D) 他將讀醫學院。
   * ***practice medicine*** 行醫　　***first aid*** 急救

2. (**B**) The woman told her sons to stretch out the tablecloth on
   the table. What were they to do?
   這位女士叫她的兒子將桌上的桌巾攤開。/ 他們要做什麼?
   (A) 摺起桌上的桌巾　　　　　　(B) 將桌上的桌巾攤開
   (C) 捲起桌上的桌巾　　　　　　(D) 將桌上的桌巾拿開
   * ***stretch out*** 攤開　　tablecloth〔'tebḷ,klɔθ〕*n.* 桌巾
   fold〔fold〕*v.* 摺疊　　spread〔sprɛd〕*v.* 攤開
   roll〔rol〕*v.* 捲起

3. (**B**) The barometer is one of many devices used by the weather
   experts. What does a barometer measure?
   氣壓計是氣象專家所使用許多裝置中的一種。/ 氣壓計測量什麼?
   (A) 測量雨量　　　　　　　　　(B) 測量大氣壓力
   (C) 測量氣溫　　　　　　　　　(D) 測量風速
   * barometer〔bə'rɑmətə〕*n.* 氣壓計　　device〔dɪ'vaɪs〕*n.* 裝置;設計
   rainfall〔'ren,fɔl〕*n.* 雨量　　atmospheric〔,ætməs'fɛrɪk〕*adj.* 大氣的
   pressure〔'prɛʃə〕*n.* 壓力　　velocity〔və'lɑsətɪ〕*n.* 速度

4. (**A**) Tired and bored, he left the theater before the movie
   ended. When did he leave?
   因為又疲倦又無聊,電影還沒有結束他就離開戲院了。
   他何時離開?
   (A) 電影結束前。　　　　　　　(B) 電影結束後。
   (C) 電影開始前。　　　　　　　(D) 電影開始後。

5. (**D**) When you meet a person between 6:00 a.m. and noon, what do you say?

早上六點到中午時見到人時要說什麼？

(A) 午安。   (B) 晚安。

(C) 晚安。（道別時用語）   (D) <u>早安。</u>

6. (**B**) What is made in a textile mill?

紡織工廠裏製做什麼？

(A) 鋼   (B) <u>布</u>   (C) 收音機   (D) 麵粉

* textile（'tɛkstḷ, -taɪl）*adj.* 紡織的   mill（mɪl）*n.* 工廠
steel（stil）*n.* 鋼   flour（flaʊr）*n.* 麵粉

7. (**C**) Charles was promised a new watch by his father. What will Charles' father do?

查爾斯的父親答應給他一支新錶。／查爾斯的父親將要做什麼？

(A) 違反諾言   (B) 爲他母親買一條項鍊

(C) <u>給他一支新錶</u>   (D) 答應他一個願望

* ***break one's promise*** 背信   necklace（'nɛklɪs）*n.* 項鍊
grant（grænt）*v.* 答應

8. (**D**) Sometimes Captain Miller gives examples to clarify his statements. Why does he give examples?

有時候米勒船長會舉例使人明白他的話。／爲什麼他要舉例？

(A) 下達命令   (B) 回答問題

(C) 完成他的話   (D) <u>解釋他的話</u>

* clarify（'klærə,faɪ）*v.* 使明白   statement（'stetmənt）*n.* 陳述

9. (**D**) The car fell apart when it hit the pillar. What happened to the car?

車子撞上柱子就解體了。／車子怎麼了？

(A) 撞上碼頭   (B) 完整無缺   (C) 錯過柱子   (D) <u>變成碎片</u>

* ***fall apart*** 分解   pillar（'pɪlɚ）*n.* 柱子
dock（dɑk）*n.* 碼頭   intact（ɪn'tækt）*adj.* 完整的；未受損的

10. (**D**) Bruce saluted twice. What did he do?
布魯斯行了兩次禮。╱他做了什麼？
(A) 向船長致敬　　　　　　　(B) 很快地致敬
(C) 完美地行了一次禮　　　　(D) 行了兩次禮
* salute〔səˋlut〕*v.,n.* 行禮；致敬

11. (**B**) Professor Cannon said that it was sprinkling outside. What did the professor mean?
卡能教授說外面正在下毛毛雨。╱教授是什麼意思？
(A) 雨下得很大。　(B) 下小雨。　(C) 陽光普照。　(D) 雲很多。
* sprinkle〔ˋsprɪŋkḷ〕*v.* 下小雨

12. (**A**) Mr. and Mrs. Wood watch television at home two hours every night because they like the program.
Why do they watch television?
伍德先生和伍德太太每晚在家看兩小時的電視，因為他們喜歡那個節目。╱他們為什麼要看電視？
(A) 因為他們喜歡那個節目　　(B) 伍德先生和伍德太太
(C) 每晚兩小時　　　　　　　(D) 在家

13. (**B**) Were the girls singing when the teacher arrived?
老師到的時候，這些女孩是否還在唱歌？
(A) 不，他們沒在唱歌。（ wasn't 應改為 weren't ）
(B) 是的，他們正在唱歌。
(C) 是的，他們沒在唱歌。　　(D) 不，他們在唱歌。

14. (**A**) Mary asks the clerk, "How much are the eggs?"
What should the clerk say?
瑪莉問店員：「這些蛋多少錢？」╱店員應該說什麼？
(A) 一打五十五分錢。　　　　(B) 一盒十二個。
(C) 裏面有蛋白質。　　　　　(D) 我要用水煮的。
* dozen〔ˋdʌzṇ〕*n.* 一打　　carton〔ˋkɑrtṇ〕*n.* 紙盒
protein〔ˋprotin〕*n.* 蛋白質

15. (**A**) Who is the man in the gray jacket?
那位穿灰色夾克的男士是誰？

(A) 他是我的英文老師。   (B) 他三十歲。
(C) 他穿著灰色夾克。   (D) 他站在那邊。

16. (**B**) They cried when they heard how the story ended.
What kind of story is it?
他們聽了故事的結局都哭了。／這是怎樣的一個故事？

(A) 好笑的   (B) 悲傷的   (C) 有趣的   (D) 糟糕的

17. (**C**) What does an industrial area contain?
工業區包含什麼？

(A) 農田   (B) 住宅   (C) 工廠   (D) 公園

* industrial (ɪnˈdʌstrɪəl) *adj.* 工業的   contain (kənˈten) *v.* 包含
residence (ˈrɛzədəns) *n.* 住宅

18. (**A**) He must start his work by noon.
What must he do by noon?
中午前他必須開始工作。／中午前他必須做什麼？

(A) 開始   (B) 停止   (C) 結束   (D) 改進

19. (**C**) Sergeant Bloom read a book during the trip.
What did he look at?
旅途中布魯中士讀一本書。／他看什麼？

(A) 一種武器   (B) 一種來福槍
(C) 一種出版品   (D) 一種機關槍

* sergeant (ˈsɑrdʒənt) *n.* 中士   rifle (ˈraɪfḷ) *n.* 來福槍
publication (ˌpʌblɪˈkeʃən) *n.* 出版品   ***machine gun*** 機關槍

20. (**B**) What is a similar phrase for "to love liberty"?
與「熱愛自由」的類似用語為何？

(A) 熱愛同伴   (B) 熱愛自由   (C) 熱愛朋友   (D) 熱愛生命

* phrase (frez) *n.* 片語   liberty (ˈlɪbɚtɪ) *n.* 自由

21. (**D**) My son has been looking for an interesting job for two weeks. What is he looking for?

我兒子爲了要找個有趣的工作已經找二星期了。/ 他要找什麼?

  (A) 一本書   (B) 一段文章

  (C) 一個名字   (D) 一個職位

  * passage ('pæsɪdʒ) *n.* 段落;文章   position (pə'zɪʃən) *n.* 職位

22. (**D**) This is the nicest month of the year, isn't it?

這是一年中最好的一個月,不是嗎?

  (A) 是的,它不是。   (B) 不,它是的。

  (C) 是的,我不這麼認爲。   (D) 是的,它是的。

23. (**A**) Little by little he learned to cook. How did he learn to cook?

他逐漸學會如何做菜。/ 他如何學會做菜?

  (A) 逐漸地   (B) 突然地   (C) 笑著地   (D) 很快地

  * *little by little* 逐漸地   gradually ('grædʒuəlɪ) *adv.* 逐漸地

    suddenly ('sʌdn̩lɪ) *adv.* 突然地

    laughingly ('læfɪŋlɪ) *adv.* 笑著

24. (**B**) She must have gone to Linda's for lunch. What did she probably do?

她一定去琳達家吃午飯了。/ 她可能做了什麼?

  (A) 去幫琳達作午飯   (B) 去和琳達一起吃午飯

  (C) 在午飯前離開琳達家   (D) 去幫琳達買午飯

25. (**B**) When Lieutenant Lee left the hotel, he paid for his room. What did he pay?

李中尉離開旅館時,付了他房間的錢。/ 他付了什麼?

  (A) 手續費   (B) 他的帳單

  (C) 他的皮夾   (D) 他的房間

  * lieutenant (lu'tɛnənt) *n.* 中尉   due (dju) *n.* 手續費

    bill (bɪl) *n.* 帳單   billfold ('bɪl,fold) *n.* 皮夾

26. (**B**) The boys are already eating breakfast.
這些男孩已經在吃早餐了。

(A) 他們還沒吃。

(B) 他們正在吃。

(C) 他們必須吃得很快。

(D) 他們吃早餐遲到。

27. (**A**) My sister stopped drinking coffee.
我姊姊停止喝咖啡。

(A) 她不再喝咖啡。

(B) 她停下來喝點咖啡。

(C) 她找不到咖啡喝。

(D) 她不喜歡咖啡，但還是喝。

* *no longer* 不再

28. (**B**) Air is dense at sea level.
海平面處的空氣很濃。

(A) 空氣稀薄。

(B) 空氣很濃。

(C) 空氣很熱。

(D) 空氣很涼。

* dense〔dɛns〕*adj.* 濃密的　　*sea level* 海平面

29. (**B**) I don't have many pens.
我沒有很多筆。

(A) 我沒有筆。

(B) 我有一些筆。

(C) 筆對我不大有用。

(D) 我有很多筆。

30. (**A**) This gray hat is more expensive than the yellow one.
這頂灰色的帽子比黃色那頂貴。

(A) 黃色的帽子較便宜。

(B) 灰色的帽子較便宜。

(C) 價格相同。

(D) 紅色的帽子較便宜。

31. (**B**) Jane always obeyed her father.
珍總是聽她父親的話。

(A) 珍記得她父親。

(B) 珍照她父親說的話去做。

(C) 珍不聽她父親的話。

(D) 珍的父親總是不在。

* obey〔ə'be , o'be〕*v.* 遵守　　disobey〔,dɪsə'be〕*v.* 不順從

32. (**C**)　Dennis was too late to catch the train.
丹尼斯太晚到而沒趕上火車。

(A) 丹尼斯趕上火車。　　　　　(B) 丹尼斯搭火車。

(C) 丹尼斯錯過火車。　　　　　(D) 丹尼斯通常把貨物裝上火車。

＊ load〔lod〕*v.* 裝貨

33. (**C**)　I expect Paul will go to the party.
我預期保羅會去參加宴會。

(A) 保羅不會去。　　　　　　　(B) 保羅想他不會去。

(C) 我想保羅會去。　　　　　　(D) 每個人都會去，除了保羅之外。

34. (**B**)　Robert has just a little bit of money.
羅伯特只有一點錢。

(A) 他只有錢。　　　　　　　　(B) 他只有一點錢。

(C) 他通常都有一些錢。　　　　(D) 他從來就沒有錢。

＊ amount〔ə'maʊnt〕*n.* 數量

35. (**A**)　Jim read a book and did some studying in the room.
吉姆在房間裏看了一本書，並讀了一些功課。

(A) 吉姆在家做了一點功課。　　(B) 吉姆清理客廳。

(C) 吉姆重新排列書房的書。　　(D) 吉姆挑出一個紅色封面的書。

＊ schoolwork〔'skul,wɜk〕*n.* 學校的功課
rearrange〔,riə'rendʒ〕*v.* 重新排列　　cover〔'kʌvɚ〕*n.* 封面

36. (**A**)　Tom, take charge of the class.
湯姆，好好管理全班。

(A) 管理全班。　(B) 離開班上。　(C) 研究全班。　(D) 下課。

＊ *take charge of* 負責管理　　dismiss〔dɪs'mɪs〕*v.* 解散

37. (**A**)　It seems to be raining.
似乎在下雨。

(A) 看起來在下雨。　　　　　　(B) 外面在下雨。

(C) 快要下雨了。　　　　　　　(D) 可能會下雨。

38.(**D**) I will attempt to call you tomorrow night.
　　　　我明晚會試著打電話給你。

　　(A) 我不會打電話給你。　　　　　(B) 我確定我會打電話。
　　(C) 我今晚會打電話。　　　　　　(D) 我會試著打電話。

　　＊ attempt〔ə'tɛmpt〕v. 嘗試

39.(**C**) I assume you are going to the dance this afternoon.
　　　　我想你今天下午要去跳舞。

　　(A) 我要你去。　　　　　　　　　(B) 我不要你去。
　　(C) 我相信你會去。　　　　　　　(D) 我想你不會跳舞。

　　＊ assume〔ə'sjum〕v. 以爲；假定

40.(**B**) Some cash registers are automatic.
　　　　有些收銀機是自動的。

　　(A) 他們可以信賴。　　　　　　　(B) 他們自己運作。
　　(C) 他們很受歡迎。　　　　　　　(D) 他們很大。

　　＊ *cash register* 收銀機
　　　 automatic〔͵ɔtə'mætɪk〕*adj.* 自動的
　　　 reliable〔rɪ'laɪəbḷ〕*adj.* 可信賴的
　　　 by oneself 獨自地；單獨地

41.(**D**) When we finish the exam, we will have a party.
　　　　我們考完試後要舉行一個舞會。

　　(A) 考完試我們去參加舞會。
　　(B) 如果我們準時結束，我們就可以去參加舞會。
　　(C) 下課後我們必須去參加舞會。
　　(D) 考試結束後我們將辦一個舞會。

42.(**A**) My portable TV set is out of order.
　　　　我的手提電視機壞了。

　　(A) 它壞了。　　　　　　　　　　(B) 它跑得很快。
　　(C) 我訂了一台新的。　　　　　　(D) 我買了一台新的。

　　＊ portable〔'portəbḷ〕*adj.* 手提式的　　*out of order* 壞掉

43. (**C**) Her name immediately came to my mind.
我突然想起她的名字。
(A) 我不知道她的名字。　　(B) 我記得她的樣子。
(C) 我突然記得她的名字。　(D) 我不能說她的名字。
* *come to mind* 突然想起

44. (**C**) Peter wants to buy a house.
彼德想買一棟房子。
(A) 他一定已經買了一棟房子。　(B) 他必須買一棟房子。
(C) 他想買一棟房子。　　　　　(D) 他可能已經買了一棟房子。

45. (**B**) Kelly told her sister to think it over before making the decision.
凱莉叫她妹妹在下決定前再仔細想想。
(A) 凱莉叫她注意。　　　　(B) 凱莉叫她考慮。
(C) 凱莉叫她取消那件事。　(D) 凱莉叫她忘記那件事。
* *think over* 仔細考慮　　*be aware of* 注意
delete〔dɪˈlit〕*v.* 刪除

46. (**B**) Kevin told me that his friend is always in a hurry.
凱文告訴我，他朋友總是很匆忙。
(A) 凱文的朋友老是遲到。
(B) 凱文的朋友總是匆忙。
(C) 凱文的朋友做事很慢。
(D) 凱文的朋友總是要求更多的時間以完成事情。

47. (**C**) When the group finished its work, the men got time off earlier for the job well done.
這個小組完成工作時，因為工作做得很好，工人們提早下班。
(A) 這個團體必須工作到下班時間。
(B) 這個團體回來完成工作。
(C) 這個團體被允許提早離開。
(D) 這個團體花更多時間來做這個工作。
* *get time off* 下班；休息　　permit〔pɚˈmɪt〕*v.* 允許

48. (**A**) The professor thought that it would be a good idea to go over the lesson during the period.

教授認爲在這段時間再複習這一課是個好主意。

   (A) 他想複習這一課。   (B) 他要學生寫這一課。
   (C) 他認爲這一課解釋得很好。   (D) 他認爲他忽略這一課。

  * ***go over*** 複習   review〔rɪ'vju〕*v.* 複習
    overlook〔͵ovɚ'lʊk〕*v.* 忽略

49. (**C**) I didn't bring my book and neither did Paul.

我沒帶書，保羅也沒帶。

   (A) 保羅沒帶書，而我有帶。   (B) 保羅和我已經買了書。
   (C) 保羅和我應該把書帶來。   (D) 我帶來的書是保羅的。

  * ***belong to*** 屬於

50. (**D**) She has been chosen to represent our class on the committee.

她被選上代表本班參加委員會。

   (A) 委員會選擇班代。   (B) 委員會給她一個禮物。
   (C) 她選我們去參加委員會。   (D) 她將代表我們參加委員會。

  * represent〔͵rɛprɪ'zɛnt〕*v.* 代表   committee〔kə'mɪtɪ〕*n.* 委員會
    select〔sə'lɛkt〕*v.* 選擇   representative〔͵rɛprɪ'zɛntətɪv〕*n.* 代表

51. (**A**) W : Did you notice Jenny's face when I told her the news ?

    M : Yes, suddenly her beautiful smile faded.

    What did the man say ?

女：當我告訴珍妮這個消息時，你有沒有注意到她的表情？
男：有啊，她美麗的笑容突然間就消失了。
這位男士說什麼？

   (A) 她的笑容突然間消失了。   (B) 她美麗的笑容開始出現。
   (C) 她總是有個美麗的笑容。   (D) 她還留著笑容。

  * notice〔'notɪs〕*v.* 注意   fade〔fed〕*v.* 消失
    disappear〔͵dɪsə'pɪr〕*v.* 消失   ***all at once*** 突然
    show up 出現   pretty〔'prɪtɪ〕*adj.* 美麗的   ***linger on*** 滯留

52. (**D**) W：I love the location of this apartment. But how modern is the kitchen?

M：The kitchen is equipped with the latest electrical appliances.

What did the man mean by "equipped"?

女：我喜歡這棟公寓的位置。但是廚房有多現代化呢？

男：廚房配備有最新的電器設備。

這位男士說 "equipped" 是什麼意思？

(A) 裝飾　　　(B) 缺乏　　　(C) 修理　　　(D) 配備

* location〔loˈkeʃən〕 *n.* 位置　　equip〔ɪˈkwɪp〕 *v.* 裝備
electrical〔ɪˈlɛktrɪkl〕 *adj.* 電的　　appliance〔əˈplaɪəns〕 *n.* 器具
furnish〔ˈfɜnɪʃ〕 *v.* 配備；供給

53. (**B**) M：Do you have to leave? It's only nine o'clock now.

W：I'm sorry, but I must. My parents are expecting me.

What does the woman mean?

男：妳得走了嗎？現在才九點鐘。

女：很抱歉，我必須走了。我爸媽正在等我。

這位女士是什麼意思？

(A) 她可以再待一會兒。　　　　(B) 她現在必須回家。
(C) 她父母從不擔心她。　　　　(D) 她父母太緊張了。

54. (**D**) M：Good morning, Major Taylor. What can I do for you?

W：Please fill up my gas tank.

Which statement best sums up this dialog?

男：早安，泰勒少校，我能為妳效勞嗎？

女：請把我的油箱加滿。

哪一個敘述為這則對話的最佳摘要？

(A) 服務員拒絕檢查水和油。　(B) 少校油箱想加半滿。
(C) 加油站沒有油。　　　　　(D) 少校油箱想加滿。

* major〔ˈmedʒə〕 *n.* 少校　　***fill up*** 裝滿
tank〔tæŋk〕 *n.* 油槽　　attendant〔əˈtɛndənt〕 *n.* 服務員
refuse〔rɪˈfjuz〕 *v.* 拒絕

55. (**D**) W : Do you think I'll need my eyeglasses?

M : Not if you're going to read the headlines.

What kind of printing is used for headlines?

女：你想我需要眼鏡嗎？

男：不用，如果妳要看標題的話。

標題是怎麼樣的印刷字體？

(A) 一般大小的字　　　　　(B) 很小的字

(C) 小寫字母　　　　　　　(D) <u>很大的字</u>

* headline (ˈhɛd͵laɪn) *n.* 標題　　printing (ˈprɪntɪŋ) *n.* 印刷字體

　ordinary (ˈɔrdn͵ɛrɪ , ˈɔrdnɛrɪ) *adj.* 一般的

56. (**B**) W : What kind of weather have you been having?

M : It has been drizzling a lot.

What kind of weather was the man referring to?

女：你們那兒的天氣怎樣？

男：常下毛毛雨。

這位男士指的是什麼天氣？

(A) 凍結的雨　　(B) <u>小雨</u>　　(C) 大雨　　　(D) 驟雨

* drizzle (ˈdrɪzl̩) *v.* 下小雨　　***refer to*** 指

57. (**C**) M : I'd like to go to the dance with you tonight, but
I'm going away for a few days.

W : Well, please give me a ring when you get back
to town.

What does she expect the man to do when he gets back
to town?

男：我想和妳一起去跳舞，可是我要離開幾天。

女：嗯，那你回到城裏的時候，請打電話給我。

她希望這個男人回到城裏的時候做什麼？

(A) 給她珠寶　　　　　　　(B) 拜訪她

(C) <u>打電話給她</u>　　　　　　(D) 探訪某人

* ***give*** sb. ***a ring*** 打電話給某人　　jewelry (ˈdʒuəlrɪ) *n.* 珠寶

　look sb. ***up*** 探訪某人

58. (**B**)　W：What is the teacher doing in class these days?

M：He took up a new lesson last week.

What did the teacher do last week?

女：老師最近在課堂上做什麼?

男：他上星期開始上新課。

老師上星期做什麼?

(A) 他結束新的一課。　　　　(B) 他開始新的一課。

(C) 他忘記介紹新課。　　　　(D) 他把新課擱置一旁。

＊ *take up* 開始　　*put aside* 擱置一旁

59. (**D**)　M：Why don't you have lunch in the restaurant?

W：I don't like the food.

M：Well, I find it convenient.

What does the man mean by "convenient"?

男：妳為什麼不在餐廳吃午飯呢?

女：我不喜歡這裏的食物。

男：嗯,我倒覺得很方便。

這位男士說 "convenient" 是什麼意思?

(A) 擁擠　　　(B) 很遠　　　(C) 吃東西的地方　(D) 近便的

＊ handy (ˈhændɪ) *adj.* 手邊的;近便的

60. (**C**)　W：Is Sandra working?

M：Yes, she is working in the hospital.

W：What kind of job does she have?

M：I don't know, but she is not a permanent employee.

What kind of job does Sandra have?

女：珊卓有工作嗎?

男：有,她在醫院工作。

女：她做什麼樣的工作?

男：我不知道,不過她不是永久性的員工。

珊卓做什麼樣的工作?

(A) 資深的工作　(B) 很棒的工作　(C) 暫時性的工作　(D) 終生的工作

＊ permanent (ˈpɝmənənt) *adj.* 永久的　　employee (ˌɛmplɔɪˈi) *n.* 職員

temporary (ˈtɛmpəˌrɛrɪ) *adj.* 暫時的

LISTENING TEST 8

● *Directions for questions 1-25. You will hear questions on the test tape. Select the one item A, B, C or D which answers the question correctly, and mark your answer sheet.*

1. A. a drama   B. a symphony
   C. an athletic event   D. a game

2. A. for a discovery   B. on a terrible job
   C. at a distance   D. in a district

3. A. a section of the newspaper
   B. a kind of poetry
   C. a part of a book
   D. a woman's magazine

4. A. She was glad.   B. She wanted to eat.
   C. She was very angry.   D. She was indifferent.

5. A. athletic games and races   B. winning teams
   C. school courses   D. homework

6. A. distances   B. directions
   C. the weight of objects   D. the volume of liquid

7. A. Yes, I enjoy their activity.
   B. Yes, I don't want to go.
   C. No, I'm going to go.
   D. Yes, I have gone.

8. A. San Francisco is located on a point.
   B. She points out San Francisco.
   C. She visits San Francisco.
   D. She locates San Francisco on the map.

9. A. better than David
   C. worse than David
   B. much better than David
   D. about the same as David

10. A. None of them are here.
    B. Most of them are here.
    C. Some of them are here.
    D. Many of them are here.

11. A. He's in Austin.
    C. He's thirty years old.
    B. He's a lawyer.
    D. He's very athletic.

12. A. seeing tiny particles
    C. weighing objects
    B. stopping vehicles
    D. ruling people

13. A. get on the bus
    C. get off the bus
    B. let him off at the corner
    D. stop driving the bus

14. A. leave
    C. know her way around
    B. put on weight
    D. pay her way

15. A. She was so happy that she couldn't talk.
    B. She saw her friends and wanted to talk to them.
    C. She was looking for her friends and wanted to talk
       with them.
    D. She was happy to talk to her friends.

16. A. reduce them
    C. improve them
    B. increase them
    D. eliminate them

17. A. tense
    C. at ease
    B. relaxed
    D. tired

18. A. stormy
    C. damp
    B. threatening
    D. fair

19. A. It rained.
    B. We went to play tennis.
    C. We played only half a game.
    D. We walked in the rain.

20. A. She was trying to catch a train.
    B. She was going to meet someone.
    C. She needed some money.
    D. She wanted to put some money in her account.

21. A. fix them   B. supply them
    C. forward them   D. further them

22. A. to move around   B. to move in
    C. to move over   D. to move forward

23. A. true stories   B. sorrowful stories
    C. amusing stories   D. unbelievable stories

24. A. a typewriter which is fixed to a table
    B. one that is heavy and not easy to carry
    C. one that is light and easy to carry
    D. a large standard typewriter

25. A. because it's not cheap
    B. because it's a good conductor
    C. because of its color
    D. because it is not flexible

● *Directions for questions 26-50. You will hear statements on the test tape. Select the one answer A, B, C, or D which comes closest to the meaning of the statement and mark your answer sheet.*

26. A. Rachel slipped on the road.
    B. Rachel gained much weight this winter.
    C. Rachel confided in her friend more than once.
    D. Rachel became more confident with practice.

27. A. This is the language of her country.
    B. Her spoken Italian is good.
    C. She speaks Italian as a second language.
    D. The language is spoken very seldom.

28. A. Nobody was kept from going.
    B. Nobody was permitted there.
    C. Nobody was advised to go.
    D. Nobody was eager to go.

29. A. Time seems to move fast.
    B. Time seems to go quickly.
    C. Time seems to pass slowly.
    D. Time seems to hold you back.

30. A. They are good friends.
    B. They don't know each other.
    C. They aren't friendly with each other.
    D. They haven't seen each other for a long time.

31. A. He usually fishes at night.
    B. Steven likes to eat fish.
    C. Steven likes to fish.
    D. He is very poor at fishing.

32. A. The girl met her boyfriend.
    B. You met her boyfriend.
    C. You met the girl.
    D. The boyfriend never met the girl.

33. A. He didn't walk to the red light.
   B. He ran over the light.
   C. He stopped for the red light.
   D. He didn't stop for the red light.

34. A. Sailors must prepare accurate forecasts.
   B. Sailors should have an assistant.
   C. Sailors are helped by good weather forecast.
   D. Sailors must assist the weatherman.

35. A. He said he would get a used jeep.
   B. He told me he would call for me in his jeep.
   C. He told me to sell his jeep.
   D. He said I should call him up.

36. A. The sleeves are too long.
   B. The shirt fits just right.
   C. The sleeves are O.K.
   D. The sleeves are too short.

37. A. Jerry wants to go outside.   B. The weather is warm.
   C. The weather is very cold.   D. Nick is feeling warm.

38. A. It became dirty.   B. It froze.
   C. It changed into water.   D. It piled up.

39. A. David, please get my umbrella.
   B. David doesn't want to get his umbrella.
   C. Allow me to get my umbrella.
   D. Don't get my umbrella.

40. A. Too many people came to the meeting.
   B. There were not enough people at the meeting to inspect
      the documents.
   C. We had expected more people to come to the meeting.
   D. There were not enough seats for all the people.

41. A. John will be able to buy groceries.
    B. John doesn't have enough money to buy groceries.
    C. John wouldn't buy groceries ever if he had enough money.
    D. John has no money for groceries.

42. A. We are going to meet Fred and Mary at the movies if we had time.
    B. We couldn't meet Fred and Mary at the movies because we didn't have any money.
    C. We went to the movies with Fred and Mary, but the theater was closed.
    D. We were supposed to meet Fred and Mary at the movies, but our car broke down.

43. A. The shopping center was big.
    B. Only a few were there.
    C. Many people were there.
    D. None were at the center.

44. A. Jessica said, "Is it too expensive ?"
    B. Jessica said, "Is it satisfactory ?"
    C. Jessica said, "Do you dislike it ?"
    D. Jessica said, "Is this your coat ?"

45. A. He will read it.   B. He will say it again.
    C. He will reason with you.   D. He will appeal to it.

46. A. He concealed it.   B. He showed it.
    C. He forgot it.   D. He covered it.

47. A. We want to get permission to sell a typewriter.
    B. We want to get permission to trade a typewriter.
    C. We want to get permission to buy a typewriter.
    D. We want to get permission to pursue a typewriter.

48. A. The explorers settled it.
    B. The explorers mapped it.
    C. They fought for it.
    D. They found it.

49. A. He had his car sold.   B. His car needs repairing.
    C. His car wasn't sold.   D. He will sell his car.

50. A. There is nothing wrong in Tom's room.
    B. People come in and out of Tom's room.
    C. The lights in Tom's room are O.K.
    D. Tom is having lighting troubles.

● *Directions for questions 51-60. You will hear dialogs on the test tape. Select the correct answer A, B, C, or D and mark your answer sheet.*

51. A. He spoke poorly.   B. He spoke slowly.
    C. He spoke carefully.   D. He spoke fast.

52. A. His English is poor.
    B. He is not understood.
    C. His English structure is very complex.
    D. His writing is easily understandable.

53. A. He'll be there in a few minutes.
    B. He wasn't going.
    C. He was leaving immediately.
    D. He'd take a long time.

54. A. by staying at the seashore
    B. by staying at the pool
    C. by using man-made lights
    D. by exposure to the moon

55. A. He will finish by the end of the week.
    B. He won't finish by the end of the week.
    C. He must finish by the end of the week.
    D. He might finish by the end of the week.

56. A. He was late for the briefing.
    B. He got to the briefing just in time.
    C. The manager was late for the briefing.
    D. He should go through the door.

57. A. He seldom goes.
    B. He often goes.
    C. He never goes.
    D. He frequently goes.

58. A. The woman is on the wrong plane.
    B. The woman is on the right train.
    C. The seat is already in use.
    D. The seat is not being held for anyone.

59. A. It has been running now and then.
    B. It has been running on and off.
    C. It has been running without stopping.
    D. It has been running slowly.

60. A. There were many traffic policemen on the streets.
    B. There were many pedestrians.
    C. There were many cars on the streets.
    D. The streets seemed empty.

ECL 聽力測驗 [8] 詳解

1. (**B**) Her favorite hobby is music. What kind of entertainment would she probably prefer?
   她最喜歡的嗜好是音樂。/ 她可能偏好何種娛樂?
   (A) 戲劇　　　　(B) 交響樂　　　　(C) 運動項目　　　　(D) 遊戲
   * symphony (ˈsɪmfənɪ) *n.* 交響樂　　athletic (æθˈlɛtɪk) *adj.* 運動的

2. (**D**) The postman works in an assigned territory. Where does he work?
   郵差在指定的地區工作。/ 他在哪裏工作?
   (A) 爲了發現而做　　　　　　　(B) 在一個可怕的工作
   (C) 在遠方　　　　　　　　　　(D) 在一個地區
   * assign (əˈsaɪn) *v.* 指定　　territory (ˈtɛrə,torɪ) *n.* 領土;地域
   district (ˈdɪstrɪkt) *n.* 地方;區

3. (**C**) Susan read the chapter twice. What did she read?
   蘇珊這章讀了二次。/ 她讀什麼?
   (A) 報紙的一版　　　　　　　　(B) 一種詩
   (C) 書的一部分　　　　　　　　(D) 女性雜誌
   * chapter (ˈtʃæptɚ) *n.* 章　　section (ˈsɛkʃən) *n.* 部分;段落

4. (**C**) The insult made her mad. How did she feel?
   這項侮辱令她非常生氣。/ 她覺得如何?
   (A) 她很開心。　　　　　　　　(B) 她想吃東西。
   (C) 她很生氣。　　　　　　　　(D) 她漠不關心。
   * insult (ˈɪnsʌlt) *n.* 侮辱　　indifferent (ɪnˈdɪfərənt) *adj.* 漠不關心的

5. (**A**) What are competitive sports?
   什麼是競爭激烈的運動?
   (A) 運動比賽和賽跑　　　　　　(B) 勝利的隊伍
   (C) 學校課程　　　　　　　　　(D) 回家作業
   * competitive (kəmˈpɛtətɪv) *adj.* 競爭的

6. (**A**) What are tape measures used to measure?
捲尺用來量什麼？

(A) 距離　　　　(B) 方向　　　　(C) 物體重量　　　　(D) 液體容積

* *tape measure* 捲尺　　volume〔'valjəm〕*n.* 容積
liquid〔'lıkwıd〕*n.* 液體

7. (**A**) Are you looking forward to attending the garden fete?
你期待參加園遊會嗎？

(A) 是啊，我喜歡他們的活動。　(B) 是啊，我不想去。
(C) 不，我要去。　　　　　　　(D) 是啊，我已經去了。

* *look forward to* 期待　　*garden fete* 園遊會

8. (**C**) Rita makes a point of visiting San Francisco every year.
What does she do?
莉塔習慣每年都要去舊金山。／她做什麼？

(A) 舊金山位於一點。　　　(B) 她指出舊金山。
(C) 她去舊金山。　　　　　(D) 她在地圖上指出舊金山。

* *make a point of* + *V-ing* 習慣於～　　*be located* 位於
point out 指出　　locate〔lo'ket〕*v.* 找出～的位置

9. (**D**) Matt spoke Russian as well as David.
How well did Matt speak Russian?
馬特的俄語說得和大衛一樣好。／馬特俄語說得有多好？

(A) 比大衛好。　　　　(B) 比大衛好多了。
(C) 比大衛差。·　　　　(D) 和大衛一樣。

* Russian〔'rʌʃən〕*n.* 俄語

10. (**B**) Bradley said, "All except few of them are here."
What did Bradley mean?
布萊德里說：「除了少數之外全都在這裏。」
布萊德里是什麼意思？

(A) 這裏一個都沒有。　　(B) 大部分都在這裏。
(C) 有一些在這裏。　　　(D) 很多在這裏。

11. (**A**) Where is your father now?
你爸爸現在在哪裏?

    (A) 他在奧斯汀。   (B) 他是律師。
    (C) 他三十歲。   (D) 他很有運動細胞。

    * Austin〔ˈɔstɪn〕 *n.* 奧斯汀 (美國德州首府)
      athletic〔æθˈlɛtɪk〕 *adj.* 運動的

12. (**C**) What are scales used for?
天平用來做什麼?

    (A) 看小顆粒   (B) 停止車輛   (C) 稱物體重量   (D) 管理人們

    * scale〔skel〕 *n.* 天平   particle〔ˈpɑrtɪk!〕 *n.* 微粒
      vehicle〔ˈviɪk!〕 *n.* 車輛

13. (**B**) John had the bus driver stop at the corner.
What did John have the driver do?
約翰請公車司機在街角停車。/ 約翰請司機做什麼?

    (A) 上公車   (B) 讓他在街角下車
    (C) 下公車   (D) 停止駕駛公車

    * *let sb. off* 讓某人下車

14. (**A**) Jenny is on her way out. What's she going to do?
珍妮正要出去。/ 她將要做什麼?

    (A) 離開   (B) 增重
    (C) 熟悉路途   (D) 自己付自己的費用

    * *on one's way out* 在出去途中   *put on weight* 增重
      know one's way around 熟悉路途   *pay one's way* 付自己的

15. (**A**) She looked at her friends, too happy to speak.
What happened to her?
她看著她的朋友,高興得說不出話來。/ 她怎麼了?

    (A) 她如此高興,以至於說不出話來。
    (B) 她看見她的朋友,想要和他們說話。
    (C) 她正在尋找她的朋友,想要和他們說話。
    (D) 她很高興和他們說話。

16. (**A**) We must cut down on our expenses. What must we do?

　　我們必須減少花費。/ 我們必須怎麼做？

　　(A) 減少　　　(B) 增加　　　(C) 改進　　　(D) 消除

　　* **cut down on** 減少　　eliminate〔ɪˈlɪməˌnet〕v. 消除

17. (**A**) The passengers on the bus are nervous.

　　How do they feel?

　　公車上的乘客很緊張。/ 他們覺得如何？

　　(A) 緊張　　　(B) 輕鬆　　　(C) 自在　　　(D) 疲倦

　　* nervous〔ˈnɝvəs〕adj. 緊張的 (= tense〔tɛns〕)　　**at ease** 自在的

18. (**D**) On a bright sunny day, how is the weather?

　　明亮晴朗的一天，天氣如何？

　　(A) 有暴風雨的　　　　　　(B) 要變壞的

　　(C) 潮濕　　　　　　　　　(D) 晴朗

　　* threatening〔ˈθrɛtənɪŋ〕adj. （天氣）似要轉壞的

　　　damp〔dæmp〕adj. 潮濕的

19. (**A**) If it hadn't rained, we would have played tennis.

　　What happened?

　　如果不是下雨，我們就去打網球了。/ 發生了什麼事？

　　(A) 下雨了。　　　　　　　(B) 我們去打網球。

　　(C) 我們只打了半場。　　　(D) 我們走在雨中。

20. (**C**) Ann needed to cash a check, so she hurried to get to the bank before three.

　　Why did Ann hurry to the bank?

　　安需要兌現一張支票，所以她在三點以前趕到銀行去。

　　安為何要趕到銀行？

　　(A) 她試著想趕上火車。　　(B) 她要去見某人。

　　(C) 她需要一點錢。　　　　(D) 她要把一些錢存進戶頭。

　　* account〔əˈkaʊnt〕n. 帳戶

21. (**B**) Jack should furnish his mechanics with enough tools to do the job right.
What should he do with the tools?
傑克應該供應足夠的工具給他的技工，以好好做這個工作。
對這些工具他應該做什麼？

   (A) 修理   (B) <u>供應</u>   (C) 寄送   (D) 促進

  * furnish (ˈfɜnɪʃ) v. 供給；配備   mechanic (məˈkænɪk) n. 技工
    tool (tul) n. 工具   forward (ˈfɔrwəd) v. 寄送
    further (ˈfɜðə) v. 促進

22. (**D**) As soon as the rain stopped, the army was able to progress faster.
What is another way to say "to progress"?
雨一停，軍隊就能前進得快一點。
"to progress" 的另一種說法為何？

   (A) 到處移動   (B) 搬進去   (C) 移過去   (D) <u>向前移動</u>

  * progress (prəˈgrɛs) v. 進展；前進

23. (**D**) Sailors often come home with incredible stories.
What kind of stories do sailors have?
水手回家常帶回令人難以相信的故事。／水手們有什麼樣的故事？

   (A) 真實的故事   (B) 悲傷的故事
   (C) 有趣的故事   (D) <u>難以相信的故事</u>

  * incredible (ɪnˈkrɛdəbḷ) adj. 難以相信的 (= unbelievable (ˌʌnbɪˈlivəbḷ))
    sorrowful (ˈsɑrofəl) adj. 悲傷的   amusing (əˈmjuzɪŋ) adj. 有趣的

24. (**C**) Captain White bought a portable typewriter.
What kind did he get?
懷特船長買了一台攜帶型打字機。／他買了哪一種？

   (A) 固定在桌上的打字機   (B) 笨重且難以攜帶的打字機
   (C) <u>輕巧且容易攜帶的打字機</u>   (D) 大的標準型打字機

  * captain (ˈkæptɪn) n. 船長
    portable (ˈportəbḷ) adj. 可提式的；可攜帶的
    fix (fɪks) v. 固定

25. (**B**)　Why is copper used in electrical wiring?
為什麼電線會使用銅？

(A) 因為不便宜　　　　　　　(B) 因為是良導體
(C) 因為它的顏色　　　　　　(D) 因為沒有彈性

　　* copper ('kɑpɚ) *n.* 銅　　electrical (ɪ'lɛktrɪkl̩) *adj.* 電的
　　wiring ('waɪrɪŋ) *n.* 電線　　conductor (kən'dʌktɚ) *n.* 導體

26. (**D**)　The more she skied, the more confidence Rachel gained.
滑雪滑得愈多次，瑞秋就愈有信心。

(A) 瑞秋在馬路上滑倒。
(B) 瑞秋今年冬天胖很多。
(C) 瑞秋對她的朋友吐露祕密不只一次。
(D) 瑞秋練習後更有信心。

　　* ski (ski) *v.* 滑雪　　confidence ('kɑnfədəns) *n.* 信心
　　slip (slɪp) *v.* 滑倒　　*gain weight* 增重；變胖
　　confide (kən'faɪd) *v.* 吐露祕密

27. (**A**)　Italian is her native tongue.
義大利話是她的母語。

(A) 這是她國家的語言。　　(B) 她的義大利話說得不錯。
(C) 義大利語是她的第二個語言。　(D) 這個語言很少人說。

　　* native ('netɪv) *adj.* 本國的　　tongue (tʌŋ) *n.* 語言

28. (**B**)　No one was allowed to go near the firing barn.
任何人都不准靠近著火的穀倉。

(A) 沒有人不得靠近。　　　　(B) 沒有人可以在那裏。
(C) 沒有人得到建議去那裏。　(D) 沒有人想去。

　　* barn (bɑrn) *n.* 穀倉　　*be eager to* 想要；渴望

29. (**C**)　Time drags when you have nothing to do.
沒有事做時，時間過得很慢。

(A) 時間似乎過得很快。　　(B) 時間似乎過得很快。
(C) 時間似乎過得很慢。　　(D) 時間似乎抵擋了你。

　　* drag (dræg) *v.* 拖；拖延　　*hold back* 抵擋

30. (**C**) Mr. Morgan doesn't get along with Mr. Brown.
摩根先生與布朗先生不合。

(A) 他們是好朋友。 (B) 他們彼此不認識。
(C) 他們對彼此不友善。 (D) 他們彼此好久不見。

* *get along with* 與～相處

31. (**C**) Steven is very fond of fishing.
史蒂芬很喜歡釣魚。

(A) 他通常在晚上釣魚。 (B) 史蒂芬喜歡吃魚。
(C) 史蒂芬喜歡釣魚。 (D) 史蒂芬釣魚技術很差。

* *be fond of* 喜歡

32. (**B**) This is the girl whose boyfriend you met last night.
這就是那個女孩，你昨晚見到她男朋友。

(A) 這女孩見到她男朋友。 (B) 你見到她男朋友。
(C) 你見到這女孩。 (D) 這個男朋友從未見過這女孩。

33. (**D**) Lieutenant Morison ran through a red light.
莫瑞森上尉闖紅燈。

(A) 他沒有走到紅燈處。 (B) 他複習紅燈。
(C) 紅燈他停下來了。 (D) 紅燈他沒停下來。

* lieutenant〔luˋtɛnənt〕*n.* 上尉　　*run over* 複習；輾過

34. (**C**) Accurate weather forecasts are a great assistance to sailors.
正確的天氣預報對水手是一大幫助。

(A) 水手必須準備正確的天氣預報。
(B) 水手應該有助手。
(C) 水手受到好的天氣預報的幫助。
(D) 水手必須幫助天氣預報員。

* accurate〔ˋækjərɪt〕*adj.* 正確的　　forecast〔ˋforͺkæst〕*n.* 預報
assistance〔əˋsɪstəns〕*n.* 幫助　　sailor〔ˋselɚ〕*n.* 水手
assistant〔əˋsɪstənt〕*n.* 助手
weatherman〔ˋwɛðɚͺmæn〕*n.* 天氣預報員

35. (**B**) Jeremy said he would pick me up in his jeep.
傑瑞米說他要開吉普車來載我。
(A) 他說他得到一輛二手吉普車。
(B) 他告訴我他會用吉普車接我。
(C) 他要我去賣他的吉普車。
(D) 他說我應該打電話給他。

* *pick sb. up* 接載某人　　used〔juzd〕*adj.* 二手的；中古的
jeep〔dʒip〕*n.* 吉普車　　*call for* 接載~

36. (**D**) The clerk said, "Try this shirt on." Mrs. Carn put it on and said "The sleeves are not long enough."
店員說：「試穿這件襯衫。」卡恩太太穿上後說：「袖子不夠長。」
(A) 袖子太長。　　　　　　(B) 襯衫剛剛好。
(C) 袖子可以。　　　　　　(D) 袖子太短。

* *try on* 試穿　　sleeve〔sliv〕*n.* 袖子

37. (**C**) Jerry said, "Let's go in. I'm freezing." Nick said, "I'm freezing too. Let's go."
傑瑞說：「我們進去，我冷死了。」尼克說：「我也好冷，走吧。」
(A) 傑瑞想到外面去。　　　(B) 天氣很暖和。
(C) 天氣很冷。　　　　　　(D) 尼克覺得暖和。

* freezing〔'frizɪŋ〕*adj.* 極冷的；冰凍的

38. (**C**) The snow melted during the week.
雪在這星期間融化了。
(A) 雪變得很髒。　　　　　(B) 雪結冰了。
(C) 雪變成水了。　　　　　(D) 雪堆起來了。

* melt〔mɛlt〕*v.* 融化　　*pile up* 堆積

39. (**C**) Let me get my umbrella, David.
讓我拿雨傘，大衛。
(A) 大衛，請拿我的雨傘。　(B) 大衛不想拿他的傘。
(C) 允許我去拿傘。　　　　(D) 不要拿我的傘。

40. (**C**) Fewer people came to the meeting than we had expected.
   來參加會議的人比我們預期得少。

   (A) 太多人來參加會議。
   (B) 會議中人數不夠來檢查這些文件。
   (C) 我們預期會來參加會議的人較多。
   (D) 椅子不夠全部的人坐。

   * inspect (ɪn'spɛkt) v. 檢查
     document ('dɑkjəmənt) n. 文件

41. (**B**) John has some money, but not enough to buy groceries.
   約翰有一點錢，但不夠買雜貨。

   (A) 約翰將可以買雜貨。
   (B) 約翰沒有足夠的錢買雜貨。
   (C) 即使約翰有足夠的錢，他也不會去買雜貨。
   (D) 約翰沒有錢買雜貨。

   * *even if* 即使   groceries ('grosəɪz) n.pl. 食品雜貨

42. (**B**) We were supposed to meet Fred and Mary at the movies, but we were broke.
   我們應該和佛烈德及瑪麗在電影院碰面，但是我們沒錢。

   (A) 如果我們有時間，我們將到電影院和佛烈德及瑪麗碰面。
   (B) 我們無法和佛烈德及瑪麗在電影院碰面，因為我們沒錢。
   (C) 我們和佛烈德及瑪麗去看電影，但電影院沒開。
   (D) 我們應該和佛烈德及瑪麗在電影院碰面，但我們的車故障了。

   * *be supposed to* 應該   broke (brok) adj. 身無分文的
     theater ('θiətə, 'θɪə-) n. 戲劇院；電影院
     break down 故障

43. (**C**) There was a large crowd at the shopping center.
   購物中心有一大群人。

   (A) 購物中心很大。   (B) 只有一些人在那裏。
   (C) 許多人在那裏。   (D) 沒有人在購物中心。

   * crowd (kraud) n. 群眾   *shopping center* 購物中心

44. (**B**) Jessica asked if the coat fit you.
傑西卡問這件夾克是否適合你穿。

　　(A) 傑西卡說：「太貴了嗎？」
　　(B) 傑西卡說：「滿意嗎？」
　　(C) 傑西卡說：「你不喜歡嗎？」
　　(D) 傑西卡說：「這是你的夾克嗎？」
　　* fit〔fɪt〕v. 適合

45. (**B**) The control tower operator will repeat the information
if you cannot understand it.
如果你不了解的話，塔台人員會重覆這個訊息。

　　(A) 他會讀。　　　　　　　(B) 他會再說一次。
　　(C) 他會與你說理。　　　　(D) 他會上訴。

　　* *control tower* 控制塔台　　operator〔'ɑpə,retə〕n. 管理員；操作者
　　reason〔'rizn̩〕v. 說理　　*appeal to* 上訴；吸引；訴諸

46. (**B**) The instructor always displayed his good temper.
這位講師總是表現出他的好脾氣。

　　(A) 他把它隱藏起來。　　　(B) 他把它表現出來。
　　(C) 他忘了。　　　　　　　(D) 他掩蓋它。

　　* instructor〔ɪn'strʌktə〕n. 講師　　display〔dɪ'sple〕v. 展示
　　temper〔'tɛmpə〕n. 脾氣　　conceal〔kən'sil〕v. 隱藏
　　cover〔'kʌvə〕v. 掩蓋

47. (**C**) We hoped to get permission from our officer to purchase
a typewriter.
我們希望得到軍官允許我們購買一台打字機。

　　(A) 我們想要得到賣打字機許可。
　　(B) 我們想要得到交換打字機的許可。
　　(C) 我們想要得到購買打字機的許可。
　　(D) 我們想要得到追求打字機的許可。

　　* permission〔pə'mɪʃən〕n. 許可
　　officer〔'ɔfəsə〕n. 軍官　　purchase〔'pɝtʃəs〕v. 購買
　　trade〔tred〕v. 交換　　pursue〔pə'su〕v. 追求

48. (**D**) The continent was discovered in the 15th century by the explorers.

這塊大陸在十五世紀被探險家發現。

(A) 探險家在此殖民。   (B) 探險家繪製大陸的地圖。

(C) 他們爭奪它。   (D) <u>他們發現它。</u>

* continent〔'kantənənt〕*n.* 大陸

   explorer〔ɪk'splorɚ〕*n.* 探險家

   settle〔'sɛtl̩〕*v.* 殖民   map〔mæp〕*v.* 繪製～的地圖

49. (**A**) He got his car sold.

他賣了他的車。

(A) <u>他賣了他的車。</u>   (B) 他的車需要修理。

(C) 他的車沒賣掉。   (D) 他將賣車。

* repair〔rɪ'pɛr〕*v.* 修理

50. (**D**) Tom said, "Something is wrong with the lights in my room. They keep going out."

湯姆說：「我房裏的燈有點問題。都不亮。」

(A) 湯姆的房間沒有問題。

(B) 人們來來去去湯姆的房間。

(C) 湯姆房裏的燈沒問題。

(D) <u>湯姆的燈有問題。</u>

* **go out** （燈）熄滅   lighting〔'laɪtɪŋ〕*n.* 點燈；照明

51. (**D**) M : Did you understand John?

W : No, he spoke too rapidly.

How did John speak?

男：你知道約翰在說什麼嗎？

女：不懂，他說得太快。

約翰如何說話？

(A) 他說得很差。   (B) 他說得很慢。

(C) 他說得很小心。   (D) <u>他說得很快。</u>

* rapidly〔'ræpɪdlɪ〕*adv.* 迅速地

52. (**D**)　M：How　does　David　write？
　　　　　　W：David　writes　clearly.
　　　　　　How　does　David　write？
　　　　　男：大衛寫得如何？
　　　　　女：大衛寫得很清楚。
　　　　　大衛寫得如何？

　　(A) 他的英文很差。　　　　　　(B) 他不被了解。
　　(C) 他的英文結構很複雜。　　　(D) 他的字很容易了解。

　　＊ clearly ('klırlı) adv. 清楚地
　　　 structure ('strʌktʃə) n. 結構
　　　 complex (kəm'plɛks) adj. 複雜的
　　　 understandable (,ʌndə'stændəbl) adj. 易懂的；可理解的

53. (**A**)　W：Are　you　coming　with　us, Clark？
　　　　　　M：I'll　be　there　soon.
　　　　　　What　did　the　man　say？
　　　　　女：克拉克，你要跟我們一起來嗎？
　　　　　男：我很快就到。
　　　　　這位男士說什麼？

　　(A) 他幾分鐘內就到。　　　　　(B) 他不去。
　　(C) 他很快就要離開。　　　　　(D) 他要花很長的時間。

54. (**C**)　W：How　did　you　injure　your　eyes　like　that？
　　　　　　M：By　using　too　many　artificial　lights.
　　　　　　How　did　he　injure　himself？
　　　　　女：你怎麼把眼睛傷成這樣？
　　　　　男：用太多人造電燈了。
　　　　　他如何弄傷自己的？

　　(A) 待在海邊。　　　　　　　　(B) 待在游泳池。
　　(C) 使用人造燈。　　　　　　　(D) 暴露於月亮下。

　　＊ injure ('ındʒə) v. 損傷
　　　 artificial (,ɑrtə'fıʃəl) adj. 人造的
　　　 seashore ('si,ʃor) n. 海濱　　**man-made** 人造的
　　　 exposure (ık'spoʒə) n. 暴露

55. (**D**) W : Sergeant Morgan, can you finish checking all the records by the end of the week?

M : I think so, but it depends on how many people I have to help me.

What did Sergeant Morgan mean?

女：摩根中士，這星期結束時你能檢查完所有的記錄嗎？

男：我想是的，但要看看有多少人幫我。

摩根中士是什麼意思？

(A) 這星期結束時他會完成。

(B) 這星期結束時他不會完成。

(C) 這星期結束時他必須完成。

(D) 這星期結束時他可能會完成。

　　* sergeant (ˈsɑrdʒənt) *n.* 中士　　*depend on* 視～而定

56. (**B**) M : Hi, Miss Jones! Am I late for the manager's briefing?

W : No, but you almost didn't make it. He is coming through the door now.

What did Miss Jones tell the man?

男：嗨，瓊絲小姐！經理的簡報我是否遲到了？

女：沒有，不過你差點趕不上。他現在正走過門口。

瓊絲小姐告訴這位男士什麼？

(A) 他聽簡報遲到了。　　　　(B) 他及時趕上聽簡報。

(C) 經理簡報遲到。　　　　　(D) 他應該走過門

　　* manager (ˈmænɪdʒɚ) *n.* 經理　　briefing (ˈbrifɪŋ) *n.* 簡報

　　make it 辦到；成功　　*in time* 及時

57. (**A**) W : Does your brother like to go to the movies, Henry?

M : Well, actually, he rarely goes to the movies.

How often does Henry's brother go to the movies?

女：亨利，你哥哥喜歡去看電影嗎？

男：嗯，事實上，他很少去看電影。

亨利的哥哥多常去看電影？

(A) 很少去　　　(B) 常去　　　(C) 從來不去　　　(D) 經常去

　　* rarely (ˈrɛrlɪ) *adv.* 很少地　　frequently (ˈfrikwəntlɪ) *adv.* 經常地

58. (**D**) W : Is this flight 705 to New York?
　　　　　M : Yes, it is.
　　　　　W : Is this seat taken?
　　　　　M : No, it isn't.
　　　　　What did the man tell the woman?

　　　女：這是飛往紐約的 705 號班機嗎？
　　　男：是的。
　　　女：這個位子有人坐嗎？
　　　男：沒有，沒人坐。
　　　這位男士告訴女士什麼？

　　　(A) 這位女士搭錯飛機了。　　　　(B) 這位女士在正確的火車上。
　　　(C) 位子已經有人坐了。　　　　　(D) 這個位子還沒有人坐。

　　　* flight (flaɪt) *n.* 飛行班次

59. (**C**) W : What is that noise?
　　　　　M : It's my car. The motor has been running continuously
　　　　　　　 all morning.
　　　　　What did the man say about the motor?

　　　女：那是什麼噪音？
　　　男：我的車。馬達整個早上一直都在動。
　　　這位男士說馬達怎麼了？

　　　(A) 有時會動　　(B) 斷斷續續地動　　(C) 沒有停　　(D) 動得很慢

　　　* motor ('motɚ) *n.* 馬達　　continuously (kən'tɪnjʊəslɪ) *adv.* 連續地
　　　　now and then 有時　　　*on and off* 斷斷續續

60. (**C**) M : Are you going to drive today?
　　　　　W : I don't know. The traffic is heavy.
　　　　　What did the woman mean?

　　　男：妳今天要開車嗎？
　　　女：我不知道。交通很繁忙。
　　　這位女士是什麼意思？

　　　(A) 街上有很多交通警察。　　　　(B) 很多行人。
　　　(C) 街上車子很多。　　　　　　　(D) 街道似乎空了。

　　　* heavy ('hɛvɪ) *adj.* (交通) 繁忙的
　　　　pedestrian (pə'dɛstrɪən) *n.* 行人　　empty ('ɛmptɪ) *adj.* 空的

LISTENING TEST 9

● *Directions for questions 1-25. You will hear questions on the test tape. Select the one item A, B, C or D which answers the question correctly, and mark your answer sheet.*

1. A. April
   C. November
   B. June
   D. September

2. A. red
   C. rain
   B. wool
   D. small

3. A. 1003
   C. 1445
   B. 1545
   D. 1645

4. A. March
   C. December
   B. January
   D. August

5. A. Canada
   C. Mexico
   B. Asia
   D. South America

6. A. He has a stomachache.
   C. His feet hurt him.
   B. He has a toothache.
   D. His eyes hurt him.

7. A. lesson eleven
   C. They are the same.
   B. lesson twelve
   D. Both are difficult.

8. A. your family name
   C. your mother's name
   B. your father's name
   D. your first name

9. A. cleaning
   C. buttons
   B. price tags
   D. changes

10. A. close the door
    C. answer it
    B. follow him
    D. look at him

11. A. colored
    C. cotton
    B. washed
    D. man-made

12. A. on Saturday
    C. on Thursday
    B. with George
    D. at the office

13. A. at 1002
    C. at 1530
    B. at 1205
    D. at 1615

14. A. red
    C. silk
    B. rock
    D. pink

15. A. a blue gas
    C. exhaust vapors
    B. sevēral gases together
    D. a compound

16. A. a bath
    C. a summer day
    B. a harvest
    D. a storm

17. A. They will fly.
    C. They will drive.
    B. They will walk.
    D. They will run.

18. A. close it
    C. look at it
    B. turn it on
    D. answer it

19. A. Friday
    C. Wednesday
    B. Monday
    D. Sunday

20. A. a long way
    C. a few stops
    B. not very far
    D. a short run

21. A. very clearly
    C. on the blackboard
    B. in his notebook
    D. key words

22. A. seated
    C. empty
    B. crowded
    D. half filled

23. A. in a large cage   B. in a small cage
    C. in a crowded cage   D. in a busy cage

24. A. He made it.   B. He saw it.
    C. He moved it.   D. He cut it.

25. A. She wants to have her tooth pulled out.
    B. She wanted to exchange her dress.
    C. She wants to have her hair permed.
    D. She wanted to apply for the membership to the club.

● *Directions for questions 26-50. You will hear statements on the test tape. Select the one answer A, B, C, or D which comes closest to the meaning of the statement and mark your answer sheet.*

26. A. It was a short run to the bank.
    B. He ran a short distance.
    C. He had little money on him.
    D. He had just cashed a check.

27. A. They took part in the games.
    B. They watched the games.
    C. They were partial to the games.
    D. They were interested in the games.

28. A. I interrupted Alice and Fanny.
    B. Fanny was interrupted.
    C. Fanny interrupted us.
    D. Alice interrupted us.

29. A. There are many people downtown.
    B. Many people are walking on the weekend.
    C. There are many cars on the streets.
    D. There are many lights on the streets.

30. A. It can't be seen.　　　B. It is cool.
　　C. It is not humid.　　　D. It is warm.

31. A. He saw the line.　　　B. He drew a line.
　　C. He hold the line.　　　D. He cut the line.

32. A. It is easily bent.　　　B. It is very hard.
　　C. It is bright.　　　　　D. It is heavy.

33. A. It plays too loudly.　　B. It needs repair.
　　C. It's in good condition.　D. It's a cheap recorder.

34. A. Don't wait for the lecture.
　　B. Don't be early for the lecture.
　　C. Be on time for the lecture.
　　D. Be alert in the lecture.

35. A. Classes are three blocks away.
　　B. There are three classes this afternoon.
　　C. There are classes in Room 3.
　　D. Classes are finished at three.

36. A. The troops fought harder.
　　B. The troops started their attack.
　　C. The troops charged.
　　D. The troops surrendered.

37. A. They may be quiet.　　　B. They have to be quiet.
　　C. They might not be quiet.　D. They shouldn't be quiet.

38. A. They sleep during working hours.
　　B. They sleep while on duty.
　　C. They sleep in their free time.
　　D. They sleep on time.

39. A. She asked me to stop reading.
B. She asked me to continue my reading.
C. She asked me not to read it.
D. She asked me to read it again.

40. A. We met them unexpectedly.
B. We were introduced to them.
C. We didn't go to the gas station.
D. We didn't see them at all.

41. A. You must tell him what you want.
B. You must see him right away.
C. You must encourage him.
D. You must trust him.

42. A. I won't have black tea.
B. I'm going to have black tea.
C. I haven't made up my mind yet.
D. I had black tea yesterday.

43. A. They employed a lot of them.
B. They fired a lot of them.
C. The men were retired.
D. They promoted a lot of them.

44. A. The lunch was prepared by my wife.
B. My wife and I prepared the lunch.
C. The children can't cook at all.
D. The children did all the work.

45. A. He put on his brakes suddenly.
B. He fell on his brakes.
C. He broke the brakes.
D. He repaired the brakes.

46. A. I want to sell my car.
    B. I borrowed the car from Edward.
    C. I will let Edward drive my car.
    D. I have bought this car from Edward.

47. A. The bus left at ten o'clock at night.
    B. The bus left at midnight.
    C. The bus left at two o'clock in the afternoon.
    D. The bus left at ten o'clock in the morning.

48. A. I think he is learned.
    B. I think he has new and different ideas.
    C. I think he is handsome.
    D. I think he likes to study the origins of the earth.

49. A. Peter was waiting for the barber.
    B. Eddie cut Peter's hair.
    C. The barber cut Peter's hair.
    D. The barber cut Eddie's hair.

50. A. Bill might see the doctor.
    B. Bill saw the doctor.
    C. Bill won't see the doctor.
    D. Bill will feel worse tomorrow.

● *Directions for questions 51-60. You will hear dialogs on the test tape. Select the correct answer A, B, C, or D and mark your answer sheet.*

51. A. remove a tire
    B. write down his personal information
    C. ask for help
    D. check the air pressure

52. A. only a quarter   B. less than a quarter
    C. more than a quarter   D. none at all

53. A. waiting for his laundry to dry
    B. getting his laundry
    C. delivering his dirty clothes
    D. putting his laundry in the machine

54. A. It was not true.   B. It was interesting.
    C. It was not long.   D. It was musical.

55. A. The company could not send a taxi.
    B. She did not understand the man.
    C. She will send a taxi at once.
    D. All the cabs are away.

56. A. He can't read it all.
    B. He can't read quickly.
    C. He can read it fairly well.
    D. He can read it slowly.

57. A. He wants to eat out now.
    B. He doesn't want to eat right now.
    C. He has had his dinner already.
    D. He wants to eat later.

58. A. It is new.   B. It is not pretty.
    C. It is blue.   D. It is beautiful.

59. A. They took a picture of it.
    B. They went there later.
    C. They arrived there at last.
    D. They finally changed it.

60. A. up the street from the post office
    B. inside the post office
    C. across the street from the post office
    D. outside the post office

ECL 聽力測驗 [9] 詳解

1. (**C**) What month comes before December?
十二月之前是幾月?

    (A) 四月　　　　(B) 六月　　　　(C) <u>十一月</u>　　　(D) 九月

2. (**A**) What color is your hat?
你的帽子什麼顏色?

    (A) <u>紅色的</u>　　　(B) 毛料的　　　(C) 下雨　　　(D) 小的

3. (**B**) Lieutenant Johnson was told to report to Captain Spark at 3:45. When does he have to be there?
強森上尉被告知要在三點四十五分時,向史巴克船長報告。
他何時必須到那裡?

    (A) 1003　　　(B) <u>1545</u>　　　(C) 1445　　　(D) 1645

    * lieutenant (lu'tɛnənt) *n.* 上尉
    captain ('kæptɪn) *n.* 隊長;船長

4. (**B**) What is the name of the first month of the year?
一年的第一個月是什麼?

    (A) 三月　　　(B) <u>一月</u>　　　(C) 十二月　　　(D) 八月

5. (**C**) What country is located south of the United States?
什麼國家位於美國南部?

    (A) 加拿大　　(B) 亞洲　　(C) <u>墨西哥</u>　　(D) 南美洲

    * locate (lo'ket) *v.* 位於

6. (**A**) If Tommy has an appointment with the physician, what is probably the matter with him?
如果湯米和內科醫生有個約會,那他可能發生了什麼事?

    (A) <u>他胃痛。</u>　(B) 他牙痛。　(C) 他腳痛。　(D) 他眼睛痛。

    * physician (fə'zɪʃən) *n.* 內科醫生

7. (**B**) Lesson 11 is more difficult than Lesson 12.
Which lesson is easier to learn?
第十一課比第十二課困難。／那一課較容易學習？

(A) 第十一課 　　　　　　　(B) <u>第十二課</u>
(C) 都一樣 　　　　　　　　(D) 都很困難

8. (**A**) Jenny asked, "What is your surname?"
What name did she want to know?
珍妮問：「你姓什麼？」／她想知道名字的哪一部分？

(A) <u>你的姓</u> 　　　　　　(B) 你爸爸的名字
(C) 你媽媽的名字 　　　　　(D) 你的名字

* surname (ˈsɜˌnem) *n.* 姓

9. (**D**) The salesgirl said, "I don't think the suit needs any
alterations." What did the salesgirl mean by "alterations"?
女售貨員說：「我認為這件套裝不需要任何修改。」
女售貨員說 alterations 是什麼意思？

(A) 清理 　　(B) 價格標籤 　　(C) 鈕扣 　　(D) <u>改變</u>

* salesgirl (ˈselzˌgɜl) *n.* 女售貨員
alteration (ˌɔltəˈreʃən) *n.* 變更；修改
tag (tæg) *n.* 標籤 　　button (ˈbʌtn̩) *n.* 鈕扣

10. (**C**) If your father asks you a question, what should you do?
如果你爸爸問你一個問題，你應該怎麼做？

(A) 關門 　　(B) 跟隨他 　　(C) <u>回答</u> 　　(D) 看著他

11. (**D**) Her vest is made of synthetic fabric.
What kind of fabric is it?
她的背心是合成布料做的。／是何種布料？

(A) 有顏色的 　　　　　　(B) 清洗過的
(C) 棉花的 　　　　　　　(D) <u>人造的</u>

* vest (vɛst) *n.* 背心 　　synthetic (sɪnˈθɛtɪk) *adj.* 合成的；人造的
fabric (ˈfæbrɪk) *n.* 布 　　***man-made*** 人造的

12. (**C**) Today is Friday. Yesterday we went out of town.
When did we go out of town?
今天是星期五，昨天我們出城去了。/ 我們何時出城的?

　　(A) 星期六　　　(B) 和喬治　　　(C) 星期四　　　(D) 在公司

13. (**C**) I have to be in the dentist's office at 3:30.
When do I have to be there?
我必須在三點三十分到牙醫診所。/ 我何時必須到那裏?

　　(A) 在 1002　　　(B) 在 1205　　　(C) 在 1530　　　(D) 在 1615
　　* dentist ('dɛntɪst) *n.* 牙醫

14. (**C**) What material is her shirt made of?
她的襯衫是何種料子做成的?

　　(A) 紅色的　　　(B) 石頭的　　　(C) 絲的　　　(D) 粉紅色的
　　* silk (sɪlk) *n.* 絲

15. (**B**) Air is a mixture of gases surrounding the earth.
What is air?
空氣是圍繞著地球的混合氣體。/ 空氣是什麼?

　　(A) 一種藍色氣體　　　　　　(B) 幾種氣體混在一起
　　(C) 排出的蒸氣　　　　　　　(D) 混合物
　　* mixture ('mɪkstʃɚ) *n.* 混合物　　exhaust (ɪg'zɔst) *n.* 排出
　　vapor ('vepɚ) *n.* 蒸氣　　compound ('kɑmpaʊnd) *n.* 混合物；化合物

16. (**D**) If we are having a thundershower, what are we having?
如果有雷陣雨，那我們有什麼?

　　(A) 洗澡　　　(B) 收穫　　　(C) 夏日　　　(D) 暴風雨
　　* thundershower ('θʌndɚ,ʃaʊɚ) *n.* 雷陣雨　　harvest ('hɑrvɪst) *n.* 收穫

17. (**A**) They are going to Seattle by jet.
How are they going to Seattle?
他們要搭噴射機去西雅圖。/ 他們要怎樣去西雅圖?

　　(A) 他們將會用飛的。　　　　(B) 他們將會用走的。
　　(C) 他們將會開車。　　　　　(D) 他們將會用跑的。

18. (**D**) If the telephone rings, what should you do?
如果電話響了，你應該做什麼？

(A) 把它關掉　　　　　　　(B) 把它打開
(C) 看著它　　　　　　　　(D) 接電話

* *turn on* 打開

19. (**C**) What day comes before Thursday?
星期四之前是星期幾？

(A) 星期五　　(B) 星期一　　(C) 星期三　　(D) 星期日

20. (**A**) Allen walked quite a distance. How far did he walk?
艾倫走了好一段路。／他走了多遠？

(A) 很長的一段路　　　　　(B) 不會很遠
(C) 幾站　　　　　　　　　(D) 跑了很短的距離

21. (**C**) Jim is writing a word on the blackboard. Tom is writing
many words in his notebook. Where is Jim writing?
吉姆正在黑板上寫一個字。湯姆正在他的筆記本上寫很多字。
吉姆在哪裡寫字？

(A) 非常清楚　　　　　　　(B) 在他的筆記本
(C) 在黑板上　　　　　　　(D) 關鍵字

22. (**B**) The stadium is packed with people. How is the stadium?
運動場擠滿了人。／運動場怎樣？

(A) 坐著人　　(B) 很擁擠　　(C) 空的　　(D) 半滿

* stadium〔'stedɪəm〕*n.* 有看台的運動場　　*be packed with* 擠滿
empty〔'ɛmptɪ〕*adj.* 空的

23. (**A**) The lion lives in a spacious cage. Where does he live?
獅子住在寬敞的籠子裡。／他住在哪裡？

(A) 在一個大的籠子裡。　　(B) 在一個小的籠子裡。
(C) 在一個擁擠的籠子裡。　(D) 在一個忙碌的籠子裡。

* spacious〔'speʃəs〕*adj.* 寬敞的　　cage〔kedʒ〕*n.* 籠子

24. (**B**)　John noticed a flying object in the sky.
　　　　約翰注意到在天空飛的物體。

　　　　(A) 他做到了。　　　　　　　　(B) 他看到它。
　　　　(C) 他移動它。　　　　　　　　(D) 他剪斷它。

　　　　* object (ˈɑbdʒɪkt) *n.* 物體

25. (**C**)　Lily has an appointment with her hairdresser.
　　　　What does she want to do?
　　　　麗莉和她的美髮師有個約會。 / 她想要做什麼?

　　　　(A) 她想拔牙。　　　　　　　　(B) 她想換衣服。
　　　　(C) 她想燙頭髮。　　　　　　　(D) 她想申請入會。

　　　　* hairdresser (ˈhɛrˌdrɛsə) *n.* 美髮師　　　*pull out* 拔掉
　　　　exchange (ɪksˈtʃendʒ) *v.* 交換　　　perm (pɝm) *v.* 燙頭髮
　　　　apply (əˈplaɪ) *v.* 申請

26. (**C**)　Justin said he was running short of cash.
　　　　傑斯汀說他沒有錢。

　　　　(A) 跑去銀行距離很短。　　　　(B) 他跑了一段短距離。
　　　　(C) 他錢很少。　　　　　　　　(D) 他剛兌換了一張支票。

　　　　* *run short of* 缺少　　　cash (kæʃ) *v.* 兌現

27. (**A**)　The boys participated in the games.
　　　　男孩們參加這些遊戲。

　　　　(A) 他們參加這些遊戲。　　　　(B) 他們觀賞這些遊戲。
　　　　(C) 他們偏愛這些遊戲。　　　　(D) 他們對遊戲有興趣。

　　　　* *participate in* 參加　　　*take part in* 參加
　　　　partial (ˈpɑrʃəl) *adj.* 偏愛的;偏袒的

28. (**C**)　I was talking to Alice when Fanny cut in.
　　　　我正在和愛麗絲說話時,芬妮插進來。

　　　　(A) 我打斷愛麗絲和芬妮的談話。　(B) 芬妮被打斷。
　　　　(C) 芬妮打斷我們。　　　　　　　(D) 愛麗絲打斷我們。

　　　　* *cut in* 插嘴　　　interrupt (ˌɪntəˈrʌpt) *v.* 打斷;插嘴

29. (**C**) On weekdays the traffic is heavy downtown.
在平日時，市區的交通堵塞。

(A) 市區有很多人。 　　　　(B) 許多人在週末時散步。
(C) 街上有許多車。 　　　　(D) 街上有許多燈。

* weekday〔'wik,de〕*n.* 平日（星期一到星期五）

30. (**A**) The atmosphere is invisible.
大氣是看不見的。

(A) 它無法被看到。 　　　　(B) 它是冷的。
(C) 它不是潮濕的。 　　　　(D) 它是溫暖的。

* atmosphere〔'ætməs,fɪr〕*n.* 氣氛；大氣
invisible〔ɪn'vɪzəbḷ〕*adj.* 看不見的　　humid〔'hjumɪd〕*adj.* 潮濕的

31. (**B**) Bill underlined the key words of the sentence.
比爾把句子中的關鍵字劃底線。

(A) 他看到這條線。 　　　　(B) 他畫一條線。
(C) 他沒有掛電話。 　　　　(D) 他把線剪掉。

* underline〔,ʌndə'laɪn〕*v.* 畫底線　　*hold the line*（電話）不掛斷

32. (**A**) Rubber is flexible.
橡膠有彈性。

(A) 它很容易彎曲。 　　　　(B) 它非常硬。
(C) 它很亮。 　　　　(D) 它很重。

* rubber〔'rʌbə〕*n.* 橡膠　　flexible〔'flɛksəbḷ〕*adj.* 有彈性的
bend〔bɛnd〕*v.* 彎曲

33. (**B**) This tape recorder functions poorly.
這台錄音機運轉得很差。

(A) 它放得很大聲。
(B) 它需要修理。
(C) 它情況良好。
(D) 它是一台便宜的錄音機。

* function〔'fʌŋkʃən〕*v.* 起作用；運轉

34. (**C**)　Don't be late for the lecture.
　　　　演講不要遲到。
　　　　(A) 不要等待演講。　　　　　(B) 演講不要早到。
　　　　(C) <u>演講要準時。</u>　　　　　(D) 演講要警覺一點。
　　　　* lecture〔'lɛktʃɚ〕 *n.* 演講　　*on time* 準時　　alert〔ə'lɜt〕 *adj.* 警覺的

35. (**D**)　Classes are over at three this afternoon.
　　　　課程在今天下午三點結束。
　　　　(A) 課程在三條街以外之處。　(B) 今天下午有三堂課。
　　　　(C) 三號教室有課。　　　　　(D) <u>課程在三點結束。</u>

36. (**D**)　The troops finally gave up.
　　　　軍隊最後投降了。
　　　　(A) 軍隊打得更激烈。　　　　(B) 軍隊開始攻擊。
　　　　(C) 軍隊猛攻。　　　　　　　(D) <u>軍隊投降了。</u>
　　　　* troop〔trup〕 *n.* 隊；軍隊　　*give up* 放棄；投降
　　　　fight〔faɪt〕 *v.* 打仗　　charge〔tʃɑrdʒ〕 *v.* 猛攻；猛衝
　　　　surrender〔sə'rɛndɚ〕 *v.* 投降

37. (**B**)　The students must be quiet in class.
　　　　學生在課堂上必須安靜。
　　　　(A) 他們可能安靜。　　　　　(B) <u>他們必須安靜。</u>
　　　　(C) 他們可能不會安靜。　　　(D) 他們不應該安靜。

38. (**C**)　Many people sleep in their spare time.
　　　　許多人在他們休閒時間睡覺。
　　　　(A) 他們在工作時間睡覺。　　(B) 他們在上班時間睡覺。
　　　　(C) <u>他們在空閒時間睡覺。</u>　(D) 他們準時睡覺。
　　　　* *spare time* 餘暇　　*on duty* 上班

39. (**D**)　Mrs. Peck asked me to reread the article.
　　　　派克太太要我重讀這篇文章。
　　　　(A) 她要我停止閱讀。　　　　(B) 她要我繼續閱讀。
　　　　(C) 她要我別閱讀。　　　　　(D) <u>她要我再讀一次。</u>

40. (**A**) We ran into them in the gas station.
　　　我們在加油站與他們偶遇。

　　　(A) 我們意外地遇到他們。　　　(B) 我們被介紹給他們。
　　　(C) 我們沒去加油站。　　　　(D) 我們根本沒看到他們。

　　　* **run into** 偶然遇到　　unexpectedly〔ˌʌnɪkˈspɛktɪdlɪ〕*adv.* 意外地

41. (**D**) You must be confident in your partner.
　　　你必須對你的同伴有信心。

　　　(A) 你必須告訴他你想要的。　　(B) 你必須立刻見他。
　　　(C) 你必須鼓勵他。　　　　　(D) 你必須信任他。

　　　* confident〔ˈkɑnfədənt〕*adj.* 有信心的
　　　　partner〔ˈpɑrtnɚ〕*n.* 同伴

42. (**B**) I'll have black tea please.
　　　我要喝紅茶。

　　　(A) 我不喝紅茶。　　　　　　(B) 我將會喝紅茶。
　　　(C) 我還沒決定。　　　　　　(D) 我昨天喝過紅茶。

　　　* **make up** *one's* **mind** 決定

43. (**A**) This factory hired a lot of workers last year.
　　　這家工廠去年雇用了很多工人。

　　　(A) 他們雇用許多人。　　　　(B) 他們解雇了許多人。
　　　(C) 這些人退休了。　　　　　(D) 他們升了許多人。

　　　* factory〔ˈfæktrɪ〕*n.* 工廠　　hire〔haɪr〕*v.* 雇用
　　　　employ〔ɪmˈplɔɪ〕*v.* 雇用　　retire〔rɪˈtaɪr〕*v.* 退休
　　　　promote〔prəˈmot〕*v.* 升遷

44. (**D**) The children cooked their own lunch today. I did not
　　　help them.
　　　小孩們今天自己煮午餐。我沒有幫助他們。

　　　(A) 午餐是我太太準備的。　　(B) 我太太和我準備午餐。
　　　(C) 小孩們根本不會煮。　　　(D) 小孩們做所有的工作。

45. (**A**) Thomas slammed on his brakes.
湯瑪士猛踩煞車。

(A) 他突然踩煞車。　　　　　(B) 他跌到煞車上。
(C) 他把煞車弄壞了。　　　　(D) 他修理煞車。

* slam (slæm) v. 猛力關門；猛擊　　brake (brek) n. 煞車
put on the brake(s) 踩煞車

46. (**C**) I am going to lend my car to Edward tomorrow.
我明天將把車借給愛德華。

(A) 我想賣我的車子。　　　　(B) 我跟愛德華借車。
(C) 我將讓愛德華開我的車子。　　(D) 我向愛德華買車。

47. (**A**) He got to the bus station at midnight, missing his bus by two hours.
他於午夜到達公車站，錯過公車二小時。

(A) 公車晚上十點離開。　　　(B) 公車午夜離開。
(C) 公車下午二點離開。　　　(D) 公車早上十點離開。

48. (**B**) I consider the writer full of originality.
我認為這位作家很有創造力。

(A) 我認為他知識豐富。
(B) 我認為他有新的、不同的點子。
(C) 我認為他很帥。
(D) 我認為他喜歡研究地球的起源。

* originality (ə,rɪdʒə'nælətɪ) n. 創造力
learned ('lɜnɪd) adj. 知識豐富的

49. (**D**) While waiting for Peter, Eddie had the barber cut his hair.
在等彼得時，艾迪讓理髮師剪他的頭髮。

(A) 彼得在等理髮師。　　　　(B) 艾迪剪彼得的頭髮。
(C) 理髮師剪彼得的頭髮。　　(D) 理髮師剪艾迪的頭髮。

* barber ('bɑrbɚ) n. 理髮師

50. (**A**) Bill will go to the doctor if he feels worse tomorrow.
比爾將會去看醫生，如果他明天覺得更糟的話。

(A) 比爾可能會去看醫生。   (B) 比爾看過醫生了。
(C) 比爾不會去看醫生。   (D) 比爾明天會覺得更糟。

51. (**B**) W : What are you doing?
M : The clerk asked me to fill out the application form.
What is the man supposed to do?
女：你在做什麼？
男：職員要我填申請表。
這個男士應該要做什麼？

(A) 換輪胎   (B) 寫下他的個人資料
(C) 尋求幫助   (D) 檢查氣壓

* *fill out* 填寫   *application form* 申請表   tire〔taɪr〕*n.* 輪胎

52. (**A**) W : Do you have any change on you?
M : Well, I just have a quarter.
How much money did the man have?
女：你身上有零錢嗎？
男：嗯，我只有一個二十五分的硬幣。
這個男士有多少錢？

(A) 只有二十五分   (B) 少於二十五分
(C) 超過二十五分   (D) 沒有零錢

* quarter〔'kwɔrtɚ〕*n.* 二十五分的硬幣

53. (**B**) W : Where is Sergeant Gable?
M : He is picking up his laundry.
What is Sergeant Gable doing?
女：蓋伯中士在哪兒？
男：他去拿他送洗的衣服。
蓋伯中士在做什麼？

(A) 等衣服乾   (B) 拿他的衣服
(C) 送髒衣服   (D) 把衣服放到洗衣機裏

* sergeant〔'sɑrdʒənt〕*n.* 中士
laundry〔'lɔndrɪ〕*n.* 所洗或要洗的衣服；洗衣店

54. (**B**)　M : Did you enjoy the play last night?
　　　　　W : It was not at all boring.
　　　　　What did the woman say about the play?
　　　　　男：妳喜歡昨晚那齣戲嗎？
　　　　　女：一點也不會無聊。
　　　　　這位女士認為那齣戲怎樣？

　　　　(A) 不是真的　　　　　　　　(B) 很有趣
　　　　(C) 不長　　　　　　　　　　(D) 是音樂性的

55. (**C**)　M : Hello, is this the taxi company?
　　　　　W : Yes, it is.
　　　　　M : When can you send a taxi to 307, 5th Street?
　　　　　W : Right away.
　　　　　What did the woman say?
　　　　　男：哈囉！計程車公司嗎？
　　　　　女：是的。
　　　　　男：你何時可以派輛計程車到第五街 307 號？
　　　　　女：馬上。
　　　　　這位女士說什麼？

　　　　(A) 公司無法派出計程車。
　　　　(B) 她不了解這位男士說的話。
　　　　(C) 她將立刻派一輛計程車。
　　　　(D) 所有的計程車都不在。

　　　　* *right away* 馬上；立刻　　*at once* 立刻
　　　　cab〔kæb〕*n.* 計程車

56. (**C**)　M : Can James read Chinese?
　　　　　W : He can read pretty well.
　　　　　How well can James read Chinese?
　　　　　男：詹姆士看得懂中文嗎？
　　　　　女：他可以讀得非常好。
　　　　　詹姆士的中文可以唸得多好？

　　　　(A) 他無法讀全部。　　　　　(B) 他無法讀得很快。
　　　　(C) 他可以讀得相當好。　　　(D) 他可以慢慢地讀。

57. (**A**)　W：What do you feel like doing？
　　　　　 M：I'd like to go out to dinner now.
　　　　　 What did the man mean？
　　　　　 女：你想做什麼？
　　　　　 男：我想現在出去吃晚餐。
　　　　　 這位男士什麼意思？

　　　(A) 他現在想到外面吃飯。　　　(B) 他不想馬上吃。
　　　(C) 他已經吃過晚餐了。　　　　(D) 他想要晚一點再吃

58. (**D**)　W：Paula's skirt is just like mine.
　　　　　 M：Yes, and it's pretty, isn't it？
　　　　　 What did they say about Paula's skirt？
　　　　　 女：波拉的裙子跟我的很像。
　　　　　 男：是啊，而且很漂亮，不是嗎？
　　　　　 他們說波拉的裙子怎樣？

　　　(A) 很新　　(B) 不漂亮　　(C) 是藍色的　　(D) 很漂亮

59. (**C**)　M：Where are Peter and Paul？
　　　　　 W：They finally made it to the school.
　　　　　 What did the woman mean？
　　　　　 男：彼得和保羅在哪裡？
　　　　　 女：他們最後成功地到達學校。
　　　　　 這位女士是什麼意思？

　　　(A) 他們照了相。　　　　　　(B) 他們晚一點去那裡。
　　　(C) 他們最後到達了那裡。　　　(D) 他們最後改變。

60. (**D**)　M：Where shall we meet？
　　　　　 W：Let's meet on the corner where the post office is.
　　　　　 Where will they meet？
　　　　　 男：我們要在哪兒碰面？
　　　　　 女：我們在郵局轉角那兒碰面吧！
　　　　　 他們將在哪兒碰面？

　　　(A) 郵局那條街上　　　　　　(B) 在郵局裡面
　　　(C) 郵局的對面　　　　　　　(D) 郵局外面

LISTENING TEST　10

● *Directions for questions 1-25. You will hear questions on the test tape. Select the one item A, B, C or D which answers the question correctly, and mark your answer sheet.*

1. A. It mixes fuel.　　　　　　B. It measures fuel.
   C. It checks fuel.　　　　　　D. It delivers fuel.

2. A. stopping cars　　　　　　B. breaking stones
   C. steering cars　　　　　　D. draining water

3. A. in the lamp shade
   B. in the lowest part of the vase
   C. in the light bulb
   D. in the neck of the vase

4. A. to the kitchen　　　　　　B. to the laundry
   C. to the bookstore　　　　　D. to the skating rink

5. A. in the kitchen　　　　　　B. at the cash register
   C. on the counter　　　　　　D. in the sitting area

6. A. She wants to look at tiny particles.
   B. She wants to stop her vehicle.
   C. She wants to weigh something.
   D. She wants to rule people.

7. A. a quarter to five
   B. fifteen minutes after five
   C. fifteen minutes before six
   D. a quarter past six

8. A. forget her teacher　　　　B. contact her teacher
   C. remember her teacher　　　D. touch her teacher

9. A. He fell asleep.
   B. He wouldn't be able to sleep.
   C. He wanted to sleep.
   D. He couldn't sleep.

10. A. right above her stomach   B. below her stomach
    C. in her ankle   D. in her foot

11. A. some children   B. one child
    C. two grown-ups   D. all grown-ups

12. A. Johnny Robin   B. John Robinson
    C. John Robin   D. Johnny Robinson

13. A. yesterday   B. on Friday
    C. on Saturday   D. at the office

14. A. take a rest   B. bring his plane down
    C. take off   D. fly faster

15. A. She reads regulations.   B. She works with machines.
    C. She uses recipes.   D. She looks up words.

16. A. a movie   B. a concert
    C. a play   D. a game

17. A. a place where you can buy stationery
    B. a place where doctors treat patients
    C. a place where food is sold
    D. a place where shoes are sold

18. A. rough   B. comfortable
    C. long   D. hot

19. A. underwater　　　　　　B. on a tree
　　C. on a vine　　　　　　　D. underground

20. A. forty-eight　　　　　　B. five
　　C. seven　　　　　　　　　D. six

21. A. a ship to go to school
　　B. a school book
　　C. a special type of car
　　D. aid in continuing his studies

22. A. It arrived at the station.
　　B. It left the station.
　　C. It headed for the next station.
　　D. It was on the way to the next station.

23. A. for firewood　　　　　　B. to mark positions
　　C. to hide things　　　　　　D. for lumber

24. A. a pair of boots　　　　　B. a raincoat
　　C. a pair of spectacles　　　D. a hat

25. A. He called it off.　　　　　B. He called for it.
　　C. He called at it.　　　　　D. He called in it.

● *Directions for questions 26-50. You will hear statements on the test tape. Select the one answer A, B, C, or D which comes closest to the meaning of the statement and mark your answer sheet.*

26. A. It is regulated by many elements.
　　B. It requires many elements.
　　C. It excludes many elements.
　　D. It is made up of many elements.

27. A. It showed the boundary.
    B. It eliminated the boundary.
    C. It calculated the boundary.
    D. It included the boundary.

28. A. There was a good selection.
    B. They have the same color.
    C. They taste very sweet.
    D. They are cheap.

29. A. He suggested a bicycle for me.
    B. He maintained a bicycle for me.
    C. A bicycle was not available.
    D. He supplied a bicycle for me.

30. A. He directed it.   B. He counted it.
    C. He rolled it.   D. He displayed it.

31. A. I avoided Mr. Lee yesterday.
    B. I met Mr. Lee yesterday.
    C. I did not see Mr. Lee yesterday.
    D. My car hit Mr. Lee's car yesterday.

32. A. He will come.   B. He won't come.
    C. He didn't understand.   D. I didn't ask him to come.

33. A. I like to work hard.   B. I like to study a lot.
    C. I like to take a bath.   D. I like to relax.

34. A. He does not like to study.
    B. Studying does not bother him.
    C. He never looks at his lessons.
    D. Studying is not his preferred activity.

35. A. He will read every sentence.
    B. He read all the sentences.
    C. He didn't read every sentence.
    D. He read nothing in the paper.

36. A. They do not mix.   B. They do not boil.
    C. They do not absorb.   D. They do not melt.

37. A. She thought about getting a raise in pay.
    B. She got a raise in pay.
    C. She asked for a raise in pay.
    D. She considered a raise in pay.

38. A. Paggy thought that the city was on the map.
    B. Paggy surrounded the city on the map.
    C. Paggy colored the city on the map.
    D. Paggy found the city on the map.

39. A. She labeled the sheets of paper.
    B. She cut the sheets of paper.
    C. She joined the sheets of paper together.
    D. She stamped the sheets of paper.

40. A. It should be wasted.   B. It should be implemented.
    C. It should be limited.   D. It should be dropped.

41. A. The price has been increased.
    B. The price has been reduced.
    C. The chair has been sold.
    D. The chair is not to be sold.

42. A. Allow him to stay inside.
    B. Keep away from him.
    C. Be friendly to him.
    D. Keep him warm.

43. A. It was very delicious.
    B. It was too tough.
    C. It was well cooked.
    D. It was not cooked enough.

44. A. It was reinforced.   B. It was successful.
    C. It was fought off.   D. It was ordered.

45. A. He taught his student the right answer.
    B. He wanted his student to teach him the right answer.
    C. He believed his student had the right answer.
    D. His student taught him the right answer.

46. A. John has to go.   B. John could go.
    C. John may go.   D. John should go.

47. A. It's been used before.
    B. It is not a new car.
    C. It's a completely new car.
    D. It's a second-hand car.

48. A. I'm buying it.   B. I'm sharing it.
    C. I'm making it.   D. I'm comparing it.

49. A. I have a severe heachache.
    B. I still have a lot of work despite my headache.
    C. I was given medicine for my headache.
    D. The medicine cured me of my headache.

50. A. He passed it easily.   B. He wasn't successful.
    C. He hasn't taken it yet. D. He got a good score.

● *Directions for questions 51-60. You will hear dialogs on the test tape. Select the correct answer A, B, C, or D and mark your answer sheet.*

51. A. He talked honestly and openly.
    B. He talked quietly and slowly.
    C. He talked quickly and energetically.
    D. He talked calmly and thoughtfully.

52. A. It occurred just in time.   B. It occurred gradually.
    C. It occurred all at once.   D. It occurred tediously.

53. A. He would go to town.
    B. He has gone to town.
    C. He should go to town.
    D. He should have gone to town.

54. A. They told us to go slowly.
    B. They told us to separate.
    C. They told us to cooperate.
    D. They told us to hurry.

55. A. She gained a few pounds.
    B. She selected the right scale.
    C. She improved her weight lifting.
    D. She lost a little weight.

56. A. He's taking driving lessons.
    B. He hopes to change his mind.
    C. He's afraid to drive.
    D. He'll take driving lessons soon.

57. A. It was held in the morning.
    B. It was held as scheduled.
    C. It was held in a different place.
    D. It was postponed.

58. A. It stopped.   B. It ran very fast.
    C. It was in an accident.   D. It has a flat tire.

59. A. It turns.   B. It closes.
    C. It stops.   D. It starts.

60. A. usually   B. never
    C. occasionally   D. often

When visiting my friend, Mary, I was surprised to
hear her lovingly address her three-month-old baby as
"Coffee."

"Is that really her name?" I asked curiously.

"No," Mary sighed. "My husband and I call her that
because she keeps us awake at night."

拜訪我的朋友瑪麗時，我很驚訝聽到她溫柔地叫她三個月大的
寶寶「咖啡」。

我很好奇地問道：「那眞是她的名字嗎？」

「不，」瑪麗歎了口氣，「我先生和我這麼叫她，因爲她總是
讓我們晚上無法睡覺。」

ECL 聽力測驗 [10] 詳解

1. (**D**) The pump supplies fuel under pressure.
   What does the pump do?
   幫浦在壓力下供應燃料。/ 幫浦做什麼?

   (A) 混合燃料　(B) 測量燃料　　(C) 檢查燃料　　(D) 運送燃料

   * pump (pʌmp) *n.* 幫浦;抽水機　　fuel ('fjuəl) *n.* 燃料
     deliver (dɪ'lɪvɚ) *v.* 運送

2. (**C**) What is the wheel of a car used for?
   車子的方向盤作用是什麼?

   (A) 停止車子　(B) 打破石頭　　(C) 駕駛車子　　(D) 排水

   * wheel (hwil) *n.* 輪子;方向盤　　steer (stɪr) *v.* 駕駛;操縱
     drain (dren) *v.* 排水

3. (**B**) The base of the vase has a crack. Where is the crack?
   花瓶的底部有裂痕。/ 裂痕在哪裏?

   (A) 燈的陰影處　　　　　　(B) 花瓶的最低處
   (C) 燈泡裏　　　　　　　　(D) 花瓶的頸處

   * base (bes) *n.* 底部　　crack (kræk) *n.* 破裂;裂痕
     bulb (bʌlb) *n.* 電燈泡

4. (**A**) Where do you take your dirty dishes?
   你把髒盤子拿到哪裏?

   (A) 到廚房　　(B) 到洗衣店　　(C) 到書店　　(D) 到溜冰場

   * laundry ('lɔndrɪ) *n.* 洗衣店　　rink (rɪŋk) *n.* 溜冰場

5. (**D**) The teacher left her books in a booth in a restaurant.
   Where are her books?
   老師把她的書遺留在餐廳的座位上。/ 她的書在哪裏?

   (A) 在廚房　　(B) 在結帳處　　(C) 在櫃台　　(D) 在座位區

   * booth (buθ) *n.* 隔間;座位　　*cash register* 收銀機
     counter ('kauntɚ) *n.* 櫃台

6. (**A**) Mandy is going to use the magnifier.
    What does she want to do?
    曼蒂將使用放大鏡。／她要做什麼?

    (A) 她想看微小的粒子。   (B) 她想把車停住。
    (C) 她想要秤一些東西。   (D) 她想要統治人們。

    * magnifier〔'mægnə,faɪɚ〕 *n.* 放大鏡   tiny〔'taɪnɪ〕 *adj.* 微小的
      particle〔'partɪkl̩〕 *n.* 粒子

7. (**D**) It is 6:15. What time is it?
    現在是六點十五分。／現在是幾點?

    (A) 四點四十五分   (B) 五點十五分
    (C) 五點四十五分   (D) 六點十五分

    * quarter〔'kwɔrtɚ〕 *n.* 四分之一;一刻鐘

8. (**B**) Tina wants to get in touch with her teacher.
    What does she want to do?
    堤娜想要和她老師聯絡。／她想做什麼?

    (A) 忘記她的老師   (B) 聯絡她的老師
    (C) 記起她的老師   (D) 摸她的老師

    * *get in touch with* ~ 與~聯絡   contact〔kən'tækt〕 *v.* 聯絡

9. (**C**) Jack said that he felt sleepy.
    What did he say?
    傑克說他想睡覺。／他說了什麼?

    (A) 他睡著了。   (B) 他不能睡覺。
    (C) 他想要睡覺。   (D) 他不能睡覺。

10. (**A**) Susan had a pain in her chest.
    Where was the pain?
    蘇珊的胸部會痛。／哪裏會痛?

    (A) 就在胃的上方   (B) 在胃的下方
    (C) 腳踝   (D) 腳

    * chest〔tʃɛst〕 *n.* 胸部   ankle〔'æŋkl̩〕 *n.* 踝

11. (**D**) Every adult should read this book.
Who should read this book?
每個成人都應該唸這本書。／誰應該唸這本書？

　(A) 一些小孩子　　　　　　(B) 一個小孩
　(C) 二個大人　　　　　　　(D) <u>所有的大人</u>

　* adult (ə'dʌlt) *n.* 成人　　grown-up ('gron,ʌp) *n.* 成人

12. (**D**) His name is Johnny Robinson Jr.
What is his father's name?
他的名字是小強尼・羅賓森。／他爸爸叫什麼名字？

　(A) 強尼・羅賓　　　　　　(B) 約翰・羅賓森
　(C) 約翰・羅賓　　　　　　(D) <u>強尼・羅賓森</u>

　* Jr. = junior　年少的（指同名父子中的兒子）

13. (**B**) Today is Thursday. I will see George tomorrow.
When will I see George?
今天是星期四，我明天要去看喬治。／我何時去看喬治？

　(A) 昨天　　(B) <u>星期五</u>　　(C) 星期六　　(D) 在公司

14. (**B**) The pilot can land now. What can the pilot do?
飛行員現在可以著陸了。／飛行員能做什麼？

　(A) 休息　　　　　　　　　(B) <u>將飛機降下來</u>
　(C) 起飛　　　　　　　　　(D) 飛得更快

　* pilot ('paɪlət) *n.* 飛行員　　land (lænd) *v.* 著陸
　take off 起飛

15. (**D**) Conny often consults the dictionary.
What does Conny do?
康妮常常查字典。／康妮做什麼？

　(A) 她閱讀規則。　　　　　(B) 她操作機器。
　(C) 她使用食譜。　　　　　(D) <u>她在查單字。</u>

　* consult (kən'sʌlt) *v.* 查閱　　recipe ('rɛsəpɪ) *n.* 食譜
　look up 查閱

16. (**C**) They went to the National Theater last night.
    What did they see?
    他們昨晚去國家戲劇院。/ 他們看什麼呢?

    (A) 一部電影　　(B) 一場音樂會　(C) <u>一齣戲劇</u>　　(D) 一場比賽

17. (**B**) George caught a cold and went to the clinic.
    What kind of place is a clinic?
    喬治感冒了,到診所去。/ 診所是什麼樣的地方?

    (A) 你可以買到文具的地方　　(B) <u>醫生治療病人的地方</u>
    (C) 賣食物的地方　　　　　　(D) 賣鞋的地方

    * clinic (ˈklɪnɪk) *n.* 診所　　stationery (ˈsteʃənˌɛrɪ) *n.* 文具

18. (**A**) The trip was made over bumpy roads.
    What kind of roads were they?
    這趟旅程路上都很顛簸。/ 路怎麼樣?

    (A) <u>崎嶇不平</u>　　(B) 很舒服　　(C) 很長　　(D) 很熱

    * bumpy (ˈbʌmpɪ) *adj.* 顛簸崎嶇的 ,　rough (rʌf) *adj.* 崎嶇不平的

19. (**C**) This fruit grows on a vine. Where does it grow?
    這水果長在葡萄籐上。/ 它長在哪裏?

    (A) 在水裡　　(B) 在樹上　　(C) <u>在葡萄籐上</u>　(D) 在地下

    * vine (vaɪn) *n.* 葡萄籐

20. (**D**) My brother works every day except Monday.
    How many days a week does he work?
    我哥哥除了星期一之外每天工作。/ 他一個禮拜工作幾天?

    (A) 四十八　　(B) 五　　　(C) 七　　　(D) <u>六</u>

21. (**D**) The student obtained a scholarship. What did he get?
    這個學生得到獎學金。/ 他得到什麼?

    (A) 到學校的船　　　　　(B) 一本學校的書
    (C) 一部樣式特別的車子　(D) <u>得到援助,得以繼續其學業</u>

    * scholarship (ˈskɑləˌʃɪp) *n.* 獎學金

22. (**A**) The train finally pulled into the station.
　　　　What did the train do?
　　　　火車終於駛進車站。／火車怎麼樣了？

　　　　(A) 到達車站　　　　　　　　(B) 離開車站
　　　　(C) 開往下一個車站　　　　　(D) 到下一站的路上

　　　　* **pull into** （火車）進站　　**head for** 前往

23. (**C**) This tree can be used for camouflage.
　　　　What can we use the tree for?
　　　　這棵樹可以用來偽裝。／我們可以用這棵樹來做什麼？

　　　　(A) 做柴火　　　(B) 標明位置　　　(C) 隱藏東西　　　(D) 作爲木材

　　　　* camouflage (ˈkæməˌflɑʒ) *n.* 偽裝；隱瞞
　　　　　lumber (ˈlʌmbɚ) *n.* 木材

24. (**B**) It's raining cats and dogs outside.
　　　　What does Tom need to get out?
　　　　外面下大雨。／湯姆出去需要什麼？

　　　　(A) 一雙靴子　　(B) 雨衣　　　(C) 一副眼鏡　　(D) 一頂帽子

　　　　* **rain cats and dogs** 下大雨　　spectacles (ˈspɛktəkl̩z) *n. pl.* 眼鏡

25. (**A**) Mr. Johnson has canceled the meeting.
　　　　What did he do?
　　　　強森先生取消了這場會議。／他做什麼？

　　　　(A) 他取消會議。　　　　　　(B) 他要求開會
　　　　(C) 他拜訪它。　　　　　　　(D) 他要求收回它。

　　　　* **call for** 要求　　**call at** 拜訪（地方）　　**call in** 要求收回

26. (**D**) The compound consists of many elements.
　　　　這個化合物由許多元素所組成。

　　　　(A) 它由許多元素所管理。　　(B) 它需要很多元素。
　　　　(C) 它排除許多元素。　　　　(D) 它由許多元素所組成。

　　　　* **consist of** 由～組成　　element (ˈɛləmənt) *n.* 元素
　　　　　regulate (ˈrɛgjəˌlet) *v.* 管理；規定　　exclude (ɪkˈsklud) *v.* 排除
　　　　　be made up of 由～組成

27. (**A**) The marker indicated the boundary.
這個記號指出邊界所在。

(A) 它顯示出邊界。   (B) 它除去邊界。
(C) 它計算邊界。   (D) 它包含邊界。

* marker (ˋmɔrkɚ) *n.* 記號   indicate (ˋɪndəˌket) *v.* 指出
boundary (ˋbaʊndərɪ) *n.* 分界線；邊界
eliminate (ɪˋlɪməˌnet) *v.* 除去   calculate (ˋkælkjəˌlet) *v.* 計算

28. (**A**) They had a large variety of candy.
他們有各種糖果。

(A) 有許多選擇。   (B) 他們顏色相同。
(C) 他們嚐起來很甜。   (D) 他們很便宜。

* selection (səˋlɛkʃən) *n.* 選擇

29. (**D**) He provided a bicycle for me.
他提供一輛腳踏車給我。

(A) 他為我建議一輛腳踏車。   (B) 他為我保留一輛腳踏車。
(C) 買不到腳踏車。   (D) 他供應一輛腳踏車給我。

* available (əˋveləbḷ) *adj.* 可獲得的

30. (**A**) The manager controlled the operation skillfully.
經理有技巧地控制這項運作。

(A) 他引導它。   (B) 他計算它。
(C) 他旋轉它。   (D) 他展示它。

* roll (rol) *v.* 旋轉   display (dɪˋsple) *v.* 展示

31. (**B**) I came across Mr. Lee yesterday in the hospital.
我昨天在醫院偶然遇見李先生。

(A) 昨天我避開李先生。
(B) 昨天我遇到李先生。
(C) 昨天我沒看到李先生。
(D) 昨天我的車撞到李先生的車。

* *come across* 偶遇

32. (**A**) I invited him to my party and he accepted it.
　　　我邀請他來我的舞會，而他接受了。

　　　(A) 他將會來。　　　　　(B) 他將不會來。
　　　(C) 他不了解。　　　　　(D) 我沒要他來。

33. (**D**) When I am at home, I like to take it easy.
　　　當我在家時，我喜歡輕鬆一下。

　　　(A) 我喜歡努力工作。　　　(B) 我喜歡讀很多書。
　　　(C) 我喜歡洗澡。　　　　　(D) 我喜歡放鬆。

　　　* *take it easy* 輕鬆一下

34. (**B**) The boy doesn't mind studying his lessons.
　　　這個男孩不介意讀書。

　　　(A) 他不喜歡唸書。　　　　(B) 讀書不會困擾他。
　　　(C) 他從不看他的功課。　　(D) 讀書不是他所喜愛的活動。

35. (**C**) Sergeant Walker doesn't have enough time to read every sentence in the paper.
　　　沃克中士沒有足夠的時間來看報上的每個句子。

　　　(A) 他將會看每個句子。　　(B) 他看所有的句子。
　　　(C) 他不是每個句子都看。　(D) 他沒看報紙上的東西。

　　　* sergeant (ˈsɑrdʒənt) *n.* 中士

36. (**A**) Oil and water do not combine.
　　　油和水不能結合在一起。

　　　(A) 它們不能混合。　　　　(B) 它們不能煮。
　　　(C) 它們不能吸收。　　　　(D) 它們不能熔化。

　　　* combine (kəmˈbaɪn) *v.* 聯合；結合　　boil (bɔɪl) *v.* 煮
　　　　absorb (əbˈsɔrb) *v.* 吸收　　melt (mɛlt) *v.* 熔化

37. (**C**) Sonia demanded a raise in pay.
　　　桑妮亞要求加薪。

　　　(A) 她考慮要加薪。　　　　(B) 她加了薪。
　　　(C) 她要求加薪。　　　　　(D) 她考慮加薪。

　　　* demand (dɪˈmænd) *v.* 要求　　raise (rez) *n.* 加薪

38. (**D**) Paggy located the city on the map.
佩姬在地圖上找出這個城市的位置。

    (A) 佩姬認爲這個城市在地圖上。
    (B) 佩姬在地圖上把這個城市包圍起來。
    (C) 佩姬將地圖上的這個城市著色。
    (D) 佩姬在地圖上發現這個城市。

    * locate〔lo'ket〕*v.* 找出~的位置　　surround〔sə'raʊnd〕*v.* 包圍

39. (**C**) Rachel attached the sheets of paper together.
瑞秋把紙張貼在一起。

    (A) 她把紙張貼上標籤。　　(B) 她把紙張剪掉。
    (C) 她把紙張接在一起。　　(D) 她把紙張貼上郵票。

    * attach〔ə'tætʃ〕*v.* 貼上　　label〔'lebl〕*v.* 貼上標籤
    stamp〔stæmp〕*v.* 貼上郵票

40. (**B**) Rosa has such a good plan that I think it should be put into practice.
羅莎有一個如此好的計畫，我覺得應該實施。

    (A) 它應該被浪費掉。　　(B) 它應該被實施。
    (C) 它應該被限制。　　(D) 它應該被丟棄。

    * *put into practice* 實施　　implement〔'ɪmplə,mɛnt〕*v.* 實施

41. (**B**) This chair is on sale.
這種椅子在拍賣。

    (A) 價格已提高。　　(B) 價格已減低。
    (C) 椅子已賣出。　　(D) 椅子不賣。

    * *on sale* 拍賣　　reduce〔rɪ'djus〕*v.* 減低

42. (**B**) Avoid anyone with a cold.
避免與感冒的人接觸。

    (A) 允許他留在裡面。　　(B) 遠離他。
    (C) 對他友善。　　(D) 使他保持溫暖。

    * avoid〔ə'vɔɪd〕*v.* 避免

43.(**D**) The fish was too rare.
魚太生了。

    (A) 魚美味可口。   (B) 魚太硬了。

    (C) 魚煮得很好。   (D) <u>魚煮得不夠熟。</u>

    * rare〔rɛr〕*adj.* 未完全煮熟的   tough〔tʌf〕*adj.* （肉等）硬的

44.(**C**) The attack was repelled.
攻擊被擊退。

    (A) 攻擊被增強。   (B) 攻擊很成功。

    (C) <u>攻擊被擊退。</u>   (D) 攻擊命令被下達。

    * repel〔rɪ'pɛl〕*v.* 擊退   reinforce〔͵riɪn'fors〕*v.* 增強
    fight off 擊退

45.(**C**) The teacher thought his student had the right answer.
老師認為他的學生有正確答案。

    (A) 他教他學生正確答案。   (B) 他想要他學生教他正確答案。

    (C) <u>他相信他學生有正確的答案。</u> (D) 他的學生教他正確答案。

46.(**A**) John must go to the dentist today.
約翰今天必須去看牙醫。

    (A) <u>約翰必須去。</u>   (B) 約翰能去。

    (C) 約翰可能會去。   (D) 約翰應該去。

    * dentist〔'dɛntɪst〕*n.* 牙醫

47.(**C**) I bought a brand-new car yesterday.
我昨天買了一輛全新的車子。

    (A) 車子以前被用過。   (B) 不是新車。

    (C) <u>是一輛全新的車。</u>   (D) 是一輛二手車。

    * ***brand-new*** 全新的   ***second-hand*** 二手的

48.(**C**) I am preparing the coffee now.
我現在正在準備咖啡。

    (A) 我正在買。   (B) 我正在分配。

    (C) <u>我正在煮。</u>   (D) 我正在比較。

49. (**D**) The medicine for my headache works.

治我頭痛的藥有效。

    (A) 我頭疼得很厲害。   (B) 儘管我頭痛，我仍有許多工作。

    (C) 有人給我頭痛藥。   (D) <u>這藥治好了我的頭痛。</u>

50. (**B**) The student failed the examination.

學生考試不及格。

    (A) 他輕鬆地過了。   (B) <u>他沒成功。</u>

    (C) 他還沒考試。   (D) 他得到好成績。

    * fail〔fel〕*v.* 不及格

51. (**A**) M：Did you have a good talk with Edward？

    W：Yes, he talked very frankly.

How did Edward talk？

男：你和愛德華聊得好嗎？

女：是啊，他說話很坦白。

愛德華講話如何？

    (A) <u>他講話誠實且開放。</u>   (B) 他講話安靜而緩慢。

    (C) 他講話速度很快且充滿活力。   (D) 他講話鎮定而體貼。

    * frankly〔'fræŋklɪ〕*adv.* 坦白地

    energetically〔ˌɛnəˈdʒɛtɪkəlɪ〕*adv.* 充滿活力地

    calmly〔'kɑmlɪ〕*adv.* 鎮定地   thoughtfully〔'θɔtfəlɪ〕*adv.* 體貼地

52. (**C**) M：How did the accident occur？

    W：I don't know. It happened suddenly.

How did the accident occur？

男：意外如何發生？

女：我不知道，突然發生的。

意外是如何發生的？

    (A) 及時發生   (B) 逐漸發生

    (C) <u>突然發生</u>   (D) 沈悶地發生

    * suddenly〔'sʌdn̩lɪ〕*adv.* 突然地   ***in time*** 及時

    gradually〔'grædʒuəlɪ〕*adv.* 逐漸地   ***all at once*** 突然

    tediously〔'tidɪəslɪ〕*adv.* 沈悶地

53. (**B**) M : Where is Samuel?

W : He's gone to town.

What did the woman say about Samuel?

男：山繆爾在哪裡？

女：他進城去了。

這位女士說了山繆爾怎樣了？

(A) 他會進城。　　　　　　　(B) 他已進城了。

(C) 他應該進城。　　　　　　(D) 他早該進城了。

54. (**B**) M : Why aren't you with your sister?

W : Because they told us to split up.

What did the woman say?

男：妳爲何不跟妳的姊姊一起？

女：因爲他們告訴我們要分開。

這位女士說什麼？

(A) 他們告訴我們走慢一點。

(B) 他們告訴我們要分開。

(C) 他們告訴我們要合作。

(D) 他們告訴我們快點。

* *split up* 分開　　separate ('sɛpə,ret) *v.* 分開

cooperate (ko'ɑpə,ret) *v.* 合作

55. (**A**) M : Well Jenny, how is your mother?

W : She picked up a little weight.

What did the woman mean?

男：珍妮，妳媽媽如何？

女：她體重有點增加。

這位女士是什麼意思？

(A) 她胖了幾磅。　　　　　　(B) 她選擇了正確的磅秤。

(C) 她的舉重改善了。　　　　(D) 她減了一些重量。

* *pick up weight* 體重增加　　select (sə'lɛkt) *v.* 選擇

scale (skel) *n.* 磅秤　　improve (ɪm'pruv) *v.* 改善

weight lifting 舉重　　*lose weight* 體重減少

56. (**C**) W : Are you taking driving lessons?

M : No, I am afraid to drive a car.

W : Well, I hope you'll change your mind.

What did the man say?

女：你正在上駕駛課嗎？

男：不，我害怕開車。

女：好吧！我希望你會改變你的心意。

這位男士說什麼？

(A) 他正在上駕駛課。　　　　(B) 他希望改變心意。

(C) 他害怕開車。　　　　　　(D) 他很快會去上駕駛課。

　* *change one's mind* 改變心意

57. (**D**) M : I thought the panel discussion was going to be held this afternoon.

W : It was put off.

What happened to the panel discussion?

男：我想小組討論今天下午會舉行。

女：延期了。

小組討論怎麼了？

(A) 在早上舉行　　　　　(B) 按照計劃舉行

(C) 在不同的地方舉行　　(D) 延期

　* panel (ˊpænḷ) *n.* 討論小組　　　*put off* 延期

　　as scheduled 按照計畫　　postpone (postˊpon) *v.* 延期

58. (**A**) W : Why didn't you arrive on time?

M : My car stalled on the highway.

What happened to the man's car on the highway?

女：為何你沒有準時到達？

男：我的車子在高速公上無法發動。

這位男士的車子在高速公路上發生了什麼事？

(A) 停住了　　　　　(B) 開得很快

(C) 發生意外　　　　(D) 爆胎

　* stall (stɔl) *v.* （車子）無法發動

　　flat tire 爆胎

59.(**A**) W：That's a powerful engine. Does it have a propeller?

M：Yes, it does, and it rotates at a very fast rate of speed.

What did he say the propeller does?

女：那個引擎很有力。有推進器嗎？

男：有，而且旋轉得非常快速。

他說推進器怎樣？

(A) 會轉動　　(B) 關起來　　(C) 停止　　(D) 開始

* propeller〔prə'pɛlə〕*n.* 推進器　　rotate〔'rotet〕*v.* 旋轉

60.(**C**) M：I thought you sent your maid out to do your shopping.

W：Well, sometimes I go shopping by myself.

How often does the woman go shopping?

男：我以爲妳派女傭來買東西。

女：嗯，有時候我會自己買。

這位女士多常去購物？

(A) 經常　　(B) 從未　　(C) <u>偶爾</u>　　(D) 常常

* occasionally〔ə'keʒənlɪ〕*adv.* 偶爾

It doesn't matter if you win or lose, until you lose.

你的輸贏並不重要，直到你輸了爲止。

LISTENING TEST 11

● *Directions for questions 1-25. You will hear questions on the test tape. Select the one item A, B, C or D which answers the question correctly, and mark your answer sheet.*

1. A. to eat a lot
   B. to buy an encyclopedia
   C. to solve her mental troubles
   D. to look up the meanings of words

2. A. to get his suit pressed   B. to have a drink
   C. to get a haircut   D. to do some shopping

3. A. lively   B. intense
   C. vital   D. tense

4. A. There were reservations for one room.
   B. One man was at the hotel.
   C. Only one room was ready to be used.
   D. There was one room at the hotel.

5. A. They are turning on the lights.
   B. They are turning the lights on and off.
   C. They are turning off the lights.
   D. They are watching the lights.

6. A. to meet his friend's plane   B. on the civilian side
   C. by taxi   D. only twenty minutes

7. A. four miles   B. a high school
   C. a three-story building   D. three months

8. A. factories   B. animals
   C. schools   D. reserves

9. A. a fight   B. a night
    C. a flight   D. a light

10. A. the sheet   B. the screen
    C. the shirt   D. the sleeves

11. A. a light that burns steadily
    B. a flying object
    C. a dim light
    D. the condition for seeing things at a distance

12. A. the size of the box   B. the form of the box
    C. the color of the box   D. the make of the box

13. A. in a shopping center
    B. in an area of private homes
    C. in a large motel
    D. in a small apartment house

14. A. by looking at it   B. by driving it
    C. by paying for it   D. by repairing it

15. A. Yes, it will arrive early.   B. No, it won't be canceled
    C. Yes, it came yesterday.   D. No, it is a private plane.

16. A. to board the ship   B. to see her friends off
    C. to get a haircut   D. to see the factory

17. A. Janet's brother   B. Janet's friend
    C. Janet herself   D. Janet's father

18. A. a non-commissioned officer   B. a private
    C. a commissioned officer   D. a major

19. A. every one of them   B. most of them
    C. several of them   D. lots of them

20. A. much   B. few
    C. some   D. several

21. A. the inside of a house
    B. the outside of a building
    C. the contents of a magazine
    D. the cover of a book

22. A. the name of the author   B. the name of the book
    C. the publisher of the book   D. the author of the book

23. A. an invisible plane   B. a jet plane
    C. a fleet of aircraft   D. a flying saucer

24. A. stamping packages   B. depositing letters
    C. filing envelopes   D. collecting stamps

25. A. It'll stay in good condition.   B. It'll decay quickly.
    C. It'll remain unchanged.   D. It'll be safe to eat.

● *Directions for questions 26-50. You will hear statements on the test tape. Select the one answer A, B, C, or D which comes closest to the meaning of the statement and mark your answer sheet.*

26. A. There was a single sound of thunder.
    B. There was thunder at the beginning.
    C. There wasn't any thunder.
    D. There was thunder now and then.

27. A. He was a lazy player.
    B. He was a fair player.
    C. He was an outstanding player.
    D. He was an average player.

28. A. The unexpected typhoon took many lives.
B. The mild typhoon took many lives.
C. The lively typhoon took many lives.
D. The dreadful typhoon took many lives.

29. A. They had some trouble.
B. They had a great deal of trouble.
C. They had a bit of trouble.
D. They have very little trouble.

30. A. Air can be spent.
B. Air can be heated.
C. Its volume will be decreased.
D. Its volume can be increased.

31. A. He is very alert.
B. He is used to them.
C. He is not sure about them.
D. He knows all the names.

32. A. You shouldn't skip class.
B. You shouldn't be in class today.
C. You shouldn't attend class.
D. You should never go to class.

33. A. He is touching something.
B. He is feeling a color.
C. He is feeling sad.
D. He is wearing in blue.

34. A. I have a business appointment.
B. I have a social appointment.
C. I have a medical appointment.
D. I don't know the date today.

35. A. It is a liquid.   B. It will burn easily.
    C. It is a fuel.   D. It will not burn.

36. A. Cindy must go out of town.
    B. Cindy must go to the city center.
    C. Cindy must go to town.
    D. Cindy must go to the suburbs.

37. A. She had mostly paper money.
    B. She had mostly coins.
    C. She had lots of money with her.
    D. She had very little money with her.

38. A. He was afraid.   B. He was nervous.
    C. He was relaxed.   D. He was unhappy.

39. A. Get on the television.   B. Turn the television.
    C. Give it power.   D. Put it out.

40. A. She had to go to the dentist.
    B. She liked going to the dentist.
    C. She feared going to the dentist.
    D. She wanted to pay the dentist.

41. A. It is not warm.   B. It is not new.
    C. It has been sold.   D. It is made of gold.

42. A. It looks out on Fifth Avenue.
    B. It is near Fifth Avenue.
    C. It is across from Fifth Avenue.
    D. It is away from Fifth Avenue.

43. A. He repaired the car.
    B. He watched the car for an hour.
    C. He replaced the car.
    D. He cleaned the car.

44. A. It was very warm.　　　B. I couldn't see the sun.
　　C. It was windy.　　　　　D. I couldn't see the ground.

45. A. They are too big.
　　B. They are too small.
　　C. They are the wrong color.
　　D. They are the correct size.

46. A. I'm old.　　　　　　　B. I'm not angry.
　　C. I'm rich.　　　　　　　D. I'm weak.

47. A. He has the money.　　　B. He bought the car.
　　C. He will sell it.　　　　D. He may buy it.

48. A. Don't hurry.　　　　　B. Take ten cents.
　　C. Take your tin cup.　　　D. Hurry, you're late.

49. A. The weather got worse today.
　　B. The clouds went away this afternoon.
　　C. It was cloudy last night.
　　D. It was clear yesterday.

50. A. He was afraid to fly solo.
　　B. He wasn't afraid to fly solo.
　　C. He wasn't frightened by the noise.
　　D. He wasn't going to fly solo.

● *Directions for questions 51-60. You will hear dialogs on the test*
　tape. Select the correct answer A, B, C, or D and mark your
　answer sheet.

51. A. Mrs. Arnold was tired after 30 years.
　　B. Mrs. Arnold stopped working after 30 years.
　　C. Mrs. Arnold stopped working for 30 years.
　　D. Mrs. Arnold tried to work for 30 years.

52. A. a loan   B. a dollar bill
     C. a quarter   D. a stamp

53. A. The coffee is good.
     B. The restaurant is always open.
     C. The restaurant is close to the office.
     D. The food is good.

54. A. a wrench   B. the scissors
     C. a file   D. the hammer

55. A. wait a minute   B. take the telephone line
     C. hang up the phone   D. open the telephone book

56. A. He answered, "No."   B. He answered, "Sometimes."
     C. He answered, "Yes."   D. He answered, "Maybe."

57. A. It runs around west.   B. It runs straight to the west.
     C. It runs about west.   D. It runs from the west.

58. A. He couldn't go to the party.
     B. He might go to the party.
     C. He would go to the party.
     D. He would let her know.

59. A. The hotel has no rooms for Mr. Woolf.
     B. The hotel cannot make any reservations.
     C. Mr. Woolf will return in a month.
     D. The hotel will keep a double room for him.

60. A. Each system is the specific job of an engineer.
     B. Each system is planned to do a particular job.
     C. Each system must have several functions.
     D. Designing the system is a particular job.

ECL 聽力測驗 [11] 詳解

1. (**D**) Sonia often keeps a dictionary at hand.
Why does she need it?
桑妮雅經常隨身帶著一本字典。/ 爲何她需要它？

    (A) 爲了吃很多   (B) 爲了買一本百科全書
    (C) 爲了解決她的精神問題   (D) <u>爲了查字義</u>

    * *at hand* 在手邊　　encyclopedia (ɪn͵saɪklə'pidɪə) *n.* 百科全書
    mental ('mɛntḷ) *adj.* 心理的；精神的　　*look up* 查閱

2. (**C**) Why is Tad going to the barber shop?
泰德爲何去理髮廳？

    (A) 去燙西裝   (B) 去喝一杯   (C) <u>去理髮</u>   (D) 去購物

    * barber ('bɑrbɚ) *n.* 理髮師　　*barber shop* 理髮廳
    suit (sut , sɪut , sjut) *n.* 套裝；西裝　　press (prɛs) *v.* 燙 (衣服)

3. (**A**) The book has a vivid description of the scenery in Italy.
What kind of description does the book have?
這本書對義大利的風景有生動的描述。/ 該書有何種描述？

    (A) <u>生動的</u>   (B) 劇烈的
    (C) 生命的；非常重要的   (D) 緊張的

    * vivid ('vɪvɪd) *adj.* 生動的　　scenery ('sinərɪ) *n.* 風景
    description (dɪ'skrɪpʃən) *n.* 描述
    lively ('laɪvlɪ) *adj.* 生動的；寫實的　　intense (ɪn'tɛns) *adj.* 劇烈的
    vital ('vaɪtḷ) *adj.* 生命的；非常重要的　　tense (tɛns) *adj.* 緊張的

4. (**C**) The front desk clerk said that there was only one room
available at the hotel. What did the clerk mean?
櫃台職員說旅館只剩一個房間。/ 職員的意思爲何？

    (A) 有一個房間被預訂。   (B) 旅館有一個人。
    (C) <u>只有一個房間可供使用。</u>   (D) 旅館有一個房間。

    * *front desk* 櫃台　　available (ə'veləbḷ) *adj.* 可利用的
    reservation (͵rɛzɚ'veʃən) *n.* 預訂

5. (**B**) Shirley said, "They are blinking the lights."
What did she mean?
雪莉說：「他們將燈開開關關。」／她的意思為何？

(A) 他們打開燈。　　　　　　　　(B) <u>他們將燈又開又關。</u>
(C) 他們關掉燈。　　　　　　　　(D) 他們看著燈。

* blink〔blɪŋk〕*v.* 閃光　　***turn on*** 打開
　on and off 斷斷續續地　　***turn off*** 關掉

6. (**C**) How did Jack return from the airport?
傑克如何從機場回來？

(A) 去接朋友的飛機　　　　　　　(B) 站在人民立場
(C) <u>搭計程車</u>　　　　　　　　(D) 只有二十分鐘

* civilian〔sə'vɪljən〕*adj.* 人民的

7. (**A**) How far is it to the school library?
到學校圖書館有多遠？

(A) <u>四哩</u>　　　　　　　　　　(B) 一所中學
(C) 一棟三層樓建築物　　　　　　(D) 三個月

* story〔'storɪ, 'stɔrɪ〕*n.* 樓層

8. (**B**) David went to the zoo yesterday. What did he see there?
大衛昨天去動物園。／他在那裏看到什麼？

(A) 工廠　　　　(B) <u>動物</u>　　　　(C) 學校　　　　(D) 保留區

* factory〔'fæktrɪ〕*n.* 工廠　　reserve〔rɪ'zɜv〕*n.* 保留區

9. (**C**) Louis is planning for a long flight.
What is he planning for?
路易斯正籌劃一次遠程的飛行。／他正在籌劃什麼？

(A) 一場格鬥　　　　　　　　　　(B) 一夜
(C) <u>一次飛行</u>　　　　　　　　(D) 一盞燈

* flight〔flaɪt〕*n.* 飛行　　fight〔faɪt〕*n.* 格鬥；打架

10. (**D**) Mark doesn't like his sweater because the sleeves are too short. What is too short?

馬克不喜歡他的毛衣，因爲袖子太短了。/ 什麼東西太短？

(A) 被單　　　(B) 屏風　　　(C) 襯衫　　　(D) 袖子

* sleeve (sliv) *n.* 袖子　　sheet (ʃit) *n.* 被單
screen (skrin) *n.* 屏風；遮簾

11. (**D**) What is visibility?

何謂能見度？

(A) 持續點燃的燈　　　　　(B) 飛行物體
(C) 幽暗的燈光　　　　　　(D) 從遠處所見物體的狀況

* visibility (,vɪzə'bɪlətɪ) *n.* 能見度　　burn (bɝn) *v.* 點燃
steadily ('stɛdəlɪ) *adv.* 持續地　　object ('ɑbdʒɪkt) *n.* 物體
dim (dɪm) *adj.* 幽暗的　　distance ('dɪstəns) *n.* 距離

12. (**B**) Nancy wanted to know the shape of the box. What did she want to know?

南西想知道盒子的形狀。/ 她想知道什麼？

(A) 盒子的大小　　　　　　(B) 盒子的形狀
(C) 盒子的顏色　　　　　　(D) 盒子的製造牌子

* shape (ʃep) *n.* 形狀　　form (fɔrm) *n.* 形狀
make (mek) *n.* 製造品牌

13. (**B**) Adam lives in a residential area. Where does he live?

亞當住在住宅區。/ 他住在哪裏？

(A) 購物中心　　　　　　　(B) 私人住宅區
(C) 大型汽車旅館　　　　　(D) 小公寓

* residential (,rɛzə'dɛnʃəl) *adj.* 居住的
private ('praɪvɪt) *adj.* 私人的　　motel (mo'tɛl) *n.* 汽車旅館

14. (**B**) How do you check the performance of the new car?

你如何檢查新車的性能？

(A) 觀看它　　(B) 開它　　(C) 付錢買它　　(D) 修理它

* performance (pɚ'fɔrməns) *n.* 表現

15. (**B**) Will this flight be canceled?

這班飛機將被取消嗎?

(A) 是的,它會提早到達。　　　　(B) 不,不會取消。

(C) 是的,它昨天到。　　　　　　(D) 不,它是私人飛機。

* cancel〔'kænsḷ〕v. 取消

16. (**B**) Why did Vicky go to the airport?

維琪爲何去機場?

(A) 去搭船　　(B) 爲朋友送行　　(C) 剪頭髮　　(D) 參觀工廠

* board〔bord〕v. 上船　　*see off* 送行　　haircut〔'hɛr,kʌt〕n. 剪髮

17. (**C**) Janet fixed the broken chair herself. Who fixed the chair?

珍娜自己修好了那張壞掉的椅子。/ 誰修好了那張椅子?

(A) 珍娜的哥哥　　　　　　　(B) 珍娜的朋友

(C) 珍娜自己　　　　　　　　(D) 珍娜的爸爸

18. (**A**) Who is a sergeant?

中士是何許人物?

(A) 軍士　　(B) 士兵　　　　(C) 軍官　　(D) 少校

* sergeant〔'sɑrdʒənt〕n. 中士　　commission〔kə'mɪʃən〕v. 任命

 non-commissioned officer 軍士;士官　　private〔'praɪvɪt〕n. 士兵

 commissioned officer 軍官　　major〔'medʒɚ〕n. 少校

19. (**B**) Practically all American homes have TVs.

How many homes have TVs?

幾乎所有的美國家庭都有電視。/ 有多少家庭有電視?

(A) 每一家　　(B) 大部分家庭　　(C) 好幾家　　(D) 很多家

* practically〔'præktɪkḷɪ〕adv. 幾乎

20. (**A**) Linda has a lot of time.

What is the meaning of "a lot of"?

琳達有許多時間。/ "a lot of" 的意思爲何?

(A) 很多　　(B) 很少　　　　(C) 一些　　(D) 數個

21. (**A**) What does an interior designer design?
　　室內設計師設計什麼？

　　(A) 房屋的內部　　　　　　　(B) 建築物的外部
　　(C) 雜誌的目錄　　　　　　　(D) 書本的封面

　　* interior (ɪn'tɪrɪɚ) *adj.* 內部的　　designer (dɪ'zaɪnɚ) *n.* 設計師
　　　contents ('kɑntɛnts) *n. pl.* 目錄　　cover ('kʌvɚ) *n.* 封面

22. (**B**) What is the title of a book?
　　一本書的書名是指什麼？

　　(A) 作者的名字　　　　　　　(B) 本書的名稱
　　(C) 本書的出版商　　　　　　(D) 本書的作者

　　* title ('taɪtl̩) *n.* 題目；名稱　　author ('ɔθɚ) *n.* 作者
　　　publisher ('pʌblɪʃɚ) *n.* 出版社；出版商

23. (**D**) What is a UFO?
　　幽浮是什麼？

　　(A) 看不見的飛機　　　　　　(B) 噴射機
　　(C) 一隊飛機　　　　　　　　(D) 飛碟

　　* UFO ('ju'ɛf'o , 'jufo) *n.* 幽浮；不明飛行物體
　　　(= *unidentified flying object*)
　　　invisible (ɪn'vɪzəbl̩) *adj.* 看不見的
　　　jet (dʒɛt) *n.* 噴射機　　fleet (flit) *n.* 一隊
　　　aircraft ('ɛr,kræft) *n.* 飛行器
　　　saucer ('sɔsɚ) *n.* 飛碟；碟狀物

24. (**B**) What is a mailbox used for?
　　郵筒的用途是什麼？

　　(A) 貼郵票於包裹上　　　　　(B) 存放信件
　　(C) 將信封歸檔　　　　　　　(D) 收集郵票

　　* mailbox ('mel,bɑks) *n.* 郵筒
　　　stamp (stæmp) *v.* 貼上 (郵票) *n.* 郵票
　　　package ('pækɪdʒ) *n.* 包裹　　deposit (dɪ'pɑzɪt) *v.* 存放
　　　file (faɪl) *v.* 編檔保存　　envelope ('ɛnvə,lop) *n.* 信封
　　　collect (kə'lɛkt) *v.* 收集

25. (**B**) Some food spoils easily if it's not put in the refrigerator. What happens if some food is not placed in the refrigerator?

如果沒有放在冰箱，有些食物很容易便壞掉。

有些食物如果沒有放在冰箱會怎樣？

 (A) 保持在良好狀況   (B) 很快腐壞

 (C) 保持不變   (D) 很安全可以吃

 * spoil〔spɔɪl〕 v. 變壞   refrigerator〔rɪ'frɪdʒə‚retə〕 n. 冰箱
   decay〔dɪ'ke〕 v. 腐壞   remain〔rɪ'men〕 v. 保持

26. (**D**) During the shower, there was occasional thunder.

陣雨中偶有打雷。

 (A) 只有一聲雷聲。   (B) 剛開始有打雷。

 (C) 沒有打雷。   (D) 偶爾有打雷。

 * occasional〔ə'keʒənl〕 adj. 偶爾的   single〔'sɪŋgl〕 adj. 單獨的
   now and then 有時候；偶爾

27. (**C**) Tom was an eminent basketball player.

湯姆是位傑出的籃球選手。

 (A) 他是位懶惰的選手。   (B) 他是位普通的選手。

 (C) 他是位傑出的選手。   (D) 他是位普通的選手。

 * eminent〔'ɛmənənt〕 adj. 傑出的   fair〔fɛr〕 adj. 普通的
   outstanding〔aʊt'stændɪŋ〕 adj. 傑出的
   average〔'ævərɪdʒ〕 adj. 普通的

28. (**D**) The terrible typhoon that swept through the country took many lives.

橫掃全國的可怕颱風奪走許多人命。

 (A) 突如其來的颱風奪走許多人命。

 (B) 輕度颱風奪走許多人命。

 (C) 活潑的颱風奪走許多人命。

 (D) 可怕的颱風奪走許多人命。

 * terrible〔'tɛrəbl〕 adj. 可怕的   mild〔maɪld〕 adj. 溫和的
   lively〔'laɪvlɪ〕 adj. 活潑的   dreadful〔'drɛdfəl〕 adj. 可怕的

29. (**B**) They had considerable troubles in getting their application approved.

在申請獲准過程中，他們遇到不少麻煩。

(A) 他們有一些麻煩。   (B) 他們有許多麻煩。

(C) 他們有一點麻煩。   (D) 他們的麻煩很少。

* considerable〔kən'sɪdərəbḷ〕 *adj.* 數量大的；不少的

　application〔͵æplə'keʃən〕 *n.* 申請

　approve〔ə'pruv〕 *v.* 核准　　***a great deal of*** 很多的

30. (**D**) Air can be expanded.

空氣可以膨脹。

(A) 空氣可以消耗。   (B) 空氣可以加熱。

(C) 它的體積會縮小。   (D) 它的體積可以增大。

* expand〔ɪk'spænd〕 *v.* 擴大；膨脹　　heat〔hit〕 *v.* 使變熱

　volume〔'vɑljəm〕 *n.* 體積　　decrease〔dɪ'kris〕 *v.* 減少

31. (**C**) The child is confused by all the names.

這位小孩將所有的名字搞混了。

(A) 他非常機警。   (B) 他習慣於它們。

(C) 他對所有名字不確定。   (D) 他知道所有的名字。

* confused〔kən'fjuzd〕 *adj.* 迷惑的；混亂的

　alert〔ə'lɝt〕 *adj.* 機警的　　***be used to*** 習慣於

32. (**A**) You should never cut class.

你絕對不可以翹課。

(A) 你不應該翹課。   (B) 你今天不應該來上課。

(C) 你不應該去上課。   (D) 你應該永遠不上課。

33. (**C**) The student is feeling a little blue today.

這位學生今天心情沮喪。

(A) 他正在碰某樣東西。   (B) 他在感覺一個顏色。

(C) 他覺得難過。   (D) 他穿著藍色的衣服。

* blue〔blu〕 *adj.* 憂鬱的；沮喪的

34. (**B**) I have a date with my boyfriend this evening.
今晚我和男友有約會。

(A) 我有個商務約會。　　　　(B) 我有個社交約會。
(C) 我有個醫療約會。　　　　(D) 我不知道今天的日期。

＊ date〔det〕*n.* 約會；日期　　social〔'soʃəl〕*adj.* 社交的
medical〔'mɛdɪkḷ〕*adj.* 醫療的；需就醫的

35. (**B**) Gasoline is flammable.
汽油易燃。

(A) 它是種液體。　　　　(B) 它容易燃燒。
(C) 它是種燃料。　　　　(D) 它不會燃燒。

＊ gasoline〔'gæsḷ,in , ,gæsḷ'in〕*n.* 汽油
flammable〔'flæməbḷ〕*adj.* 可燃性的；易燃的

36. (**B**) Cindy has to go downtown.
辛蒂必須去市中心。

(A) 辛蒂必須出城。　　　　(B) 辛蒂必須去市中心。
(C) 辛蒂必須進城。　　　　(D) 辛蒂必須去市郊。

＊ downtown〔'daʊn'taʊn〕*adv.* 在市中心
center〔'sɛntɚ〕*n.* 中心　　suburb〔'sʌbɝb〕*n.* 市郊

37. (**D**) She had hardly any money with her.
她幾乎沒有錢。

(A) 她的錢大多是紙鈔。　　　　(B) 她的錢大多是硬幣。
(C) 她有許多錢。　　　　(D) 她的錢非常少。

＊ hardly〔'hɑrdlɪ〕*adv.* 幾乎不
mostly〔'mostlɪ〕*adv.* 多半地；主要地

38. (**C**) Bob talked easily to everybody.
鮑伯很容易和人談起話來。

(A) 他很害怕。　　(B) 他很緊張。　　(C) 他很隨和。　　(D) 他不愉快。

＊ nervous〔'nɝvəs〕*adj.* 緊張的
relaxed〔rɪ'lækst〕*adj.* 隨和的；不拘形式的

39. (**C**) Turn that television on.
打開電視機。

(A) 爬到電視機上。　　　　　(B) 旋轉電視機。
(C) 給它動力。　　　　　　　(D) 熄滅它。

* *turn on* 打開
  get on 爬上；登上　　*put out* 熄滅

40. (**C**) Alice said that she dreaded going to the dentist.
愛麗絲說她害怕去看牙醫。

(A) 她必須去看牙醫。　　　　(B) 她喜歡去看牙醫。
(C) 她害怕去看牙醫。　　　　(D) 她想付錢給牙醫。

* dread (drɛd) v. 害怕　　dentist ('dɛntɪst) n. 牙醫
  fear (fɪr) v. 害怕

41. (**B**) This table lamp is old.
這個檯燈舊了。

(A) 它不暖和。　　　　　　　(B) 它不是新的。
(C) 它已經賣掉了。　　　　　(D) 它是金子做的。

* lamp (læmp) n. 燈

42. (**A**) My room faces Fifth Avenue.
我的房間面對著第五街。

(A) 它面向第五街。　　　　　(B) 它靠近第五街。
(C) 它在第五街對面。　　　　(D) 它遠離第五街。

* face (fes) v. 面對　　avenue ('ævə,nu , -,nju) n. 大街
  look out 面向

43. (**A**) The mechanic fixed my car in one hour.
技工在一小時內修理好我的車。

(A) 他修理車子。　　　　　　(B) 他觀察車子一小時。
(C) 他更換車子。　　　　　　(D) 他清理車子。

* mechanic (mə'kænɪk) n. 技工　　repair (rɪ'pɛr) v. 修理
  replace (rɪ'ples) v. 更換

44. (**B**) The sky was overcast before the typhoon.
在颱風之前，天空烏雲密佈。
(A) 天氣非常暖和。　　　　(B) 我看不到太陽。
(C) 風很強。　　　　　　　(D) 我無法看到地面。
* overcast ('ovəˌkæst , ˌovə'kæst) *adj.* 多雲的；陰暗的

45. (**D**) These boots fit me.
這靴子合我的腳。
(A) 它們太大。　　　　　　(B) 它們太小。
(C) 它們的顏色不對。　　　(D) 它們的尺寸正確。
* boot (but) *n.* 靴子　　fit (fɪt) *v.* 適合

46. (**D**) I feel under the weather today.
我今天覺得不舒服。
(A) 我老了。　(B) 我沒有生氣。　(C) 我很有錢。　(D) 我覺得虛弱。
* *under the weather* 身體不適

47. (**D**) He will buy the car if he has the money.
如果他有錢，他就會買那部車。
(A) 他有錢。　　　　　　　(B) 他買了那部車。
(C) 他將賣了它。　　　　　(D) 他可能會買下它。

48. (**A**) Take your time.
慢慢來。
(A) 別急。　　　　　　　　(B) 拿十分錢。
(C) 拿你的錫杯。　　　　　(D) 快點，你遲到了。
* *take one's time* 慢慢來　　hurry ('hɜɪ) *v.* 匆忙　　tin (tɪn) *n.* 錫

49. (**B**) The weather was cloudy this morning but it cleared up
in the afternoon.
今天早上天氣多雲，可是下午就轉晴了。
(A) 今天的天氣變得愈糟。　(B) 今天下午雲散了。
(C) 昨晚天氣多雲。　　　　(D) 昨天天氣晴朗。
* cloudy ('klaʊdɪ) *adj.* 多雲的

50. (**B**) Strauss was not scared to fly solo.
史特勞斯不怕單獨飛行。

(A) 他害怕單獨飛行。　　　　　(B) 他不怕單獨飛行。
(C) 他沒有被噪音嚇倒。　　　　(D) 他沒有要單獨飛行。

* scared〔skɛrd〕*adj.* 害怕的　　solo〔'solo〕*adv.* 單獨地
frighten〔'fraɪtn̩〕*v.* 使驚嚇

51. (**B**) W：When did Mrs. Arnold retire?
M：She retired after working for thirty years.
What does the man mean?
女：亞諾太太何時退休?
男：工作三十年後她就退休了。
這位男士的意思為何?

(A) 三十年後亞諾太太疲倦了。　(B) 三十年後亞諾太太停止工作。
(C) 亞諾太太停止工作三十年。　(D) 亞諾太太嘗試工作三十年。

* retire〔rɪ'taɪr〕*v.* 退休

52. (**C**) W：What did you give your nephew when you saw him?
M：A coin.
What did the man give his nephew?
女：當你見到你姪子時,你給他什麼東西?
男：一枚硬幣。
這位男士給他的姪子什麼?

(A) 貸款。　　　　　　　　　　(B) 一元紙鈔。
(C) 一個二角五分的硬幣。　　　(D) 一張郵票。

* nephew〔'nɛfju〕*n.* 姪子　　loan〔lon〕*n.* 貸款

53. (**B**) M：Why do you usually eat at this restaurant?
W：I like to eat here because it never closes.
What did the woman say about the restaurant?
男：妳為什麼常在這家餐廳吃飯?
女：我喜歡在這裏用餐,因為它從不打烊。
這位女士說餐廳如何?

(A) 咖啡很好。　　　　　　　　(B) 餐廳總是營業中。
(C) 餐廳靠近辦公室。　　　　　(D) 食物很好。

54. (**A**) M : Hand me that tool over there.

W : What do you need to do?

M : I need to tighten this bolt.

What tool does he need?

男：拿那邊的那支工具給我。

女：你要做什麼用？

男：我要鎖緊門閂。

他需要什麼工具？

(A) 扳手　　　　(B) 剪刀　　　　(C) 文件夾　　　　(D) 鐵鎚

　* tool〔tul〕*n.* 工具　　tighten〔'taɪtn〕*v.* 使堅固；勒緊
　bolt〔bolt〕*n.* 門閂　　wrench〔rɛntʃ〕*n.* 扳手
　scissors〔'sɪzəz〕*n.* 剪刀　　file〔faɪl〕*n.* 文件夾
　hammer〔'hæmə〕*n.* 鐵鎚

55. (**A**) M : Hello, is Vicky there?

W : Hold the line.

What does she want the man to do?

男：喂，維琪在嗎？

女：請稍等。

她要這位男士做什麼？

(A) 等一下　　　　　　　　(B) 拿起電話
(C) 掛斷電話　　　　　　　(D) 打開電話簿

　* *hold the line* 稍等　　*hang up* 掛斷

56. (**A**) M : Did Henry finally answer your question?

W : He certainly did and his answer was negative.

What did Henry answer?

男：亨利最後回答了妳的問題嗎？

女：當然，而且他的回答是否定的。

亨利回答什麼？

(A) 他回答：「不。」　　　　(B) 他回答：「有時候。」
(C) 他回答：「是。」　　　　(D) 他回答：「也許。」

　* negative〔'nɛgətɪv〕*adj.* 否定的

57. (**B**) M：Excuse me, Madam. I want to drive west. Should I stay on this road?

W：This road runs directly west.

How does the road run?

男：對不起，女士。我想往西開，我應該繼續走這條路嗎？

女：這條路筆直往西沿伸。

這條路如何延伸？

 (A) 它環繞西部延伸。   (B) 它往西筆直延伸。

 (C) 它在西部四處延伸。   (D) 它從西邊開始延伸。

 * directly〔dəˈrɛktlɪ〕*adv.* 筆直地

  straight〔stret〕*adv.* 一直線地；直地

58. (**C**) M：Will James be at the party tomorrow?

W：He said he'll go.

What did he say?

男：詹姆士明天會去舞會嗎？

女：他說他會去。

他說什麼？

 (A) 他無法去舞會。   (B) 他可能會去舞會。

 (C) 他會去舞會。   (D) 他會讓她知道。

59. (**C**) M：I enjoyed my stay in your hotel very much. In fact, I would like to make a reservation for two nights for next month.

W：Very good, Mr. Woolf.

What do we learn from this conversation?

男：我在貴旅館住得非常愉快。事實上，我想再預訂下個月二個晚上。

女：太好了，吳爾夫先生。

從對話中我們得知什麼？

 (A) 旅館沒有房間可給吳爾夫先生。

 (B) 旅館無法預訂。

 (C) 吳爾夫先生一個月後會再來。

 (D) 旅館會為他保留一間雙人房。

60. (**B**) W : I'd like to buy this car, but I didn't understand what you said about its systems.

M : Each system in an automobile is designed to do a specific job.

What did the man mean?

女：我想買這部車，可是我不了解你所說的系統。

男：一部車的每個系統都被設計來專司某項工作。

這位男士的意思為何？

(A) 每個系統都是工程師的指定工作。

(B) 每個系統都被設計來執行某項特殊的工作。

(C) 每個系統必須具備幾種功能。

(D) 設計系統是項特殊的工作。

* design (dɪ'zaɪn) v. 設計
specific (spɪ'sɪfɪk) adj. 指定的
engineer (͵ɛndʒə'nɪr) n. 工程師
particular (pə'tɪkjələ) adj. 特殊的
function ('fʌŋkʃən) n. 功能

How come it takes so little time for a child who is afraid of the dark to become a teen-ager who wants to stay out all night?

　　為什麼從一個怕黑的小孩，到成為一個整晚只想待在外面的青少年，只需要這麼短的時間？

LISTENING TEST 12

● *Directions for questions 1-25. You will hear questions on the test tape. Select the one item A, B, C or D which answers the question correctly, and mark your answer sheet.*

1. A. put some money in the bank
   B. look at his account
   C. take money out of his account
   D. account for the cashier's money

2. A. her father's mother
   C. her brother's father
   B. her father who is 90
   D. her mother's father

3. A. none
   C. a lot
   B. little
   D. very little

4. A. Yes, I like them.
   B. Yes, they are friends.
   C. Yes, they look the same.
   D. Yes, they will go on a trip.

5. A. buy some medicine
   C. get a private room
   B. see a doctor
   D. give some help

6. A. a swinging blade
   C. a jumping blade
   B. a vibrating blade
   D. a revolving blade

7. A. languages
   C. machines
   B. flowers
   D. animals

8. A. transformed
   C. composed
   B. translated
   D. transposed

9. A. at 5:30 a.m.   B. in the morning
   C. at 5:30 p.m.   D. at night

10. A. the temperature   B. the size
    C. the name   D. the color

11. A. Saturday   B. Tuesday
    C. Thursday   D. Friday

12. A. August   B. June
    C. April   D. September

13. A. Panama   B. Mexico
    C. Brazil   D. Argentina

14. A. He wants to get credit for it.
    B. He likes learning about animals.
    C. He doesn't like studying by himself.
    D. He feels the course is good for him.

15. A. erase the word   B. answer the door
    C. translate the sentence D. copy the paper

16. A. I have several coins.
    B. I weigh 130 pounds.
    C. I have eaten 3 times today.
    D. I have changed rooms many time.

17. A. Yes, I would like to correct it.
    B. Yes, I would like to destroy it.
    C. Yes, I like the size of the paper.
    D. Yes, I bought the paper to use here.

18. A. two days ago   B. yesterday
    C. a week ago   D. three days ago

19. A. No, she won't be smoking soon.
　　B. No, she isn't getting used to smoking.
　　C. Yes, she uses cigarettes when he smokes.
　　D. Yes, but she doesn't smoke now.

20. A. his lesson　　　　　B. will finish
　　C. his homework　　　 D. in a few minutes

21. A. have the letter written　　B. have the letter addressed
　　C. have the letter delivered　 D. have the letter sealed

22. A. animals　　　　　B. stars
　　C. plants　　　　　 D. machines

23. A. a list of telephone numbers
　　B. a group of workers
　　C. a place to eat
　　D. a new medicine

24. A. whether there was a reservation or not
　　B. whether the rooms were ready or not
　　C. whether there were vacant rooms or not
　　D. whether there were any clerks at the hotel or not

25. A. The wire is not good.
　　B. The wire is not covered for protection.
　　C. The wire is not carrying electricity.
　　D. The wire is not visible.

● *Directions for questions 26-50. You will hear statements on the test tape. Select the one answer A, B, C, or D which comes closest to the meaning of the statement and mark your answer sheet.*

26. A. He is a careful pilot.　　　B. He is a negligent pilot.
　　C. He is nervous pilot.　　　D. He is a careless pilot.

27. A. She saw a light in town.
    B. She saw a light far away.
    C. She saw a light at the station.
    D. She saw a light nearby.

28. A. You have to speak French.
    B. You enjoy speaking French.
    C. You have a chance to speak French.
    D. You like to speak French.

29. A. Steve will use the elevator.
    B. Steve will run the elevator.
    C. Steve will repair the elevator.
    D. Steve will study the elevator.

30. A. Tommy is 30, Jerry 15, Henry 25
    B. Tommy is 15, Jerry 20, Henry 30
    C. Tommy is 25, Jerry 30, Henry 20
    D. Tommy is 20, Jerry 15, Henry 30

31. A. Clark can go with James.
    B. James can't go with Clark.
    C. Clark can't go with Kevin.
    D. Kevin and James can go with Clark.

32. A. I will listen to every tape.
    B. He listened to all the tapes.
    C. I didn't listen to every tape.
    D. He listened to nothing in the tapes.

33. A. The crew stayed in the jet.
    B. The crew made repairs.
    C. The crew left the jet.
    D. The crew made some changes.

34. A. It doesn't have much power.
    B. It won't go up the hill.
    C. It won't go backward.
    D. It won't begin running.

35. A. He likes foods out of the garden.
    B. He likes a lot of food.
    C. He likes very sweet foods.
    D. He likes different kinds of foods.

36. A. I want to sell this radio.   B. I will buy this radio.
    C. I will follow this radio.   D. I have bought this radio.

37. A. Bruce called Louis.   B. Bruce hurt Louis.
    C. Bruce telephoned Louis.   D. Bruce met Louis.

38. A. She goes to parties with her friends.
    B. She rates her friends carefully.
    C. She jokes with her friends.
    D. She becomes annoyed with her friends.

39. A. He decided to get a shot.
    B. He decided to call it off.
    C. He decided to shoot at it.
    D. He decided to try it.

40. A. Look off the road.
    B. Watch the road closely.
    C. Stay away from the road.
    D. Close your eyes carefully.

41. A. He always works very hard.
    B. He is always sick.
    C. He is always very clean.
    D. He is always very strange.

42. A. He hears a highway noise.
    B. He hears an unfamiliar noise.
    C. He hears a familiar noise.
    D. He hears no noise.

43. A. All examinations have over 50 questions.
    B. All examinations have less than 50 questions.
    C. This examination has 100 questions.
    D. This examination doesn't have 100 questions.

44. A. The TV programs pay the big companies.
    B. Most TV programs sell cars and soft drinks.
    C. The TV companies produce soft drinks and breakfast foods.
    D. The big companies pay for the TV programs.

45. A. It is too heavy.
    B. It is dirty.
    C. It can be seen through.
    D. It is made of light metal.

46. A. He told me to lie down.
    B. He told me about his flight.
    C. He didn't tell me the truth.
    D. He didn't tell me it was mine.

47. A. The airlines pay him for flying.
    B. He flies for the Air Force.
    C. He flies for sport.
    D. He sells airplanes.

48. A. It is broken.   B. It is straight.
    C. It is thick.   D. It is not straight.

49. A. He got some checks.
    B. He deposited some money.
    C. He obtained some money.
    D. He withdrew some money.

50. A. It looks very easy.   B. I solved it easily.
    C. I don't understand it.   D. It's not too difficult.

● *Directions for questions 51-60. You will hear dialogs on the test tape. Select the correct answer A, B, C, or D and mark your answer sheet.*

51. A. 3 : 00   B. 3 : 30
    C. 4 : 00   D. 4 : 30

52. A. the commissary
    B. the non-commissioned officer's club
    C. the officer's club
    D. the cafeteria

53. A. They will go by air.   B. economy
    C. first-class   D. They'll make reservations.

54. A. the general   B. the major
    C. the commandant   D. the admiral

55. A. a star   B. a rectangle
    C. a circle   D. a wall

56. A. drop Laurie off at her place
    B. take Laurie to the movie
    C. tell Laurie to use her eye drops
    D. visit Laurie

57. A. the large room   B. the wrong room
    C. the room on the left D. the correct room

58. A. He only watches TV.
    B. He saw a space shuttle on TV.
    C. There's a space shuttle on the TV set.
    D. There was a TV set in the space shuttle.

59. A. let the water run
    B. stop the flow of water
    C. make the water run more slowly
    D. make the water run more quickly

60. A. The weather is bad.   B. The weather is fine.
    C. The day is cloudy.   D. The wind is blowing.

While traveling on a British Rail train, I was amused to hear our conductor ask over the loudspeaker: "Is the driver on the train? If he is, will he contact the conductor?"

坐在英國的火車上時，聽到車掌透過擴音機的廣播，我覺得很有趣。「司機在火車上嗎？如果在的話，請他和車掌聯絡好嗎？」

ECL 聽力測驗 [**12**] 詳解

1. (**A**) The cashier told Fred he could open an account.
What could Fred do?
出納員告訴弗烈德他可以開一個帳戶。／弗烈德可以做什麼呢？

(A) 存些錢在銀行　　　　　　(B) 看看他的帳戶
(C) 從他的帳戶提錢出來　　　(D) 對櫃台職員的錢負責

＊ cashier (kæˋʃɪr) *n.* 出納員　　account (əˋkaunt) *n.* 帳戶
account for 對～負責

2. (**A**) Sandy saw her grandmother yesterday. Whom did she see?
珊蒂昨天看見她的祖母。／她看見誰？

(A) 她爸爸的媽媽　　　　　　(B) 她九十歲的爸爸
(C) 她弟弟的爸爸　　　　　　(D) 她媽媽的爸爸

3. (**C**) Josephine spent a great deal of time in the west.
How much time did she spend there?
約瑟芬在西部花了許多時間。／她在那兒花了多少時間？

(A) 完全沒有　　　　　　　　(B) 幾乎沒有
(C) 許多　　　　　　　　　　(D) 非常少

＊ ***a great deal of*** 大量；許多

4. (**C**) Aren't those two girls alike?
那兩個女孩不是很相像嗎。

(A) 是的，我喜歡她們。　　　(B) 是的，她們是朋友。
(C) 是的，她們看來一樣。　　(D) 是的，她們將去旅行。

5. (**D**) Lisa wants to serve in the hospital.
What does she want to do in the hospital?
麗莎想在醫院服務。／她想在醫院做什麼？

(A) 買些藥　　　　　　　　　(B) 看醫生
(C) 有個私人房間　　　　　　(D) 幫忙

6. (**D**) What kind of blade makes a helicopter rise into the air?
哪一種螺旋槳讓直升機升空？

(A) 搖晃式的螺旋槳
(B) 震動式的螺旋槳
(C) 跳躍式的螺旋槳
(D) 旋轉式的螺槳

* blade〔bled〕*n.* 螺旋槳　helicopter〔'hɛlɪ͵kɑptə〕*n.* 直升機
swing〔swɪŋ〕*v.* 搖晃　vibrate〔'vaɪbret〕*v.* 震動
revolving〔rɪ'vɑlvɪŋ〕*adj.* 旋轉的

7. (**C**) Michael goes to a technical school.
What does he study?
麥可到一間技術學校去上課。／他學些什麼？

(A) 語言　　(B) 花朵　　(C) 機器　　(D) 動物

* technical〔'tɛknɪkl̩〕*adj.* 技術的

8. (**A**) Water can be changed into steam by heating.
What do we mean by "change"?
水可以由加熱轉變爲蒸氣。／「轉變」是什麼意思？

(A) 變化　　(B) 翻譯　　(C) 組成　　(D) 調換

* transform〔træns'fɔrm〕*v.* 轉換；變化
translate〔træns'let〕*v.* 翻譯　compose〔kəm'poz〕*v.* 組成
transpose〔træns'poz〕*v.* 調換

9. (**C**) Willy starts football practice every afternoon at 5:30.
When does he begin?
每天下午五點半威利開始他的足球練習。
他什麼時候開始？

(A) 上午五點半
(B) 在早上
(C) 下午五點半
(D) 在晚上

10. (**B**) Jack said, "What is the width of this room?"
What did Jack want to know?
傑克說，「這房間多寬？」／傑克想知道什麼？

(A) 溫度　　(B) 大小　　(C) 名字　　(D) 顏色

11. (**A**) Jeffrey goes to the park on Saturday of every week.
When does he go to the park?
傑弗瑞每個星期六去公園。／他何時去公園?

    (A) <u>星期六</u>　　　(B) 星期二　　　(C) 星期四　　　(D) 星期五

12. (**C**) What month comes right after March?
三月後是幾月?

    (A) 八月　　　(B) 六月　　　(C) <u>四月</u>　　　(D) 九月

13. (**D**) What country is located in the southernmost part of
South America?
哪一個國家位於南美洲的最南端?

    (A) 巴拿馬　　　(B) 墨西哥　　　(C) 巴西　　　(D) <u>阿根廷</u>

    * southernmost ('sʌðən‚most) *adj.* 最南端的
      Brazil (brə'zɪl) *n.* 巴西　　　Argentina (‚ɑrdʒən'tinə) *n.* 阿根廷

14. (**D**) Jason is taking the anthropology course for self-
improvement. Why is he taking the course?
傑生爲了自我進步,正在選修人類學課程。
他爲何要選修這個課程?

    (A) 他想要得到榮譽。　　　(B) 他喜歡學習關於動物的事。
    (C) 他不喜歡獨自讀書。　　　(D) <u>他覺得這個課程對他有益。</u>

    * anthropology (‚ænθrə'pɑlədʒɪ) *n.* 人類學
      get credit for 因~得到榮譽

15. (**B**) If someone knocks at the door, what should you do?
如果有人在敲門,你該怎麼做?

    (A) 把字擦掉　(B) <u>去應門</u>　(C) 翻譯句子　(D) 影印這張紙

    * erase (ɪ'res) *v.* 消除;擦掉

16. (**A**) How much change do you have?
你有多少零錢?

    (A) <u>我有一些硬幣。</u>　　　(B) 我體重一百三十磅。
    (C) 我今天吃了三次。　　　(D) 我已經換了很多次房間。

17. (**A**) Would you like to revise this paper?
   你願意訂正這份報告嗎?
   (A) 是的,我願意更正它。　　　(B) 是的,我願意毀了它。
   (C) 是的,我喜歡這報告的大小。　(D) 是的,我買這紙在這裏用。
   * revise 〔 rɪ'vaɪz 〕 v. 更正

18. (**A**) Lieutenant Hope said, "I haven't seen Carl since the day
   before yesterday." When was the last time Lieutenant
   Hope saw Carl?
   霍普上尉說:「從前天起,我就沒有見到卡爾。」
   霍普上尉最後見到卡爾是什麼時候?
   (A) 兩天前　　　　　　　　　　(B) 昨天
   (C) 一星期前　　　　　　　　　(D) 三天前
   * lieutenant 〔 lu'tɛnənt 〕 n. 上尉

19. (**D**) Didn't she use to smoke?
   她不是曾經吸煙嗎?
   (A) 不,她很快就不吸煙了。　　(B) 不,她不習慣吸煙。
   (C) 是,當他吸煙時,她使用香煙。 (D) 是,但她現在不抽了。

20. (**D**) Bob said, "I will finish my homework in five minutes."
   When will Bob complete his homework?
   鮑伯說:「我將在五分鐘內完成我的作業。」
   鮑伯何時會完成他的作業?
   (A) 他的課程　　　　　　　　　(B) 將要完成
   (C) 他的作業　　　　　　　　　(D) 幾分鐘內

21. (**C**) I'll go to mail the letter at the post office.
   What will I do with the letter?
   我將去郵局寄這封信。/ 我將如何處理這封信?
   (A) 寫完它　　　　　　　　　　(B) 寫上地址
   (C) 寄這封信　　　　　　　　　(D) 封好這封信
   * address 〔 ə'drɛs 〕 v. 寫地址　　deliver 〔 dɪ'lɪvə 〕 v. 遞送
   seal 〔 sil 〕 v. 密封

22. (**A**) I read a book on zoology. What is the book about?
    我讀了一本有關動物學的書。／這本書是有關什麼?

    (A) 動物　　　(B) 星星　　　(C) 植物　　　(D) 機器

    * zoology〔zoˈɑlədʒɪ〕*n.* 動物學

23. (**C**) I know the man talking about the snack bar.
    What was he talking about?
    我認識那個正在談論小吃店的男人。／他正在談論什麼?

    (A) 一個電話號碼名單　　　(B) 一群工人
    (C) 一個吃東西的地方　　　(D) 一種新藥品

    * snack〔snæk〕*n.* 零食;小吃

24. (**C**) A guest asked if there were any rooms available in the
    hotel. What did the guest want to know?
    有個客人問這旅館還有沒有空房間。／這客人想知道什麼?

    (A) 是否有預訂　　　(B) 房間是否準備好了
    (C) 是否有空房間　　　(D) 旅館裏是否有職員

    * available〔əˈveləbḷ〕*adj.* 可使用的
      reservation〔ˌrɛzəˈveʃən〕*n.* 預訂　　vacant〔ˈvekənt〕*adj.* 空的

25. (**B**) Tom said "The wire is not insulated."
    What did Tom mean?
    湯姆說:「這電線沒有被絕緣。」／湯姆的意思是什麼?

    (A) 這電線不好。　　　(B) 這電線沒有用保護層遮蓋。
    (C) 這電線不傳電。　　　(D) 這電線看不見。

    * insulate〔ˈɪnsəˌlet〕*v.* 隔離;絕緣　　visible〔ˈvɪzəbḷ〕*adj.* 看得見的

26. (**A**) Lieutenant Norton is a very cautious pilot.
    諾頓上尉是個很謹慎的飛行員。

    (A) 他是個小心的飛行員。　　　(B) 他是個疏忽的飛行員。
    (C) 他是個緊張的飛行員。　　　(D) 他是個粗心的飛行員。

    * pilot〔ˈpaɪlət〕*n.* 飛行員　　cautious〔ˈkɔʃəs〕*adj.* 謹慎的
      negligent〔ˈnɛglədʒənt〕*adj.* 疏忽的　　nervous〔ˈnɝvəs〕*adj.* 緊張的
      careless〔ˈkɛrlɪs〕*adj.* 粗心的

27. (**B**) Mrs. Eagleton saw a light in the distance.
伊格頓太太看到遠方有燈光。

(A) 她看到城裏有光。　　(B) 她看到遠處有光。
(C) 她看到車站有光。　　(D) 她看到近處有光。

* *in the distance* 在遠方　　*far away* 遠處

28. (**C**) Visiting Canadian homes gives you an opportunity to speak French.
拜訪加拿大家庭讓你有機會說法語。

(A) 你必須說法語。　　(B) 你喜歡說法語。
(C) 你有機會說法語。　　(D) 你喜歡說法語。

* Canadian (kə'nedɪən) *adj.* 加拿大的

29. (**B**) The hotel manager said that Steve would operate the elevator today.
旅館經理說史蒂夫今天會操控電梯。

(A) 史蒂夫將使用電梯。　　(B) 史蒂夫將運作電梯。
(C) 史蒂夫將修理電梯。　　(D) 史蒂夫將研究電梯。

* operate ('ɑpə,ret) *v.* 操作　　elevator ('ɛlə,vetə) *n.* 升降梯

30. (**D**) Tommy is older than Jerry, but Henry is the eldest.
湯米比傑瑞年長，但亨利年紀最大。

(A) 湯米三十歲，傑瑞十五歲，亨利二十五歲。
(B) 湯米十五歲，傑瑞二十歲，亨利三十歲。
(C) 湯米二十五歲，傑瑞三十歲，亨利二十歲。
(D) 湯米二十歲，傑瑞十五歲，亨利三十歲。

31. (**B**) Kevin can go with Clark, but James can't.
凱文可以和克拉克去，但詹姆士不行。

(A) 克拉克可以和詹姆士去。
(B) 詹姆士不能和克拉克去。
(C) 克拉克不能和凱文去。
(D) 凱文和詹姆士可以和克拉克去。

32. (**C**) I didn't have enough time to listen to all of the tapes.
我沒有足夠的時間聽完所有的錄音帶。
(A) 我將聽每一捲錄音帶。　　　(B) 他聽了所有的錄音帶。
(C) 我沒有聽完每一捲錄音帶。　(D) 他在錄音帶裏什麼也沒聽到。

33. (**C**) The crew abandoned the jet after the landing.
降落後，全體機員遺棄了這架噴射機。
(A) 機員們留在機上。　　　　(B) 機員們做了一些修復。
(C) 機員們離開了飛機。　　　(D) 機員們做了一些改變。
* abandon (əˋbændən) v. 捨棄　　crew (kru) n. 全體機員 (集合名詞)

34. (**D**) I have trouble starting the engine.
我發動引擎有困難。
(A) 它沒有動力。　　　　(B) 它不能上坡。
(C) 它不往後走。　　　　(D) 它不能起動。
* engine (ˋɛndʒən) n. 引擎

35. (**D**) Douglas likes a variety of food.
道格拉斯喜歡各種食物。
(A) 他喜歡花園外的食物。　　(B) 他喜歡很多食物。
(C) 他喜歡很甜的食物。　　　(D) 他喜歡不同種類的食物。
* variety (vəˋraɪətɪ) n. 多種；各種

36. (**B**) I'm going to purchase this radio.
我將要買這台收音機。
(A) 我要賣這台收音機。　　　(B) 我將買這台收音機。
(C) 我將跟隨這台收音機。　　(D) 我已經買了這台收音機。
* purchase (ˋpɝtʃəs) v. 購買

37. (**D**) On his way home, Bruce bumped into Louis at the drug-store.
在回家途中，布魯斯湊巧在藥房遇見路易斯。
(A) 布魯斯叫路易斯。　　　　(B) 布魯斯傷了路易斯。
(C) 布魯斯打電話給路易斯。　(D) 布魯斯遇見路易斯。
* *bump into* 偶遇

38. (**D**) Sometimes, Cynthia becomes irritated with her friends.
有時候，辛西亞被她的朋友觸怒。

(A) 她和朋友去參加宴會。　　(B) 她小心地評價她的朋友。

(C) 她和朋友開玩笑。　　(D) <u>她因朋友而變得惱怒。</u>

* irritate (ˈɪrə͵tet) v. 激怒　　rate (ret) v. 評價
annoy (əˈnɔɪ) v. 使苦惱

39. (**D**) At the last minute, he decided to have a shot at it.
在最後一分鐘，他決定試試看。

(A) 他決定打一針。　　(B) 他決定取消它。

(C) 他決定射它。　　(D) <u>他決定試試。</u>

* *have a shot at* ~ 試試~　　shot (ʃɑt) n. 注射　　shoot (ʃut) v. 射擊

40. (**B**) Keep your eye on the road.
注意看馬路。

(A) 別看路。　　(B) <u>小心看路。</u>

(C) 離馬路遠些。　　(D) 小心地閉上你的眼睛。

* *keep one's eye on* 注意

41. (**C**) Nick is a very neat person.
尼克是個非常整潔的人。

(A) 他總是努力工作。　　(B) 他總是生病。

(C) <u>他總是很乾淨。</u>　　(D) 他總是很奇怪。

42. (**B**) He hears a strange noise.
他聽到一個奇怪的吵雜聲。

(A) 他聽到高速公路的吵雜聲。　　(B) <u>他聽到不尋常的吵雜聲。</u>

(C) 他聽到熟悉的吵雜聲。　　(D) 他沒有聽到吵雜聲。

* unfamiliar (͵ʌnfəˈmɪljɚ) adj. 不熟悉的

43. (**C**) Generally, the examination has fifty questions, but this one has a hundred.
一般說來，考試有五十題，但這次有一百題。

(A) 所有考試都超過五十題。　　(B) 所有考試都不到五十題。

(C) <u>這次考試有一百題。</u>　　(D) 這次考試沒有一百題。

44. (**D**) In our country, most TV programs are paid for by big companies that make such products as cars, soft drinks and cosmetics.

在我們國內，大多數電視節目的費用，是由製造汽車、飲料、化粧品等產品的大公司來支付。

(A) 電視節目付錢給大公司。
(B) 大部分電視節目賣車和飲料。
(C) 電視公司製造飲料和早餐食物。
(D) 大公司為電視節目支付費用

* cosmetics〔kɑz'mɛtɪks〕*n. pl.* 化粧品

45. (**D**) The chair is made of aluminum.

這椅子是鋁製的。

(A) 它太重了。　　　　　(B) 它是髒的。
(C) 它可以被看透。　　　(D) 它是由輕金屬製成。

* aluminum〔ə'lumɪnəm〕*n.* 鋁

46. (**C**) My friend told me a lie.

我朋友告訴我謊話。

(A) 他叫我躺下。　　　　(B) 他告訴我有關他的飛行。
(C) 他沒有告訴我實話。　(D) 他沒有告訴我它是我的。

47. (**A**) Mr. Jones is a commercial pilot.

瓊斯先生是個商業飛行員。

(A) 航空公司付他飛行的費用。　(B) 他為空軍服務。
(C) 他以飛行為運動。　　　　　(D) 他販賣飛機。

* commercial〔kə'mɝʃəl〕*adj.* 商業的

48. (**D**) The wire is twisted.

這電線是扭曲的。

(A) 它是破的。　　　　(B) 它是直的。
(C) 它是厚的。　　　　(D) 它不是直的。

* twist〔twɪst〕*v.* 扭曲

49. (**C**) Johnson went to the bank and cashed his check.
　　　強生去銀行兌現支票。

　　　(A) 他得到一些支票。　　　　　(B) 他存了一些錢。
　　　(C) 他得到一些錢。　　　　　　(D) 他提了一些錢。

　　　* cash〔kæʃ〕v. 兌現　　deposit〔dɪˈpazɪt〕v. 存款
　　　withdraw〔wɪðˈdrɔ〕v. 提款

50. (**C**) This setup looks puzzling.
　　　這結構看來令人困惑。

　　　(A) 它看來很容易。　　　　　(B) 我輕易地解決了它。
　　　(C) 我不了解它。　　　　　　(D) 它並不難。

　　　* setup〔ˈsɛtˌʌp〕n. 結構　　puzzling〔ˈpʌzlɪŋ〕adj. 令人困惑的

51. (**C**) M : I'd like to see you for about half an hour this
　　　　　　afternoon.
　　　　　W : How about meeting me here about 3:30?
　　　　　When should their meeting be finished?
　　　男：我今天下午想和妳見個面，大約半個小時。
　　　女：三點半來這裡找我如何？
　　　他們的會面何時會結束？

　　　(A) 三點　　(B) 三點半　　(C) 四點　　(D) 四點半

52. (**C**) W : Sergeant Taylor, where are you going in such a
　　　　　　hurry?
　　　　　M : I am going to the club for dinner.
　　　　　Where will Sergeant Taylor eat?
　　　女：泰勒中士，你急著去哪裏？
　　　男：我要去俱樂部吃晚餐。
　　　泰勒中士要在哪裏用餐？

　　　(A) 餐廳　　　　　　　　　　(B) 非軍官俱樂部
　　　(C) 軍官俱樂部　　　　　　　(D) 自助餐廳

　　　* sergeant〔ˈsɑrdʒənt〕n. 中士　　commissary〔ˈkɑməˌsɛrɪ〕n. 餐廳
　　　commission〔kəˈmɪʃən〕v. 任命爲軍官
　　　cafeteria〔ˌkæfəˈtɪrɪə〕n. 自助餐廳

53. (**A**) M : Our friends are going to Florida next month.

W : Yes, I know. This morning they told me they will be going by jet plane.

How are they getting to Florida?

男：我們的朋友下個月要去佛羅里達。

女：我知道，今天早上他們告訴我他們將搭飛機前往。

他們如何去佛羅里達？

(A) 搭飛機　　　　　　　　(B) 坐經濟艙

(C) 坐頭等艙　　　　　　　(D) 他們會訂位

54. (**C**) M : Where did Captain Johnson go?

W : He went to the headquarters. He has to report to the Commandant at 2:50.

Who does the Captain have to be there to meet?

男：強森上尉去哪裏？

女：他去總部。他必須在二點五十分時向司令官作報告。

上尉必須去那裏見誰？

(A) 將軍　　　　　　　　　(B) 少校

(C) 司令官　　　　　　　　(D) 海軍上將

　* captain (ˈkæptɪn) *n.* 上尉　　headquarters (ˈhɛdˈkwɔrtəz) *n.* 總部
　 commandant (ˌkɑmənˈdænt) *n.* 司令官　　general (ˈdʒɛnərəl) *n.* 將軍
　 major (ˈmedʒə) *n.* 少校　　admiral (ˈædmərəl) *n.* 海軍上將

55. (**C**) M : Have you noticed anything unusual about the moon tonight?

W : There is a ring around it.

What does the woman see?

男：妳有沒有注意到今晚的月亮有任何不同？

女：它的周圍有道光圈。

這位女士看到什麼？

(A) 一顆星　　　　　　　　(B) 一個長方形

(C) 一個圓圈　　　　　　　(D) 一面牆

　* ring (rɪŋ) *n.* 環狀物　　rectangle (ˈrɛktæŋgl) *n.* 長方形
　 circle (ˈsɝkl) *n.* 圓圈

56.(**D**) W : Have you seen Laurie recently?

M : No, but I spoke to her on the phone and told her
I'd drop in this evening after the movie.

What does the man plan to do?

女：你最近見過羅莉嗎？

男：沒有，但我和她講過電話，而且我告訴她，今天晚上看完電影
後，我會去拜訪她。

這位男士打算做什麼？

(A) 讓羅莉在她家下車　　　　(B) 帶羅莉去看電影

(C) 告訴羅莉用她的眼藥水　　(D) 拜訪羅莉

* recently ('risntlɪ) *adv.* 最近

speak to *sb.* **on the phone** 和某人講電話　　**drop in** 拜訪

drop *sb.* **off** 讓某人下車　　**eye drops** 眼藥水

57.(**D**) M : Did you send the student to Mr. Brown's office?

W : Yes, I hope he went to the right room.

Which room did she want the student to go to?

男：妳叫那名學生到布朗先生的辦公室嗎？

女：是的，希望他走對房間。

她要該名學生進哪間房間？

(A) 大的房間　　　　(B) 錯誤的房間

(C) 在左邊的房間　　(D) 正確的房間

58.(**B**) W : Have you seen a space shuttle?

M : Only on TV.

What does the man mean?

女：你看過太空梭嗎？

男：只有在電視上看過。

這名男士是什麼意思？

(A) 他只看電視。

(B) 他在電視上看到一架太空梭。

(C) 電視機上方有一架太空梭。

(D) 太空梭裏有一架電視機。

* **space shuttle** 太空梭

59. (**B**) W : What should I do ?

M : Turn off the faucet.

What does the man want the woman to do ?

女：我該做什麼？

男：把水龍頭關掉。

這位男士要女士做什麼？

(A) 讓水流 (B) <u>停止水流</u>

(C) 讓水流得更慢 (D) 讓水流得更快

* faucet〔ˈfɔsɪt〕 *n.* 水龍頭 　　flow〔flo〕 *n.* 流動

60. (**B**) M : How is the weather in Boston today ?

W : The sun is shining and the sky is clear.

What did the woman say about the weather ?

男：波士頓今天的天氣如何？

女：陽光普照晴空萬里。

這位女士說天氣如何？

(A) 天氣不好。 (B) <u>天氣很好。</u>

(C) 白天多雲。 (D) 風在吹。

In a perfect world, potato chips might have calories, but if you ate them with dip, the calories would be neutralized.

　　在完美的世界中，洋芋片可能含有卡路里，可是如果你沾醬吃，卡路里就可以被中和掉。

LISTENING TEST 13

- *Directions for questions 1-25. You will hear questions on the test tape. Select the one item A, B, C or D which answers the question correctly, and mark your answer sheet.*

1. A. who will be using this car
   B. who wants to use this car
   C. who used this car frequently
   D. who used this car first

2. A. what time you ate breakfast
   B. what time you dressed
   C. what time you opened your eyes
   D. what time you got out of bed

3. A. He didn't think he could come.
   B. He was sure he could come.
   C. He didn't want to come.
   D. He was eager to come.

4. A. perfectly normal
   C. very lonesome
   B. quite happy
   D. somewhat tense

5. A. both
   C. hot dog
   B. neither
   D. hamburger

6. A. air humidity
   C. temperature
   B. blood pressure
   D. wind velocity

7. A. the Pacific Ocean
   C. Lake Michigan
   B. the Atlantic Ocean
   D. the Gulf of Mexico

8. A. some rest
   C. a little rest
   B. little rest
   D. a lot of rest

9. A. a slope   B. a lake
    C. a plane   D. a ski

10. A. so as not to seek a cold   B. so as not to bring a cold
     C. so as not to cure a cold   D. so as not to catch a cold

11. A. clean   B. untidy
     C. neat   D. empty

12. A. wool   B. silk
     C. cotton   D. chemicals

13. A. because of the cold weather
     B. because of the work at home
     C. because of the heat
     D. because of the humidity

14. A. go to a race   B. report to the commander
     C. watch a parade   D. read a newspaper

15. A. He is going for a boat ride.
     B. He is going to sell a boat.
     C. He is going to a sale.
     D. He is going to look at some boats.

16. A. put the coat on   B. buy the coat
     C. check the price   D. find another like it

17. A. fast speed   B. broken
     C. excellent condition   D. pretty color

18. A. after sitting down   B. after the sun went down
     C. after the sun came up   D. during sunrise

19. A. new cars and houses   B. international news
     C. baseball and football   D. the comic strips

20. A. yesterday   B. tomorrow
    C. the day before yesterday   D. the day after tomorrow

21. A. your family name   B. your phone number
    C. where your house is   D. your car plate

22. A. put it on the desk   B. put a new cover on it
    C. check words in it   D. correct it

23. A. a sport played with a rope
    B. a sport played only with hands
    C. a sport played with feet and head
    D. a sport played with a racket

24. A. the price   B. the prize
    C. the surprise   D. the pies

25. A. a dime   B. a dollar
    C. a quarter   D. fifty cents

● *Directions for questions 26-50. You will hear statements on the test tape. Select the one answer A, B, C, or D which comes closest to the meaning of the statement and mark your answer sheet.*

26. A. He sent a letter.
    B. He and his mother sent a letter.
    C. His mother sent a letter.
    D. The letter was written by his mother.

27. A. He is arriving very shortly.
    B. His departure was canceled.
    C. He is departing in a short time.
    D. He is coming today.

28. A. She is reading the newspaper.
    B. She is searching for the newspaper.
    C. She was reading the newspaper.
    D. She is looking for the newspaper.

29. A. Sidney won a yellow car.
    B. Sidney will race a yellow car.
    C. Sidney often refers to his yellow car.
    D. Sidney prefers a yellow car.

30. A. They are imaginary.　　B. They are popular.
    C. They are boring.　　　 D. They are favorable.

31. A. He gets to class quickly.
    B. He is late to class most of the time.
    C. He gets to class on time once in a while.
    D. He gets to class on time most of the time.

32. A. He thinks German is easy.
    B. He thinks it is hard to learn.
    C. He thinks it is a dead language.
    D. He thinks it is different.

33. A. The motor cools off too fast.
    B. The motor becomes too hot.
    C. The motor runs too slow.
    D. The motor uses too much oil.

34. A. He produced it.　　 B. He sold it.
    C. He worshipped it.　 D. He bought it.

35. A. She does not need a haircut tomorrow.
    B. She should get a haircut.
    C. Her hair is too short.
    D. Haircuts are better today.

36. A. I have little time to prepare.
    B. I have some time to prepare.
    C. I have enough time to prepare.
    D. I have a few minutes to prepare.

37. A. You must study.
    B. You must have the child study.
    C. You must study with the child.
    D. Your child may study.

38. A. We will finish them.   B. We must finish them.
    C. We should finish them.   D. We won't finish them.

39. A. There were many tickets for sale.
    B. We could not get the tickets.
    C. There are no more games.
    D. We are lucky to get the tickets.

40. A. He will soon leave.   B. He will soon come.
    C. He will soon talk.   D. He will soon follow.

41. A. it went around it fast.
    B. It landed roughly on it.
    C. It moved smoothly over it.
    D. It jumped quickly away from it.

42. A. One table is better.   B. One table is smaller.
    C. The tables are alike.   D. The tables are different.

43. A. I have influenza.   B. I have something new.
    C. I was told what to do.   D. I need to fly more.

44. A. Neil enjoys swimming.
    B. Alan enjoys swimming.
    C. Alan doesn't swim for pleasure.
    D. Neil doesn't swim.

45. A. He bought the clock.
    B. He taught the clock.
    C. He looked for the clock.
    D. He was thinking about buying it.

46. A. It was already closed.
    B. It wasn't closed yet.
    C. It stays open.
    D. It's always closed when I go there.

47. A. He called them by phone.
    B. He visited them.
    C. He wrote them some letters.
    D. He saw them accidentally.

48. A. He was driving nails in the board.
    B. He was making holes in it.
    C. He was sawing the board.
    D. He was plugging holes.

49. A. He freed himself from the crowd.
    B. He got some news from the crowd.
    C. He joined the crowd.
    D. He encircled the crowd.

50. A. They fixed their baggage.
    B. They deposited their baggage.
    C. They sold their baggage.
    D. They found their baggage.

● *Directions for questions 51-60. You will hear dialogs on the test
tape. Select the correct answer A, B, C, or D and mark your
answer sheet.*

51. A. a sticky material
    C. cardboard
    B. scissors
    D. long nails

52. A. slippery
    C. slipping
    B. safe
    D. wide

53. A. It is misty.
    C. It is raining.
    B. It is sleeting.
    D. It is snowing.

54. A. beneficial
    C. dangerous
    B. light
    D. concentrated

55. A. move forward
    C. fire
    B. retreat
    D. relax

56. A. He won the first place.
    C. He broke his arm.
    B. He had his finger cut.
    D. He sprained his ankle.

57. A. She's tired of teaching.
    C. She's changing jobs.
    B. She was fired.
    D. The school was too far.

58. A. 6 : 50
    C. 6 : 05
    B. 7 : 25
    D. 7 : 05

59. A. $ 20
    C. $ 35
    B. $ 40
    D. $ 70

60. A. She got up later than usual.
    B. The bus was late.
    C. She forgot her class.
    D. Her clock was broken.

ECL 聽力測驗 [13] 詳解

1. (**D**) Mary asked, "Who used this car originally?"
What did she want to know?
瑪麗問：「最初是誰使用這部車？」／ 她想知道什麼？

(A) 誰將使用這部車　　　　　　(B) 誰想使用這部車
(C) 誰時常使用這部車　　　　　(D) 誰最初使用這部車

* originally〔ə'rɪdʒənḷɪ〕*adv.* 原本；最初

2. (**D**) "What time did you get up?" Bill asked.
What did Bill want to know?
比爾問道：「你幾點起床？」／ 比爾想知道什麼？

(A) 你幾點吃早餐　　　　　　　(B) 你幾點穿衣服
(C) 你幾點睜開眼睛　　　　　　(D) 你幾點下床

* dress〔drɛs〕*v.* 穿衣服

3. (**A**) I asked Joe whether he could come tomorrow. He said he
didn't suppose he could come. What did Joe mean?
我問喬明天是否能來。他說他想他不能來。／ 喬的意思為何？

(A) 他不認為他可以來。　　　　(B) 他確定他可以來。
(C) 他不想來。　　　　　　　　(D) 他渴望過來。

* suppose〔sə'poz〕*v.* 猜測；認為　　eager〔'igə〕*adj.* 渴望的

4. (**D**) The new student is nervous. How does he feel?
這位新生很緊張。／ 他感覺如何？

(A) 完全正常　　　　　　　　　(B) 相當快樂
(C) 非常寂寞　　　　　　　　　(D) 有些緊張

* nervous〔'nɜvəs〕*adj.* 緊張的
perfectly〔'pɜfɪktlɪ〕*adv.* 完全地
normal〔'nɔrmḷ〕*adj.* 正常的　　lonesome〔'lonsəm〕*adj.* 寂寞的
somewhat〔'sʌm,hwɑt〕*adv.* 有幾分；有些
tense〔tɛns〕*adj.* 緊張的

5. (**A**) John would love to have a hamburger and a hot dog. What does he prefer?

約翰想要一個漢堡和一根熱狗。／他偏愛什麼？

    (A) 兩者   (B) 都不是   (C) 熱狗   (D) 漢堡

    * prefer (prɪˋfɝ) *v.* 偏愛

6. (**C**) What is a thermometer used to measure?

溫度計用來測量什麼？

    (A) 空氣濕度   (B) 血壓   (C) 溫度   (D) 風速

    * thermometer (θəˋmɑmətɚ , θɚ-) *n.* 溫度計
    measure (ˋmɛʒɚ) *v.* 測量   humidity (hjuˋmɪdətɪ) *n.* 濕度
    pressure (ˋprɛʃɚ) *n.* 壓力   temperature (ˋtɛmprətʃɚ) *n.* 溫度
    velocity (vəˋlɑsətɪ) *n.* 速度

7. (**B**) What body of water is located east of the United States?

什麼水系位於美國以東？

    (A) 太平洋   (B) 大西洋   (C) 密西根湖   (D) 墨西哥灣

    * locate (loˋket) *v.* 位於   gulf (gʌlf) *n.* 海灣

8. (**D**) Everybody should get plenty of rest. What should everybody get?

每個人都應該得到充裕的休息。／每個人應該得到什麼？

    (A) 一些休息   (B) 少量的休息
    (C) 一點休息   (D) 大量的休息

    * plenty (ˋplɛntɪ) *adj.* 充裕的；大量的

9. (**A**) The girl saw the steep descent from a distance. What did she see?

這位女孩從遠處看到一個很陡的下坡。／她看到什麼？

    (A) 斜坡   (B) 一座湖   (C) 一架飛機   (D) 一片滑雪板

    * steep (stip) *adj.* 陡峭的   descent (dɪˋsɛnt) *n.* 下坡
    slope (slop) *n.* 斜坡   ski (ski) *n.* 滑雪板

10. (**D**) Why should you wear a sweater when it is cold?
為何你在天氣寒冷時應該穿毛衣？

(A) 為了不要尋找感冒   (B) 為了不要帶來感冒
(C) 為了不要治癒感冒   (D) <u>為了不要罹患感冒</u>

* *catch a cold* 患感冒

11. (**B**) His desk is always quite messy. How is his desk?
他的書桌總是很亂。／他的書桌如何？

(A) 乾淨   (B) <u>不整齊</u>   (C) 整齊   (D) 空的

* messy ('mɛsɪ) *adj.* 亂七八糟的
    untidy (ʌn'taɪdɪ) *adj.* 不整齊的   neat (nit) *adj.* 整齊的

12. (**D**) What are synthetic fabrics made from?
合成布料由什麼製成？

(A) 羊毛   (B) 絲   (C) 棉   (D) <u>化學製品</u>

* synthetic (sɪn'θɛtɪk) *adj.* 化學合成的；人造的
    fabric ('fæbrɪk) *n.* 織布；纖維   silk (sɪlk) *n.* 絲
    cotton ('katn̩) *n.* 棉   chemical ('kɛmɪkl̩) *n.* 化學製品

13. (**A**) Since it was so cold, he stayed at home.
Why did he remain at home?
因為天氣如此寒冷，所以他待在家裏。／他為何留在家？

(A) <u>因為天氣寒冷</u>   (B) 因為家裏的工作
(C) 因為暑氣   (D) 因為濕氣

* remain (rɪ'men) *v.* 停留   heat (hit) *n.* 暑氣；暑熱

14. (**D**) Andrew wants to see the headline. What will he do?
安德魯想看頭條新聞。／他將做什麼？

(A) 去比賽   (B) 向指揮官報告
(C) 觀看遊行   (D) <u>看報紙</u>

* headline ('hɛd,laɪn) *n.* 頭條新聞   race (res) *n.* 比賽
    commander (kə'mændə) *n.* 指揮官
    parade (pə'red) *n.* 遊行

15. (**A**) David is going sailing. What is he going to do?
大衛將要出航。／他將做什麼？

(A) 他將駕船航行。 　　　　　(B) 他將賣掉船。
(C) 他將去拍賣會。 　　　　　(D) 他將去看船。

* sail〔sel〕v. 航行

16. (**A**) I want to try on this coat. What do I want to do?
我想試穿這件外套。／我想做什麼？

(A) 穿上外套 　　　　　(B) 買外套
(C) 查價錢 　　　　　(D) 找另一個類似的

* ***try on*** 試穿　　***put on*** 穿上；戴上

17. (**C**) The computer is in very good shape.
What is the meaning of "very good shape?"
這台電腦的情況良好。／"very good shape" 的意思為何？

(A) 快速 　　　　　(B) 損壞的
(C) 極佳的狀況 　　　　　(D) 漂亮的顏色

* shape〔ʃep〕n. 情況

18. (**B**) Bob quit working after sunset. When did Bob quit?
鮑伯在日落後停止工作。／鮑伯何時停止？

(A) 坐下後 　　　　　(B) 太陽下山後
(C) 太陽出來後 　　　　　(D) 日出時

* sunset〔'sʌn,sɛt〕n. 日落　　sunrise〔'sʌn,raɪz〕n. 日出

19. (**C**) David always reads the sports section in the newspaper.
What does he read about?
大衛總是讀報紙的體育版。／他讀些什麼？

(A) 新車和房子 　　　　　(B) 國際新聞
(C) 棒球和美式足球 　　　　　(D) 連環漫畫

* section〔'sɛkʃən〕n. 版；部門　　comic〔'kɑmɪk〕n. 漫畫
strip〔strɪp〕n. 長條；連環漫畫

20. (**C**) We went to the concert the day before yesterday.
When did we go to the concert?
我們前天去聽音樂會。 / 我們何時去聽音樂會?

(A) 昨天　　　　(B) 明天　　　　(C) <u>前天</u>　　　　(D) 後天

21. (**C**) John asked "What is your address?"
What did he want to know?
約翰問:「你的地址是哪裏?」/ 他想知道什麼?

(A) 你的姓　　　　　　　　(B) 你的電話號碼
(C) <u>你家在哪裏</u>　　　　　　(D) 你的車牌

* plate〔plet〕 *n.* 車牌

22. (**C**) You should consult your dictionary.
What should you do with it?
你應該查字典。 / 你該怎麼處理它?

(A) 將它放在桌上　　　　　　(B) 放個新封面在它上面
(C) <u>查裏面的字</u>　　　　　　(D) 訂正它

* consult〔kən'sʌlt〕 *v.* 查閱　　cover〔'kʌvɚ〕 *n.* 封面
correct〔kə'rɛkt〕 *v.* 訂正

23. (**C**) Bill practices soccer every afternoon.
What does he practice?
比爾每天下午練習足球。 / 他練習什麼?

(A) 用繩索的運動　　　　　　(B) 只能用手的運動
(C) <u>用腳和頭的運動</u>　　　　(D) 用球拍的運動

* soccer〔'sɑkɚ〕 *n.* 足球　　rope〔rop〕 *n.* 繩索
racket〔'rækɪt〕 *n.* 球拍

24. (**B**) That girl will get the prize. What will she get?
那位女孩將得到獎品。 / 她將得到什麼?

(A) 價錢　　　　(B) <u>獎品</u>　　　　(C) 驚喜　　　　(D) 派

* prize〔praɪz〕 *n.* 獎品

25. (**D**) Joe went to the post office and bought five 10-cent
stamps. How much did they cost?
喬到郵局買了五張十分錢的郵票。/ 它們的費用多少？

    (A) 一角   (B) 一元   (C) 二角五分   (D) <u>五十分</u>

    * dime〔daɪm〕*n.* 一角的硬幣

26. (**A**) Bill mailed a letter to his mother.
比爾寄一封信給他母親。

    (A) <u>他寄一封信。</u>   (B) 他和他母親寄一封信。
    (C) 他的母親寄一封信。   (D) 這封信是他母親寫的。

27. (**C**) Jason is leaving soon.
傑森很快就要離開了。

    (A) 他馬上就到達。   (B) 他取消離開。
    (C) <u>他短時間內會離開。</u>   (D) 他今天要來。

    * shortly〔'ʃɔrtlɪ〕*adv.* 不久；馬上
      departure〔dɪ'partʃɚ〕*n.* 離開；出發
      depart〔dɪ'part〕*v.* 離開

28. (**A**) She is looking at the newspaper now.
她現在正在看報紙。

    (A) <u>她正在讀報紙。</u>（現在進行式）
    (B) 她正在找報紙。
    (C) 她正在讀報紙。（過去進行式）
    (D) 她正在找報紙。

    * search〔sɜtʃ〕*v.* 尋找   ***look for*** 尋找

29. (**D**) Sidney would rather have a yellow car.
席尼寧願有部黃色的車子。

    (A) 席尼贏了一部黃色的車子。   (B) 席尼將開一部黃色的車子。
    (C) 席尼常提到他的黃色汽車。   (D) <u>席尼偏愛黃色的車子。</u>

    * ***would rather*** 寧願   race〔res〕*v.* 使跑
      refer to 言及；提到

30. (**A**)　The adventures of Indiana Jones are fictional.
印第安那瓊斯的歷險記是虛構的。

　　(A) 它們是想像的。　　　　　　(B) 它們受到歡迎。
　　(C) 它們很無聊。　　　　　　　(D) 它們是有利的。

　　* adventure (əd'vɛntʃə) *n.* 冒險　　fictional ('fɪkʃənḷ) *adj.* 虛構的
　　imaginary (ɪ'mædʒə,nɛrɪ) *adj.* 想像的
　　favorable ('fevrəbḷ) *adj.* 有利的

31. (**D**)　Edward usually attends class on time.
愛德華通常準時上課。

　　(A) 他很快開始上課。　　　　　(B) 他上課大多遲到。
　　(C) 他偶爾準時上課。　　　　　(D) 他大多準時上課。

　　* attend (ə'tɛnd) *v.* 出席　　*on time* 準時

32. (**B**)　Steven thinks German is a difficult language.
史蒂芬認為德文是個困難的語言。

　　(A) 他認為德文很簡單。　　　　(B) 他認為它很難學。
　　(C) 他認為那是個死的語言。　　(D) 他認為它不同。

33. (**B**)　The motor sometimes gets overheated.
這個馬達有時加熱過度。

　　(A) 馬達冷卻得太快。　　　　　(B) 馬達變得太熱。
　　(C) 馬達轉動太慢。　　　　　　(D) 馬達消耗太多油。

　　* overheat (,ovə'hit) *v.* 使過熱

34. (**A**)　He created a picture.
他創作了一幅畫。

　　(A) 他製作它。　　(B) 他賣掉它。　　(C) 他崇拜它。　　(D) 他買下它。

　　* create (krɪ'et) *v.* 創作　　worship ('wɜʃəp) *v.* 崇拜

35. (**B**)　She'd better get a haircut tomorrow.
她明天最好去剪頭髮。

　　(A) 她明天不需要剪頭髮。　　　(B) 她應該剪頭髮。
　　(C) 她的頭髮太短。　　　　　　(D) 今天剪頭髮比較好。

36.(**C**) I have plenty of time to prepare.
我有充足的時間準備。

(A) 我有很少的時間準備。　　　(B) 我有一些時間可準備。

(C) 我有足夠的時間可準備。　　　(D) 我有幾分鐘可準備。

37.(**B**) You must make your child study.
你必須讓你的孩子念書。

(A) 你必須念書。　　　　　　　(B) 你必須讓孩子念書。

(C) 你必須和孩子一起念書。　　　(D) 你的孩子可以念書。

38.(**C**) We ought to finish our assignments by 6:00 p.m.
我們應該在下午六點前完成我們的任務。

(A) 我們將完成它們。　　　　　(B) 我們必須完成它們。

(C) 我們應該完成它們。　　　　(D) 我們將不會完成它們。

* *ought to* 應該　　assignment (ə'saɪnmənt) *n.* 任務

39.(**D**) We are very fortunate to get the tickets for the game.
我們非常幸運可以拿到比賽的票。

(A) 有許多票在販售。　　　　　(B) 我們無法拿到票。

(C) 已經沒有比賽了。　　　　　(D) 我們很幸運可以拿到票。

* fortunate ('fɔrtʃənɪt) *adj.* 幸運的

40.(**B**) John will soon arrive.
約翰不久將到達。

(A) 他不久將離開。　　　　　　(B) 他不久將來到。

(C) 他不久將說話。　　　　　　(D) 他不久將跟隨。

41.(**C**) The airplane glided over the lake.
飛機從湖面上滑翔而過。

(A) 它快速地繞著它走。　　　　(B) 它粗魯地降落在它上面。

(C) 它平穩地從它上面移動而過。　(D) 它迅速跳離開它。

* glide (glaɪd) *v.* 滑翔　　roughly ('rʌflɪ) *adv.* 粗魯地
smoothly ('smuðlɪ) *adv.* 平穩地

42. (**C**) This table is like that one.
　　這張桌子像那一張。
　　(A) 有一張桌子比較好。　　　(B) 有一張桌子比較小。
　　(C) 這些桌子類似。　　　　　(D) 這些桌子不同。

43. (**A**) The doctor says I have the flu.
　　醫生說我得了流行性感冒。
　　(A) 我得了流行性感冒。　　　(B) 我有新東西。
　　(C) 我被告知該如何做。　　　(D) 我需要飛行更久。
　　* flu〔flu〕*n.* 流行性感冒　　influenza〔,ɪnflu'ɛnzə〕*n.* 流行性感冒

44. (**B**) Neil asked, "Do you enjoy swimming?"
　　Alan replied, "Yes, it is my favorite sport."
　　尼爾問：「你喜歡游泳嗎？」。
　　艾倫回答：「是的，那是我最喜歡的運動。」
　　(A) 尼爾喜歡游泳。　　　　　(B) 艾倫喜歡游泳。
　　(C) 艾倫不是爲樂趣而游泳。　(D) 尼爾不游泳。

45. (**D**) He thought about buying the clock.
　　他考慮買那個鐘。
　　(A) 他買那個鐘。　　　　　　(B) 他敎那個鐘。
　　(C) 他尋找那個鐘。　　　　　(D) 他考慮要買它。

46. (**B**) The drugstore was still open when I went there.
　　當我到那兒時，藥房仍在營業。
　　(A) 它已經打烊。　　　　　　(B) 它還沒打烊。
　　(C) 它持續開著。　　　　　　(D) 我去的時候總是打烊了。
　　* drugstore〔'drʌg,stor〕*n.* 藥房；雜貨店

47. (**B**) Mr. Jones called on his friends.
　　瓊斯先生拜訪他的朋友。
　　(A) 他打電話給他們。　　　　(B) 他拜訪他們。
　　(C) 他寫幾封信給他們。　　　(D) 他碰巧看見他們。
　　call on 拜訪　　accidentally〔,æksə'dɛntḷɪ〕*adv.* 意外地

48. (**B**) He was drilling the board.
　　 他正在木板上鑽孔。

　　(A) 他正把釘子釘在木板上。　　(B) 他正在打洞。
　　(C) 他正在鋸木板。　　　　　　(D) 他正在把洞塞住。
　　＊ drill〔drɪl〕v. 鑽　　　drive〔draɪv〕v. 釘
　　　 saw〔sɔ〕v. 鋸　　　　plug〔plʌg〕v. 塞住

49. (**A**) He broke away from the crowd.
　　 他逃離人群。

　　(A) 他脫離人群。
　　(B) 他從人群中得到一些消息。
　　(C) 他加入人群。
　　(D) 他圍繞群眾。
　　＊ ***break away*** 逃走　　encircle〔ɪn'sɝkl〕v. 圍繞

50. (**B**) The students checked their baggage before getting on the plane.
　　 學生們在上飛機前先寄存他們的行李。

　　(A) 他們固定行李。　　　　(B) 他們寄放行李。
　　(C) 他們賣掉行李。　　　　(D) 他們找到行李。
　　＊ check〔tʃɛk〕v. 寄存　　deposit〔dɪ'pɑzɪt〕v. 存放

51. (**A**) W : I have to put these two pieces of glass together.
　　 M : Well, to hold two pieces of glass together, you should
　　　　　use strong glue.
　　 What should the woman use?
　　 女：我必須將這兩塊玻璃合在一起。
　　 男：嗯，要將兩塊玻璃固定在一起，妳應該使用強力膠。
　　 這位女士應該使用什麼？

　　(A) 有黏性的物質　　　　(B) 剪刀
　　(C) 硬紙板　　　　　　　(D) 長釘子
　　＊ glue〔glu〕n. 膠　　sticky〔'stɪkɪ〕adj. 黏稠的
　　　 cardboard〔'kard,bord, -,bɔrd〕n. 硬紙板

52. (**A**)　M : Isn't it cold today?

W : Yes, and the streets are covered with ice.

How are the streets?

男：今天冷不冷？

女：冷，而且街道上結滿了冰。

街道如何？

(A) 很滑 　　　　　　　　　(B) 很安全

(C) 滑動的 　　　　　　　　(D) 很寬

* slippery (ˈslɪpərɪ) *adj.* 滑的　　slipping (ˈslɪpɪŋ) *adj.* 滑動的

53. (**C**)　M : Doesn't the weather change quickly here?

W : Yes, we're having a shower now.

What did the woman say about the weather?

男：這裏的天氣變化快不快？

女：快，現在正下著陣雨。

這位女士說天氣如何？

(A) 起霧 　　　　　　　　　(B) 正在下霰

(C) 正在下雨 　　　　　　　(D) 正在下雪

* misty (ˈmɪstɪ) *adj.* 有霧的

sleet (slit) *v.* 下霰（夾著雨的雪）

54. (**C**)　W : Do you smell anything?

M : Yes, I do, and those fumes are poisonous.

What kind of fumes are they?

女：你聞到什麼嗎？

男：是的，我聞到了，而且那種氣體有毒。

那是什麼種氣體？

(A) 有益的 　　　　　　　　(B) 味道淡的

(C) 危險的 　　　　　　　　(D) 濃縮的

* smell (smɛl) *v.* 聞　　fume (fjum) *n.* 氣體

poisonous (ˈpɔɪsṇəs) *adj.* 有毒的

beneficial (ˌbɛnəˈfɪʃəl) *adj.* 有益的

concentrated (ˈkɑnsṇˌtretɪd) *adj.* 濃縮的

55. (**A**)　W : What are the soldiers doing now?

　　　　　M : They are in battle, but they couldn't advance.

　　　　　What couldn't the soldiers do?

　　　　　女：士兵們正在做什麼？

　　　　　男：他們正在交戰，但是卻無法前進。

　　　　　士兵們無法做什麼？

　　　　　　(A) <u>往前進</u>　　　　(B) 撤退　　　　(C) 開火　　　　(D) 放鬆

　　　　　　＊ advance〔əd'væns〕*v.* 前進

　　　　　　　forward〔'fɔrwəd〕*adv.* 往前地

　　　　　　　retreat〔rɪ'trit〕*v.* 撤退

56. (**D**)　M : Which of the boys is Henry Smith?

　　　　　W : The one with the yellow coat using the crutches.

　　　　　What is the probable reason for Henry's using crutches?

　　　　　男：哪個男孩是亨利史密斯？

　　　　　女：身穿黃外套、拄著拐杖的那位。

　　　　　亨利使用拐杖可能的原因為何？

　　　　　　(A) 他贏得第一名。　　　　　　(B) 他的手指割傷。

　　　　　　(C) 他摔斷手臂。　　　　　　　(D) <u>他扭傷腳踝。</u>

　　　　　　＊ crutch〔krʌtʃ〕*n.* 拐杖

　　　　　　　sprain〔spren〕*v.* 扭傷　　　ankle〔'æŋkl̩〕*n.* 腳踝

57. (**B**)　M : Mary, why isn't Jane teaching here this semester?

　　　　　W : Don't you know she was dismissed?

　　　　　Why isn't Jane teaching here any more?

　　　　　男：瑪麗，珍這學期為什麼沒在這裏教書？

　　　　　女：你不知道她被解雇了嗎？

　　　　　為何珍不繼續在這兒教書？

　　　　　　(A) 她對教書感到厭倦。

　　　　　　(B) <u>她被炒魷魚。</u>

　　　　　　(C) 她正在換工作。

　　　　　　(D) 學校太遠了。

　　　　　　＊ semester〔sə'mɛstə〕*n.* 學期

　　　　　　　dismiss〔dɪs'mɪs〕*v.* 解雇

58. (**D**)　W : What time does the opera start?

M : At 7:30. We have 25 minutes to get there.

What time is it now?

女：歌劇幾點開始？

男：七點三十分。我們有二十五分可以到那兒。

現在是什麼時刻？

(A) 六點五十分　　　　　　(B) 七點二十五分

(C) 六點零五分　　　　　　(D) 七點零五分

* opera ('ɑpərə) *n.* 歌劇

59. (**A**)　M : Do you sell jogging shoes, ma'am?

W : Yes, we do. They're on special this week at $ 20

a pair or two pairs for $ 35.

How much is one pair of jogging shoes?

男：小姐，你們有賣慢跑鞋嗎？

女：是的，我們有。這個星期特價，一雙二十元或者二雙三十五元。

一雙慢跑鞋多少錢？

(A) 二十元　　　(B) 四十元　　　(C) 三十五元　　　(D) 七十元

60. (**A**)　M : Why were you late for class this morning?

W : I overslept and missed the bus.

Why was the woman late?

男：妳今天早上為何上課遲到？

女：我睡過頭，沒趕上公車。

這位女士為何遲到？

(A) 她比平常晚起床。　　　(B) 公車誤點。

(C) 她忘了有課。　　　　　(D) 她的鐘壞了。

* oversleep ('ovə'slip) *v.* 睡過頭

LISTENING TEST 14

- *Directions for questions 1-25. You will hear questions on the test tape. Select the one item A, B, C or D which answers the question correctly, and mark your answer sheet.*

1. A. Ruth only   B. Mr. Blake
   C. only Woody   D. Ruth or Woody

2. A. exactly 9 : 00   B. around noon
   C. before 9 : 00   D. after 9 : 00

3. A. clean   B. flat
   C. heavy   D. loose

4. A. asked   B. notified
   C. blamed   D. reviewed

5. A. attitude   B. relaxed
   C. stiff   D. altitude

6. A. very short   B. a part
   C. gradually   D. graciously

7. A. bumpy   B. wavy
   C. smooth   D. tough

8. A. A prize was gave to me.
   B. I gave a prize.
   C. I give a prize.
   D. A prize was given to me.

9. A. a list of men   B. a group of women
   C. a list of the food available   D. a list of members

10. A. The construction was good.
    B. The fixture was good.
    C. The plan was good.
    D. The texture was good.

11. A. He left his unit.   B. He assumed control.
    C. He found his unit.   D. He lost control.

12. A. She rejected the prize.
    B. She received the prize.
    C. She accepted the prize.
    D. She didn't win the prize.

13. A. a plant   B. a car
    C. an animal   D. a building

14. A. Yes, he won't.   B. No, she won't.
    C. No, he won't.   D. Yes, she won't.

15. A. a box   B. a beverage
    C. a liquid   D. a container

16. A. 9 : 30   B. 10 : 00
    C. 11 : 30   D. 10 : 30

17. A. Let's review it.   B. Let's skip it.
    C. Let's finish it.   D. Let's forget it.

18. A. a big car   B. a small car
    C. a new car   D. an old car

19. A. Crenson   B. Jack
    C. Paul   D. Jack Paul

20. A. dishes   B. cars
    C. clothes   D. glasses

21. A. rough   B. polished
    C. sharp   D. bright

22. A. broken   B. bad
    C. costly   D. cheap

23. A. 50 dollars   B. 100 dollars
    C. 115 dollars   D. 148 dollars

24. A. get on board   B. get off the plane
    C. eat brunch   D. check in at the hotel

25. A. measuring   B. painting
    C. holding   D. sharpening

● *Directions for questions 26-50. You will hear statements on the test tape. Select the one answer A, B, C, or D which comes closest to the meaning of the statement and mark your answer sheet.*

26. A. He objected to it.   B. He ignored it.
    C. He forgot it.   D. He tested it.

27. A. Mary believed in him.   B. Mary relieved him.
    C. Mary helped him.   D. Mary relied on him.

28. A. She crawled on the ladder.
    B. She jumped down the ladder.
    C. She went down the ladder.
    D. She pulled down the ladder.

29. A. David perfected his duties.
    B. David took over his duties again.
    C. David forgot his duties.
    D. David did not do his duties.

30. A. We heard an argument.　　B. We heard the band.
　　C. We heard the bell.　　　　D. We heard a talk.

31. A. He explained the progress.
　　B. He explained the process.
　　C. He explained the dialog.
　　D. He explained the enrollment.

32. A. He didn't hear the question.
　　B. He couldn't answer the question.
　　C. He couldn't read the question.
　　D. He thought the answer was easy.

33. A. The brakes are operating properly.
　　B. The brake system is not functioning properly.
　　C. The brake system has foul odor.
　　D. The brake fluid is flowing freely.

34. A. Stop what you are doing.　　B. Lie down over here.
　　C. Go back to work.　　　　　D. Continue working.

35. A. Richard forgot the key to the lock.
　　B. Richard resisted the lock on the door.
　　C. Richard locked the door quickly.
　　D. Richard closed the lock on the door.

36. A. A few wanted to leave.
　　B. Several wanted to leave.
　　C. Most wanted to leave.
　　D. None wanted to leave.

37. A. Soft cover books are more expensive.
　　B. Hardcover books are less expensive.
　　C. Hardcover books are cheaper.
　　D. Soft cover books are less expensive.

38. A. Nickie's roommate went to the post office.
    B. Nickie went to the post office.
    C. Nickie and her roommate went there.
    D. Nickie's roommate didn't go to the post office.

39. A. He returned the parcel.
    B. He didn't write his return address.
    C. He forgot to return the parcel.
    D. He wrote his return address.

40. A. Sophie's friend is learning to drive.
    B. Sophie taught her friend to drive.
    C. Sophie still hasn't learned to drive.
    D. A friend gave Sophie driving lessons.

41. A. She arrived just before 11 : 00.
    B. She arrived immediately after Mr. Brown.
    C. She arrived a few minutes after eleven.
    D. She arrived with Mr. Brown.

42. A. The fuel system was running low.
    B. Everything was working properly.
    C. The system was not working properly.
    D. The oil supply was sufficient.

43. A. He will finish his work today.
    B. He doesn't want to finish it today.
    C. He is able to work today.
    D. He will not finish his work today.

44. A. He always drinks coffee.
    B. He does not like coffee.
    C. He is accustomed to drinking coffee.
    D. He never drinks coffee.

45. A. He lost the gold.   B. He found the gold.
    C. He shaped the gold.   D. He melted the gold.

46. A. He left a new student in class.
    B. He found a new student in class.
    C. The class found a new student.
    D. He presented a new student.

47. A. The plane will take off at nine.
    B. The train will arrive at nine.
    C. The train will depart at nine.
    D. Both will depart at the same time.

48. A. It is to be sold at a higher price.
    B. It is already sold.
    C. It is reduced in price.
    D. It is being sold for a limited time.

49. A. He wore his new suit to work.
    B. He liked his new suit very much.
    C. He found a small hole in it.
    D. He made a hole in it.

50. A. We gave many of our books to the library.
    B. The library has only hardcover books on art topics.
    C. There are a large number of art books in the library.
    D. There are many paintings in the library.

● *Directions for questions 51-60. You will hear dialogs on the test*
  tape. Select the correct answer A, B, C, or D and mark your
  answer sheet.

51. A. none   B. two
    C. twenty-two   D. everyone knows

52. A. Dr. Hardy will come by plane.
    B. Dr. Hardy arrives this week.
    C. Dr. Hardy will come straight home.
    D. Dr. Hardy will come home after he visits Texas.

53. A. She wanted to go to town.
    B. She wanted to meet the captain's parents.
    C. She wanted to go to the airport.
    D. She wanted to grant his request.

54. A. eat a piece of candy
    B. eat something light
    C. drink something tasteful
    D. eat a big meal

55. A. Most of them are shipped to Manchester.
    B. Most cars are made outside of Manchester.
    C. Most of them are damaged in Manchester.
    D. Most of them are made in Manchester.

56. A. looking for something   B. looking for water
    C. planting something   D. getting dirty

57. A. 3 : 30   B. 2 : 50
    C. 3 : 00   D. 2 : 30

58. A. a supermarket   B. a department store
    C. a pharmacy   D. a garage

59. A. France   B. Italy
    C. Spain   D. England

60. A. hang clothes   B. sail a boat
    C. catch a horse   D. fish

ECL 聽力測驗 [**14**] 詳解

1. (**D**) Mr. Blake said either Ruth or Woody could go.
Who did Mr. Blake say could go？
布雷克先生說露絲或伍迪可以去。
布雷克先生說誰可以去？

(A) 只有露絲　　　　　　　(B) 布雷克生生
(C) 只有伍迪　　　　　　　(D) 露絲或伍迪

2. (**A**) The program is going to start at 9:00 sharp.
When will the program begin？
節目將在九點整開始。／節目何時開始？

(A) 正好九點　　　　　　　(B) 正午左右
(C) 九點前　　　　　　　　(D) 九點後

* sharp〔ʃɑrp〕*adv.* 準時地；整　　exactly〔ɪg'zæktlɪ〕*adv.* 精確地

3. (**B**) In addition to being square, what other characteristics
describe the mirror？
除了方形之外，還有什麼特色是描述鏡子？

(A) 乾淨的　　　　　　　　(B) 平坦的
(C) 沈重的　　　　　　　　(D) 寬鬆的

* *in addition to* 除了～之外　　square〔skwɛr〕*adj.* 方形的
characteristic〔ˌkærɪktə'rɪstɪk〕*n.* 特色
describe〔dɪ'skraɪb〕*v.* 描述　　mirror〔'mɪrə〕*n.* 鏡子
flat〔flæt〕*adj.* 平坦的　　loose〔lus〕*adj.* 寬鬆的

4. (**B**) The secretary was informed of the situation.
What do we mean by "informed"？
這位秘書被告知情況。／"informed" 是什麼意思？

(A) 請求　　　(B) 通知　　　(C) 責備　　　(D) 複習

* inform〔ɪn'fɔrm〕*v.* 報告；通知　　notify〔'notəˌfaɪ〕*v.* 通知
review〔rɪ'vju〕*v.* 複習

5. (**C**) During the landing, we all sat in a rigid position.
In what position did we sit?
在降落的時候，我們都保持僵硬的姿勢。／我們採用何種姿勢？

    (A) 態度   (B) 放鬆的   (C) 僵硬的   (D) 高度

    * rigid (ˋrɪdʒɪd) *adj.* 僵硬的   position (pəˋzɪʃən) *n.* 姿勢
    attitude (ˋætə͵tjud) *n.* 態度   stiff (stɪf) *adj.* 僵硬的
    altitude (ˋæltə͵tjud) *n.* 高度

6. (**C**) Little by little, I began to understand the meaning.
What is the meaning of the phrase "little by little"?
漸漸地，我開始了解這個意思。
"little by little" 這個片語的意思為何？

    (A) 非常短暫   (B) 一部份   (C) 逐漸地   (D) 和藹可親地

    * *little by little* 逐漸地   phrase (frez) *n.* 片語
    gradually (ˋgrædʒuəlɪ) *adv.* 逐漸地
    graciously (ˋgreʃəslɪ) *adv.* 和藹可親地

7. (**C**) We had a nice trip; it was not rough.
How was the trip?
我們有個愉快的旅行；它並不辛苦。／旅行如何？

    (A) 顛簸的   (B) 起伏的   (C) 順利的   (D) 艱苦的

    * bumpy (ˋbʌmpɪ) *adj.* 顛簸的   wavy (ˋwevɪ) *adj.* 起伏的

8. (**D**) They gave me a prize. What happened?
他們給我一個獎品。／發生什麼事？

    (A) 有個獎品給了我。（文法錯誤）   (B) 我給人一個獎品。
    (C) 我給人一個獎品。（時態錯誤）   (D) 有個獎品給了我。

9. (**C**) The student asked for a menu. What did she want?
這名學生要求看菜單。／她要什麼東西？

    (A) 一個男人的名單   (B) 一群女人
    (C) 可吃的食物的名單   (D) 成員名單

    * available (əˋveləbl) *adj.* 可獲得的

10. (**A**) The structure of the business building was excellent.
What was excellent?
這棟商業大樓的結構非常好。/ 什麼非常好?

(A) 結構很好 (B) 設備很好
(C) 設計圖很好 (D) 質地很好

* structure (ˈstrʌktʃɚ) *n.* 結構 construction (kənˈstrʌkʃən) *n.* 結構
fixture (ˈfɪkstʃɚ) *n.* 固定裝置;設備 texture (ˈtɛkstʃɚ) *n.* 質地

11. (**B**) Captain Miller took over the unit. What did he do?
米勒上尉接管該單位。/ 他做了什麼?

(A) 他離開他的單位。 (B) 他擔任管理。
(C) 他找到他的單位。 (D) 他失去控制。

* ***take over*** 接管 assume (əˈsjum) *v.* 擔任

12. (**A**) Mary refused to accept the prize. What did Mary do?
瑪麗拒絕接受獎品。/ 瑪麗做了什麼?

(A) 她拒絕了獎品。 (B) 她收到獎品。
(C) 她接受獎品。 (D) 她沒有得到獎品。

* reject (rɪˈdʒɛkt) *v.* 拒絕

13. (**C**) What is a horse?
馬是什麼?

(A) 植物 (B) 車子 (C) 動物 (D) 建築物

14. (**C**) Will Mr. Sutter be here?
沙特先生將來這裡嗎?

(A) 是的,他將不會。 (B) 不,她將不會。
(C) 不,他將不會。 (D) 是的,她將不會。

15. (**D**) The jam was in a jar. What was the jam in?
果醬在瓶子裏。/ 果醬在什麼裏面?

(A) 盒子 (B) 飲料 (C) 液體 (D) 容器

* beverage (ˈbɛv(ə)rɪdʒ) *n.* 飲料 liquid (ˈlɪkwɪd) *n.* 液體
container (kənˈtenɚ) *n.* 容器

16. (**D**) It was half past ten when the students took the test.
 When did they take the test?
 學生們在十點半考試。／學生們何時考試?

 (A) 九點三十分   (B) 十點
 (C) 十一點三十分   (D) 十點三十分

17. (**A**) The teacher said, "Let's go over the chapter."
 What did the teacher mean?
 老師說:「我們來複習這一章」。／老師的意思爲何?

 (A) 我們來複習它。   (B) 我們略過它。
 (C) 我們來完成它。   (D) 我們忘記它。

 * *go over* 複習   skip〔skɪp〕*v.* 略過

18. (**B**) Bill wants to trade his big car for a smaller one.
 What does he want?
 比爾要把他的大車換成小一點的車。／他想要什麼?

 (A) 大車   (B) 小車   (C) 新車   (D) 舊車

19. (**A**) The boy's name is Jack Paul Crenson.
 What is the boy's surname?
 這位男孩的姓名是傑克・保羅・奎恩森。／這位男孩姓什麼?

 (A) 奎恩森   (B) 傑克   (C) 保羅   (D) 傑克保羅

20. (**C**) Mrs. Taylor bought a washing machine.
 What can the machine wash?
 泰勒太太買了一台洗衣機。／這台機器可以洗什麼?

 (A) 盤子   (B) 汽車   (C) 衣服   (D) 眼鏡

21. (**C**) That piece of metal has a keen end.
 How is its end?
 那塊金屬一端很尖銳。／它一端如何?

 (A) 粗糙   (B) 有光澤   (C) 銳利   (D) 明亮的

 * keen〔kin〕*adj.* 尖銳的   polished〔'palɪʃt〕*adj.* 有光澤的
 sharp〔ʃarp〕*adj.* 銳利的

22. (**C**) Pat bought an expensive watch. How was the watch?

派特買了一支昂貴的手錶。／那支錶如何？

　(A) 壞掉　　　(B) 不好　　　(C) 昂貴　　　(D) 便宜

　* costly (ˈkɔstlɪ) *adj.* 昂貴的

23. (**D**) The salesman wants approximately 150 dollars for the TV set. How much does he charge for the TV set?

這位推銷員想以一百五十元左右賣掉電視機。
這台電視機他索價多少？

　(A) 五十元　　　　　　　　(B) 一百元
　(C) 一百一十五元　　　　　(D) 一百四十八元

　* approximately (əˈprɑksəmɪtlɪ) *adv.* 大概；左右

24. (**A**) The embarkation time is 10:30.
What should we do at 10:30?

登機時間是十點半。／我們應該在十點半做什麼？

　(A) 上飛機　　(B) 下飛機　　(C) 吃早午餐　　(D) 到旅館登記住宿

　* embarkation (ˌɛmbɑrˈkeʃən) *n.* 登機
　　get on 上車（船、飛機等交通工具）
　　get off 下車（船、飛機等交通工具）
　　brunch (brʌntʃ) *n.* 早午餐　　***check in*** 登記住宿

25. (**A**) Bob has a new tape measure in his work shop.
What does he use it for?

鮑伯的工廠裏有一卷新的捲尺。／他用它來做什麼？

　(A) 測量　　(B) 畫圖　　　(C) 握住　　　(D) 削尖

　* ***tape measure*** 捲尺　　measure (ˈmɛʒɚ) *v.* 測量
　　sharpen (ˈʃɑrpən) *v.* 使尖銳

26. (**A**) William protested the Lieutenant's decision.

威廉抗議中尉的決定。

　(A) 他反對它。　　　　　(B) 他不理它。
　(C) 他忘記它。　　　　　(D) 他測試它。

　* protest (prəˈtɛst) *v.* 抗議　　object (əbˈdʒɛkt) *v.* 反對
　　ignore (ɪgˈnor) *v.* 忽視；不理

27. (**D**) Mary depended on her boyfriend for help.
瑪麗依賴男友的幫助。

    (A) 瑪麗相信他。   (B) 瑪麗解救他。
    (C) 瑪麗幫助他。   (D) <u>瑪麗依靠他。</u>

    * ***depend on*** 依賴   relieve〔rɪ'liv〕 *v.* 解救
    rely on 依靠

28. (**C**) She climbed down the ladder during the fire drill.
她在消防演習時爬下梯子。

    (A) 她爬上梯子。   (B) 她從梯子上跳下來。
    (C) <u>她從梯子上下來。</u>   (D) 她將梯子拉下來。

    * drill〔drɪl〕 *n.* 練習   crawl〔krɔl〕 *v.* 爬行

29. (**B**) David resumed his duties.
大衛重回他的崗位。

    (A) 大衛將工作做得盡善盡美。   (B) <u>大衛再度接管他的工作。</u>
    (C) 大衛忘記他的工作。   (D) 大衛沒有執行他的工作。

    * resume〔rɪ'zjum〕 *v.* 再繼續   perfect〔pə'fɛkt〕 *v.* 使完美
    take over 接管

30. (**D**) We went to a lecture this afternoon.
我們今天下午去聽一場演講。

    (A) 我們聽到爭論。   (B) 我們聽樂團演奏。
    (C) 我們聽到鈴聲。   (D) <u>我們聽了一場演說。</u>

    * lecture〔'lɛktʃə〕 *n.* 演講   argument〔'argjəmənt〕 *n.* 爭論

31. (**B**) The engineer explained the procedure.
工程師解說這個程序。

    (A) 他解說進展。   (B) <u>他解說過程。</u>
    (C) 他解說對話。   (D) 他解說登記。

    * procedure〔prə'sidʒə〕 *n.* 程序   progress〔'prɑgrɛs〕 *n.* 進展
    process〔'prɑsɛs〕 *n.* 過程   enrollment〔ɪn'rolmənt〕 *n.* 登記

32. (**B**)　The boy said that he didn't know the answer.

這位男孩說他不知道答案。

(A) 他沒有聽到問題。　　　　　　(B) 他無法回答問題。

(C) 他無法讀問題。　　　　　　　(D) 他認為答案很簡單。

33. (**B**)　The brake system is fouled up.

煞車系統壞掉了。

(A) 煞車運作正常。　　　　　　　(B) 煞車系統運作不正常。

(C) 煞車系統有臭味。　　　　　　(D) 煞車油任意流出。

* brake〔brek〕*n.* 煞車　　*foul up* 弄壞　　foul〔faul〕*adj.* 惡臭的
odor〔'odɚ〕*n.* 氣味　　fluid〔'fluɪd〕*n.* 流體

34. (**A**)　Alex is getting mad. You'd better lay off.

亞歷士快發瘋了。你最好停止。

(A) 停止你正在做的事。　　　　　(B) 在這裏躺下。

(C) 回去工作。　　　　　　　　　(D) 繼續工作。

* *lay off* 停止

35. (**D**)　Richard fastened the lock on the door.

理查將門鎖鎖上。

(A) 理查忘了門的鑰匙。　　　　　(B) 理查抵住門鎖。

(C) 理查快速將門鎖上。　　　　　(D) 理查關上門鎖。

* fasten〔'fæsn̩〕*v.* 繫牢；關上　　resist〔rɪ'zɪst〕*v.* 抵抗

36. (**C**)　The majority of them wanted to leave.

他們大多數人都想離開。

(A) 有一些想離開。　　　　　　　(B) 有幾個想離開。

(C) 大部分想離開。　　　　　　　(D) 沒有人想離開。

* majority〔mə'dʒɔrətɪ〕*n.* 大多數

37. (**D**)　Soft cover books are cheaper than hardcover books.

平裝書比精裝書便宜。

(A) 平裝書比較貴。　　　　　　　(B) 精裝書較不貴。

(C) 精裝書較便宜。　　　　　　　(D) 平裝書較不貴。

* *soft cover* 平裝本　　hardcover〔'hard'kʌvɚ〕*n.* 精裝本

38. (**A**) Nickie did not want to go to the post office so her roommate went there alone.

妮琦不想去郵局，所以她的室友自己去。

(A) 妮琦的室友去郵局。   (B) 妮琦去郵局。

(C) 妮琦和她的室友去那兒。   (D) 妮琦的室友沒有去郵局。

39. (**B**) Lieutenant Smith forgot to put his return address on the parcel.

史密斯中尉忘了將寄件人地址寫在包裹上。

(A) 他歸還包裹。   (B) 他沒有寫寄件人地址。

(C) 他忘了歸還包裹。   (D) 他寫了寄件人地址。

* parcel (ˈpɑrsḷ) *n.* 包裹

40. (**D**) Sophie wanted to learn to drive. Therefore, her friend taught her.

蘇菲想學開車，所以她的朋友教她。

(A) 蘇菲的朋友在學開車。   (B) 蘇菲教朋友開車。

(C) 蘇菲尚未學開車。   (D) 一位朋友教蘇菲駕駛課程。

41. (**A**) Mrs. Brown arrived just before eleven and Mr. Brown arrived just after eleven.

布朗太太在十一點前一些到達，而布朗先生在十一點後一些到達。

(A) 她在十一點前一些到達。

(B) 她在布朗先生到後隨即到達。

(C) 她在十一點過後幾分鐘到達。

(D) 她和布朗先生一起到達。

42. (**C**) There was a malfunction in the system.

系統故障。

(A) 燃料系統運作緩慢。   (B) 每樣東西都正常運作。

(C) 系統運作不正常。   (D) 供油充足。

* malfunction (mælˈfʌŋkʃən) *n.* 故障
sufficient (səˈfɪʃənt) *adj.* 充足的

43. (**D**) Dr. Wright would like to finish his work today, but he won't be able to.
　　萊特醫師想在今天完成工作，但是他無法辦到。

　　(A) 他將在今天完成工作。　　　(B) 他不想在今天完成。
　　(C) 他今天可以工作。　　　　　(D) 他今天將不會完成工作。

44. (**C**) He is used to drinking coffee for lunch.
　　他習慣午餐喝咖啡。

　　(A) 他總是喝咖啡。　　　　　　(B) 他不喜歡咖啡。
　　(C) 他習慣喝咖啡。　　　　　　(D) 他從不喝咖啡。

　　* *be used to* 習慣於　　accustom〔əˋkʌstəm〕v. 使習慣

45. (**B**) He discovered the gold.
　　他發現黃金。

　　(A) 他遺失黃金。　　　　　　　(B) 他找到黃金。
　　(C) 他塑造黃金。　　　　　　　(D) 他將黃金熔化。

　　* shape〔ʃep〕v. 塑造　　melt〔mɛlt〕v. 熔化

46. (**D**) The teacher introduced the new student to the class.
　　老師向全班介紹新同學。

　　(A) 他將一位新同學留在班上。　　(B) 他發現班上有位新同學。
　　(C) 班上發現一位新生。　　　　　(D) 他介紹一位新生。

　　* present〔prɪˋzɛnt〕v. 介紹

47. (**C**) The plane doesn't leave at 9 o'clock, but the train does.
　　飛機不是九點起飛，但火車是。

　　(A) 飛機將在九點起飛。　　　　　(B) 火車將在九點到達。
　　(C) 火車將在九點離開。　　　　　(D) 兩者同時離開。

　　* *take off* 起飛　　depart〔dɪˋpɑrt〕v. 離開；出發

48. (**C**) The merchandise is on sale.
　　商品在特價。

　　(A) 它將以較高的價格賣出。　　　(B) 它已經賣出。
　　(C) 它的價格降低。　　　　　　　(D) 它要在限定的時間賣出。

　　* merchandise〔ˋmɝtʃənˏdaɪz〕n. 商品

49. (**D**) He tore a hole in his new suit.
　　　他將新西裝扯破一個洞。

　　　(A) 他穿新西裝去上班。　　　(B) 他非常喜歡他的新西裝。
　　　(C) 他發現上面有小洞。　　　(D) 他在上面弄了一個洞。

　　　* tear 〔tɛr〕 v. 扯破

50. (**C**) This library has many books on art.
　　　這座圖書館有許多關於藝術的書。

　　　(A) 我們把許多書捐給圖書館。
　　　(B) 圖書館只有藝術主題的精裝書。
　　　(C) 圖書館有很多藝術書籍。
　　　(D) 圖書館裏有許多畫。

　　　* topic 〔'tɑpɪk〕 n. 主題　　　*a large number of* 許多；大量的
　　　painting 〔'pentɪŋ〕 n. 畫

51. (**B**) W : How many computers are there on the table?
　　　　　　M : There are only two, I think.
　　　　　How many computers are on the table?
　　　　　女：桌上有幾台電腦？
　　　　　男：只有兩台，我想。
　　　　　桌上有幾台電腦？

　　　(A) 沒有　　　　　　　　　(B) 兩台
　　　(C) 二十二台　　　　　　　(D) 每個人都知道

52. (**D**) M : Will Dr. Hardy get back next week?
　　　　　　W : Yes, he will. He plans to stop in Texas for a few
　　　　　　　　days and then he will come home.
　　　　　What did the woman say about Dr. Hardy?
　　　　　男：哈蒂醫師下星期會回來嗎？
　　　　　女：是的，他會。他計畫在德州停留幾天，然後就回來。
　　　　　這位女士說哈蒂醫師如何？

　　　(A) 哈蒂醫師將搭飛機回來。　　(B) 哈蒂醫師將於本週抵達。
　　　(C) 哈蒂醫師將直接回家。　　　(D) 哈蒂將在拜訪德州後回來。

53. (**C**)　W : Captain, my parents are coming to town to visit me. I would like time off on the seventeenth to meet them at the airport.

　　　　　M : Request granted.

　　　　　What did the woman want?

　　　女：上尉，我父母親要來城裏探望我。我想在十七日請假去機場接他們。

　　　男：請求獲准。

　　　這位女士想做什麼?

　　　(A) 她想進城。　　　　　　　　(B) 她想要見上尉的父母親。

　　　(C) 她想去機場。　　　　　　　(D) 她想批准他的請求。

　　　* request (rɪˋkwɛst) *n.* 請求　　grant (grænt) *v.* 批准

54. (**C**)　W : Are you thirsty?

　　　　　M : Yes, I'd like some juice.

　　　　　What would the man like to do?

　　　女：你口渴嗎?

　　　男：是的，我想喝些果汁。

　　　這位男士想做什麼?

　　　(A) 吃一塊糖果　　　　　　　　(B) 吃清淡的東西

　　　(C) 喝好喝的東西　　　　　　　(D) 吃一頓大餐

55. (**D**)　M : Where were these cars manufactured?

　　　　　W : Most British cars were made in Manchester.

　　　　　What did the woman say about the British cars?

　　　男：這些汽車在哪裏製造?

　　　女：大部分的英國車都在曼徹斯特製造。

　　　這位女士說英國車如何?

　　　(A) 它們大部分被運到曼徹斯特。

　　　(B) 大部分的汽車在曼徹斯特以外的地方製造。

　　　(C) 它們大部分在曼徹斯特銷毀。

　　　(D) 它們大部分在曼徹斯特製造。

　　　* manufacture (ˏmænjəˋfæktʃɚ) *v.* 製造

　　　Manchester (ˋmænˏtʃɛstɚ) *n.* 曼徹斯特

56.(**C**) W : May I watch what you are doing?

M : Sure. You dig a hole, put in the seed, cover it with dirt, and then water it.

What is the man doing?

女：我可以看你在做什麼嗎？

男：當然。挖個洞、放進種子、蓋上泥土，然後再澆水。

這位男士在做什麼？

(A) 找東西　　　(B) 找水　　　(C) <u>種東西</u>　　　(D) 弄髒

57.(**B**) M : Miss, what time is flight 101 for Boston due to depart?

W : It leaves at 3:50, but you must check in one hour prior to departure.

At what time must the passenger be at the airport for flight 101?

男：小姐，往波士頓的 101 號班機預定何時起飛？

女：三點五十分起飛，不過你必須在起飛前一小時辦登機手續。

該乘客要搭 101 號班機必須在何時到機場？

(A) 三點三十分　　　　　(B) <u>二點五十分</u>

(C) 三點　　　　　　　　(D) 二點三十分

* due〔dju〕*adj.* 預期的　　***check in*** 辦登機手續
prior to 在～之前　　departure〔dɪˋpartʃɚ〕*n.* 離開

58.(**C**) W : May I have this prescription filled here? I have a terrible headache.

M : Yes, but you will have a 15-minute wait.

Where did this conversation most probably take place?

女：我可以在這裡配這幅處方嗎？我頭痛得厲害。

男：可以，不過你得等十五分鐘。

這段對話最可能發生在哪裏？

(A) 超級市場　　(B) 百貨公司　　(C) <u>藥房</u>　　(D) 車庫

* prescription〔prɪˋskrɪpʃən〕*n.* 處方
fill a prescription 配藥　　pharmacy〔ˋfɑrməsɪ〕*n.* 藥房
garage〔gəˋrɑʒ, -ˋrɑdʒ〕*n.* 車庫

59. (**C**) W：Where did you and Sue go on your vacation?

M：We spent three days in England, one week in Italy, and five days in France.

Which of the following countries was not mentioned?

女：你和蘇到哪兒去度假？

男：我們在英國待三天，義大利待一星期，法國待五天。

下列那個國家沒有被提到？

(A) 法國　　　　(B) 義大利　　　　(C) 西班牙　　　(D) 英國

60. (**D**) W：Can you help me? I haven't done this before.

M：It's easy. All you do is put the worm on the hook, loose the line, and cast it.

What is the man showing the woman how to do?

女：你能幫助我嗎？我以前沒做過這個。

男：很簡單。妳只要將蟲放在鉤子上，鬆開線，然後拋出去。

這位男士向女士示範什麼？

(A) 掛衣服　　　(B) 航行船隻　　(C) 捉一匹馬　　(D) 釣魚

* hook〔huk〕n. 鉤子　　　loose〔lus〕v. 釋放；鬆開

cast〔kæst〕v. 拋出　　　hang〔hæŋ〕v. 掛

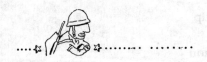

No one has more driving ambition than the boy who wants to buy a car.

沒有人比一個想買車的男孩更有開車的雄心壯志。

LISTENING TEST 15

● *Directions for questions 1-25. You will hear questions on the test tape. Select the one item A, B, C or D which answers the question correctly, and mark your answer sheet.*

1. A. in the cafeteria   B. He has a good appetite.
   C. at 4 o'clock   D. bread and meat

2. A. if I wanted anything except coffee
   B. if I carried some coffee
   C. if I wanted some coffee
   D. if I sold any coffee

3. A. Classes begin at eight o'clock.
   B. Only young children go to school there.
   C. The school is three miles from here.
   D. The school is closed for the day.

4. A. He stole nothing.   B. He escaped.
   C. He returned the goods.   D. He was arrested.

5. A. large   B. windy
   C. cold   D. lacks fresh air

6. A. the ability to speed up
   B. the color of the car
   C. the slowing-down action
   D. the stopping action

7. A. soccer   B. baseball
   C. football   D. swimming

8. A. a directional light   B. a new headlight
   C. a spare tire   D. a warning device

9. A. because she goes on a vacation
   B. because she is sick of working all the time
   C. because she is sick
   D. because she is fired

10. A. He got it at a store.
    B. He read it slowly.
    C. He looked at it for a long time.
    D. He read it quickly.

11. A. She received many flowers.
    B. She sent me many flowers.
    C. She sent me to the hospital.
    D. She was very kind.

12. A. He thanked us.
    B. He gave us a test earlier.
    C. He announced a test.
    D. He told us he was sorry.

13. A. to board the ship   B. to take a train
    C. to see the mountain   D. to get on the plane

14. A. a bowl   B. sugar
    C. coffee   D. nothing

15. A. both   B. neither
    C. a hot dog   D. a sandwich

16. A. William's   B. George's
    C. to New York   D. to Boston

17. A. temporarily   B. forever
    C. for a short time   D. for a vacation

18. A. black   B. with sugar and cream
    C. with cream   D. with sugar only

19. A. meek   B. tough
    C. lazy   D. disloyal

20. A. He thought the price is too high.
    B. He thought the price is too low.
    C. He thought the price is reasonable.
    D. He agreed with the man.

21. A. some wine   B. a sign
    C. a vine   D. bind

22. A. a period of rest   B. a mistake
    C. a complaint   D. a visitor

23. A. gay   B. unpleasant
    C. easy   D. strange

24. A. to have some food preserved
    B. to have some rooms reserved
    C. to make some friends
    D. to make some money

25. A. a section   B. a name
    C. a sheet   D. a number

● *Directions for questions 26-50. You will hear statements on the test tape. Select the one answer A, B, C, or D which comes closest to the meaning of the statement and mark your answer sheet.*

26. A. They were not clear.   B. They were hard.
    C. They were not correct.   D. They were easy.

27. A. He was strong.　　　　B. He was sick.
　　C. He was lazy.　　　　　D. He was weak.

28. A. There was no lights on it. B. There was grassy on it.
　　C. There was water on it.　 D. There were birds on it.

29. A. It does not change.　　 B. It changes.
　　C. It is inconsistent.　　　D. It is variable.

30. A. The weather is pleasant.
　　B. The weather is hot and dry.
　　C. The weather is humid.
　　D. The weather is cool.

31. A. Someone else was talking on the line.
　　B. There were many wires busy.
　　C. The line was out of order.
　　D. Paul was too busy to call.

32. A. The man was given a fine.
　　B. The man was found innocent.
　　C. The man was sentenced to prison.
　　D. The man was found guilty.

33. A. He killed the sick horse.
　　B. He killed the fat horse.
　　C. He killed the injured horse.
　　D. He killed the dying horse.

34. A. The pay was more than usual.
　　B. The pay was less than usual.
　　C. There was little pay.
　　D. There was some pay.

35. A. It was not worth much.
    B. It was not very expensive.
    C. It cost more than it was worth.
    D. It cost a lot.

36. A. He got a high score.
    B. He missed a few questions.
    C. His score was unsatisfactory.
    D. He received help on the examination.

37. A. She plans to have five children.
    B. Her children are sick.
    C. She stays with sick children.
    D. She has five children that are grown up.

38. A. I review my lesson now and then.
    B. I don't have time to study my lesson.
    C. I review my lesson one time.
    D. I overlook studying my lesson sometimes.

39. A. I am nearest to the phone.
    B. He is not near the phone.
    C. He is nearest to the phone.
    D. I doubt there is a phone.

40. A. The road was level.
    B. We lived in an apartment.
    C. We lay down on the highway.
    D. One of our tires lost its air.

41. A. He must go to class often.
    B. He must study unconsciously.
    C. He must not study too much.
    D. He must pay close attention to his lessons.

42. A. He became satisfied.
    B. He became exhausted.
    C. He became happy.
    D. He became scared.

43. A. His guest is a problem for him.
    B. He doesn't know about the gas.
    C. I have an idea about his problem.
    D. His problem is greater than mine.

44. A. He will write twice on his trip.
    B. He would write twice a day.
    C. He would not write the second week.
    D. He promised to write two times each week.

45. A. Gary had more homework than Susan.
    B. Gary worked with Susan at home.
    C. Gary told Susan to do her homework at home.
    D. Gary asked Susan to look at his homework.

46. A. I wanted a light-colored suit.
    B. I don't like the suit at all.
    C. The suit is not dark enough.
    D. I don't like the style of it.

47. A. They will be at the station on time.
    B. They won't catch the train.
    C. They will get on the train.
    D. They won't miss their train.

48. A. They asked us for a suggestion.
    B. They invited us to their house.
    C. We wanted to invite them for a visit.
    D. We suggested a place for them to visit.

49. A. It is highly polished.   B. It is not clean.
    C. It is being painted.   D. It is covered with paper.

50. A. We enjoy the editorials.
    B. We enjoy the newspaper staff.
    C. We enjoy the news of our city.
    D. We enjoy international news.

● *Directions for questions 51-60. You will hear dialogs on the test tape. Select the correct answer A, B, C, or D and mark your answer sheet.*

51. A. Tom is speaking with a lawyer.
    B. The tall man and Tom are law students.
    C. Tom's students are discussing law.
    D. The tall man is Tom's student.

52. A. It was too rigid.   B. It was too artificial.
    C. It was too soft.   D. It was too dirty.

53. A. separating them   B. fastening them
    C. loosening them   D. removing them

54. A. a snack   B. the main course
    C. cream   D. dessert

55. A. He will order dinner.   B. He will make dinner.
    C. He will charge for dinner. D. He will eat dinner.

56. A. There was something wrong with her car.
    B. She got up too late to catch the bus.
    C. She was broke and couldn't afford the bus.
    D. Her car got stuck in the driveway.

57. A. She went jogging.
　　B. She went to the store.
　　C. She went for a walk.
　　D. She went to get a newspaper.

58. A. She is sick.
　　B. She said she would come later.
　　C. She decided to stay home.
　　D. She had a date.

59. A. too hard-working　　　　　B. rather boastful
　　C. very dependable　　　　　D. strong in math

60. A. a butcher　　　　　　　　B. an electrician
　　C. a carpenter　　　　　　　D. a plumber

Patient: "This hospital is no good. They treat us like dogs."
Orderly: "Mr. Jones, you know that's not true. Now, roll over."

病人：「這家醫院不好，對我們像狗一樣。」
護理員：「瓊斯先生，你知道這不是真的。現在，翻過去。」

ECL 聽力測驗 [15] 詳解

1. (**C**) Mr. Jones has supper at four o'clock, he eats in the
cafeteria, and he always has a good appetite.
When does Mr. Jones have supper?
瓊斯先生四點吃晚餐，他在自助餐廳吃，而且他的胃口一直都很好。
瓊斯先生何時吃晚餐？

    (A) 在自助餐廳　　(B) 他胃口很好　　(C) <u>四點</u>　　(D) 麵包和肉

    * supper ('sʌpə) *n.* 晚餐　　cafeteria (ˌkæfə'tɪrɪə) *n.* 自助餐廳
appetite ('æpəˌtaɪt) *n.* 食慾

2. (**C**) John said "How about a cup of coffee?"
What did he want to know?
約翰說：「要不要喝杯咖啡？」。／他想知道什麼？

    (A) 我是不是要咖啡以外的東西。　　(B) 我是不是有帶咖啡。

    (C) <u>我是不是要喝咖啡。</u>　　(D) 我是不是有賣咖啡。

3. (**C**) How far is it to the school?
到學校要多遠？

    (A) 八點開始上課。　　(B) 只有小孩到那裏上學。

    (C) <u>學校離這裏三哩。</u>　　(D) 學校白天關閉。

4. (**D**) The thief was caught with the stolen goods.
What happened to him?
那個小偷人贓俱獲被逮住了。／他怎麼了？

    (A) 他什麼也沒偷。　　(B) 他逃走了。

    (C) 他歸還東西。　　(D) <u>他被捕了。</u>

    * arrest (ə'rɛst) *v.* 逮捕

5. (**D**) The room is very stuffy. How is the room?
房間很悶。／房間怎麼樣？

    (A) 很大　　(B) 有風　　(C) 很冷　　(D) <u>缺少新鮮空氣</u>

    * stuffy ('stʌfɪ) *adj.* 通風不良的；窒悶的

6. (**A**) Scott was pleased with the acceleration of the car. What was he pleased with?

史考特對車子的加速性能十分滿意。／他對什麼很滿意？

(A) 加速性能　　(B) 車子的顏色　　(C) 減速的動作　　(D) 煞車的動作

* acceleration〔æk͵sɛlə'reʃən〕 *n.* 加速

   speed up 加速（↔ *slow down* 減速）

7. (**C**) Football is considered a major sport in college; swimming a minor sport. Which is a major sport?

美式足球被認爲是大學裏一項主要的運動；游泳則是次要運動。哪一個是主要的運動？

(A) 足球　　　　(B) 棒球　　　　　(C) 美式足球　　　(D) 游泳

* football〔'fut͵bɔl〕 *n.* 美式足球

   minor〔'maɪnɚ〕 *adj.* 次要的　　soccer〔'sɑkɚ〕 *n.* 足球

8. (**D**) Eric bought a new horn for his car. What did he buy?

艾瑞克替車子買了新喇叭。／他買了什麼？

(A) 方向燈　　　(B) 新的頭燈　　　(C) 備胎　　　　　(D) 警告裝置

* horn〔hɔrn〕 *n.* 喇叭　　headlight〔'hɛd͵laɪt〕 *n.*（車的）頭燈

   spare〔spɛr〕 *adj.* 備用的　　device〔dɪ'vaɪs〕 *n.* 裝置

9. (**C**) Jane is taking sick leave from work for the summer. Why is Jane absent from work?

珍在夏天時請了病假，沒去上班。／珍爲什麼沒去上班？

(A) 因爲她去度假。　　　　　　　(B) 因爲她厭惡一直工作。

(C) 因爲她生病了。　　　　　　　(D) 因爲她被解雇了。

* *take a sick leave* 請病假　　*be sick of* ~　厭惡~

10. (**D**) Jason glanced through the book. What did he do?

傑生把那本書大略瀏覽一下。／他做了什麼？

(A) 他在商店裏買了這本書。　　　(B) 他慢慢地讀這本書。

(C) 這本書他注視了很久。　　　　(D) 他很快地讀完這本書。

* glance〔glæns〕 *v.* 匆匆看；稍微看一下

11. (**B**) It was kind of Susan to send me flowers when I was in hospital. What did Susan do?

蘇珊人眞好，我住院時她送花給我。／蘇珊做了什麼？

(A) 她收到很多花。　　　　　　(B) 她送我很多花。

(C) 她送我去醫院。　　　　　　(D) 她人很好。

12. (**D**) The professor apologized to us for not announcing the test earlier. What did he do?

教授因爲沒早一點宣布考試的消息，而向我們道歉。

他做了什麼？

(A) 他向我們道謝。　　　　　　(B) 他提早考試。

(C) 他宣布要考試。　　　　　　(D) 他對我們說他很抱歉。

＊ apologize〔ə'pɑlə,dʒaɪz〕v. 道歉　　announce〔ə'naʊns〕v. 宣布

13. (**A**) Why did Frank go to the harbor?

法蘭克爲何要去港口？

(A) 搭船　　　(B) 搭火車　　　(C) 看山　　　(D) 搭飛機

＊ harbor〔'hɑrbə〕n. 港口　　board〔bord〕v. 搭乘

　　get on 上車（船、飛機等）

14. (**B**) There was a bowl of sugar on the coffee table. What was on the table?

咖啡桌上有一碗糖。／桌上有什麼？

(A) 一個碗　　　(B) 糖　　　(C) 咖啡　　　(D) 什麼都沒有

＊ bowl〔bol〕n. 碗

15. (**D**) Sara would rather have a sandwich than a hot dog. What would she prefer?

莎拉寧可吃三明治，也不願吃熱狗。／她比較喜歡什麼？

(A) 兩個都喜歡　　　　　　　(B) 兩個都不喜歡

(C) 熱狗　　　　　　　　　　(D) 三明治

＊ ***would rather*** A ***than*** B 寧願A 也不願B

　　sandwich〔'sændwɪtʃ〕n. 三明治

16. (**B**) William drove George's car from New York to Boston. Whose car was he driving?

威廉開著喬治的車,從紐約開到波士頓。/ 他開的是誰的車?

(A) 威廉的   (B) 喬治的
(C) 去紐約   (D) 去波士頓

17. (**B**) Mary is leaving her job for good. How long is Mary leaving her job?

瑪麗將永遠離開她的工作。/ 瑪麗要離職多久?

(A) 暫時   (B) 永遠   (C) 短時間   (D) 去度假

* *for good* 永遠 (= *forever*)
   temporarily ('tɛmpə‚rɛrəlɪ) *adv.* 暫時地~

18. (**D**) He likes sugar in his coffee, and nothing else. How does he like his coffee?

他的咖啡只要加糖就好。/ 他想要什麼樣的咖啡?

(A) 黑咖啡   (B) 加糖和奶精   (C) 加奶精   (D) 只要加糖

* black (blæk) *adj.* (咖啡) 純的

19. (**B**) Which one of the following words describes a strong person?

下列哪個字可用來描述強壯的人?

(A) 柔順的   (B) 強壯的   (C) 懶惰的   (D) 不忠實的

* meek (mik) *adj.* 柔順的   tough (tʌf) *adj.* 強壯的
   disloyal (dɪs'lɔɪəl) *adj.* 不忠的

20. (**B**) The man offered $1000 for the car, but John shook his head. What did John mean?

這部車那個人出價一千元,但約翰搖搖頭。/ 約翰的意思是什麼?

(A) 他認為價錢太高。   (B) 他認為價錢太低。
(C) 他認為價錢合理。   (D) 他同意那個人的說法。

* offer ('ɔfɚ) *v.* 出價
   reasonable ('riznəbḷ) *adj.* 合理的

21. (**C**) The front of May's house is covered with a honeysuckle vine. What covers the front of May's house?

梅的房子前面長滿了忍冬的藤蔓。/ 梅的房子前面長滿了什麼?

(A) 一些酒　　　　(B) 號誌　　　　(C) 藤蔓　　　　(D) 綁

* honeysuckle 〔'hʌnɪ,sʌk!〕 *n.* 忍冬　　vine 〔vaɪn〕 *n.* 藤蔓
bind 〔baɪnd〕 *v.* 綁

22. (**A**) We are allowed some breaks on the job each day. What is a break?

每天工作時我們會有一些休息時間。/ 休息時間是指什麼?

(A) 休息時間　　　(B) 錯誤　　　　(C) 抱怨　　　　(D) 訪客

* break 〔brek〕 *n.* 休息時間　　complaint 〔kəm'plent〕 *n.* 抱怨

23. (**B**) She told me of her painful experience. How was her experience?

她告訴我她的痛苦經驗。/ 她的經驗如何?

(A) 愉快的　　　　　　　　　(B) 不愉快的
(C) 容易的;舒適的　　　　　(D) 奇怪的

* gay 〔ge〕 *adj.* 愉快的　　unpleasant 〔ʌn'plɛznt〕 *adj.* 不愉快的

24. (**B**) I am going to make reservations for my trip. What am I going to do?

我要去預訂旅行的住宿及交通等等。/ 我要做什麼事?

(A) 保存一些食物　　　　　　(B) 預留一些房間
(C) 交一些朋友　　　　　　　(D) 賺一些錢

* *make reservations* 預訂　　preserve 〔prɪ'zɜv〕 *v.* 保存

25. (**C**) A leaf was torn out of my book. What was torn out?

我的書有一頁被撕掉了。/ 什麼被撕掉了?

(A) 一個章節　　　　　　　　(B) 一個名字
(C) 一頁　　　　　　　　　　(D) 一個號碼

* tear 〔tɛr〕 *v.* 撕掉　　section 〔'sɛkʃən〕 *n.* (書、文章) 節;段落
sheet 〔ʃit〕 *n.* 一張;一頁

26. (**B**) The questions were difficult.
這些問題很難。

(A) 問題不清楚。　　　　　　(B) <u>問題很難。</u>
(C) 問題不正確。　　　　　　(D) 問題很簡單。

27. (**A**) Charles was very powerful.
查爾斯很有力量。

(A) <u>他很強壯。</u>　　　　　　(B) 他生病了。
(C) 他很懶惰。　　　　　　　(D) 他很虛弱。

* powerful ('pauəfəl) *adj.* 有力的

28. (**C**) The pilot landed the plane on a wet runway.
飛行員將飛機降落在潮濕的跑道上。

(A) 跑道沒有燈。　　　　　　(B) 跑道上有草。
(C) <u>跑道上有水。</u>　　　　　(D) 跑道上有鳥。

* pilot ('paɪlət) *n.* 飛行員　　land (lænd) *v.* 降落
runway ('rʌn,we) *n.* 跑道

29. (**A**) The earth's gravity is a constant force.
地心引力是一股持續不變的力量。

(A) <u>它不會改變。</u>　　　　　(B) 它會改變。
(C) 它是不一致的。　　　　　(D) 它是很善變的。

* gravity ('ɡrævətɪ) *n.* 重力；地心引力
constant ('kɑnstənt) *adj.* 持續不變的
inconsistent (,ɪnkən'sɪstənt) *adj.* 不一致的；反覆無常的
variable ('vɛrɪəbḷ) *adj.* 變化無常的；善變的

30. (**C**) The air is 98 percent saturated.
空氣的濕度高達百分之九十八。

(A) 天氣很宜人。　　　　　　(B) 天氣又熱又乾燥。
(C) <u>天氣潮濕。</u>　　　　　　(D) 天氣涼爽。

* saturate ('sætʃə,ret) *v.* 使濕透；使飽和
humid ('hjumɪd) *adj.* 潮濕的；多濕氣的

31. (**A**) Paul tried to call you but the line was busy.
保羅想打電話給你，但是都佔線。

    (A) <u>有別人在講這一線。</u>   (B) 有很多線佔線。

    (C) 線路故障。   (D) 保羅忙得無法打電話。

    * busy ('bɪzɪ) *adj.* （電話）佔線的（ = *engaged* ）
      wire (waɪr) *n.* （電話）線路   ***out of order*** 故障

32. (**B**) The man was not guilty of the charge.
那個人無罪。

    (A) 那個人被處以罰款。   (B) <u>那個人是清白的。</u>

    (C) 那個人被判刑入獄。   (D) 那個人有罪。

    * guilty ('gɪltɪ) *adj.* 有罪的   charge (tʃɑrdʒ) *n.* 指控；罪狀
      fine (faɪn) *n.* 罰款   innocent ('ɪnəsn̩t) *adj.* 清白的
      sentence ('sɛntəns) *v.* 判刑；宣判
      prison ('prɪzn̩) *n.* 監牢

33. (**A**) He killed the diseased horse.
他殺了那匹生病的馬。

    (A) <u>他殺了那匹生病的馬。</u>   (B) 他殺了那匹很肥的馬。

    (C) 他殺了那匹受傷的馬。   (D) 他殺了那匹垂死的馬。

    * diseased (dɪ'zɪzd) *adj.* 生病的   injured ('ɪndʒəd) *adj.* 受傷的

34. (**A**) We received extra pay last month.
上個月我們收到了一筆額外的報酬。

    (A) <u>這筆報酬比平常多。</u>   (B) 這筆報酬比平常少。

    (C) 這筆報酬數目很小。   (D) 這筆報酬只有一些。

    * extra ('ɛkstrə) *adj.* 額外的   pay (pe) *n.* 薪水；報酬

35. (**D**) The gift was very valuable.
這份禮物很昂貴。

    (A) 禮物價值不高。   (B) 禮物不是很貴。

    (C) 禮物的價格比實際的價值高。   (D) <u>禮物值很多錢。</u>

    * valuable ('væljuəbl̩) *adj.* 昂貴的

36. (**C**) Robert failed his last examination.
羅伯特上次考試不及格。

(A) 他分數很高。　　　　　　(B) 他有些題目沒寫。
(C) 他的分數不令人滿意。　　(D) 他在考試時有人幫忙。

* fail〔fel〕*v.*（考試）不及格　　score〔skor〕*n.* 分數
unsatisfactory〔͵ʌnsætɪsˊfæktrɪ〕*adj.* 不能令人滿意的

37. (**D**) This woman has brought up five children.
這個女人把五個孩子撫養長大。

(A) 她打算生五個小孩。　　　(B) 她的小孩生病了。
(C) 她和生病的小孩在一起。　(D) 她有五個長大成人的孩子。

* ***bring up*** 撫養

38. (**A**) I look over my lesson from time to time.
我有時會複習一下功課。

(A) 我有時會複習一下功課。　(B) 我沒時間唸書。
(C) 我的功課只複習一次。　　(D) 我有時會忽略我的課業。

* ***look over*** 複習（= *review*〔rɪˊvju〕）
from time to time 有時（= *now and then* = *sometimes*）
overlook〔͵ovəˊluk〕*v.* 忽視

39. (**C**) Mr. Crane can answer the phone. He is closer to it than any of us.
克倫先生可以接電話。他離電話比我們都近。

(A) 我最靠近電話。　　　　　(B) 他離電話不是很近。
(C) 他最靠近電話。　　　　　(D) 我懷疑那裏有電話。

* ***answer the phone*** 接電話

40. (**D**) We had a flat tire on the highway.
我們在公路上爆胎。

(A) 路是平的。　　　　　　　(B) 我們住在公寓裏。
(C) 我們躺在公路上。　　　　(D) 我們有個輪胎沒氣了。

* flat〔flæt〕*adj.*（輪胎）洩了氣的　　***flat tire*** 爆胎
level〔ˊlɛvḷ〕*adj.* 平坦的　　***lie down*** 躺臥

41. (**D**) John must concentrate on his lessons or he will fail.
   約翰必須專心唸書，否則就會不及格。

    (A) 他必須常去上課。   (B) 他必須毫無意識地唸書。
    (C) 他不可以讀太多書。   (D) 他必須非常專心地唸書。

    * *concentrate on* 專心於～
      unconsciously〔ʌn'kɑnʃəslɪ〕*adv.* 無意識地
      pay close attention to 密切注意～；非常專心

42. (**B**) The physical training made him very tired at the end of the day.
   體能訓練讓他在晚上非常累。

    (A) 他變得很滿意。   (B) 他變得筋疲力盡。
    (C) 他變得很快樂。   (D) 他變得很害怕。

    * *physical training* 體能訓練
      exhausted〔ɪg'zɔstɪd〕*adj.* 筋疲力盡的   scared〔skɛrd〕*adj.* 害怕的

43. (**C**) I don't know about his problem, but I can guess what it is about.
   我不知道他的問題是什麼，不過我猜得出來。

    (A) 他的客人對他而言是個問題。   (B) 他不懂汽油。
    (C) 我大概知道他的問題。   (D) 他的問題比我嚴重。

    * guest〔gɛst〕*n.* 客人   gas〔gæs〕*n.* 瓦斯；汽油

44. (**D**) Tom said, "I will write twice a week on my trip."
   湯姆說：「旅行時，我一週會寫兩次信。」

    (A) 他在旅行時會寫兩次信。   (B) 他一天會寫兩次信。
    (C) 他第二週不會寫信。   (D) 他答應每週要寫兩次信。

45. (**D**) Gary had Susan check his homework.
   蓋瑞請蘇珊檢查他的作業。

    (A) 蓋瑞的作業比蘇珊多。
    (B) 蓋瑞和蘇珊在家工作。
    (C) 蓋瑞告訴蘇珊在家做她的作業。
    (D) 蓋瑞要求蘇珊看看他的作業。

46. (**C**) I like the style of the suit, but it's not as dark as I
wanted.
我喜歡這西裝的款式，但顏色不如我想要的深。

(A) 我要一套淺色的西裝。
(B) 我一點也不喜歡這套西裝。
(C) <u>這套西裝的顏色不夠深。</u>
(D) 我不喜歡它的款式。

* suit (sut , sjut) *n.* 西裝
dark (dɑrk) *adj.* 暗的；（顏色）深的

47. (**B**) The students are going to miss their train.
這些學生搭不上火車了。

(A) 他們會準時到達車站。　　　(B) <u>他們無法搭上火車。</u>
(C) 他們會搭上火車。　　　　　(D) 他們不會搭不上火車。

* *on time* 準時

48. (**B**) They suggested we visit them.
他們建議我們去拜訪他們。

(A) 他們要求我們提出建議。　　(B) <u>他們邀請我們去他們家。</u>
(C) 我們要邀請他們來拜訪。　　(D) 我們建議一個地方讓他們拜訪。

49. (**B**) The car is covered with dirt.
那部車沾滿了泥巴。

(A) 車被擦得雪亮。　　　　　　(B) <u>車子不乾淨。</u>
(C) 車子被漆了油漆。　　　　　(D) 車子被紙所覆蓋。

* dirt (dɜt) *n.* 泥土　　　polish ('pɑlɪʃ) *v.* 擦亮

50. (**C**) We always enjoy reading the local news.
我們一直很喜歡看地方新聞。

(A) 我們喜歡看社論。　　　　　(B) 我們喜歡報紙的工作人員。
(C) <u>我們喜歡看本市的新聞。</u>　(D) 我們喜歡看國際新聞。

* local ('lokḷ) *adj.* 當地的
editorial (,ɛdə'torɪəl) *n.* 社論　　staff (stæf) *n.* 工作人員

51. (**A**)　M : Who is that tall fellow with Tom? Is he a student?

　　　　　W : Oh, no. The man talking with Tom is a lawyer.

　　　　　What does the woman mean?

　　　　　男：和湯姆在一起的那個高個子是誰？是學生嗎？

　　　　　女：喔，不！和湯姆說話的那個人是律師。

　　　　　這位女士意指什麼？

　　　　　(A) 湯姆正在和一位律師說話。

　　　　　(B) 那個高個子和湯姆都是法律系學生。

　　　　　(C) 湯姆的學生正在討論法律。

　　　　　(D) 那個高個子是湯姆的學生。

52. (**A**)　W : Can you bend that plastic board?

　　　　　M : No, it's too stiff.

　　　　　Why couldn't the man bend the board?

　　　　　女：你能把那塊塑膠板弄彎嗎？

　　　　　男：不行，太硬了。

　　　　　為何這位男士無法將板子弄彎？

　　　　　(A) 板子太硬了。　　　　　(B) 板子太不自然了。

　　　　　(C) 板子太軟了。　　　　　(D) 板子太髒了。

　　　　* bend〔bɛnd〕*v.* 使彎曲

　　　　　plastic〔'plæstɪk〕*adj.* 塑膠的　　board〔bord〕*n.* 板子

　　　　　stiff〔stɪf〕*adj.* 硬的（= *rigid*〔'rɪdʒɪd〕）

　　　　　artificial〔ˌɑrtə'fɪʃəl〕*adj.* 人造的；不自然的

53. (**B**)　W : What are you doing with those pieces of rope?

　　　　　M : I'm securing them.

　　　　　What is the man doing?

　　　　　女：你要如何處理這些繩子？

　　　　　男：我要把它們繫緊一點。

　　　　　這位男士要做什麼？

　　　　　(A) 將繩子分開　　　　　(B) 將繩子繫緊

　　　　　(C) 鬆開繩子　　　　　(D) 移開繩子

　　　　* *do with* 處理　　rope〔rop〕*n.* 繩子

　　　　　secure〔sɪ'kjur〕*v.* 繫緊（= *fasten*〔'fæsn̩〕）

　　　　　loosen〔'lusn̩〕*v.* 鬆開　　remove〔rɪ'muv〕*v.* 移開

54. (**D**) M : Did you enjoy the meal?

W : Yes, and I ate something sweet at the end of the meal.

What do we call the sweet food eaten at the end of the meal?

男：用餐愉快嗎？

女：很愉快，在飯後我還吃了甜食。

餐後的甜食我們稱之為什麼？

(A) 點心　　　　(B) 主菜　　　　(C) 奶精　　　　(D) <u>甜點</u>

* meal〔mil〕*n.* 一餐　　snack〔snæk〕*n.* 點心；零食

main course 主菜　　dessert〔dɪˈzɜt〕*n.* 甜點

55. (**B**) W : What are you going to fix for dinner today?

M : I'm going to prepare steak and eggs for a change.

What will the man do?

女：今天晚餐你要做些什麼？

男：我要煎牛排和蛋，換換口味。

這位男士要做什麼？

(A) 他要點晚餐。　　　　　　　　(B) <u>他要做晚餐。</u>

(C) 他要收取晚餐的費用。　　　　(D) 他要吃晚餐。

* fix〔fɪks〕*v.* 烹調（餐飲）　　charge〔tʃɑrdʒ〕*v.* 收費

56. (**A**) M : What happened to you? You're so late.

W : My car broke down on the highway, and I had to walk.

Why did the woman have to walk?

男：妳怎麼了？這麼晚才來！

女：我的車在路上拋錨了，我只好走路來。

為什麼那女人必須走路？

(A) <u>她的車子出了問題。</u>　　　　(B) 她太晚起床，沒搭上公車。

(C) 她沒錢，搭不起公車。　　　　(D) 她的車子被困在車道上。

* *break down* 故障

broke〔brok〕*adj.* 沒錢的　　*get stuck* 動彈不得

driveway〔ˈdraɪˌwe〕*n.* 私人車道

57. (**B**) M：Where is Diane?

M：We ran out of milk and she went out to get some. Where is Diane?

男：黛安在哪裏？

女：我們沒有牛奶了，她出去買。

黛安在哪裏？

(A) 她去慢跑。   (B) <u>她去商店。</u>

(C) 她去散步。   (D) 她去買報紙。

* *run out of* ~ ~用完了

58. (**A**) M：Gail is supposed to be here at the meeting tonight. Where is she?

W：She came down with the flu and had to stay home. Why didn't Gail attend the meeting?

男：蓋兒今天晚上應該來開會的。她上哪兒去了？

女：她得了流行性感冒，必須待在家裏休息。

爲何蓋兒沒來開會？

(A) <u>她生病了。</u>   (B) 她說她會晚點來。

(C) 她決定要待在家裏。   (D) 她有約會。

* *be supposed to* 應該   *come down with* ~ 因~而病倒

flu (flu) *n.* 流行性感冒 (= *influenza* (ˌɪnfluˈɛnzə))

59. (**C**) W：I do hope Peter does well in his studies this semester.

M：When our son promises to get good grades, you can count on him.

What kind of student does the man consider his son?

女：我眞希望彼德這學期功課能好一點。

男：當我們兒子保證說他會得高分，你就可以信賴他。

那男人覺得他的兒子是怎麼樣的學生？

(A) 太用功了   (B) 很愛吹牛

(C) <u>十分值得信賴</u>   (D) 數學很強

* *count on* 信賴 (= *depend on*)

boastful (ˈbostfəl) *adj.* 自誇的

dependable (dɪˈpɛndəbl̩) *adj.* 可信賴的

60. (**D**) W : I'm glad you could come today. The drain became
stopped up yesterday afternoon.

M : Don't worry. I'll have it open for you in no time.
What is the man?

女：很高興你今天能來。水管昨天下午塞住了。

男：別擔心。我馬上替你通。

那男人是做什麼的？

(A) 屠夫 　　　　(B) 電工 　　　　(C) 木匠 　　　　(D) 水管工人

* drain〔dren〕*n.* 排水管　　　stop〔stɑp〕*v.* 阻塞
  in no time 立刻 (= *at once*) 　　butcher〔'bʊtʃɚ〕*n.* 屠夫
  electrician〔ɪ,lɛk'trɪʃən〕*n.* 電工　carpenter〔'kɑrpəntɚ〕*n.* 木匠
  plumber〔'plʌmɚ〕*n.* 水管工人

At the exclusive restaurant where I work, a party of
diners was exhausting the waiter with relentless
demands. Through it all, he remained professional.

Finally one of the patrons asked the waiter to take
the group's picture. He did — from the neck down.

在我工作的那家高級餐廳中，一群用餐者毫不留情地要求服
務生，讓他疲於奔命。從頭到尾，他都維持他的職業風度。

最後，其中一位客人請服務生替全部人照張相，他照了 — 從
脖子以下照起。

LISTENING TEST 16

● *Directions for questions 1-25. You will hear questions on the test tape. Select the one item A, B, C or D which answers the question correctly, and mark your answer sheet.*

1. A. beef noodles   B. roast beef
   C. apple pie   D. curry and rice

2. A. indifferent   B. interested
   C. worried   D. wonderful

3. A. with the cooperation of others
   B. with no assistance
   C. without stopping
   D. with consideration of others

4. A. thirty   B. forty
   C. forty-five   D. forty-eight

5. A. with great fear
   B. as a wonderful experience
   C. as a routine activity
   D. without fear

6. A. 3 : 15   B. 2 : 15
   C. 1 : 15   D. 1 : 45

7. A. writing Spanish   B. speaking Spanish
   C. both   D. neither

8. A. take care of the dog   B. look at the dog
   C. take after the dog   D. take away the dog

9. A. for a month   B. for two weeks
    C. for many years   D. for a year

10. A. He is heart broken.   B. He has no money.
     C. He is sick.   D. He is thirsty.

11. A. besides him   B. opposite him
     C. in front of him   D. beside him

12. A. eighteen   B. fourteen
     C. ten   D. sixteen

13. A. inoculated   B. insulated
     C. live wire   D. coiled wire

14. A. a field that requires a special skill
     B. a field that requires very little training
     C. a field that requires a lot of strength
     D. a field that requires a lot of practice

15. A. Yes, she could.   B. Yes, she may.
     C. Yes, she must.   D. Yes, she won't

16. A. one day after class   B. two days after class
     C. before class   D. during class

17. A. every one   B. no one
     C. a seven-year-old boy   D. the police

18. A. strawberry pie   B. apple pie
     C. cheese pie   D. blackberry pie

19. A. He'll become thinner.   B. He'll look older.
     C. He'll become fatter.   D. He'll be richer.

20. A. helped them   B. shook hands with them
    C. raised their hands   D. clapped for them

21. A. a half   B. one third
    C. none   D. some

22. A. twenty minutes   B. hundreds of miles
    C. half an hour   D. a hundred miles

23. A. 2 : 45   B. 2 : 30
    C. 3 : 15   D. 3 : 30

24. A. a birthday card   B. a birthday cake
    C. flowers   D. a necklace

25. A. He is shorter than his mother.
    B. He is taller than his father.
    C. He is as tall as his mother.
    D. He is almost as tall as his father.

● *Directions for questions 26-50. You will hear statements on the test tape. Select the one answer A, B, C, or D which comes closest to the meaning of the statement and mark your answer sheet.*

26. A. Mary was speaking too loudly.
    B. Mary was not speaking.
    C. Mary was speaking eloquently.
    D. Mary was not speaking loud enough.

27. A. She will fasten them together.
    B. She will compare them.
    C. She will refuse to pay.
    D. She will send Bill the check.

28. A. Brian has the money.
    B. Brian loaned Peter the money.
    C. Peter doesn't need the money.
    D. Brian didn't have the money.

29. A. He sold the best tools.
    B. He picked out the best tools.
    C. He overlooked the best tools.
    D. He didn't see the best tools.

30. A. Christmas is leaving.　　　　B. Christmas is over.
    C. Christmas is coming.　　　　D. Christmas has passed.

31. A. Yesterday Stanley played basketball very well.
    B. The girl plays basketball very well.
    C. The girl saw Stanley play basketball yesterday.
    D. Stanley didn't see the girl yesterday.

32. A. He has reached the same level.
    B. He is still behind them.
    C. He dropped behind them.
    D. He is ahead of them.

33. A. Loan me a pack of cigarettes.
    B. Get me a pack of cigarettes.
    C. Take away the pack of cigarettes.
    D. Sell me a pack of cigarettes.

34. A. It looks very easy.　　　　B. I solved it easily.
    C. I don't understand it.　　　D. It's not too difficult.

35. A. He wants to sell some chalk.
    B. He wants to give me some chalk.
    C. He wants some chalk from me.
    D. He wants no chalk from anyone.

36. A. He likes to repair cars.
    B. He thinks it's necessary to repair cars.
    C. His car should be repaired.
    D. He wants a car to repair.

37. A. The pub is opposite the drugstore.
    B. The pub is around the corner from the drugstore.
    C. The pub is next to the drugstore.
    D. The pub is at the other end of the drugstore.

38. A. He liked to drink.
    B. He went drinking with the people.
    C. He continued helping the drinkers.
    D. He continued looking at the drinkers.

39. A. He must repeat very fast.
    B. He must talk very fast.
    C. He must respond very fast.
    D. He must relieve very fast.

40. A. They have lunch in their rooms.
    B. They study while having lunch.
    C. They study before lunch.
    D. They study after lunch.

41. A. He sleeps until seven.
    B. He always sleeps at 7 a.m.
    C. He eats breakfast at seven.
    D. He isn't awake at seven.

42. A. They are lost.
    B. They have become old and worn.
    C. They are on the table.
    D. They have changed colors.

43. A. He is lecturing.
    B. He is letting the students speak.
    C. He is talking to the students.
    D. He is talking too much.

44. A. Joe could not go to the dentist.
    B. The dentist might visit Joe.
    C. Joe needs a new tooth.
    D. Joe should go to the dentist.

45. A. It was on the steamship.
    B. It was very far from the steamship.
    C. It was away from the steamship.
    D. It was at the side of the steamship.

46. A. He took a chance on the movie being good.
    B. He had the money to see the movie.
    C. He had an opportunity to see a movie.
    D. He had no time to see a movie.

47. A. There are a lot of ports on the East Coast.
    B. There is much commerce carried on.
    C. There are many miles between the areas.
    D. There is a lot of training conducted.

48. A. We plan to arrive late at night.
    B. We may arrive late at night.
    C. We can arrive early at night.
    D. We must arrive late at night.

49. A. The size is the same.
    B. The color is similar.
    C. Mine is different from yours.
    D. The cloth is alike.

50. A. They have not eaten yet.
    B. They are eating now.
    C. They want to eat early.
    D. They were late for lunch.

● *Directions for questions 51-60. You will hear dialogs on the test tape. Select the correct answer A, B, C, or D and mark your answer sheet.*

51. A. She is very unhappy with her studies.
    B. She has no great interest in her studies.
    C. She wants to change courses.
    D. She is very interested in her studies.

52. A. 5   B. 4
    C. 3   D. 2

53. A. She likes roller skating better.
    B. She has no choice.
    C. She prefers the movies.
    D. She doesn't like either one.

54. A. He was undecided.
    B. He is going with Jane.
    C. He decided not to go with Jane.
    D. He went to the game.

55. A. to quit smoking
    B. to reduce his smoking
    C. that he didn't need to smoke regularly
    D. that he could continue smoking

56. A. Wiwtner   B. Winnter
    C. Wittner   D. Wittmer

57. A. history
    B. chemistry
    C. home economics
    D. business administration

58. A. They went to Paris.
    B. They couldn't afford a honeymoon.
    C. They are still planning to go to Paris.
    D. They went to Rome.

59. A. She will go to the concert.
    B. She will watch her neighbors' children.
    C. She will go to a dinner party.
    D. She will visit her neighbors.

60. A. vegetables   B. cookies
    C. meat   D. fruit

Business conventions are important because
they demonstrate how many people a company can
operate without.

商務會議是很重要的，因為它們可以顯示一個公司沒有
多少人還能夠運作。

ECL 聽力測驗 [16] 詳解

1. (**C**) Thomas ate some dessert at noon. What did he eat?
湯瑪士中午吃了一些甜點。/ 他吃了什麼?

(A) 牛肉麵   (B) 烤牛肉   (C) 蘋果派   (D) 咖哩飯

* dessert (dɪ'zɜt) *n.* 甜點   roast (rost) *adj.* 燒烤的
curry ('kɜɪ) *n.* 咖哩

2. (**C**) The social workers are very concerned about the child.
How do the social workers feel about him?
社工人員非常擔心這個小孩。/ 社工人員對他的感覺如何?

(A) 漠不關心   (B) 感興趣   (C) 擔心   (D) 奇妙

* indifferent (ɪn'dɪfərənt) *adj.* 冷漠的

3. (**B**) This student studies independently.
How does he study?
這位學生獨立念書。/ 他如何念書?

(A) 靠別人的合作   (B) 沒有受到援助
(C) 沒有停止   (D) 靠別人的體諒

* independently (͵ɪndɪ'pɛndəntlɪ) *adv.* 獨立地
assistance (ə'sɪstəns) *n.* 幫助   consideration (kən͵sɪdə'reʃən) *n.* 體諒

4. (**D**) A man works 8 hours a day. He works every day except
Sundays. How many hours does he work in one week?
有個人每天工作八小時。除了星期天之外,他每天工作。
他一星期工作幾小時?

(A) 三十   (B) 四十   (C) 四十五   (D) 四十八

5. (**A**) Some people dread public speaking. How do they view it?
有些人害怕在公開場合講話。/ 他們如何看待它?

(A) 極度害怕   (B) 奇妙的經驗   (C) 例行的活動   (D) 毫無畏懼

* dread (drɛd) *v.* 害怕   routine (ru'tin) *adj.* 例行的

6. (**D**) The class should have begun at 1:15, but the professor was half an hour late. When did the professor arrive?
課應該一點十五分開始,可是教授遲到半小時。 / 教授幾點到?

(A) 三點十五分　　　　　　(B) 兩點十五分

(C) 一點十五分　　　　　　(D) 一點四十五分

7. (**C**) Louise writes Spanish as well as she speaks it. Which does she do better?
露薏絲的西班牙文寫得和說得一樣好。 / 她哪一樣比較好?

(A) 寫西班牙文　　　　　　(B) 說西班牙文

(C) 兩者都好　　　　　　　(D) 兩者都不好

8. (**A**) While we're on vacation, Mary will look after the dog. What will Mary do?
我們去度假時,瑪麗將會照顧小狗。 / 瑪麗將做什麼?

(A) 照顧小狗　　(B) 注視小狗　　(C) 追趕小狗　　(D) 帶走小狗

* **look after** 照顧　　**take care of** 照顧　　**take after** 追趕

9. (**C**) Emma hasn't gone to a movie for years. How long hasn't Emma seen a movie?
艾瑪已經有好多年沒去看電影。 / 艾瑪多久沒看過電影?

(A) 一個月　　(B) 兩星期　　(C) 許多年　　(D) 一年

10. (**B**) Sergeant Blake told me that he is broke. What did he mean?
布雷克中士跟我說他破產了。 / 他的意思為何?

(A) 他的心碎了。　(B) 他沒有錢。　(C) 他生病。　(D) 他口渴。

* broke (brok) *adj.* 破產的

11. (**D**) James is sitting next to Paul. Where is he sitting?
詹姆斯坐在保羅隔壁。 / 他坐在哪裏?

(A) 除了他　　(B) 他對面　　(C) 他前面　　(D) 他旁邊

* **next to** 隔壁　　opposite ('ɑpəzɪt) *prep.* 在對面

12. (**D**) They expected eight people at the party, but twice that many showed up. How many people went to the party?
他們預計八個人到舞會，可是出現了兩倍的人數。
有多少人參加舞會？

(A) 十八　　　　(B) 十四　　　　(C) 十　　　　(D) 十六

13. (**B**) The wire had a rubber covering. What kind of wire was it?
這條電線有塑膠套。/ 這是何種電線？

(A) 接種過的　　　　　　　　(B) 絕緣的
(C) 通電的電線　　　　　　　(D) 捲起來的電線

* inoculated (ɪn'ɑkjə,letɪd) *adj.* 接種過的
insulated ('ɪnsə,letɪd , 'ɪnsjʊ-) *adj.* 絕緣的　　　live (laɪv) *adj.* 通電的
coiled (kɔɪld) *adj.* 捲起的

14. (**A**) After Jack took his aptitude test, he was scheduled for training in the technical field. What kind of field is it?
傑克在性向測驗後，被安排接受技術領域的訓練。/ 這是何種領域？

(A) 需要專門技術的領域　　　(B) 需要極少訓練的領域
(C) 需要很大力量的領域　　　(D) 需要很多練習的領域

* aptitude ('æptə,tjud) *n.* 才能；傾向　　schedule ('skɛdʒʊl) *v.* 安排
technical ('tɛknɪkḷ) *adj.* 技術的

15. (**C**) Frances has to get more gasoline.
Does she have to go to the gas station?
法蘭西絲需要更多的汽油。/ 她必須去加油站嗎？

(A) 是的，她可以。　　　　　(B) 是的，她可能。
(C) 是的，她必須。　　　　　(D) 是的，她不用。

16. (**C**) You should study your lesson in advance.
When should you study your lesson?
你應該事先研讀課程。/ 你應該何時研讀課程？

(A) 上課後一天　　(B) 上課後兩天　　(C) 上課前　　(D) 上課中

* ***in advance*** 事先

17. (**C**) No one but the seven-year-old boy saw the terrible accident. Who saw the accident?
除了那位七歲的男孩，沒有人目睹這場可怕的車禍。／誰看到車禍？

 (A) 每個人　　　　　　　　(B) 沒有人
 (C) <u>一位七歲的男孩</u>　　　　(D) 警方

18. (**A**) John prefers strawberry pie, but his wife always bakes apple pie. Which does John like better?
約翰比較喜歡草莓派，可是他太太總是烤蘋果派。
約翰比較喜歡何者？

 (A) <u>草莓派</u>　(B) 蘋果派　(C) 起司派　(D) 黑莓派

19. (**C**) Henry is afraid he'll gain weight if he stops smoking. What does Henry worry about if he stops smoking?
亨利擔心如果他戒煙，體重會增加。／如果戒煙亨利擔心什麼？

 (A) 他會變瘦。　　　　　　(B) 他看起來會比較老。
 (C) <u>他會變胖。</u>　　　　　　(D) 他會更富有。

 * gain〔gen〕*v.* 增加　　weight〔wet〕*n.* 重量

20. (**D**) The audience gave the orchestra a big hand. What did the audience do?
聽眾給予樂團熱烈的鼓掌。／觀眾做了什麼？

 (A) 幫助他們　　　　　　　(B) 和他們握手
 (C) 舉起他們的手　　　　　(D) <u>爲他們鼓掌</u>

 * audience〔'ɔdɪəns〕*n.* 聽眾　　orchestra〔'ɔrkɪstrə〕*n.* 管絃樂團
 give sb. a big hand 熱烈鼓掌　　clap〔klæp〕*v.* 鼓掌

21. (**C**) The tickets for tonight's show are sold out. How many tickets are left?
今晚節目的票已經售完。／還剩多少票？

 (A) 一半　　　　　　　　　(B) 三分之一
 (C) <u>一張也沒有</u>　　　　　　(D) 一些

 * *sell out* 賣完

22. (**D**) It was worth driving a hundred miles to see the basketball game. How far did we drive to see the game?

開一百哩的路程去看那場籃球賽是值得的。／我們開多遠去看比賽?

(A) 二十分鐘   (B) 幾百哩   (C) 半小時   (D) <u>一百哩</u>

* worth〔wɜθ〕*adj.* 值得的

23. (**A**) The next bus for the city center is due to depart at a quarter to three. When will the next bus leave?

往市中心的下一班公車預定三點前一刻開車。／下班公車何時開?

(A) <u>兩點四十五分</u>   (B) 兩點半
(C) 三點十五分   (D) 三點半

* due〔dju〕*adj.* 預定的   depart〔dɪ'pɑrt〕*v.* 出發;離開
    quarter〔'kwɔrtɚ〕*n.* 一刻鐘

24. (**B**) Mrs. Peterson was pleased that her husband got her a lovely birthday cake. What did he give her?

彼德生太太很高興她先生送她一個可愛的生日蛋糕。／他送她什麼?

(A) 生日卡   (B) <u>生日蛋糕</u>   (C) 花   (D) 項鍊

* necklace〔'nɛklɪs〕*n.* 項鍊

25. (**D**) Daniel is taller than his mother and nearly the same height as his father. How tall is Daniel?

丹尼爾比他母親高,而且幾乎和他父親一樣高。／丹尼爾多高?

(A) 他比母親矮。   (B) 他比父親高。
(C) 他和母親一樣高。   (D) <u>他幾乎和父親一樣高。</u>

* height〔haɪt〕*n.* 身高;高度

26. (**D**) Tom said, "I can hardly hear Mary."

湯姆說:「我幾乎聽不到瑪麗說話。」

(A) 瑪麗說得太大聲。   (B) 瑪麗沒有說話。
(C) 瑪麗說得滔滔不絕。   (D) <u>瑪麗說得不夠大聲。</u>

* eloquently〔'ɛləkwəntlɪ〕*adv.* 雄辯地;滔滔不絕地

27. (**A**) Susan is going to attach the check to the bill.
蘇珊將把支票附在帳單上。

(A) 她將把它們釘在一起。 (B) 她將比較它們。
(C) 她將拒絕付錢。 (D) 她將寄支票給比爾。

* attach〔ə'tætʃ〕*v.* 縛；繫 fasten〔'fæsṇ〕*v.* 釘牢
compare〔kəm'pɛr〕*v.* 比較

28. (**D**) If Brian had had the money, he would have loaned it to Peter.
如果布萊恩有錢，他早就借給彼得。

(A) 布萊恩有錢。 (B) 布萊恩借錢給彼得。
(C) 彼得不需要錢。 (D) 布萊恩沒有錢。

* loan〔lon〕*v.* 借貸

29. (**B**) Mr. Johnson chose the best tools for the job.
強森先生選擇最好的工具做事。

(A) 他賣掉最好的工具。 (B) 他挑選最好的工具。
(C) 他忽略最好的工具。 (D) 他沒有看到最好的工具。

* *pick up* 挑選 overlook〔,ovɚ'luk〕*v.* 忽略

30. (**C**) Christmas is around the corner.
聖誕節即將來臨。

(A) 聖誕節就要離去。 (B) 聖誕節結束了。
(C) 聖誕節就要來臨。 (D) 聖誕節已經過了。

* *around the corner* 即將來臨

31. (**B**) The girl Stanley saw yesterday plays basketball very well.
史丹利昨天看到的那個女孩籃球打得非常好。

(A) 昨天史丹利籃球打得非常好。
(B) 那位女孩籃球打得非常好。
(C) 那位女孩昨天看到史丹利打籃球。
(D) 史丹利昨天沒有看到那女孩。

32.(**A**) Lieutenant Regan has finally caught up with them in their studies.

雷根中尉終於在課業上趕上他們。

(A) 他達到相同的程度。　　(B) 他仍然落後他們。

(C) 他落後他們。　　(D) 他超前他們。

* *catch up with sb.* 趕上某人　*drop behind* 落後　*ahead of* 超前

33.(**B**) Pick up a pack of cigarettes for me.

拿一包煙給我。

(A) 借我一包煙。　　(B) 拿一包煙給我。

(C) 拿走這包煙。　　(D) 賣我一包煙。

* pack〔pæk〕*n.* 一包

34.(**C**) This sentence looks like a puzzle to me.

這個句子對我而言如同難題。

(A) 它看起來很容易。　　(B) 我輕鬆地解決它。

(C) 我不了解它。　　(D) 它不會太難。

* puzzle〔′pʌzl〕*n.* 拼圖；難題

35.(**C**) The teacher said, "Please give me some chalk."

老師說：「請給我一些粉筆。」

(A) 他想賣一些粉筆。　　(B) 他想給我一些粉筆。

(C) 他想向我要一些粉筆。　　(D) 他不想向任何人要粉筆。

* chalk〔tʃɔk〕*n.* 粉筆

36.(**C**) John's car needs repairing.

約翰的車需要修理。

(A) 他喜歡修車。　　(B) 他認為修車有必要。

(C) 他的車應該要修理。　　(D) 他想要一輛車去修理。

37.(**A**) The pub is across from the drugstore.

酒吧在藥房的對面。

(A) 酒吧在藥房對面。　　(B) 酒吧在藥房那條路的街角。

(C) 酒吧在藥房旁邊。　　(D) 酒吧在藥房的另一端。

38. (**D**) Kevin kept watching the people drink.
凱文一直看著那些人喝酒。

(A) 他喜歡喝酒。
(B) 他和那些人去喝酒。
(C) 他不斷幫助那些喝酒的人。
(D) 他不斷看著那些喝酒的人。

39. (**C**) A pilot must react very fast.
飛行員必須反應迅速。

(A) 他必須迅速重覆。　　　(B) 他必須講話迅速。
(C) 他必須反應迅速。　　　(D) 他必須迅速解脫。

* pilot ('paɪlət) *n.* 飛行員　　react (rɪ'ækt) *v.* 反應
respond (rɪ'spɑnd) *v.* 反應　　relieve (rɪ'liv) *v.* 解脫

40. (**D**) After having lunch, many of the students go to their rooms and study.
吃過午餐後，許多學生回房讀書。

(A) 他們在房間吃午餐。　　(B) 他們邊吃午餐邊讀書。
(C) 他們在午餐前讀書。　　(D) 他們在午餐後讀書。

41. (**A**) Bill always wakes up at 7 a.m.
比爾總是在早上七點醒來。

(A) 他睡到七點。　　　　　(B) 他總是在早上七點睡覺。
(C) 他七點吃早餐。　　　　(D) 他到七點還沒醒來。

* wake (wek) *v.* 醒來　　awake (ə'wek) *adj.* 清醒的

42. (**A**) My socks have disappeared.
我的襪子不見了。

(A) 它們不見了。　　　　　(B) 它們變得破舊。
(C) 它們在桌上。　　　　　(D) 它們改變顏色。

* disapper (,dɪsə'pɪr) *v.* 消失　　worn (wɔrn) *adj.* 破舊的

43. (**B**) The instructor is listening and not talking.

老師在聽沒有在說。

(A) 他正在講課。   (B) 他讓學生講話。

(C) 他在對學生講話。   (D) 他講得太多。

* lecture〔ˈlɛktʃɚ〕v. 演講

44. (**D**) Joe needs to visit the dentist for treatment of his tooth.

喬需要去看醫生治療牙齒。

(A) 喬無法去看牙醫。   (B) 牙醫可能會拜訪喬。

(C) 喬需要一顆新牙齒。   (D) 喬應該去看牙醫。

* treatment〔ˈtritmənt〕n. 治療

45. (**D**) The small fishing boat was anchored alongside the big steamship.

這艘小漁船停靠在大汽船旁邊。

(A) 它在汽船上。   (B) 它離汽船非常遠。

(C) 它遠離汽船。   (D) 它在汽船的旁邊。

* anchor〔ˈæŋkɚ〕v. 拋錨；停泊   alongside〔əˈlɔŋˈsaɪd〕prep. 靠旁邊

46. (**C**) He had a chance to see a good movie while he was in town.

他在城裏時有機會看到一部好電影。

(A) 他碰運氣希望電影好看。   (B) 他有錢看電影。

(C) 他有機會看電影。   (D) 他沒有時間看電影。

* ***take a chance*** 碰運氣   opportunity〔ˌɑpɚˈtjunətɪ〕n. 機會

47. (**B**) There is a lot of trade between the East Coast and the West Coast.

東西兩岸之間的貿易量很大。

(A) 東岸有許多港口。   (B) 有許多貿易在進行。

(C) 兩地相隔許多哩。   (D) 有許多訓練在進行。

* commerce〔ˈkɑmɚs〕n. 貿易；商業   ***carry on*** 經營

48. (**B**) We are likely to arrive in San Antonio late at night.
我們可能在深夜抵達聖安東尼奧。

(A) 我們計畫在深夜抵達。　　(B) <u>我們可能在深夜抵達。</u>
(C) 我們可以在黃昏抵達。　　(D) 我們必須在深夜抵達。

49. (**D**) The material of your suit is the same as mine.
你套裝的質料和我的一樣。

(A) 尺寸一樣。　　　　　(B) 顏色類似。
(C) 我的和你的不同。　　(D) <u>布料相近。</u>

* cloth 〔 klɔθ 〕 *n.* 布料

50. (**B**) The students are already eating lunch.
學生已經在吃午餐。

(A) 他們還沒吃。　　　(B) <u>他們正在吃。</u>
(C) 他們想早點吃。　　(D) 他們午餐遲到。

51. (**D**) M : How is your daughter doing in school?
W : She is highly motivated in her studies.
What did the woman say about her daughter?
男：妳女兒在學校裏的表現如何？
女：她的求知慾很強。
這位女士說她女兒如何？

(A) 她不喜歡讀書。　　　　(B) 她對讀書沒有多大興趣。
(C) 她想換課程。　　　　　(D) <u>她對讀書很有興趣。</u>

* motivate 〔'motə,vet〕 *v.* 動機

52. (**D**) W : Louie, how did your football team do last season?
M : We won three times, lost five times, and tied twice.
How many times did they tie?
女：路易，你們的橄欖球隊上個球季表現如何？
男：我們贏三場，輸五場，兩場平手。
他們平手幾場？

(A) 五　　　　(B) 四　　　　(C) 三　　　　(D) <u>二</u>

* tie 〔 taɪ 〕 *v.* 平手

53. (**C**) M : Maggie, would you like to go to the movies or
the skating rink?

W : Skating is great, but I'd rather go to the movies.

What did the woman mean?

男：瑪姬，妳想去看電影或是去溜冰？

女：溜冰很棒，可是我比較想去看電影。

這位女士的意思為何？

(A) 她比較喜歡輪鞋溜冰。　　(B) 她沒有選擇。

(C) 她比較喜歡看電影。　　(D) 她兩種都不喜歡。

* skating (ˈsketɪŋ) *n.* 溜冰　　rink (rɪŋk) *n.* 溜冰場
roller (ˈrolɚ) *n.* 滾輪

54. (**C**) W : Mike, did you go to the game with Jane?

M : I thought I would, but then I changed my mind.

What did Mike mean?

女：麥克，你和珍去看比賽了嗎？

男：我以為我會去，可是後來我改變主意。

麥克的意思為何？

(A) 他還沒有決定。　　(B) 他將和珍去。

(C) 他決定不和珍去。　　(D) 他去看比賽。

* *change one's mind* 改變主意
undecided (ˌʌndɪˈsaɪdɪd) *adj.* 未決定的

55. (**A**) W : What did the doctor say, John?

M : He told me to cut out smoking.

What did the doctor tell John?

女：約翰，醫生怎麼說？

男：他要我戒煙。

醫生告訴約翰什麼？

(A) 戒煙　　(B) 少抽煙

(C) 他不需要經常抽煙。　　(D) 他可以繼續抽煙。

* *cut out* 停止　　quit (kwɪt) *v.* 停止
reduce (rɪˈdjus) *v.* 減少

56. (**C**)　W : Would you please spell your name for me, sir?

　　　　　M : Sure. W… I… double T… N… E… R.

　　　　What's the man's name?

　　　　女：先生，請拼出您的名字好嗎？

　　　　男：當然。W, I, 兩個 T, N, E, R。

　　　　這位男士的名字是什麼？

　　　　(A) Wiwtner　　　　　　　　(B) Winnter

　　　　(C) Wittner　　　　　　　　(D) Wittmer

57. (**D**)　M : I heard Marilyn is going to college. What's she
　　　　　　　studying?

　　　　　W : She's taking courses in statistics, economics, and
　　　　　　　accounting.

　　　　What career does Marilyn probably plan to follow?

　　　　女：我聽說瑪麗蓮要上大學了。她要攻讀什麼？

　　　　男：她將要修統計、經濟、會計等課程。

　　　　瑪麗蓮可能計劃從事那種事業？

　　　　(A) 歷史　　　(B) 化學　　　(C) 家政　　　(D) 企業管理

　　　*　statistics (stə'tɪstɪks) *n.* 統計學
　　　　economics (,ikə'nɑmɪks) *n.* 經濟學
　　　　accounting (ə'kaʊntɪŋ) *n.* 會計學　　*home economics* 家政
　　　　administration (əd,mɪnə'streʃən) *n.* 管理

58. (**D**)　W : Where did Joe and Nancy go for their honeymoon?

　　　　　M : They intended to go to Paris, but they couldn't afford
　　　　　　　it, so they went to Rome instead.

　　　　Where did Joe and Nancy go on their honeymoon?

　　　　女：喬和瑪麗去哪裏度蜜月？

　　　　男：他們打算去巴黎，但是他們負擔不起，所以改去羅馬。

　　　　喬和瑪麗去哪裏度蜜月？

　　　　(A) 他們去巴黎。　　　　　　(B) 他們負擔不起蜜月。

　　　　(C) 他們仍計劃去巴黎。　　　　(D) 他們去羅馬。

　　　*　intend (ɪn'tɛnd) *v.* 打算　　afford (ə'ford, ə'fɔrd) *v.* 負擔得起

59.(**B**) M : Are you going to the concert tonight?

W : No. I promised to babysit for my neighbors while they go to a dinner party.

What will the woman do tonight?

男：妳今天晚上要去聽演唱會嗎？

女：不，我答應鄰居要在他們去晚宴時幫忙帶小孩。

這位女士今晚將做什麼？

(A) 她要去聽演唱會。　　　(B) 她要幫忙看鄰居的小孩。

(C) 她要去參加晚宴。　　　(D) 她要拜訪鄰居。

* babysit ('bebɪ,sɪt) v. 當臨時褓姆

60.(**D**) M : What's in that big bag over there?

W : I bought some pears. grapes, apples, and melons.

What did the woman buy?

男：那邊的大袋子裏裝了什麼？

女：我買了一些桃子、葡萄、蘋果，還有甜瓜。

這位女士買了什麼？

(A) 蔬菜　　　(B) 餅乾　　　(C) 肉　　　(D) 水果

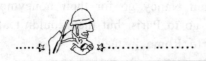

Wife, loaded down with packages, to husband: "I disposed of our disposable income."

　　大包小包的太太對先生說：「我已經處理掉我們可以任意處理的收入了。」

Editorial Staff

- **編著** / 程　明
- **執編** / 蔡琇瑩
- **校訂** / 劉　毅・吳濱伶・謝靜芳・莊心怡
- **校閱** / Tom Branigan
- **封面設計** / 張鳳儀
- **版面設計** / 張鳳儀
- **打字** / 黃淑貞・吳秋香・蘇淑玲

||||||||||||● 學習出版公司門市部 ●||||||||||||||

台北地區：台北市許昌街 10 號 2 樓 TEL：(02)2331-4060・2331-9209
台中地區：台中市綠川東街 32 號 8 樓 23 室
TEL：(04)2223-2838

|||||||||||||||||||||||||||||||||||||||||||||||||

ECL 聽力測驗詳解

編　　著／程　明
發　行　所／學習出版有限公司　　　　　☎ (02) 2704-5525
郵 撥 帳 號／0512727-2 學習出版社帳戶
登　記　證／局版台業 2179 號
印　刷　所／裕強彩色印刷有限公司
台 北 門 市／台北市許昌街 10 號 2 F　　　☎ (02) 2331-4060・2331-9209
台 中 門 市／台中市綠川東街 32 號 8 F 23 室　　☎ (04) 2223-2838
台灣總經銷／紅螞蟻圖書有限公司　　　　☎ (02) 2795-3656
美國總經銷／Evergreen Book Store　　　☎ (818) 2813622
本公司網址　www.learnbook.com.tw
電子郵件　　learnbook@learnbook.com.tw

售價：新台幣三百八十元正

2004 年 5 月 1 日一版三刷

ISBN 957-519-499-3